Book Three:
A Story of Reighton,
Yorkshire 1714 to 1720

Whisper to the Bees

Joy Stonehouse

Grosvenor House
Publishing Limited

This book is published by
Grosvenor House Publishing Ltd
Link House
140 The Broadway, Tolworth, Surrey, KT6 7HT.
www.grosvenorhousepublishing.co.uk

A CIP record for this book
is available from the British Library

ISBN 978-1-83975-768-6

For Joanne, Hannah and Dominic

Acknowledgements

I would like to thank the helpful and friendly staff at the Treasure House, Beverley, and the Hull History Centre; they are always helpful and both sites make research a pleasure.

A huge thank you goes to members of the Hornsea Writers Group. They have continued to offer support and encouragement as well as online critiques during lockdown.

Special thanks must go to Lisa Blosfelds for her transcript of the Reighton parish records – an invaluable aid. She has also been most helpful in loaning local history books and allowing access to her collection of documentary evidence and maps.

Last but by no means least, thanks to Pam Williams for the first reading and editing, and for painting the book cover (again) and for being the first port of call when the technology goes wrong.

Author's Note

While inspired by the parish records, and although I have carried out extensive research into East Yorkshire in the early 18th century, I must stress that the stories in the series are works of fiction. Though the names of most of the characters are taken from the parish records, some are not. Any omissions and deviations from these records have been made for the sake of narrative interest.

The main characters, and those of higher social standing, speak in Standard English. Lesser characters and the older generation speak with a slight East Yorkshire accent.

Although Reighton is mentioned throughout as a village, the people of the time would have called it a town. As for Bridlington, the town was formerly known as Burlington and was often referred to as Bollin'ton.

Contents

Part One

Young Mary

Chapter 1

1714

It was the week before Christmas. The low sun had risen as high as it would reach that day and the ice on the thatch of Uphall had begun to thaw. Water dripped from the eaves in the still December air. William Jordan stood in the doorway of his father's half-empty barn, staring as if looking would increase the stock of corn. The pitiful harvest meant a meagre Christmas and an even leaner time to come. He didn't know how his mother would feed the hired lads as well as all his brothers.

As he turned and gazed at the yard, white-over with frost, he feared for his own growing family and, especially, for his daughter. Young Mary, now five years old, was always hungry and was getting a reputation in Reighton for begging. Old Ben called her a swill-kite. Unlike her older brother, she had no qualms about asking for small treats and leftovers. He imagined her cocking her head on one side, her chestnut curls falling loose from her bonnet. Folk needed only to look into those hazel eyes, and they'd give her anything. His wife and his mother would have none of it though. They saw young Mary as trouble; the girl was both clumsy and disobedient.

'That lass'll be death o' me,' his mother often complained. 'She's gotten above 'erself, that's what. Vicar 'as taught 'er over much. It's alright for *'is* daughters to read an' write, but what good will it do young Mary?'

Almost every day when he went home for supper, his wife met him with some story about the girl's latest mischief. Yesterday had been no exception.

'I can't do a thing with her,' Mary had grumbled. 'If she's not rushing round the fields and village with her dog, she's in the house unsettling her brothers with some nonsense or other. Why today, while I was busy feeding John, she somehow sneaked past me into the garden. God alone knows what she was up to out there, but she came back filthy.'

He hid a smile. His daughter liked to make mud pies, but it was obviously too frosty. He shook his head, wondering what to do. It was a pity his sister Jane was not more help. He'd hoped that, with her living in, she'd keep his wife happier, make the chores lighter and keep an eye on young Mary. It was not to be.

William sighed as he walked back across the yard, his boots ringing on the frozen ground. Avoiding the worst of the ice, he headed down the hill for home, pausing only to glance across Filey Bay. The dark distant cliffs appeared ominously close in the clear, cold air – a sure sign of worse weather from the north. The sea, granite-grey, offered no reprieve. Deep in thought, he blew on his hands to warm them and carried on. In mid-winter he regretted his decision to live down St Helen's Lane, right at the bottom of Reighton. By late morning, the hill took all the light so that his house was gloomy as well as damp. And now the hours of daylight were so few. He cheered up at the thought of seeing young Mary; no doubt, she'd been up to something today.

On entering the kitchen, he found his wife standing over their daughter. A candle was alight beside them and she was trying to get a comb through the girl's hair. It was the usual tangle, and the two boys were keeping well away. Suddenly, his wife threw down the comb in horror. William approached and, on closer inspection, saw that the girl's head had gone scaly. There were also some bald spots. It didn't bode well.

'Have you been scratching?' his wife demanded.

'No.'

'You have! Your head's a real mess.'

William leaned over to see for himself. 'It's ringworm,' he announced calmly.

'I'm not surprised, the way she rummages all over the foldyard and plays with her dog in the muck. Well, my lady,' she continued almost gleefully, 'you'll have to get your head shaved.'

The girl smiled. 'Good, I won't have to have my hair combed anymore. I'll be like a man under his wig.'

If William hadn't been there, Mary would have slapped her.

Francis and his small brother sat very still and watched while their mother cut off the natural ringlets.

William blinked back a tear as the lovely hair fell to the floor. When the dog sniffed among the curls, he moved it away with his foot.

'Come here, Stina,' coaxed young Mary. 'It's alright. I'm still here.' She knelt down and wrapped her arms round the dog.

It was nearly Christmas again and William remembered how happy she'd been last year when he'd surprised her with the tiny black puppy.

'Leave that dog alone,' Mary chided. 'I haven't finished. William – fetch your razor.'

William soaped his daughter's head into a lather and then, with great care, shaved her whole head.

Francis giggled. His sister looked such a funny little thing with a bald head.

'Don't laugh – it might be you next,' his mother warned. As she swept away the curls, she said with some regret, 'I'm sorry, Mary, I'll get some ointment for you from Sarah Ezard. Then I think you'd better keep your bonnet on. And wipe that smile off your face, Francis. I'm coming to check *your* head – see if *you've* caught it.'

He shut up at once. Luckily, for him, his head was clean.

While William missed his daughter's beautiful hair, she revelled in her new head. She didn't care what she looked like and was happy not to suffer her mother getting the knots out anymore. The one thing she didn't like was the ointment massaged daily into her scalp. It stank of garlic.

William feared for young Mary being bald at Christmas. When they went to Uphall for the day, he didn't want to hear any of his mother's comments on the shaved head. Perhaps he could persuade Mary to keep her bonnet on at all times.

Early on Christmas morning, William went alone to Uphall. He was aiming to be the first to greet everyone. When he entered the yard, Dickon, the foreman, had unsettling news. John Dawson's wife was with child again. William was quite aware that, to most people, this would have been good news; John was Uphall's best ploughman, hardworking and honest, and deserving of some luck. William's sister Dorothy would be *very* upset, to say the least. Since John had been obliged to wed the pregnant Susannah Hovington, his sister had been almost a recluse. Everyone in Reighton, including Dorothy, had believed John would marry her, not some stranger from Burton Fleming. This latest news would ruin her day.

Dickon rubbed his whiskery chin. 'God 'elp thee, William. Someone 'as to tell tha mother. John's not even allowed in 'ouse an' I don't want to get involved.'

William sighed and turned to go and do the deed. The news would blight the day's celebrations, but he could hardly put it off. Someone else was bound to find out and tell his mother. He had wanted to be the first to enter Uphall that morning and carried a branch of holly on purpose. Now he was bringing trouble rather than good luck. As he walked down the passage, he heard voices from the kitchen. His mother was not alone.

On entering, he saw the hired lads finishing their breakfast. After waving his holly branch and wishing them all a merry Christmas, he stepped over to his mother. She was stirring the pot by the fire. He passed on the news.

'Oh Lord!' she cried and sat down heavily on the stool. She put a hand over her mouth and shook her head. 'Whatever am I goin' to say to Dorothy? She still 'as 'er 'eart set o' John. She was 'opin' lass wouldn't be able to 'ave anymore bairns – not after last one delivered dead. Oh, William, she was 'opin' Susannah might leave John an' go back where she came from.'

'That's not going to happen,' William concluded.

The lads sitting round the kitchen table pulled long faces. They knew full well such news would spoil the day.

Their mistress glared at them. 'Thoo lads 'ad better keep tha mouths shut. *I'll* see to Dorothy – no need for any o' thee to say owt.' Turning to William, she added, 'I'd best tell 'er straightaway.' With that, she rushed to the bedchamber.

Her daughter was still dressing and seemed in good spirits for a change. She held up a pair of ribbons. 'Does this suit the gown or this one?'

'I'm not sure, Dorothy, I just can't think. Listen, sit 'ere wi' me for a bit, eh?'

They sat side by side on the edge of the bed.

Taking a deep breath, she began. 'I've summat to tell thee. It's about John Dawson.'

'What? He's alright, isn't he? He's not ill?'

'Nay… nay.' She took hold of her daughter's hand. 'It's his wife. I'm afraid she's wi' child again.'

'What? She can't be – she's hardly got over the last one.'

'I know it's sudden. It's true 'er body 'asn't 'ad much time to recover. Listen, Queen Anne 'ad a dozen stillborn children. It doesn't mean Susannah'll 'ave any better luck with 'er next one.'

This didn't console Dorothy. She leapt up and strode to the window. Scraping away the coating of ice with her fingernails, she let the tears fall.

Her mother bit her lips in anger. She'd never forgiven John for marrying Susannah, and it was cruel to hear this news on Christmas Day.

'Listen,' she said, walking over to the window, 'there'll be someone else fo' thee, I'm sure.' She put an arm round her. 'Finish dressin' an' come down an' join rest of us. Make most o' Christmas food – there'll be little enough after.'

Dorothy didn't go down for breakfast but sat alone upstairs, occasionally going to the window to see the comings and goings. She might avoid breakfast, but she couldn't avoid attending church.

Dorothy sat with the rest of her family in the Jordan pew. Her wretchedness at losing John Dawson was a sore she chafed continually; she couldn't stop herself turning to sneak a peek behind. He was still Uphall's best ploughman, but because he was no longer welcome in the house, she never got to see him anymore – only in church or as he passed the window on his way to work. She turned as if to admire the decorations of holly and ivy. He was sitting bolt upright near the back of the church with his wife at his side. If anything, he was more handsome than ever, his black hair shining in the candlelight. It was a horrid thought that married life was suiting him, making him bolder and almost taller. His wife kept her eyes to the floor. And so she should, thought Dorothy. John could never have been the father of that stillborn child. She was sure he'd been tricked into marriage. And what a big nose Susannah had – she'd seen smaller beaks on geese.

Sitting in the pew right behind Dorothy were William and his immediate family. Young Mary was fidgeting more than usual. She was forbidden to remove her close-fitting bonnet and was dying to scratch her head. As a distraction, she turned round to see who her aunt was looking at. William could not stop her in time as she stood up and pointed at John Dawson. Her mother, sitting further down the pew, grabbed her arm and yanked her back down.

'Sit still for God's sake!'

'Why is Aunt Dorothy looking at John Dawson?'

'I don't know. Shush. It's none of your business. William – you keep her quiet.'

He took his daughter's hand, kissed it and winked at her.

'It's nothing for you to worry about,' he whispered, 'but you'd better behave when we go to Uphall and *don't* mention John Dawson to Dorothy.' He put her hand back onto her lap. She moved it straight to her head. 'And *will* you stop scratching!'

Chapter 2

Young Mary stepped eagerly into her grandmother's kitchen. After being in the cold, the heat was overwhelming. There was a delicious smell of roast goose and, as she lifted up her nose, there were so many indefinable spicy aromas. Her eyes widened at the sight of the food set out on the thick oak table. There was salted beef, pickled pigs' knuckles, plum pudding and mutton pies. There were even slabs of gingerbread. The family members and hired hands were already in their places, wielding their spoons at the ready though the goose still spat and crackled over the fire. Young Mary watched the fat ooze and drip into the large tin beneath.

'It makes your mouth water, doesn't it?' said her father. 'Just look at that crispy skin.' He went to the fire to warm his hands and then turned to warm his bottom. It had been cold sitting in church. 'That's better,' he announced. 'I have some feeling back at last.' He showed his children where to sit at the small pine table to one side.

Mary was sorry there was no room for her at the main table and wished she could be with her young uncles. The hired lads and maids were also at another table, the one with hollows carved out to hold their food. She kept an eye on the goose. She watched her grandmother, hot and bothered, ease the bird from the spit, put it onto a large platter and set it on the table. Her gran's bonnet was damp and her face red and greasy. Aunt Dorothy didn't look too happy either and sulked while grace was said.

As young Mary's grandfather began to carve the bird, her two aunts carried food to the children and the hired hands. Back and forth they went with the dishes, filling the tankards with ale. Aunt Jane laughed with the lads and gave special attention to Tom. Aunt Dorothy didn't even smile.

'Eat plenty o' pie first,' her grandmother shouted across to the lads. 'It'll fill tha bellies better an' lay longer in 'em.'

Young Mary liked Tom. He'd been at Uphall all her life and had eyes like the shepherd's dog. She saw him blush when Jane poured his drink right to the top. The lad next to Tom noticed and nudged him when he tried to drink it. The ale spilled down his shirt.

'Eh up, lad,' said Dickon, 'make most o' mistletoe later. Don't forget.'

Tom rolled his eyes. Dickon was always egging him on with Jane.

Young Mary turned to her food. It was boring to sit apart with her brothers. There was much more fun on the other tables where the hired lads burped and farted. Next to her, Francis was being fussy about his food. *Good*, she thought. *At least there'll be more for me*. She had to watch young William though. Not quite three yet, you never knew what he'd stuff into his mouth. At the moment, he was happy enough to suck on a lump of pork gristle. Her other brother, six months old, was sitting in their mother's lap. At some point, Mother would have to leave the table and feed him.

At the main tables, there was much banter and laughter, interspersed with silences for serious eating. Drinks were topped up and finally, as the plates emptied, the lads called for entertainment. Dickon had no trouble in persuading young Mary to stand on a stool and sing a carol. She chose 'I Saw Three Ships' and everyone joined in. The lads clanked their tankards in time and, at the end of each verse, swilled down more ale. By the end of the song, they were shouting. Young Mary would have remained on the stool and sung more carols, but her mother dragged her off.

'That's enough, madam.'

William intervened. 'Let her be. She's enjoying it and so's everyone else.'

'No. The lads aren't singing anymore. They're seeing who's loudest *and* they're drunk.'

William could hardly disagree. As his daughter gazed hopefully at him, he shook his head.

'I'm sorry, your mother's right. I think we'd best be getting back home. See – your brothers are yawning.'

Young Mary glared at them. Her brothers were such a disappointment. She liked the noise and all the attention and the cram of people in the kitchen. If they went home, she'd be put straight to bed. She was sure there was still food to be had and the games hadn't even started. Last year, John Dawson had got his face burnt playing Snap-apple, and Aunt Dorothy had soothed it for him.

'Can't we stay a bit more?' she pleaded and grabbed her father's hand.

He was about to give in, but his wife was watching them with a certain look on her face.

'No, best not,' he decided. 'Tell you what – you can ride home on my shoulders. And,' he whispered, 'I'll tell you about John Dawson and Dorothy.'

After wishing everyone a merry Christmas once more, William and his family left Uphall. It was early evening and black as pitch outside. Francis carried the lantern and held his brother's hand while young Mary was hoisted onto William's shoulders. Their mother was left to carry the baby. The lantern cast a small circle of light in front, making it a cautious walk back down the hill to St Helen's Lane. It was such a still evening. The sea was a faint background murmur. There was the clink of a chain and a fox barking at some distant farm. Young Mary clung tight to her father's head and stared at the black sky already sprinkled with stars.

'You haven't told me yet about John Dawson and Aunt Dorothy,' she reminded him, her breath steaming in the cold air. 'And why has Aunt Jane stayed at Uphall and not come home with us?'

Her mother intervened. 'Jane deserves a night off – a night free from having to deal with you and your brothers. Besides, she needs some rest in winter. You know she gets a bad chest.'

'Will she be back tomorrow?' Young Mary hoped so. Jane was much kinder than Mother.

'Yes, she'll probably be back before breakfast.'

'Good. Now what about Aunt Dorothy?'

'Well,' answered her father, 'you know she'd taken a strong fancy to John Dawson… but he'd misbehaved at the hirings.'

'Whoa!' her mother interrupted. 'Young Mary has big ears and an even bigger mouth. It's best she doesn't know any more.'

'Sorry, Mary. Your mother's right. Some other time perhaps – when you're older.'

Young Mary shrugged. She wasn't that interested anyway. So long as her father was paying her attention, she was more than happy.

At Uphall, Dorothy Jordan attempted at last to join in the fun. She found it hard and noticed that her brother John had also kept in the background. Always a man of few words, the recent poor harvests had made him even quieter and withdrawn. She didn't want to end up like him – in his early thirties and still living at home, unmarried.

She peered around at the hired lads, many of them newly arrived last month, and thought not one of them worth looking at. If they didn't have spots or pox marks, they had ginger hair and freckles. When the games began, she left them all to it and went early to bed. Alone in the bedchamber, she lay with her hands over her ears to blot out the racket beneath. She remembered John Dawson arriving with his sister five years ago. Even then, he was striking, with black curly hair. He'd reminded her of a strong young ox. She sighed as she recalled him at the ploughing match, his broad shoulders and tapered waist revealed beneath his damp shirt. His dark hair had been stuck to his forehead. She wondered how he was enjoying his first Christmas with his new wife, and prayed he still remembered her fondly.

John Dawson was doing his best. He was sad not to be at Uphall but was aware that his wife was a long way from her own family and was probably missing her mother. All he could do was try to make amends. Susannah was proving a dutiful wife and, with another child on the way, their futures seemed fixed. There was no point thinking what might have been. The couple ate a simple meal together in their tiny cottage and avoided talking about anything that could lead to regrets.

As John Dawson and his wife were blowing out the candle and preparing to sleep, the games at Uphall were in full swing. No one there except Dorothy had retired early, although John had also escaped, giving some excuse about settling the horses. Jane was enjoying being at home for the night and free from tending William's family. She looked forward to sleeping in the old bedchamber, and now gave all her attention to the seasonal fun.

Dickon was intent on matchmaking. He thrust Jane under the garland of mistletoe and beckoned to Tom. Once the couple were in position, he shuffled round them in a strange dance and began to sing.

> 'Pick a berry off mistletoe
> For ev'ry kiss that's given.
> When berries 'ave all gone
> There's an end to kissin'.

Jane had no option. She took a kiss from Tom, who, with a nudge and a wink from Dickon, was encouraged to steal more kisses. Her brothers and the hired hands cheered Tom on and hurried to follow suit with the maids.

As soon as the mistletoe was stripped bare, they returned to the tables. With a great deal of pushing and shoving, they finished off the remains of the plum pudding and replenished their drinks.

Tom feared that, if they were too rowdy, they'd get no more ale. He decided to appease his master and mistress by getting everyone to perform the customary Christmas song. They were not in tune but meant well.

'We wish thee a merry Kesmas an' a happy new year,
    A pokeful o' money an' a cellarful o' beer,
      A good fat pig an' a new-calven coo,
   Good master an' mistress, 'ow dost thoo do?'

Francis Jordan and his wife Dorothy acknowledged this with a nod of their heads.

'We'll fill tha tankards – one last time, mind,' she warned. 'Thoo's all 'ad more than enough.' Forever keen to economise where possible, she was unhappy about the amount of food and drink consumed as well as the number of candles used. The mistletoe garland alone was taking up four, and this Christmas feast was going to leave them short of food next year. She hinted that the feast was over.

'It's time thoo was i' bed.'

'Just one more game,' Tom pleaded. 'Let us play Snapdragon. I promise it'll be the last.'

His mistress narrowed her eyes but then told Jane to fetch a flat dish. She scattered in a few raisins and poured brandy over them. Jane carried it carefully to the table, where her father set it alight with a spill from the hearth.

Tom was the first to go. He licked his fingers to wet them and then snatched out a raisin.

'Cheat, cheat!' the lads cried. ''E wet 'is fingers!'

To show off, they tried to grab a raisin without cheating. Tom laughed when they succeeded but singed the hair on their hands.

When all the raisins had gone, Jane sprinkled salt into the dish and, as they watched the flame turn green, they made their silent wishes. Jane wished for good health. Tom wished for Jane. Dorothy, above them in bed, imagined the flaming brandy and dared to wish for a future with John Dawson.

Chapter 3

1715

By the end of January, William and Mary rationed their food further. Young Mary found it difficult to feed her dog, resorting in the end to letting it eat rats. Continually hungry, she went to bed each night with a growling stomach. She found it hard to sleep, was tense and restless, and lay awake thinking of hunks of barley bread dipped in stew, or mutton pies cut open and steaming. She tried various ways of getting to sleep – like counting her breaths. If this didn't work, she went through the alphabet and thought of foods beginning with each letter. She pretended to touch them, smell them and eat them.

When the few vegetables from the garden had been used up, and the last of the apples eaten, all that was left was the bin of dried peas. Mary simmered these in stock with pepper and salt and served them up every day. She did her best to give the peas a different taste by adding edible weeds as well as herbs, but without much success. The whole family soon tired of the watery soup. There was very little bread and she stopped making oatcakes, preferring to use what was left of the oatmeal for the breakfast porridge. Although there were no more eggs, the cow supplied milk each day.

Gradually, as the weeks passed, both Mary and William had less energy and less inclination to improve their lot. William couldn't be bothered to repair the roof and found himself worn out walking up the hill to Uphall. He fretted that his wife was too thin and, because she was still breastfeeding the baby, needed more nourishment. On the odd occasion, old Ben brought them something special – a woodcock to pluck and roast, or a rabbit to stew. Stinky Skate still came round selling his salted cod and dried skate, but they were sick of salty food. Only once did Mary succumb, and then wished she hadn't because the kitchen stank of boiled fish for a week.

George Gurwood, the vicar, became a grandfather that winter. His daughter Jane, married to Robert Read and living in Speeton, had a boy who she named after him. While delighted, he was suffering like everyone else with his remaining seven growing girls to feed. He knew that folk were beginning to eat all kinds of birds and animals they wouldn't normally touch and hoped to make them feel better about it. He found an appropriate Bible passage in Timothy to read to them.

'For every creature of God is good, and nothing to be refused, if it be received with thanksgiving: For it is sanctified by the word of God and prayer.'

Old Ben thought this just as well, having recently dug up and eaten a hibernating hedgehog.

One cold afternoon at the end of February, William returned from Uphall with an unexpected treat – an ox tongue. Yet another animal had been slaughtered due to the lack of fodder, but this time he was glad. Mary seized the tongue from him and put it in the pot to boil.

The children hung around the fire to keep warm and to smell the cooking meat. They licked their lips as the tongue was lifted at last from the pot. Francis balked at the size. Hungry as he was,he didn't fancy it.

'That's horrid,' he commented. 'It's so big, and why is it white like that?'

'Oh, stop complaining,' his mother barked. 'Look, I'm going to peel off all this white skin.'

Francis was relieved to find the meat dark pink underneath. He watched his mother slice the solid, lean tongue and share it into their bowls.

'Francis – go and call your father. He's in the garden.'

As soon as the two returned, the family sat at the table. There was a hushed moment as they put their hands together in prayer to say grace. It was like being in church. Then, as if taking part in a solemn rite, they began to eat the meat slowly. No one said a word. They savoured each mouthful before swallowing. When they'd eaten all they could, they sat back and burped.

Francis giggled and pointed at his sister. 'Look at your tummy!'

Her stomach, like everyone else's, had swollen.

That night they couldn't sleep for indigestion, but over the next few days, they felt the benefit of their feast.

Despite the vicar's sermons on love and neighbourliness, they did not lead to charity. Instead of helping each other, folk turned in on themselves and grasped what food they could for their own survival. At mealtimes, they watched each other like hawks. Within each family, there were discussions as to who should have the most to eat; invariably, the man of the house was chosen.

George Gurwood tried to stem the selfishness but wasted his breath. Many were dizzy and faint in church and found it hard to concentrate when their stomachs ached for food. Their only thought was for themselves. Any vagrants who dared to wander near the village were soon pelted with stones by the children and chased away.

The lack of food made folk vulnerable to disease. Mary's children had a prolonged bout of diarrhoea, leaving them weak and dehydrated. For weeks afterwards, young Mary was too weak to attend lessons at the vicarage and, unusually for her, she sat still for hours at a time with her young brothers. They stared at the fire, not even having the energy to play.

William and Mary worried that the food shortage would have long-term effects on their youngest. One evening, when the children were in bed, William voiced their fears. They were sitting by the fire staring at the last embers. William stood up suddenly and put his finished pipe on the shelf. He turned to Mary.

'This lack of food's going to stop young William growing. He's already got something wrong with his spine. You must have noticed he walks with a list to one side.'

Mary was well aware. She'd often wondered if it was her fault. Perhaps she'd swaddled him badly as a baby.

'It's not just young William,' he continued. 'If John doesn't get more nourishment soon, then it'll be too late. He'll end up a simpleton.'

'He won't,' she countered. Tears filled her eyes. Helpless, she looked at William. He had hollow cheeks and his arms and legs had lost much of their muscle.

'We're all suffering,' she murmured. She didn't mention that her nails kept splitting, that her hair was dull and brittle and fell out when she brushed it. She added quietly, 'At least young Mary's hair is growing back.'

'Hmm… small consolation.'

Their brief conversation ended, and they went to bed. William thought about his daughter's hair. It had grown into a velvety fuzz, and she enjoyed rubbing her fingers through it. 'It's soft as moss. Feel it,' she'd say. He always obliged. No one else in the family was that interested. Yet, whenever he ran his hand over her head, he was afraid the curls would never grow back quite the same or be as shiny.

The winter and the lack of nourishment affected William's sister, Jane. She lived with the family as Mary's help, though continuing to work for her mother at Uphall. Sleeping under the leaky thatched roof did not help. Jane became ill and her cough returned. At first, William thought it was a bad cold. She was hot and shivery and soon out of breath, but then she complained of sharp pains in her chest. One evening, when Jane had one of her coughing fits, the phlegm was pink with blood. William was so alarmed that he rushed straight away to see Sarah Ezard.

While he was gone, Mary told the children to stay away from Jane. Whatever it was, she didn't want them to catch it.

Jane sat alone in a corner by the fire, wrapped in her shawl to keep warm. She tried not to breathe in too deeply or she'd start coughing again. Perhaps, she hoped, it was nothing more serious than a lack of proper food. When she glanced at the children, they stared back at her from the other side of the room, wide-eyed and frightened. Young William began to run towards her. It broke her heart to see him restrained; he would not understand why he had to keep away.

Sarah Ezard returned with William. She listened to Jane's chest and felt her forehead. Then, afraid of catching any disease, she washed her hands in vinegar and rinsed out her nose and mouth.

William and Mary exchanged worried glances.

Sarah dried her hands, took the couple aside and spoke in a whisper.

'I can't give 'er much until spring when I gather fresh 'erbs. An' thoo can't feed 'er up – thoo 'as enough of a struggle to feed tha bairns as it is.'

She walked back to Jane to offer some encouragement. 'Best thing is to drink a pint o' cold water ev'ry morn an' wash thy 'ead afterwards. Thoo can always try drinkin' nettle water as soon as nettles are up – it won't do any 'arm an' it might clean tha blood.'

Jane bit her lip. She had hoped for better remedies.

'Don't worry, lass. Come spring, I'll 'ave summat. Till then, don't work over 'ard. Get more rest.'

Mary listened in the background. When she let Sarah out of the house, she asked how best to tend Jane. She wondered if it would be better if Jane went back to Uphall.

'I've been keeping Jane away from the children,' she explained, 'but it's not easy.'

'Put 'er to bed. Keep 'er i' one place. An' then only thoo need see to 'er.'

'I was thinking maybe her own mother should be the one to tend her. I'll go and see her today, see what she thinks.'

When Mary visited her mother-in-law, she got short shrift.

'Nay! O' no account bring Jane to Up'all. Why, we 'ave so many livin' 'ere – we can't 'ave 'em fall ill. An' don't look at me like that – I can't spare anyone to 'elp thee.'

Mary had expected as much. In despair, she searched the yard for Tom and found him pouring water into the troughs.

'Morning, Tom. I've been looking for you. I know how fond you are of Jane, but I'm sorry to tell you she's taken badly again.'

He threw down the empty bucket. 'I knew it. I knew 'er cough was much worse than 'er mother thought. I just knew it.' Controlling his anger, he apologised. 'I'm sorry, it's not your fault. But what's to be done? You know I'll 'elp anyway I can.'

Mary touched his arm and stroked it. 'I know you'll help, Tom. I'll keep Jane in bed, and you can come whenever you want to keep her spirits up. She's going to get very lonely up there in the loft.'

'Aye, that she will. An' she's not used to lyin' idle neither.'

'No, she's like her mother in that respect. But listen, maybe Sarah Ezard'll come up with something good in the spring. I'm sure she'll get better.'

Tom was as good as his word and visited Jane daily. Each morning, as she woke to the sound of birds scuffling on the thatch above her head, her first thought was of Tom. She looked forward to the sound of his voice and found her heart beating faster as he climbed the ladder up to the loft.

He called to her quietly in case she was asleep, and always brought a present – a slice of bacon or a sausage sneaked from Uphall, or a bunch of violets. The visits were the best part of their day. Although it was dim up in the loft and smelled of old onions, it was cosy. He'd sit on the edge of her bed and hold her hand with the excuse of feeling how hot or cold she was. Before long, it became a regular habit to hold hands. When he sat so close, she found the scent of him comforting and homely, reminding her of Uphall, where she was not allowed.

'Thoo's still clammy,' he remarked one day.

'At least my hands aren't shovels like yours.'

That made him grin. She knew he liked to be teased.

'You are handsome this afternoon,' she added, 'in this dim light!'

Tom grinned again.

She complained that the wind frightened her. The March winds were stopping her sleeping. 'I'm scared the thatch might be torn off, or the chimney might fall on my bed.'

He tried to reassure her. 'Thoo'll be safe 'ere i' Reighton.'

'But you must have heard what happened in Beverley last month. A windmill was destroyed.' When he didn't answer, she added, 'And don't forget there were two villages on the Wolds that had the tops of their church spires blown off.'

'Yes, but it's sheltered down 'ere o' St 'Elen's Lane. Thoo'll be fine, I promise.' He smiled and gave her a wink.

Though always overjoyed to see her, he worried over her loss of weight and her pale complexion. He was concerned that she wasn't getting any fresh air or exercise cooped up in her space under the roof.

In desperation, Tom called on Sarah Ezard and explained Jane's situation. The woman nodded her head wisely and agreed that Jane should be allowed outside when the weather was fine. So, whenever he could get some other lads to fill in for him, he strolled with Jane to the cliff top to breathe in the sea air. The fresh breezes soon put colour into her cheeks, and she regained her appetite.

With the spring weather came a new food supply. Large numbers of dotterels flew in and landed briefly on the top fields. Enough birds were captured to feed the whole village for a week. As promised, Sarah Ezard brought new medicines for Jane – syrup of hyssop and a sweet jelly made from boiled seaweed. When the hens began to lay again, and the cow gave more milk, Jane was prescribed another cure – a pint of fresh milk, to be drunk while still warm, and with the white of a new-laid egg beaten in. She was told to drink this each morning for a month, and not have anything else for an hour afterwards.

Jane continued to have daily visits from Tom, who always coaxed her to eat some treat or other. She was sad whenever he left and wondered about his future. If he became the main stockman, as well he might, he could continue to live at Uphall. And if she married him, they'd both be together at Uphall forever. That would be a dream worth praying for – if he felt the same.

Chapter 4

As spring progressed, life became less stressful for the animals at least. The cows and sheep were grazing on the new grass while, for the people of Reighton, food shortages continued. The good news was that Jane Jordan was making a fine recovery. By April, she was looking and feeling so much better that she was allowed to work again at Uphall. There, she relished the bustle and banter but also heard an unsettling story.

Around the table at breakfast, Dickon passed on what he'd heard from the blacksmith.

'There were a widow i' Bridlington – she were called Jane – an' she committed some crime or other – I can't remember what – it doesn't matter. Anyway, she were to be whipped all along Main Street. What's strange, she'd broken 'er neck some'ow while i' care o'constable. 'Er whippin' 'ad to be postponed.'

The lads found this amusing, but Jane couldn't help wondering if the woman had tried to hang herself. Whipping was such an ordeal. The thought of the poor woman's plight kept her awake at night.

William also passed on disturbing news. He'd been to Bridlington market with his brother John and had returned in a sombre mood. As he strolled home with Jane, he told her that John was even quieter than usual, had hardly said a word on the journey.

'I think it's the riots that have upset him,' he confided.' There's a lot of trouble in some parts. I've heard so many different rumours today, but most folk think it's because of the general election next month.'

'It might be last year's bad harvest,' Jane offered. 'People get desperate when food prices are so high.'

'That could be. John's taken the poor harvests to heart. The vicar will know more. Let's see on Sunday – he's bound to have something to say.'

George Gurwood knew of the riots, deemed them political, and chose his next service to show support for King George. Pointing towards the doorway, he warned his congregation of the Catholic threat to the throne.

'There are papists and Scots out there now.'

Old Ben flinched. He was nearest to the door.

'They want James Stuart to be king,' the vicar continued. 'They're plotting rebellion against King George and causing havoc.' He leant forward and lowered his voice for dramatic effect. 'They've already attacked chapels and smashed up the pews. They've broken windows and pulpits. They've even set fire to places of worship.'

'Aye,' mumbled old Ben, 'an' I bet they dared to shout "Damn King George".'

Sarah Ezard, sitting next to him, was quick to reply. 'Let's 'ope them chapel folk 'ad swords an' shotguns to fight back.'

George Gurwood waited for the congregation to settle. He held up his right arm.

'Don't worry. There *will* be an end to this dissension and violence. The government has passed a Riot Act. If more than a dozen folk gather to disturb the peace, they must disperse within the hour. If they don't, they'll be forced to – and any injuries will be deemed their own fault.' When he saw many heads nod in agreement, he let his arm fall to his side. 'And those who ignore this law may be sentenced to three years in prison at least – or given hard labour.'

The congregation murmured among themselves; they dreaded a Jacobite uprising and approved of stiff measures against papists.

On leaving church, the blacksmith signalled to the men to follow him to the forge. His blood was up, and he wanted action. As soon as everyone gathered round, he stood on an upturned log and provoked them.

'Are we goin' to stand 'ere an' do nowt? Are we mice or men? Are we goin' to let a few papists beat us?'

'Nay,' they mumbled, unsure where this was leading.

'Oh, come on!' cried Phineas. 'Thoo's got red blood i' tha veins. I'll ask again. Are we goin' to let a few papists rule over us?'

'Nay,' they shouted.

'Right then, 'ands up all them that 'as a scythe.'

Many hands were raised.

'We have more scythes at Uphall,' William offered.

'Aye,' added Dickon, 'an' we 'ave even more sickles that lasses use at 'arvest time.'

'Alright then,' replied Phineas, rubbing his huge calloused hands together. 'We must be prepared. If word comes that them Frenchies or Scots want to land 'ere, or they come marchin' round 'ere, we can give 'em summat they'll not forget.'

The men, now stirred up, cheered him on.

'Aye, that's right, be ready. Get tha scythes an' sickles sharpened. Bart Huskisson – thoo can give us poles. We can fix blades onto 'em. Oh, an' make sure poles is long enough to out-reach any pikes.'

Dickon frowned and raised his arm. He had a question. 'What 'appens if we 'ave to fight at 'aymakin' or 'arvest?'

'Aye,' they murmured. It was a reasonable enough question. They wouldn't be prepared, as their scythes and sickles would be in use.

Phineas sighed and rested his hands on his hips. 'Look 'ere,' he said, 'we'll get news of any invasion. We'll not be taken by surprise. We 'ave beacons, 'aven't we? They'll be lit. Don't worry about it. Go back 'ome an' be prepared.'

As they turned to leave, he shouted after them, 'Don't say owt to tha womenfolk, mind. No need to trouble *their* 'eads.'

The women *were* troubled. They heeded the sermon and grew suspicious of the Scottish pedlar, Speckledy Golightly. Only John Dawson's wife Susannah now bought anything from the woman. As a result, the pedlar's visits were less frequent. When she did visit the village, the children threw sticks and stones at her and yelled, 'Papist traitor!' Their parents did nothing to stop them.

The pedlar had no option but to leave the area for good. She made one last call on Susannah and sat outside in the garden to share a jug of milk and a curd cheesecake.

'I'm sorry thoo's leavin',' Susannah said as she poured the milk. 'I've made no friends 'ere.'

'There's a shame, lassie, but ah'm a wanderer. Wi'oot ma pal Stinky Skate, ah'd've bin long gone.' She laid a freckly hand on Susannah's arm. 'Ah thank ye for aw ye've done. Ye've made me aye welcome, but it's time ah was away.'

'It's goodbye, then,' Susannah replied with a tear in her eye. 'I wish thoo well.'

Speckledy Golightly stood up to go. She shouldered her pack and picked up her basket. With one last wave, she left the garden. Already, she was looking forward to travelling once more. There was a wonderful freedom in being on the road. All she need do was move from one town to another and aim towards the northwest, where she'd be more welcome. She'd endure the weather if it was bad and enjoy it when fine. She'd eat when she was hungry and sleep when she was tired, choose to be with people or avoid them. The Jacobite threat, she decided, had done her a good turn.

Susannah missed the Scottish pedlar and was now friendless during her last wearying weeks of pregnancy. It played on her mind that folk had never forgiven her for tricking John Dawson into marriage, especially when he should have wed young Dorothy Jordan. It was a sultry day in mid-June when she went into labour.

She walked by herself to fetch Sarah Ezard. Knowing it might be hours yet before the baby was born, she kept calm. Nothing, she thought, could be worse than the last time – delivering a dead baby and then having to face a new and reluctant husband with the news.

Sarah made sure Susannah was comfortable and then went to Uphall to inform John. He was sitting sharpening his scythe outside the barn.

'Tha wife's started 'er labour pains. Thoo must stay away.'

He shrugged. 'I did think to spend me gander month 'ere at Up'all, but master an' mistress say it won't do.'

'No, I see it's not fair o' Dorothy. Wherever will thoo go?'

'I can stay at Matthew Smith's place.'

'Of course – I was forgettin' Ellen's tha sister. Dost tha think, per'aps, Ellen can 'elp me wi' Susannah?'

John set off straight away to ask his sister. She left her children with her mother-in-law and rushed to Susannah's cottage. When she arrived, she was not surprised to find Sarah Ezard the only other woman present. Susannah did not have a single friend or relative with whom to share her experience, and it was too late to send word to her mother. With an aching heart, Ellen watched her shuffle round and round the tiny parlour. Every so often, when a contraction came, Susannah halted and bent over in pain.

'Keep walkin',' Sarah instructed. 'Keep walkin' an' I'll rub tha back.'

As the pains became more frequent and grew in strength, Sarah told Ellen to draw the curtain and light the candles. Minutes later, Ellen was told to boil up the water – the baby was coming quicker than expected.

'Can I kneel?' wailed Susannah. 'I don't want to lie down. I'd rather kneel.'

A particularly strong contraction made her cry out. Then, as the pain subsided and she waited for the next one, she dropped to her knees on the low bed. She inhaled deeply, preparing herself. At that moment, her waters broke and flooded the sheet and straw mattress beneath.

'Don't worry,' said Sarah, 'jus' think o' pushin'. Won't be long now.'

Susannah swayed on her knees, sweating with the effort. Each contraction was exhausting, but when the time came, she found the strength to push until her eyes turned bloodshot.

'I can see its 'ead,' Sarah announced calmly. 'Steady now. I'll ease it out. Don't push yet.'

Ellen knelt on the floor by the bed and stroked Susannah's hair.

Sarah thought the two women could not be more different. While Ellen had thick, wavy black hair and looked as fit and healthy as a calf, Susannah was pale and washed out, her fair hair hanging limp and damp.

'Thoo's doin' real well,' Ellen encouraged as she drew Susannah's hair from her eyes. 'Sarah's a wonderful midwife. She delivered both o' mine an' ev'rythin' went fine. Do just as she says an' thoo'll be alright.'

Sarah inserted her fingers to ease out the head. When the baby's face appeared, it was blue and wrinkled, and smeared with blood and mucus. Sarah remained calm and gave orders to Ellen.

'Fetch me yon bowl o' water an' that cloth. Bairn's comin' out now.'

Seconds later, the baby slid out onto the cloth. Sarah held the baby upside down. It gasped a few times and then squalled loudly, turning pink as it gulped in more air.

Susannah remained on her knees, crying with relief, and not caring to know what sex it was.

'Thoo's got a daughter,' Sarah announced as she cut and tied the cord.

Ellen washed the baby girl and swaddled her up tightly. Then she passed the bundled child to Susannah, who was now lying on her back and resting.

'Put 'er to tha breast,' Sarah said, 'an' mind she takes in all o' tha nipple. We don't want 'er suckin' just on end of it. Otherwise, tha'll get sore.'

Susannah gazed at her baby girl. 'She 'as a proper nose already,' she remarked.

'Aye,' agreed Sarah. 'She's goin' to take after thee.'

Ellen was disappointed that the girl was not going to have her brother's dark good looks. She didn't know that Susannah's dead baby had been the image of John. As she watched the baby's mouth play around the nipple, she was sorry that Susannah could not celebrate the birth with any friends. She tried to offer consolation.

'If I ever 'ave another bairn, an' it's a lass, I'll name 'er after thee.'

Susannah smiled. 'Thoo's been a great 'elp an' I'm most grateful. I'd like thoo an' Matthew to be godparents.'

'We'd be only too pleased,' Ellen replied. 'What name 'as tha chosen?'

'I don't know. I might name 'er Rebecca, after me mother.'

Sarah massaged Susannah's womb and, as the afterbirth came away, Ellen went into the poky kitchen to make the porridge. When she took the dish through to the parlour, Sarah had finished cleaning up and was giving some last instructions.

'I'll put bairn i' yon drawer. She can sleep there for a few hours, then she'll need feedin'. Keep 'er i' same room 'ere – at least till she's been baptised. We don't want evil eye bein' put on 'er. I'll tell 'em about bairn at

Up'all – whether they want to know or not – an' I'll visit later on.'

As Sarah left the cottage, she spoke to Ellen on the doorstep. 'Susannah needs someone to come ev'ry day an' see 'er an' bairn are thrivin'. When thoo visits, bring a bit o' food an' drink to celebrate. I know she may 'ave done wrong, but poor lass is all alone.'

At Uphall, the news of Susannah's baby was received like a cold draught. It was of no comfort to young Dorothy that mother and daughter were doing well; she hoped the baby, if it lived, would not take after its mother.

Chapter 5

The Jordans soon had more pressing worries than Dorothy's misery over John Dawson and his wife. The month of June, normally sunny and dry, had been wet. Hardly a day passed without rain, and Francis Jordan was concerned about the hay harvest. At each sunset, he left Uphall and walked to the top of the hill to study the weather. There he sensed the wind and the amount of heat left in the air, knowing he'd been caught out before by a late frost. Although he usually chose the right time to mow, the weather this year posed a challenge.

One evening, when Francis Jordan returned from his weather watching, his wife waved a piece of paper at him. He hadn't time to sit down before she thrust it in his face.

'Just look at this! As if we 'aven't troubles enough.'

He saw that it was a letter to them both and signed by their son, John. Sitting at the table, he read it twice in the candlelight.

Dorothy paced the kitchen waiting for his response. 'Well?' she demanded, stopping in front of him and folding her arms. 'What dost tha make of it?'

Francis pushed the letter slowly across the table with one finger. He raised his head.

'I don't know what to say – it's a shock.'

'Why would John all of a sudden take it into 'is 'ead to leave 'ome an' become a carrier? Why, fo' God's sake?'

'Well, 'e does explain. It's our bad 'arvests. 'E's lost 'ope an' 'e thinks it's best for everyone. Like 'e writes, we're not short o' sons to do 'is work.'

'Thoo can't be sidin' with 'im! What if they all take off?' She leant over the table and prodded the letter hard with her finger. 'What if William gives up, an' Thomas? Why, it sets a bad example to Samuel an' Richard.'

'They won't leave. Look – 'e says 'e's sorry, says we'll 'ave one less mouth to feed.' Suddenly overcome with fatigue, he rubbed his eyes with both hands. They'd be one man short for the haymaking. Perhaps it was his fault. Perhaps he'd taken John for granted, used him like a hired hand. But then all his sons had to work hard. It was the way of things.

Dorothy leant over the table and snatched up the letter. She screwed it up and threw it on the fire. 'Ungrateful devil! An' such a coward 'e couldn't even say goodbye.' She watched the paper burn. 'Well, that's that! *I* won't mention 'im again – an' neither will thoo,' she warned, 'nor anyone else.'

Francis gazed into the fire. He knew better than to argue. Rising from the table, he announced he didn't want any supper. He was going to bed. Tomorrow, he'd have to tell everyone about John and do it discreetly, well out of Dorothy's earshot. There was also a decision to be made about the hay harvest.

Next morning, the farmers gathered at the forge to discuss a mowing date. They were fully aware of the need to mow when the grass was in flower, for then the hay would be sweetest and most nutritious. The longer they waited, the less goodness there'd be and, if they waited too long, the hay would be almost useless as fodder. As soon as a day could be decided, George Gurwood would announce it at the Sunday service. A spell of dry weather was crucial to allow enough time to mow and the hay to dry. They observed the clouds and shook their heads. Dickon voiced their fears.

'Mack'rel sky, mack'rel sky, never long wet, never long dry.'

'Aye,' they mumbled and stared miserably at their boots. There was a very real danger the hay would be spoilt.

'It's a shame,' added Dickon. 'A lot o' penny grass is witherin' down there. Now's right time to mow.'

They waited for Francis Jordan to make his decision.

'Alright,' he said at last, 'I reckon we try i' two days' time. We'll get it mown some'ow, even if it's 'ard work – an' if it's wet, we'll just 'ave to pile it into cocks an' 'ope it dries enough off ground.'

A few grumbled. It was much harder to mow wet grass when the swathes fell so heavily over their scythes. What was the point in mowing if the rain came and ruined the hay anyway?

'We'll need four good days, Francis,' Matthew Smith reminded him. 'Hadn't we better start straight away?'

'Aye,' agreed Dickon, 'but swallows is flyin' low this week. We shouldn't do owt yet. Air's over moist. Wait till swallows is flyin' 'igh, then we can start.'

'We 'ave to mow soon,' Francis replied. 'It can't wait. I' two days, I say we begin.'

They deferred to his judgement; he was seldom wrong.

When William heard the news of his brother John, he found it hard to believe. John, never one to talk about his feelings, had given no hint of his intentions. William waited until the children were in bed before telling Mary. She was equally shocked and stopped knitting.

'*You're* not thinking of giving up farming, are you?'

'No, of course not. Don't worry – I'm bound forever to this life. And our sons will be too.'

'But you must have known John was leaving. You two worked together every day.'

'No, I had no idea – none whatsoever. He never said a word.' He did wonder if it was the reason for John being so quiet. Perhaps John had been making plans for some time.

'But you were so close,' Mary argued. 'You used to take a sledge to Bridlington in the winter to fetch supplies, and John went with you to the Michaelmas Fair. You remember that time you took the children? And John helped you carry in the Yule log each year.' She shook her head. 'I don't know – I'll never understand it.' She began to knit again, shaking her head and sighing. 'The children will miss him.'

'The whole of Uphall will miss him. Tom will have to take over the horses and oxen.'

'Perhaps John wanted to work with horses more.'

'That could explain his move. The only time he spoke with any enthusiasm was when we admired the carriage horses in Bridlington.' He realised how happy John would be in charge of a large stable.

'Well,' said Mary, her knitting needles clicking again at top speed, 'at least your brothers are of an age now to work harder. I bet your mother's upset though.'

'You wouldn't know it. She doesn't mention John at all. And Father says we're not to mention his name in front of her.'

'No, she's hard as nails, your mother.'

'Maybe. She has a lot to put up with.' He was tired of the conversation. 'I think I'll go to bed now. I'll be up early tomorrow to help Tom and Dickon. There'll be more job sorting to be done.'

On the appointed morning for the start of the hay harvest, the mowers were in position down in the meadow by 5 o'clock. There was a heavy dew, but the sun was shining. Boughs had already been set up to mark the area of grass to be mown that day. William had taken along his son. The boy was nearly eight years old, and it was high time he learnt to work. The men stood around leaning on their scythes and had a last grumble. It didn't help when Francis announced that his son John would not be working with them anymore and had left Reighton. They looked at each other and pulled faces. It didn't bode well when stalwart members of the village gave up and left.

'Come on,' urged Francis, 'we'd better make on.'

'Aye, we'd best get goin',' Dickon agreed, 'better get done before dinner. See up there – sun's over glary. It won't stay fine.'

Dickon was right. By 11 o'clock, they were mowing in a sea mist and the sun could barely be seen. They moved as a group in a staggered line with William as the foreman and kept pace as best they could to avoid cutting across the next man. William's son Francis stayed at a safe distance on the edge of the meadow. When the men paused to sharpen their scythes, William called his son over.

'Come here, Francis. Look and learn. I'm going to grease my strickle.' He removed a flat piece of wood from his belt.

Francis could see the strickle was full of neat little holes pricked in rows. His father showed him his grease horn.

'See, there's hog lard in one end,' William explained, 'and sand in the other. Now watch.' He uncorked the horn with his teeth and greased the piece of wood. Then he sprinkled sand over the holes. 'Look, I can now run the strickle over the scythe blade until it's sharp again.'

As the grass was damp, the scythes had to be sharpened more often, making the work slow. The men took few rests and never ceased worrying about the changeable weather. Normally, they'd spread the hay out to dry the next day, but in view of the damp conditions, Francis sent word round the village for help in raking it into small bundles.

Tom was not pleased to see Jane arrive with the women. He was afraid the damp and heavy work would make her ill again. While he mowed, he kept an eye on her. She worked quickly, taking swathes of hay and folding the ends in like a muff so that any rain would fall off. He prayed that her work would not be in vain.

Late in the evening, everyone left the meadow. They were wet through to the skin, unsure whether it was from their sweat, the mist or the grass. Tom walked Jane home, concerned that she must get dry as soon as possible and have something to eat. He felt her shivering as she strolled unsteadily, holding onto his arm, and knew she'd overdone it. When they reached William's house, he stood her in front of him and looked her straight in the eye.

'Promise me thoo'll eat before tha goes to bed.'

She promised and he kissed her on the cheek, saying he'd see her tomorrow.

'Don't come out to work i' meadow if thoo's not fit,' he added. 'Promise?' He tweaked her tiny snub nose.

'Aye,' she murmured, too tired to talk, and opened the door.

She staggered into the kitchen. She ignored Mary and only had the strength to remove her wet outer clothes before climbing the ladder to the loft. After pushing the hatch door open with her head, she crawled through and collapsed onto her bed exhausted.

Mary sent William up to see how she was. He took her some hot soup, but she was already fast asleep. He left the dish by the bed, hoping she might wake and have the soup later.

The next morning, Jane was feverish. She took one glance at the bowl of cold soup and gagged. Grease had congealed over it.

When she returned it untouched, William frowned. 'Come on, Jane. You must eat something, or you won't be fit for work.'

'No, I'm fine. I feel a bit sick, but it'll wear off. What I need is fresh air. I'll be better outside than in all day.'

'At least have your porridge,' coaxed Mary. 'You can't lift hay on an empty stomach.'

Jane sat at the table and was handed a bowl. She pushed the porridge around with her spoon and finally managed to swallow a few mouthfuls washed down with water.

The children stared. They didn't want Aunt Jane to be ill again.

When Jane arrived at the meadow, Tom could tell by her flushed cheeks and bright eyes that she was going to be ill again. She ignored his protests and began spreading the mown grass with the other women.

The day had started misty. By mid-morning, the sun came through and steam began to rise from the damp grass. Tom hoped that, with luck, the weather would stay dry, and the grass could be raked into rows the next day. He noticed with concern that Jane was sweating and, like the other women, was removing her overskirt. She might catch a chill.

It was mid-afternoon when Jane started to feel strange. The top of the hill shimmered in the heat, and she saw black spots dancing in front of her eyes. Her back ached from the raking and she felt sick. When she stood and stretched, the sky spun round. The next thing she knew, she was lying on her back with Tom peering over her.

He carried her back to William's house. It was the end of her haymaking.

Chapter 6

Young Mary paid little attention to Jane's recurring illness. Though her brother Francis was upset and missed Jane's presence in the kitchen, her own life did not revolve around the home. It was June 28th, and she couldn't wait to go out. She was going to the vicarage where the Gurwood girls would be preparing for St Peter's Day.

'You do know it's tomorrow?' Cecilia reminded her when she arrived. 'I hope you realise how important it is. The landowners will walk round the village. They'll check that everything is in order and good repair.' She paused to think, eyeing up Mary and her dog. 'I think we can manage best here without you. Why don't you go back home and help your mother?'

Young Mary's bottom lip trembled.

Cecilia realised she'd been too sharp. 'Alright then, if you want, you can come back this afternoon and help with the rush gathering.'

Mary returned home to find her mother scrubbing the table. The linen had already been washed and was now drying on the hedge, and her father had mended the roof and weeded the garden. Her mother grabbed her by the arm and warned her to keep out of the way.

'I'm not having Dorothy Jordan coming round to find our house dirty and untidy. I'd be so ashamed, and I'd never hear the end of it, so you just stay outside and sit still.'

Young Mary was not the only one excluded. Jane stayed up in the loft, not well enough to work. She lay in the darkness and listened with regret to the noise of preparations going on below and in the village.

In the afternoon, young Mary and Francis headed down to the meadow with all seven Gurwood girls. The young Jordan boys from Uphall met them on the way, eager to help gather the rushes that grew by the ditch. Mary skipped on ahead with Stina while the Gurwood girls followed sedately. On arrival, the eldest began to cut the smooth green stems while the others piled the rushes into bundles.

Mary and Francis helped for a while and then were sent to get wild flowers to decorate the church. Buttercups and daisies grew among the grass along the cliff top, and they found cranesbill and bog pimpernel in the marsh by Reighton Gill. Mary rushed on ahead, eager to find different flowers, while Francis was content to fill his basket with whatever was nearest. He didn't think much to her idea of picking groundsel.

'That's just food for rabbits,' he complained.

'God made rabbits, didn't he?' she countered. 'I should think he'd be pleased to see any flowers he'd made.'

Francis couldn't be bothered to argue. He turned and walked away, knowing she wouldn't let it end there. She'd go on and on, showing off what she'd learnt in the Bible. He returned to the others with his basket and sat down to wait for her.

Mary soon tired of picking flowers and began to throw sticks for Stina instead. The dog would chase after anything and fetch it back, as if retrieving things was her sole purpose in life. Even when panting with protruding eyes and in a state of collapse, the dog would return with the stick and crouch with her head low and feet apart in readiness for the next throw. Stina's eyes never left the stick for a second and, as Mary became more skilful at throwing, she pretended to hurl it one way to fool the dog, and then spin and throw it in the opposite direction. Engrossed in her game, she threw the stick too far in the wrong direction; it flew over the cliff edge.

She cried out in horror as the dog chased it, leapt up high and caught the stick in mid-air before falling out of sight. She raced to the edge, afraid she'd caused the dog harm. With her heart pounding, she saw that Stina had managed to get a foothold on the wet clay halfway down the cliff.

'Stina!' she called. 'Come here, girl, come on.'

The dog began to scrabble upwards. Once within reach, Mary yanked her by the scruff of her neck and hauled her over the tufts of grass overhanging the edge. Stina's white paw and chest were covered in mud, and she had a strange grin. Mary didn't know why the dog's lips were parted like that, as if smiling.

When she returned to the others, Cecilia's mouth fell open.

'I'm appalled! Just look at you. I can't leave you for a moment. Only you could get that filthy. And I don't know who's muddier – you or your dog.'

Mary's cousins giggled, but Francis was neither amused nor surprised. 'You don't have to live with her,' he grumbled. Then he noticed the dog's odd smile and remarked on it.

'I think there's something in its mouth,' said Richard Jordan. 'Have you looked inside, Mary?'

'No,' she replied, and knelt down to prise the jaws apart. She tilted her head to get a better look. 'I think there's a bit of my stick back there.' She poked in her fingers and tried to pull out the piece of wood. 'It's stuck fast right across. I can't budge it.'

'Let me try,' offered Thomas, the eldest. He bent down and stroked the dog for a while before risking his hand in her mouth. 'You're right. I can't shift it.' He straightened up and wiped the saliva from his hand down his breeches. 'That stick's wedged tight. We'll need something stronger to free it. The blacksmith has lots of pliers. He'll do it for us. At least your dog isn't in any pain.'

They trooped back to the village, each with a bundle of rushes, followed by the dog with the smirk on her face.

First, they delivered the rushes to the vicarage where George Gurwood set bundles aside for decoration. Then his wife took two of her daughters to the church to strew the rest of the rushes down the cobbled aisle and between the pews. Cecilia stayed behind with her other sisters to organise the decoration of the remaining bundles. Young Mary and the boys, in no hurry to start decorating, preferred to see to the dog.

'Come on,' said Mary, 'let's go to the blacksmith.'

Phineas Wrench was vexed at seeing a group of children standing outside his forge. He wondered what on earth they wanted. When Mary sidled in with her grinning dog and explained the reason for it, he laughed.

The boys still hung back. They were in awe of the blacksmith. He wasn't tall, yet he was broad and strong. His arms were almost as thick as his thighs. They watched from a distance as, with expert ease, Phineas pulled the dog between his knees and held her there.

Stina was very trusting and let him open her mouth wide, but when he tried to remove the stick with his fingers, he soon realised how tightly it was wedged. He pitied the dog; her teeth must be aching under the pressure. He reached for his small pliers and managed to get a grip. After a bit of wiggling, he released the piece of wood. He held it up and they marvelled at its shape and size – perfect for slotting exactly into the back of the dog's mouth.

'Anyone want it?' the blacksmith asked as he waved the stick about.

It had blood and saliva on it. They shook their heads.

'Right then, Mary, take tha dog to yon sleck trough an' give 'er a drink.'

As Mary led her dog to the trough, she worried that Stina's mouth was still bleeding.

Phineas guessed her concern. 'Don't worry. That water's good for any ailments. A mouthful o' that an' Stina's mouth'll soon be mended.'

The dog drank and dribbled a little but was otherwise fine. After thanking Mr Wrench politely, they ambled back to the vicarage, the dog no longer smiling.

They found Cecilia still bossing her sisters and arranging the decorations. In no mood to be organised, Mary and the boys did whatever they wanted with their own bundles, and with various results. The Gurwood girls decorated their rushes by making cross and heart patterns with the flowers. They'd even incorporated the roots of sweet-scented flags to make the church smell like myrtle. Mary and the boys stuffed their rushes in a haphazard fashion with every flower possible.

Cecilia didn't pass comment but narrowed her eyes.

Mary didn't care. She was pleased with her efforts. 'At least my bundle's full of colours,' she mumbled.

The next morning, on St Peter's Day, the children met up again at the vicarage. They were clean and dressed in their Sunday best, and villagers turned out to watch them carry the decorated rushes in a procession to the church. Cecilia, in solemn mood, led the way alongside the two churchwardens. Her older brother John, home for the day, played 'The Rush Bearers' March' on his fiddle as he followed behind with his younger sisters.

It was the first time young Mary had taken part and she believed her bundle was the brightest. She grinned as she marched in time to the music. As the bundle was as tall as her, onlookers saw only a moving heap of green and yellow bobbing its way to church.

Francis, taking it all very seriously, was afraid that his clumsy sister would trip and spoil the procession.

His mother and grandmother watched with equal concern.

Chapter 7

Once inside the church, the children were told to place the largest and best bundles by the altar and pulpit. Young Mary's was one of those dismantled and strewn under the pews and along the nave. She decided that next year she'd make a daisy chain instead, one so long it would hang in loops between every pew. They wouldn't take that to pieces. As she sat with her family, her eyes wandered over the decorations. She twisted her head to see the back of the church. The font was hardly recognisable, draped in bright green moss with a cross leant against it made from ivy, moss and creamy white roses. When she turned back to look at the vicar, he gave her a wink.

George Gurwood kept the service brief, not wishing to curtail the day's festivities. As soon as he'd uttered the final prayer and blessing, his wife and son went to the church door. Susanna carried a box of gingerbread and John held a fiddle under his arm. The children filed past, each receiving a piece of gingerbread dried hard and crunchy.

As young Mary reached for her treat, she noticed her aunt Elizabeth being ushered away by her husband.

'Why is Aunt Lizzie going home?' she asked her mother. 'Doesn't she want to stay?'

'If Robert goes, she goes. That's what wives do. Come on, eat your gingerbread.'

'But she'll miss the fun.'

'Look, Robert's never been one for fun and games. Lizzie knows that, knew when she married him. Eat your gingerbread.'

John Gurwood picked up his fiddle and began to play a jig, leading everyone to the small grassy field below the church where the wrestling matches would be held. Two barrels of ale had been set up and the women had brought hardboiled eggs, cheeses and cold meats. Soon, men arrived from Speeton and Hunmanby, eager to take part in the wrestling. They checked on the rules and put money into a hat. It was winner takes all. Their names were put into another hat and the draw was made. Young Mary was thrilled when her father's name was pulled out first. He was to wrestle with her uncle Thomas.

Her grandfather frowned. He did not look pleased. 'That's not a fair match, William,' he complained. 'Thoo should 'ave been facin' John *if* 'e'd still been 'ere. Why, Thomas is only 17 – just a lad.'

Thomas stripped off his shirt and boasted. 'See my muscles? I think I can manage.'

William also stripped off his shirt and both took off their shoes. They squared up, one pace apart, leaning towards each other and with their feet planted firmly on the turf.

Mary never liked to see her father without his shirt. His body was so white compared with his face and arms and he had black hair on his chest. She peered around, surprised to see her mother not taking any notice of the wrestling.

Her mother was sitting with the other women and their youngest children at the top of the field. It was a rare day of rest. Young William sat at her feet, content to search for beetles in the grass, and baby John lay cradled in her lap. She relaxed as the sun warmed her back and gazed dreamily across the bay to Filey. Her only regret was that Jane and Elizabeth could not join them. It was a shame for them to be indoors on such a beautiful day. She thought of her sister's dutiful life looking after Robert's father. Elizabeth cared for him every single day, had no option since he lived with them. Surely though, Robert could have allowed her a few hours respite. As for Jane, perhaps Tom would visit her and keep her company.

Young Mary was alert, her attention now solely on the wrestlers. Her father and uncle bent their arms and held up their hands. Suddenly, her father feigned a move. When Thomas tried to counter it, her father grabbed him in a waist hold. She shivered with excitement as he tripped Thomas onto the grass. Her uncle submitted, but he won the next time. In their final wrestle, her father's longer reach and knowledge of his opponent gave him victory. She ran up to him and hugged him round the legs.

'Watch out, Will,' joked old Ben, 'she might pull thee over.'

'Can girls wrestle?' Mary asked, full of hope. 'Can they, Father?'

'No, lass, girls don't wrestle. But I'm sure you'd be the best one if they did.'

That gave her something to think about. While the other men wrestled, she persuaded her brother Francis and her youngest uncle, Richard, to have a wrestling match with her. Though she grunted and fought with all her strength, she was hopelessly outmatched. Even Francis could beat her, which made her more determined than ever to beat him at something else.

On returning to the main crowd, they found a group of boys standing to one side having a spitting competition, to see who could spit the furthest. Young Mary marched up to them and stood in line. She was dying to have a go, but they kept shoving her back and didn't allow her a turn. All she could do was stand and watch.

She was ashamed of Francis. He just couldn't get the hang of a good spit. She'd have done much better. While the others laughed at him, she hated to see his pathetic attempts. As an older brother, he was such a disappointment. She'd always disliked his girlish face and gentle ways, and the way he never stood up for himself.

She strode forwards. 'Look at you!' she shouted and prodded him with her finger. 'You can't even spit half a yard.'

When Francis reddened and seemed about to cry, it angered her more. She grabbed him by his belt and yanked him out of the line of boys queuing up for spits. She shook him and screamed, as her mother sometimes did to her.

'You're useless! You can't do anything! What are you? Useless!'

She would have carried on, but one of the Gurwood girls had been watching. Milcah rushed over to them and intervened. Without fuss, she pulled on Mary's arm.

'Leave Francis alone,' she said quietly and with authority.

Mary was so surprised that she let go of Francis and stepped away. Her face was dark with anger, and she scowled at him as he walked away to join their mother.

The boys had now lost interest in the spitting. They'd been surprised by Mary's sudden and unprovoked assault and thought it was mean of her to embarrass Francis in front of them. They left Milcah and Mary alone together and wandered off to watch the wrestling.

Milcah rested her hands on her hips. 'Oh, Mary,' she cried, 'why did you hurt your brother so?'

'Don't know.' Mary was now close to tears. She couldn't look Milcah in the eye and couldn't explain. The loss of temper had frightened her, and she didn't want the vicar to hear about it. He might stop her lessons or forbid his daughters to read aloud her favourite stories.

'I don't know,' she shouted and turned her back on Milcah. Then she stomped off in a sulky mood to see what her father was doing.

Only four men remained to battle it out, William being one of them. While everyone paused for food and drink, old Ben mischievously challenged Dickon to an impromptu fight.

'Come on, Dickon, thoo was a good wrestler once,' he teased. 'I reckon us two could 'ave a decent match. We could show them young'uns a thing or two.'

Dickon grinned. 'I'm game, but I'm a lot younger than thoo. Should thoo be wrestlin' at thy age?'

'Oh, come on – I'm fit as a lop.'

Young Mary watched them grapple like a pair of old, cantankerous bears. They shoved each other in all directions, making folk move quickly out of the way to avoid being trampled. Neither man could find an advantage. They puffed and wheezed and cleared their throats and spat. After a quarter of an hour, Mary's grandfather tapped them on their shoulders.

'Enough, you two. I think we should call it a draw.'

'Aye,' shouted Sarah Ezard, spluttering with a large chunk of cheese in her mouth. 'I don't want to waste all me embrocations on a couple o' broken-winded nags as them two.'

The two men loosened their grips and shook hands. They were both relieved though they'd never admit it.

Young Mary wondered why even old men were allowed to wrestle. As she chewed on her pie, she glanced around. As well as her father, her uncle Matthew, Robert Read from Speeton and the blacksmith were still in the contest. She crossed her fingers and hoped her father would not draw the blacksmith.

Chapter 8

John Dawson wasn't at the wrestling. Still unwelcome wherever the Jordan family gathered, he stayed behind at the Smiths' farm, weeding their garden and carrying out odd repairs. His wife was alone too, in her darkened parlour, nursing the new baby. Both heard the cheers and shouts from the field and wished they could partake of the feast and merriment.

Jane Jordan, also indoors, heard the noise and wished she were there.

Tom did not stay to watch the afternoon's matches. All morning, he'd been itching to visit Jane and so, as soon as everyone was busy eating, he sneaked away. He found Jane in the kitchen, huddled on a stool by the fire even though it was June, and the weather was warm.

'I'm glad to see thoo's up an' about,' he said.

'And *I'm* glad to see *you*, but don't miss the wrestling for my sake. Get back to the field. Don't stay in with me.'

He pulled up another stool and sat beside her. ''Ow could I enjoy it without thee? 'Ere's where I want to be. I love thee, Jane.'

He put an arm round her, feeling her bony shoulders under the shawl. She was thinner each day.

'Why not come out an' get some fresh air,' he coaxed. 'We could walk to cliff top. It'll do us both good.'

With reluctance, she left the fire and went out into the bright sunlight. Despite wearing a bonnet, the light hurt her eyes, and the fresh air made her cough. She held onto his arm tightly as they strolled up Oxtrope Lane. Every so often, they stopped while she got her breath back.

'Is thoo still takin' nettle tea?' he asked.

'Yes, every day. Sarah Ezard keeps telling me all young maidens should drink it.'

'Aye, I've 'eard 'er many times.' He began to imitate Sarah's gait, her back bent like when she scoured the undergrowth for herbs and fungi. He tried to imitate her voice. 'If they'd drink nettles i' March an' Mugwort i' May, so many fine maidens would not turn to clay.'

Jane laughed for the first time in ages. 'I'm also taking one of her cordials,' she added. 'It's made from herb angelica – it smells a lot better than nettles.'

'Good,' he said and smiled, though he doubted the so-called cures were effective.

By the time they reached the cliffs, the sky had clouded over, and it looked like rain. He was afraid they'd be caught in a shower. To save time, he carried her part of the way back and, because she was so weary, he decided to stay and spend the rest of the day with her. As he held her hand, he noted with alarm that she was feverish.

At the field below the church, William had drawn Matthew Smith as his opponent, and Robert Read was to face the blacksmith, Phineas Wrench. Young Mary jumped up and down at the thought of her father's next match. She desperately wanted him to win.

William and Matthew had wrestled many times before and knew each other's strengths and weaknesses. They were confident, even arrogant, as they planted their feet and faced each other. For a while, they manoeuvred in silence, no words spoken as they concentrated on each other's movements. They waved their hands about, each trying to get a good hold. Suddenly, without warning, they both fell to the ground.

Young Mary was dismayed as they performed a chain of moves that happened so rapidly she couldn't tell who was winning. As fast as her father made one hold, her uncle wriggled out of it and held her father instead. Everyone was cheering and shouting encouragement as the two wrestlers rolled about the grass, neither having the advantage for long. And then the rain came down.

The heavy shower was so sudden that most were caught unprepared. Cheeses went soggy and bonnets and clothes were drenched. Most folk ran to the church for shelter while others put sacking over their heads and braved the weather. The two wrestlers carried on, oblivious to the rain thudding around them.

Young Mary stayed to watch with her young uncles, their heads tucked under a large sheet of sackcloth. The grass beneath the men was churned into mud and still they carried on, their hands and feet slipping and sliding in the wet. Neither of them would submit. They would have continued if Francis Jordan and George Gurwood had not intervened.

'Thoo can restart this fight at Up'all,' suggested Francis. 'I'll tell rest of 'em to meet in our barn.'

'Get cleaned up first,' said George, pulling a face. 'There's that much mud on both of you, I can hardly tell you apart.'

Young Mary approached her father. Not minding the wet and dirt, she slipped her hand into his and walked with him and Uncle Matthew to Uphall. By the time they reached the yard, the rain had washed off most of the dirt, but their breeches and stockings were still streaked with mud. Mary watched them dip their heads into the trough and splash water at each other. They were like a couple of boys.

There was plenty of space in the barn for a wrestling circle and room for the spectators round the edge. The hard trodden floor made for better footholds but also for more painful falls.

It was half an hour before William finally submitted, making Matthew one of the finalists.

Young Mary couldn't understand why her father had lost. She sulked for the second time that day.

'Why did Uncle Matthew win? Did you let him?'

'No, it happens sometimes,' he explained. 'Maybe I'll beat him next year. It's nothing to be upset about. Come on, cheer up. I'm not hurt – not much anyway. Come on, lass, give me a smile.'

'Only if you put your shirt back on.'

When he'd put on a dry shirt, they snuggled up close in the fading light to watch Robert Read from Speeton take on their blacksmith. Robert was young and tall with a tanned face and piercing blue eyes. His body was muscular and yet in proportion. Stripped to the waist, both men and women admired his broad shoulders and the way his back tapered to his slim hips.

Sarah Ezard gave one of her dirty laughs. ''Is backside is good enough to eat,' she shouted. 'I could just sink me teeth into one o' them cheeks.'

Those who heard gave a bawdy cheer.

The blacksmith, in contrast, was squat. His body was top-heavy, like a barrel on legs. The muscles on his arms were huge, and the hair on his forearms was singed. His back, though white, was as freckled as his face and his shaved head looked like a badly worn brush.

The Reighton folk cheered for their blacksmith. It was obvious to them that Phineas would win. He was older, much stronger and more experienced. And he'd been the wrestling champion for years. While Robert fought with intelligence and was quick to alter his holds, he found it nigh on impossible to shift the blacksmith's balance. It was a foregone conclusion. The final would pit Phineas against Matthew Smith.

'We'll let Phineas 'ave a rest,' Francis Jordan announced. 'We can eat an' drink while 'e gets 'is breath back.'

Young Mary sat beside her father, gazing in awe at the blacksmith's bulging arms. All the children were scared of him, and the forge, with its fire and clatter, was no place for them. Though he'd helped her yesterday with Stina, she crossed her fingers and hoped her uncle would beat him.

The sun had gone behind the farmhouse by the time the last fight began. Dickon placed lanterns on the floor, and the two wrestlers cast enormous shadows against the wall. Young Mary watched the writhing shapes, imagining a hero and a monster in battle. Her father tried to explain to her the intricate moves. She only saw that Matthew's favourite arm twists were useless against Phineas; the blacksmith always reversed the holds and made Matthew cry out. All of a sudden, Matthew was thrown to the ground and pinned down with his arm twisted beneath him.

'Submit?' cried the blacksmith.

'No.'

Though Matthew banged his free hand up and down on the floor in pain, Phineas twisted the arm back even further.

'Submit?'

'No.'

Phineas waited barely a moment before jerking the arm from its socket. There was a popping sound and a cry of agony as Matthew submitted at last. He'd not be wrestling again that day. As he struggled to his knees, his arm dangled strangely and, despite biting his lip, a tear slid down his cheek.

His wife Ellen rushed to his side and helped him to his feet. 'Phineas 'as gone too far,' she protested.

Francis Jordan stood in front of them. He sensed most people agreed and yet he announced, 'It is within our rules.'

'I don't care,' chuntered Sarah Ezard as she stepped forward with William. She could see Matthew's eyes were wide but unfocused. He swayed a little as if he might faint.

William hated to see his friend in such pain. 'Shall I knock him out?' He offered.

'Nay,' said Sarah calmly. 'No need. I'll be done soon enough. It's not first time it's 'appened to 'im – maybe not same arm though. Give 'im summat to bite on. Yon thick leather strap'll do.'

Dickon unhooked a strap from the wall and passed it over. She doubled it in half.

''Ere, Matthew,' she ordered, 'put this between tha teeth an' lie down. When I count to three, bite 'ard an' give a loud grunt.'

He nodded, out of breath and almost sick with pain.

She sat on the floor with her legs astride his arm, braced one foot against his chest and held his arm by the wrist.

'Ready?' she asked. 'I'll start countin'.'

Ellen knelt beside him and smoothed the hair from his forehead.

He nodded and closed his eyes.

First, while counting one and two, Sarah raised his arm smoothly and slowly up towards his head and then, all at once, on the count of three, she twisted it.

He screamed as his arm locked into place. The strap fell from his mouth and the worst was over. Nevertheless, his hands shook as he passed the strap back to Dickon.

Sarah and Ellen helped him to sit up while he used his good arm to support the other across his chest.

He smiled. 'Thank you, that's perfect. I'm alright now. The pain's gone.'

William and Dickon got him to his feet and everyone, including Phineas, gave a round of applause.

'We thank you,' said Ellen, 'but I think Matthew's 'ad enough. We'd best get 'ome an' strap up 'is arm.'

'Aye,' he replied, 'there's no point staying.' He put on a brave face and grinned. 'I can't dance now, can I?'

As the couple left with their children, Phineas took his winnings. He received a subdued cheer. It was a poor end to the day's matches.

Out of respect for Matthew, William thought that his family should leave too.

'And we've left Jane on her own all day,' he argued. 'It's not fair.'

'I know,' replied Mary, 'but I bet Tom's been to see her, and it's been an age since we last danced together. She'll probably be asleep by now anyway.'

'Fine then, we'll stay a bit longer.'

While their parents drank and danced until late, the younger children soon fell asleep. They were bundled up together at one end of the barn like a brood of puppies. If one of them wriggled in their sleep, the rest shifted a little before settling again. At midnight, their parents took lanterns and began to untangle their offspring from the muddle of arms and legs and blankets.

As she left, young Mary glanced back at the drunken and victorious Phineas Wrench. When he wasn't looking, she stuck her tongue out at him.

Chapter 9

Tom stayed well into the evening with Jane. It was quiet in the house without the others and almost like being married the way she pulled off his boots and poured a drink for him in the kitchen. It was the stuff of his dreams.

Though happy and content in his company, Jane's face clouded over when she considered her ill health. With deep regret, she realised she was not the best of prospects for him.

'You haven't had much luck in love, Tom, what with Anna – and now me,' she said.

'Listen,' he replied instantly, 'I think I'm luckiest man alive. I've loved both tha sister an' thee, an' I've been lucky to work at Up'all. I wouldn't change places wi' no one.'

'That's kind, Tom. I love you for it.'

They sat in silence watching the fire die down, twisting their fingers in and out of each other's hands. Neither of them dared speak of a future together. They feared to tempt fate, but Jane had a suspicion that her health was permanently broken. At times, her heart raced or thumped with an irregular rhythm, and she often felt dizzy and weak.

Tom noticed her sudden sadness and tried to distract her with the latest gossip. 'Tha sister Dorothy is still grievin' over losin' John Dawson. She stays in most days.'

'That's a shame,' whispered Jane. 'I feel sorry for him too – and his poor wife.'

'No need – Ellen's become best o' friends wi' Susannah.'

'I'm pleased about that.' Jane found that she wasn't a bit jealous at this news. Her youthful passion for Ellen now seemed so long ago.

'An' vicar's lasses are growin' up fast. No doubt men'll soon come courtin'.'

This news saddened her again. She wondered who Tom would find to court if she didn't get better.

Each night, Jane lay in the loft listening in the darkness to the sound of her brother's snores beneath. Apart from Tom, her brother and Mary were her only contacts. When the family retired to bed, she heard young Mary below singing herself to sleep. It was comforting to hear the childish voice. The girl invented her own simple tunes and sang whatever came into her head, whether it was about Ben and his honeybees or about some adventure with her dog. What was unusual and endearing to Jane was that young Mary interspersed the normal, everyday events of her life with passages learnt from the Bible.

Jane always knew what kind of a day the girl had by her choice of psalm. On a bad day, when Mary thought she'd been treated unfairly, she'd sing 'Thou tellest my wanderings. Put my tears into thy bottle.' On a day when she'd been out running free with her dog in the sunshine, she'd sing 'The little hills rejoice. The pastures are clothed with flocks; the valleys are covered with corn; they shout for joy, they also sing.'

William and Mary would also lie awake listening to these improvised songs. He was proud of his daughter's learning and her amazing memory. Mary just thought the girl a queer little thing. She hardly dare speculate on the future for such a child.

Francis couldn't hope to get to sleep until his sister had finished singing. Though he enjoyed listening, he wouldn't admit it. Instead, he complained and moaned whenever she began, and held the pillow over his head.

One night, young Mary sang louder than ever, choosing an appropriate psalm. 'O sing unto the Lord a new song. Make a joyful noise unto the Lord; make a loud noise, and rejoice, and sing praise.'

'Stop! No more!' Francis shouted, his voice muffled under the pillow. He popped his head out when she paused and asked, 'Do you have to sing when we're in bed? Why can't you do your singing when you're out with Stina – miles from anybody?'

She had an immediate answer from Psalm 149. 'Let the saints be joyful in glory: let them sing aloud upon their beds.'

He groaned.

William and Mary shouted over to their daughter. 'That's enough. It's time to stop singing now. Go to sleep.'

On another evening, young Mary sang parts of Psalm 148 that she'd learnt that day at the vicarage. Her voice carried round the house, and Francis, under his pillow, pictured the things she mentioned.

'Praise the Lord from the earth, ye dragons, and all deeps, fire and hail and snow and stormy wind, mountains, and all hills, creeping things and flying fowl.'

Jane heard every word and cherished them. She sighed and slept soundly for a change, not coughing once.

George Gurwood based young Mary's education on the Bible. She could read almost as well as his youngest daughter even though she was three years younger, and she remembered everything he taught her about flowers, trees and birds. He was disappointed when Milcah told him how Mary had bullied her brother on St Peter's Day. He trusted Milcah; of all his daughters, she was the most observant and reliable. He now questioned the education he'd given young Mary and wondered if different literature might improve her character and foster a Christian conscience.

One drizzly summer's morning, the vicar pulled Bunyan's *The Pilgrim's Progress* from his shelf. When parts of it were read to young Mary, she was thrilled by the landscape of swamps, caves and mountains, and the monsters that lay in wait there. He didn't realise that whenever he left Cecilia in charge, Mary begged her to re-read the more exciting parts.

The stories fired young Mary's imagination so much that, early one morning, she decided to set off to see the Celestial City. She recalled what Christian had been given to eat on his way and, while her mother was busy seeing to Jane, she took some oatcakes and a handful of raisins and wrapped them in a cloth. Francis was in the garden weeding and John was asleep after his feed. She tied the parcel of food to her waist. Only young William was a witness, playing under the kitchen table. She'd intended to journey alone with Stina, but William crawled out and took her hand.

'You want to come with me?' she asked. 'You want to see lions and dragons – and a giant?'

He nodded, persuaded by her excitement.

She called to her dog and whispered a warning not to bark or make a fuss. Then she peered through the window to check that Francis was still busy down the garden. Everywhere was quiet as they sneaked out of the front door.

The dog ran ahead while young Mary half-dragged William along the lane. He'd never been part of her plan and his lopsided gait was slowing her progress. She stood still and glowered at him. Determined not to go back home, she decided he could be the heavy burden that weighed Christian down. As they left the lane to cut through the back field to the church, they saw Sarah Ezard out gathering herbs with her basket.

The woman hailed them, full of suspicion. 'Now then, what's thoo up to this mornin'?'

'Mother's sent us to get sticks. She's run out and wants to do some baking. She said it's time William learnt to do more work. I think Mother will probably make oatcakes.'

'Right, then.' Sarah didn't pay any more heed. She was preoccupied with her mental list of plants to collect before the day grew too hot.

Mary led her small brother further up the hill and across to the church gate, the start of her epic journey.

'See over there,' she said, pointing to Filey Brigg, where the morning sun lit up the rocks. 'That's the

Celestial City on Mount Sion. No more sadness, no more tears. You can see the King every day and walk with him. Think of that, William.'

He obeyed and looked. It was a very long way off and he was already tired after trudging up the hill.

'Listen,' she added, 'we're going downhill next. You'll find it easier.' She didn't say that the vicar had once called the low-lying field at the bottom 'The Slough of Despond'.

Stina ran on ahead down the hill, disturbing the odd rabbit that veered away in fright, and following a track between the clumps of gorse that led to the water meadow below.

The wet summer meant that there really was a miry swamp at the bottom of Reighton Hill. Soon, the children's bare feet were sinking into the boggy ground. Somewhere in the distance, they heard their names shouted. Mary knew it was her mother.

'Don't worry, William. That's probably a devil trying to tempt us. Close your ears. Now, you're my burden, so climb on my back and I'll carry you across the swamp.'

The added weight made her sink deeper, but this was just what she wanted. Her hero, Christian, she remembered, had also wallowed for a time, grievously bedaubed with dirt. Everything was as it should be.

'Do you know, William,' she said, recalling the words of the great book, 'whole cartloads of rocks and things have been swallowed up in here, and still there's room for more.'

Stina went in front, leaping and sinking until she reached the other side. Wet and filthy, she struggled out and shook herself, and then turned to see the children.

Mary was now on her knees with William hanging on, clutching her round the neck and almost choking her. She bet Christian's burden had never been this difficult. At least his burden didn't fidget and sway about and complain. The journey was harder than she'd imagined, but then it was supposed to be a test. Eventually, she crawled out of the mire and sat down, eager to get William off her back. She shielded her eyes and gazed towards the cliff top, their next target.

'Now, William, don't be afraid, although we do have to walk past some lions.' His eyes widened. 'If we keep to the middle of the path, we'll be safe. They won't harm us. You see,' she explained, 'the lions are chained up, but you can't see the chains. You just have to trust me. Come on.'

The dog ran ahead regardless of any danger. This spoiled the drama for Mary, but William was terrified and gripped her hand. He wouldn't be wearing breeches until next year and still wore a frock. He whimpered when thistles and nettles brushed against his bare legs.

After a while, Mary became bored and decided that they were safely through. For the next part of their journey, she'd need a sword. She searched around for a suitable stick but was disappointed at the lack of choice. An old broken branch of hawthorn was the nearest thing to a weapon and would have to do. She snapped off the sharp bits and waved it about.

'How's this, William, eh?'

He grinned, happy that she was pleased at last with something.

Then, as she poked around the ground with her sword, she found an old bleached jawbone of a sheep.

This reminded her of what Christian was shown in the House Beautiful.

'William, look! You'll never believe what this is.' Then she added in a dramatic whisper, 'It's the jawbone that Samson used.'

He touched it with one finger, understanding only that it was very special.

'And look here,' she said, breaking off another piece of hawthorn, 'this is the rod that Moses used in the desert. And here,' she whispered again, bending down to pick up a stone, 'this is what David used to slay Goliath!'

It was all lost on William, yet he responded with a smile to Mary's energetic prancing about.

The dog, unimpressed and eager to move on, lay and watched them with her head between her paws.

Mary sighed. 'Alright, Stina, we'll be on our way.' She stared hard at William, one hand on her hip. 'We're going to cross a valley soon, and there's a foul fiend waiting for us. I can't carry you because I'll need to fight with my sword. Come on.'

Slowly, they made their way northwards along the cliff top. William stumbled every now and then and whined that he was hungry. Also, the nettle stings on his legs were so sore.

Mary ignored his complaints. 'We can't eat until after the battle.'

As they approached Hunmanby Gap, she stopped and told him to stand still while she fought the monster. 'His name is Apollyon and he's horrible to look at.'

William flinched and turned around but saw nothing.

She remembered this part of the book word for word. 'He has scales like a fish, and wings like a dragon, and feet like a bear, and fire and smoke comes out of his belly. And his mouth is like a lion's. So keep well clear, William.'

She was unsure how to enact the great battle between Christian and Apollyon. The dog could be the monster and she could pretend to battle Stina, but Apollyon had just as good lines to say as Christian and he also got to throw darts. She opted to play both parts herself.

First, she was the monster. She lay down the 'sword' and marched with great strides away from William. Then she turned and stood with her legs and arms spread apart. She yelled in her brother's direction.

'Prepare to die! I swear thou shalt go no further. Here will I spill thy soul!' She took aim and pretended to throw flaming darts as thick as hail. Then, suddenly, she ran towards him and pretended to raise a shield in defence.

William didn't know what to do. He stood still, totally bemused by her shouting and striding about. When she played at being wounded, he grew more alarmed. First, he thought she was hit in the head. She clutched her forehead and staggered backwards. Then she yelped and shook her hand limply, and howled and hopped around as if in great pain.

'Oh, don't look so upset, William. This fight lasts half a day.' She soon tired of pretending to be wounded and moved on to the wrestling bout between Christian and Apollyon.

It was a challenge to enact both parts and in quick succession. Playing the role of Christian, she fell backwards and dropped her sword. Then, as Apollyon, she stood glowering, ready for the kill.

'I am sure of thee now!' she shouted hoarsely. Then she threw herself back onto the ground as Christian and, just as it seemed she would die, she reached for the sword and cried, 'Rejoice not against me, O mine enemy. When I fall, I shall arise!'

She thrust the hawthorn stick forwards and upwards and then shielded her face as she imagined the great creature spreading his wings and fleeing. She then got up off the grass, gave a huge sigh and glanced at William, who was standing wide-eyed and speechless.

She smiled and spoke in her normal voice. 'It's over, William. The monster's gone.' Then she remembered something else that Christian had to do. 'I must now eat these leaves of the tree of life to heal my wounds.' She smiled again. 'Then we can rest and eat.'

She pulled off a few hawthorn leaves and chewed them. Then she led William to the very edge of the cliff to sit with their legs dangling. She passed him an oatcake, saving one to throw for Stina, and counted out his share of the raisins. They had nothing to drink. It was almost noon, and their mouths were dry. Neither could find enough spit in their mouths to soothe William's nettle rash.

Now that the best part of the journey was over, Mary wished they were not so far from home and wondered if they'd ever reach their destination. Undeterred, she made William set off again.

Before long, they came to the ravine at Butcher Haven. It was just the inspiration needed for the Valley of the Shadow of Death, their last trial. She recalled that the valley was a land as black as pitch with hobgoblins and dragons. There should have been a continual howling and yelling noise, yet it was very quiet and there was bright sunlight. Even the birds had stopped singing in the heat of the day.

As they stood at the edge of the ravine, she decided they must close their eyes and walk down to the beach and on towards Filey. They must keep to a narrow path that lay between an imaginary deep ditch on one side and a dangerous quagmire on the other.

'Shut your eyes, William, and hold tight of my hand. I'll lead you through.' She fixed her eyes on the sea and then shut her eyes as well. Brandishing her stick, she walked on slowly, telling William not to mind the sparks and the noise. She imagined it to be like Phineas Wrench's forge on a dark winter's afternoon; the blazing embers, the steam, the smoke and clanging metal made it like the mouth of hell itself.

William began to cry. He'd had enough. His legs were sore, and he was more scared than ever. He wanted to be at home in the kitchen.

Mary tried to comfort him and give him courage. She quoted from the Bible. 'Though I walk through the Valley of the Shadow of Death, I will fear no evil: for thou art with me. You can open your eyes now, William. We're halfway through. The rest of the valley is full of snares and traps and deep holes, but we can see our way now. Look! See over there.'

She pointed ahead to the north, where there was a lush dark band of trees. 'That is the country of Beulah,' she explained. 'We'll soon be in heaven.'

Chapter 10

In Reighton, half the village was out looking for the two children. Only Sarah had seen them, heading southwards towards the church and the trees beyond to collect sticks. Mary swore that she'd never sent them on such an errand. She dreaded to think what her daughter was up to and was furious that she'd taken young William.

At Uphall, Dorothy Jordan was annoyed by the fuss over the missing children and complained to her husband. 'It's not right that all our lads 'ave to go out searchin'. They should be workin' i' fields.'

He was puzzled by her lack of concern. 'The children *are* part of our family after all,' he said.

'Aye,' she replied, 'an' trouble'll always return. Young Mary's been nowt but trouble since day she were born. She'll come 'ome, thoo'll see.'

Mary stayed at home with Francis and John in case the children returned. Her sister Elizabeth arrived to keep her company. Jane heard the commotion from her bed in the loft and prayed for the children's safety.

William took a horse and set off in the direction of Argam, fearing that his daughter had plans to free the bull again. Dickon and any spare lads searched around

Uphall and checked the outbuildings. The Jordan boys went down to the beach below Reighton.

Tom headed towards Speeton to see if they'd been found there. He followed the stream eastwards, stopping every now and then to call their names wherever the ravine was steepest. He was afraid they might have fallen and imagined their broken bodies in a heap at the bottom. When he returned with no news, he was told to go further south to Buckton cliffs and Bempton.

Old Ben chose to sit in his garden and wait. Young Mary often turned up without warning. Other villagers searched to the south and west of the village. Elizabeth persuaded her husband Robert to go northwards.

'Don't worry. I'll look after your father for however long it takes. Go on – find Mary.'

He agreed readily and took his favourite pathway along the cliffs. Before long, he came across a stretch of grass much trampled about. He found broken bits of hawthorn and guessed he might be on the right track.

Young Mary had hoped to find a 'sweet and pleasant' land ahead where birds sang among the flowers, where the sun shone all the time and where the Shining Ones walked. Instead, a cold wind sprang up with the incoming tide and clouds covered the sun. A smell of stewing meat hung in the wind, drifting from somewhere in front. Before she knew where she was, she'd travelled with William across another ravine and stumbled upon a gypsy camp hidden among the trees.

In an instant, one of the men grabbed Stina. Mary cried out as a rope was slung around the dog's neck. Despite growling, Stina was hauled away and tied securely to a tree. The gypsies' dogs, tethered at some distance, bared their teeth and snarled.

Mary and William stood still in shock. They'd been taught to avoid strangers, especially those with such swarthy faces and a strange way of talking. She'd heard Ben call them Egyptians. She was about to turn and run when she felt thick arms thrown around her from behind and found herself lifted into the air.

William sobbed in fright as his sister was carried, squirming and with her legs kicking, towards the campfire. A group of brown-faced children, squatting in front of a row of goatskin tents, began to laugh.

Mary was set down near the fire. The man pointed to his mouth and then to the cooking pot. It smelled of rabbit stew. She wasn't sure what he intended. Did he want to cook her or was he offering food? While she wondered what was going to happen, a young gypsy lad carried a dead rabbit into the clearing and handed it to an old woman with skin like dark leather.

In spite of her fear, Mary was distracted. She watched the woman take out a long thin knife and lay the rabbit on the ground, its white furry belly uppermost. The gypsy smoothed it out, spread wide its back legs and squeezed its lower stomach.

Suddenly, William giggled and pointed. 'It's weeing!' he shouted. He didn't find it so funny when he watched the woman slit open the rabbit's chest and, using just the tip of her knife, draw a line right down its middle.

Mary admired the speed and skill with which the old woman held the rabbit up by its front legs with one hand and used a couple of fingers on her other hand to slide the guts out. It was done in an instant. She saw William hold his nose and stare at the stinking heap of innards on the ground. Immediately, four great hairy dogs were released. They leapt forward to scrap over the remains.

Mary had her eyes on the woman, eager to see what she'd do next. The rabbit was laid on the ground once more and, with five quick chops of an axe, the legs and head were removed. The woman then chopped off the tail and, with a toothless leer, tossed the bit of fluff towards William. Then she peeled the skin back from the rabbit's stomach, freed the last bit with her knife and ripped it all off in one go. Mary's mouth hung open in awe.

William put his hands over his ears. He hated the sucking sound the skin made as it tore away from the muscle, and he didn't like the look of the rabbit's dark red and blue flesh without its fur.

The meat was thrown into a bowl of water to soak, and the gypsy wiped her hands on a sack. With her eyes on the children, she stirred the pot of stew. After a short while, she lifted out a chunk of rabbit and rubbed the white meat between her fingers. It was so tender that it fell off the bone. Seeing this, the gypsy children grinned and passed her their bowls.

Mary and William were pushed down onto the ground and made to sit cross-legged like the others. They were given a piece of rabbit meat to eat with their hands. Relieved that they were not going to be eaten after all, they relaxed, chewed their food and enjoyed sucking the juice from their fingers.

'We're from Reighton,' Mary told them, wiping her lips. 'Thank you for the rabbit, but we'd better go home now.' She glanced at the sun filtering through the trees behind and pointed. 'Look – it's getting late. Come on, William, get up. Leave that rabbit's tail here and we'll go.'

He held onto the bit of fluff, reluctant to part with it.

She stood, grabbed his hand and yanked him upwards. He dropped the tail and yelped in pain as his elbow was almost pulled out of joint. Then he burst into tears at losing the tail.

The old gypsy woman sprang forwards and picked it up. 'Scut – bring good luck,' she cried, waving it about. She grinned, showing nothing but gums, pressed the tail into his palm and closed his fingers over it. 'Keep,' she said. 'Keep. Good luck.'

'We must go home,' Mary repeated, taking a few backward steps. She waved goodbye, hoping they'd understand. 'Thank you for feeding us. Goodbye. We have to go.' She risked walking to the trees and knelt to untie Stina.

The gypsies watched and didn't stop them. Then, just as she led William and the dog out of the clearing and thought they were safe, a gypsy man jumped in front and barred their way.

Mary thought they were going to be killed.

Instead, another gypsy appeared, leading two dirty ponies with shaggy coats. The first gypsy mounted one of the ponies and Mary was hoisted up to sit behind. The second gypsy mounted the other pony and swung William up. They set off to go inland and up the ravine with Stina trotting behind.

Mary found the ride a lot easier than walking with William. Once out of the ravine, she had a good view of the sea, the cliffs and the hills from the pony. She looked at William clutching his rabbit's tail and holding on tight to the gypsy's jacket. He was smiling, but she was growing uneasy. Her cheek kept rubbing against the man's rough waistcoat and it smelled rich and rancid. Also, she was afraid. She wasn't sure that they were being taken back home.

Robert Storey carried on his search northwards. When he arrived at the gypsy camp, Mary and William were long gone. He questioned the men and then strode back to Reighton as quickly as he could. He prayed that the gypsies could be trusted and had not stolen the children.

Chapter 11

Having seen no sign of his children, William returned home expecting to find them already there safe and sound. He was puzzled by their disappearance. It was strange that, apart from Sarah Ezard, no one out in the fields or journeying through the village had seen them. He wanted another search of the Uphall buildings, though Dickon assured him that he'd been and looked everywhere. Dickon suggested that everyone in the village should check their own yards and lofts – just in case.

By mid-afternoon, William was pacing up and down the hill by the church. Word came that gypsies were in the area and, when Tom and William's younger brothers returned without any news, he feared the worst. He told Mary and old Ben to stay at home and he called on the able-bodied men to meet at Uphall. There they would decide what to do next.

The youngsters wanted a raid on the gypsies, but the older men shook their heads. Dorothy Jordan remained unmoved by the drama and kept clicking her tongue.

'Thoo's all wastin' tha time,' she grumbled. 'That lass'll turn up, thoo'll see.' She gave a wry smile and added, 'If tinkers 'ave got 'er, I reckon they'll soon bring 'er back. I'd like to see anyone put up wi' young Mary's chatter an' rubbish fo' longer than 'alf a day!'

The hired lads smirked, knowing what young Mary was like, yet the glower on William's face made them ashamed. To make amends, they offered to go out and search the hills again.

It was late in the afternoon when two gypsies rode into Reighton. They entered the main street from the north. Folk sitting outside their cottages rushed inside and slammed their doors. The villagers peeped out of their windows to see a pair of ill-fed ponies mounted by the blackest of gypsies. Seated behind the men there appeared to be gypsy children, equally grubby and unkempt. A muddy dog trailed behind.

A group of young lads had gathered round the pond to water their livestock. On seeing the gypsies, they picked up stones and began to pelt them. The gypsies raised their arms in defence and shouted something unintelligible.

Young Mary cried out, 'It's me! Stop, it's me.'

But more stones were thrown, some hitting the ponies and making them skittish. Old Ben was in his garden and heard the commotion. He hurried to the street and didn't recognise the children, their clothes and faces were so ingrained with dirt.

Mary saw him and shouted, 'Ben! Ben! Help us!'

He couldn't believe it was young Mary, filthy yet otherwise unharmed. As fast as he could, he hobbled towards her and yelled at the boys to stop throwing stones.

The lads laughed at the way he tried to run with his bandy legs, and they held onto their stones, wondering what he would do. They heard him mutter something to the gypsies and watched him lift Mary and William off the ponies. The gypsies then turned on them. They waved their fists, approached the pond and threatened them. The lads took fright and backed off. They dropped their stones and pretended to be busy with their animals.

Ben got hold of one of the biggest lads and shook him. 'Tha sackless bunchclot, where's tha sense? Run to Mary Jordan an' say 'er bairns is safe. I'll bring 'em along shortly. An' *thoo*,' he said, grabbing hold of a lanky lad with the beginnings of a downy moustache, 'thoo long stretch o' pump water, thoo'd better run to Up'all an' let 'em know there as well. Go on then, don't wait till I 'ave to clip tha lugs.'

The two lads ran off and Ben turned to face the gypsies. 'Many thanks fo' bringin' bairns back safe. 'Twas very Christian o' thee. Follow me back to their 'ouse. They'll give summat to thee i' payment.' He beckoned them and pointed towards St Helen's Lane.

They shrugged and mumbled a few words Ben couldn't understand. Suddenly, one of them spat in the direction of the pond. Without a word to Ben, they spun their ponies round, kicked them into motion and rode back where they came from.

Ben turned his attention to the two children at his side and the muddy dog. He shook his head and clicked his tongue. 'God knows what tha mother'll say.'

Mary held his hand and peered into his rheumy eyes.

'No,' he said with a deep sigh, 'it's no good, Mary. There's nowt I can do to 'elp. Thoo must be prepared for a good drubbin'. Come on. Tha mother an' father 'ave been worried sick, an' 'alf village 'as been out lookin' fo' thee.'

As they reached the house, Mary was already on her way out to meet them. She could not believe the state they were in. Her voice, when she shouted, sounded high and unnatural with worry.

'Where in God's name have you been? How could you be so thoughtless? And to take William!' She gave her daughter a hefty clout across the head, catching one ear and making it smart.

Tears flooded the girl's eyes. She pulled free of Ben and ran into the house.

The dog followed her and sat outside the door trembling.

Out in the lane, Mary took hold of her son's hand. She went down on her knees and hugged him. 'I was so afraid I'd lost you.' Then she held him at arm's length and noticed the rash on his legs. 'You poor thing! That sister of yours'll be the death of you. Come on,' she said, standing up again, 'let's get you inside and see to those legs of yours.'

As they went indoors, she turned to Ben. 'Thank you for bringing them.'

He didn't like to leave young Mary, but it was none of his business. He shuffled home, wondering if he'd ever see her free to roam the village again.

On hearing the commotion, Jane had left her bed in the loft. She began to wipe away the worst of the dirt from young Mary's face and hands. Francis watched them, glad to have his sister home again. He couldn't help feeling smug at her being in trouble and yet life was dull without her. When his mother marched in with an angry frown, he slunk into a corner.

Mary took one look at Jane with the girl. 'Leave her!' she ordered. 'She can clean her own face and then get straight to bed. Just put a bucket of water out in the garden. It's young William here needs seeing to, not her.'

Jane was shocked to see the boy's legs. The nettle rash was so severe that the stings had merged into large red patches. He could hardly bear to be touched and his arms were full of scratches.

Francis crept forward to see and found it hard to believe that such a small boy could bear that much pain. He himself hated nettle stings.

His mother took control. 'Fetch me the vinegar, Francis, and we'll dab him with it. No – better still, I'll see to the vinegar, and you go out and get a handful of dock leaves.'

'Shall I ask Sarah Ezard if she has anything? I can go that way.'

'Yes. Poor lad'll need something to ease the pain and get him off to sleep. Go now. And you, Jane, you get back to bed. Don't worry. I can see to John, and William should be home soon.'

By the time William returned from Uphall, his daughter was already in bed without any supper. He ignored his wife's complaints and went straight to young Mary and held her tight. His show of affection set her crying again.

'Listen,' he said gently, 'you must *never* go anywhere again, not without telling me first. You understand?'

She nodded and tried to tell him about her dream of getting to the Celestial City, but he could only catch the odd phrase between her sobs.

'You're too precious to me, Mary. You mustn't wander off anymore, for whatever reason. Do you hear me? Mary? Do you promise?'

She nodded again and pushed her face back into his chest as she gulped back another sob.

He didn't know what more he could do. His wife would be making their life hell for a while and his mother had already given her opinion. No doubt the whole village was thinking he was too lenient, that he gave his daughter far too much freedom. Her education was another sore point. Most were against teaching girls how to read and write. William recalled a quip that Phineas Wrench had heard and passed on. 'A very little wit is valued in a woman, as we are pleased with a few words spoken plain by a parrot.' William couldn't agree, not when it came to his own daughter.

As he wondered about young Mary's future, his son whimpered in the kitchen. Mary was doing her best to soothe the dreadful nettle rash. When Francis returned with poultices made up of groundsel, she plastered them on as a cold compress. Anxious that his legs were still sore, she chewed her nails.

'I think I'd best make some camomile tea. It might help him sleep and relieve the pain and swelling.'

It was some hours before he stopped crying and fell asleep in her arms. His hand still grasped the rabbit's tail for luck. When she put him to bed, she prised the tail away. It was a mucky thing and she thought to throw it on the fire. At the last moment, she changed her mind and put it by his side.

That night, Francis lay awake, wondering how long it would be before his sister sang in bed again.

Under the roof, Jane was the last to fall asleep. She couldn't relax after the worry over the children and coughed most of the night.

Chapter 12

Mary kept her daughter indoors. There were to be no lessons at the vicarage and no walks with the dog. Like her mother-in-law, she was still angry with the girl and annoyed that so much time and effort had been spent at such a busy time of year. She wanted to be outside herself, helping with the harvest, and now had to stay at home with her daughter and comfort young William with his nettle rash. Although she blamed the girl, she knew she'd have been hampered anyway with the year-old John. After seven days of being shadowed by a bored, sullen and clumsy helper, she gave in and allowed her daughter to go out and help with the harvest.

Each evening at sunset, young Mary rode home on her father's shoulders. It didn't matter how exhausted he was, she always charmed her way round him and he could never refuse her.

Francis walked at his father's side, trying to look tall and strong, but wished he were small enough to ride on his father's shoulders too. He didn't like to see his sister's face tanned like a hired lad. She never kept her bonnet on properly; even by midday, it was askew or hung round her neck. It was a relief that at least her hair had grown back to its usual curls. One evening, on their journey home, Francis glanced up at his sister and smirked. He repeated what his grandmother had said, imitating her voice.

'Thoo'll never get any lad to take to thee – not with a face brown as a 'Gyptian.'

'I don't care,' Mary answered, lifting her head high, 'I like the sun on my face.'

'You'll get freckles.'

'Leave her alone,' their father interrupted, 'she's fine as she is.' He admired her hair lightened by the sun; it shone with chestnut highlights. 'Mary, your hair's just like mine. It shines like a conker, except yours is like a new one, fresh from its case.'

She stuck her tongue out at Francis. His hair was dark brown and straight, without any waves or shiny bits. Even his eyes were plain – a very dark brown, almost like black beads. Her eyes, she knew from her father, were hazel, and they shimmered and changed colour depending on the weather or what she was wearing. Sometimes her eyes were golden, sometimes peagreen.

When William and the two children arrived home, worn out after a full day in the fresh air, his wife felt cheated. She envied them working outside all day and missed the companionship of the other women. With a heavy heart, she thought of the number of harvests she'd missed since being married. Often, she'd been with child or was nursing a newly born.

Young Mary had often wondered why Ben spent time every day at Uphall. If Ben was not at home, she could always find him in the stable or the field talking to the mule.

'It's not *your* mule,' she said one morning as he was about to leave for Uphall.

'No, it's not, but it's me what trained 'er an' only Tom can 'andle 'er properly. I trained 'im as well.'

'Can I ride on her?'

'No.'

She pouted as she accompanied him up the hill. Ben usually let her do anything. When they reached the field, the mule saw Ben, or smelled his arrival, and walked towards them.

'So why can't I have a ride?' she persisted.

'Because she's never 'ad a proper saddle on. It took me long enough to get 'er used to panniers.'

'I could sit on without a saddle.'

'Look – you don't understand. A mule is not like a horse and Princess Patience here is tricky – she's likely to leap sideways or bolt if a dog barks. Anything might scare 'er an' then you'd fall off.'

Young Mary frowned and thought for a while. 'Look – if you can train her to carry things, you can train her to carry me.'

He laughed. 'Aye – I bet there's a lot o' folk i' village who'd like to see thee stuffed in a pannier.'

She frowned again and put her hands on her hips. 'I didn't mean that.'

When Ben went to bed that night, he thought of ways around the problem. It could take a while, but he might be able to get the mule to suffer a child on her back. The next morning, he asked young Mary for a pair of her stockings. He also lifted her up to estimate her weight. Then they walked to Uphall, where he filled the stockings with soil. He also borrowed a small sack of grain.

'There – we'll let Princess 'ave a good look at this sack. Let 'er 'ave a sniff an' then I'll lift it onto 'er back. If she abides that, then I'll tie on tha stockings – they'll dangle like a pair o' legs.'

Mary was impressed though she was nothing like a sack of grain. She was told to stand well away and watch at a safe distance. Before Ben even lifted the sack, he allowed the mule plenty of time to smell it. All the time, he cajoled it gently. When the sack was lifted on at last, the mule backed up a few steps but made no more fuss. He led the mule once around the yard before he showed her the stockings.

Talking in the same persuasive fashion, Ben tied on a stocking. The mule pranced about under the unusual load. Ben managed to calm her down before attaching the other stocking.

'There's my beautiful princess,' he crooned. 'There's a good girl, thoo can do it. That's right, thoo's nearly there.'

Mary watched Ben lead the mule past her, back and forth. 'Do you think she'll let me on now?'

'Tomorrow maybe. We mustn't rush. Call for me i' mornin'.'

Dickon had also been watching. He nudged Tom. 'What's 'e up to now, fond old devil?'

''E'll 'ave a plan. 'E can do owt wi' that mule. Thoo'll see.'

The next day, young Mary was up early and charged out of the house saying she had an important job to do with Ben. As they walked to Uphall, he gave strict instructions.

'If Princess Patience is goin' to carry thee safely, then thoo must act as if thoo's a sack o' grain. No wrigglin'! I'll lead 'er an' talk to 'er, but thoo mustn't move an inch – not even to scratch tha nose.'

She gulped. Sitting still was the hardest thing to do.

Ben put on the halter and laid the thick cloth over the mule's back. 'Now, Mary, come 'ere. Stand i' front an' let Princess smell thee. That's it. Stand still. There, she likes thee. No – don't touch 'er! Thoo must never touch 'er ears. She doesn't like it. Don't be upset – I'm not cross wi' thee, but mules don't forget an' I want thoo to be safe.'

He waited until both Mary and the mule were bored. Then he whispered in Mary's ear. 'I'll lift thee on now, but remember to sit still as a stone. One, two, three, hup.'

The mule skittered sideways, but Ben had a tight hold of the rein. Much to his surprise, Mary did not fall off.

'There's a good girl,' he said as much to Mary as the mule. 'We'll walk round yard, that's it, just a little walk.'

With Ben leading, and walking and talking in the same rhythm, they managed a tour of the yard.

Dickon and Tom emerged from the barn and stood amazed. They saw young Mary seated like royalty, her head erect, her gaze unwavering as she stared at a point in the distance. She didn't move a muscle.

As the mule began another circuit of the yard, an exultant smile blossomed on Mary's face. When she passed by Dickon and Tom, she acknowledged them with the slightest nod of her head.

During the harvest, young Mary could escape her mother for the whole of the daylight hours and spend the day with her father. She ran to fetch him ham and cheese at the break time and, with Francis's help, poured out his beer.

William gave them a bag each. Their job was to help stand the sheaves up and gather any grains that fell to the ground. He was impressed by young Mary's readiness for hard work as he watched her rush and scrabble about, trying to pick up more than Francis. She had so much energy. When they stopped for a drink, she played hide and seek among the sheaves, and leapfrogged anyone bent over.

One day, when work resumed after a break, Dickon and the older Jordans began to sing, scything the barley to the rhythm of the song.

'The foreman goes first i' the 'ot summer glow
An' sings with a laugh, me lads, all of a row.'
Young Mary raised her head and
joined in the chorus.
'Then all of a row, then all of a row,
And tonight, we will sing, boys, all of a row.'

Unfortunately for her father, she memorised the bawdy verses and alarmed her mother that night by singing them in bed. Happy with her outdoor life, she was unaware of the amount of grain wasted by the changeable weather. So much was past saving that the hogs were brought up to Reighton field and turned loose among the sheaves. When the harvest was finished, a large portion was only good for animal fodder.

It was a relief to have the harvest behind them for another year, and the villagers attended the annual supper with as much gusto as if the harvest had been plentiful. Young Mary's eyes widened as she entered the Uphall barn and saw the food laid out. There was fresh bread and honey, mutton pies, apples and enormous joints of cold beef and ham. Casks of ale were lined up at one end of the barn with Martha Wrench standing guard. She was smiling, but her arms were folded as if daring anyone to pinch them before it was time. Young Mary sat with the rest of the Jordan family, six to a bench at each side of a table.

William missed his brother John. In former years, he and John had competed at drinking. He was wondering who he could challenge this year when he saw his young brother Thomas fetch the large pewter jug. Martha filled it with ale and Thomas announced to all present that he'd drink it in one go.

'But you're only 17,' William objected.

Thomas grabbed the jug. 'There has to be a first time for everything.'

Folk began to stamp their feet and bang their fists on the tables. Young Mary joined in.

'Drink! Drink! Drink!' they chanted until Thomas lifted the jug to his lips. Then, as he began to gulp down the ale, they made a low crooning noise that grew louder the higher the jug was tipped. A tremendous cheer went up when the last of the ale slopped over his face. He coughed and spluttered as William clapped him on the back.

'You've a lot to learn, brother. It's my turn now. Martha – refill the jug!'

Young Mary cheered with the rest, though she worried that her father would not succeed like her uncle. The jug was filled to the brim. This time, as William used both hands to lift it, John Gurwood struck up a fast tune on his fiddle. The 'drink, drink' chant was accompanied by rhythmical clapping and old Ben got up to dance in the open space.

Young Mary did not take her eyes off her father. She had her fingers crossed and held her breath while he swallowed to a rhythm of his own. Towards the end, as the jug got lighter, he raised an arm. Mary thought it was to ask for help, but it was his way of ending with a flourish. As the crooning reached its crescendo, William wiggled his fingers, encouraging the crowd. Then, all of a sudden, he held his palm open with fingers outstretched and crashed the empty jug down onto the table.

Amid the cheers, William glanced at his family. He winked at young Mary, overwhelmed by the good fortune of having such a daughter and one he loved so deeply. He smiled and wiped away a tear with his sleeve.

His wife assumed it was the effect of the ale and hoped he'd be too drunk to take her that night; all too often, she'd been caught out at harvest time.

Thomas jumped up from the bench and asked for another go with the jug. His father pushed him down and persuaded him otherwise. It was a waste of good ale if he spilled it.

'Dance with Milcah instead,' William suggested. 'Look – she's got her eyes on you.' He nodded in her direction. 'You won't impress her with your drinking. You've a better chance with singing and dancing. Go on – off you go.'

'Aye,' their father agreed. 'Young'uns should be dancin' an' courtin', not drinkin' thassens into an early grave.'

Thomas took their advice, strode confidently to where the Gurwoods were sitting and asked the quiet girl to dance. He knew she'd accept.

Soon, the centre of the barn was crammed with hot bodies as folk leapt about, bumping into each other. William's two youngest brothers, Samuel and Richard, danced with the sole intention of treading on other people's toes. No one stopped them – it was part of the fun.

Young Mary fidgeted and looked forward to a time when she could dance too. She didn't know how Francis could sit still while such lively jigs were played; she clapped her hands in time to the music and stomped her feet.

Only Tom spared a thought for Jane Jordan, left behind and alone in the house. After a couple of hours, he left the feast unnoticed, taking with him a few slices of ham and half a loaf of bread. He walked briskly down to St Helen's Lane in the hope that she might still be awake. If she were asleep, he'd sit by her side.

He fumbled with the latch in the darkness, lifted it and tiptoed in. It was even darker inside, so he lit a candle stub from the fire embers and called up to her.

She answered back at once. 'Tom? Is it you?'

'Aye. Can I come up?'

'Course you can. Come on, but you should be at the harvest supper.'

'Nay, I'd rather be wi' thee.'

As he reached the top of the ladder, he saw that she'd raised herself up in bed. When he put the candle by her side, she looked so beautiful. She also looked feverish.

'I've brought summat from feast.' He placed the ham and bread by the candle.

She took one glance at the food. 'I can't face it tonight.' Then, afraid of sounding ungrateful, she added, 'I'll be glad of it in the morning. It's kind of you. Sit here on the bed.'

She took his hands and pressed them by way of thanks. When he held on to her hands and gazed at her with those lovesick sheepdog eyes, she felt guilty. It was unfair to give him hope. Remembering her own futile affair with Ellen and the pain of unrequited love, it crossed her mind that it would be kinder to Tom if she made him fall out of love. Yet, as he kissed the palms of her hands and then each fingertip with such tenderness, she knew she couldn't do it. She wondered at the depth of his devotion and decided he deserved better.

'Tom,' she whispered and stared him full in the eye. 'Would you do something for me?' He nodded, eager to help in any way. 'I hardly dare ask, but, Tom, would you love me properly? Like a man and wife?'

'What?'

'You know what I'm asking,' she replied. Avoiding his eyes, she turned her head and bit her lip. It was so embarrassing, especially if he declined.

'Now?' he whispered. He knew they were alone in the house and would be for some time. They could do as they pleased.

She laid a hand gently on his leg and moved it slowly up to his groin. She felt his breeches tighten.

'Lie down here, Tom, next to me.'

The bed creaked as he stretched out by her side. Kissing him all the while, she helped him undo his belt and wriggle out of his clothes. When she kissed his bare stomach and ventured lower, he was overcome with gratitude as much as lust. He was in awe of her gentle touch and thought she must love every bit of him. He determined to enter her with the same love and respect, but inexperience got the better of him.

She didn't tell him it hurt or that he'd made her sore and, as they held each other afterwards, she was glad they'd done it. Suddenly, she was overcome with fatigue and began to cough.

'Tom,' she gasped, 'I think you'd best go on back to Uphall. They'll wonder where you've got to. Just kiss me again before you leave.'

'I love thee, Jane. So much!' He was in tears as he kissed her goodbye, amazed at the way his evening had turned out.

He strolled, still in wonderment, back up the hill. The sky was clear and full of stars. He was light-headed and breathless with sheer joy and yet, as he neared the churchyard, he was gripped by fear. He could not bear to lose Jane and fought against a rising image of her gravestone. To comfort himself, he argued that love could work wonders. It could even make her well again. With that in mind, he strode on past the church. He tipped his hat on a jaunty angle, stuck his thumbs in his belt and whistled a love song.

Chapter 13

The next morning, Dickon noticed a change in Tom. 'What's up wi' thee?' he asked as they checked the ploughs. 'Summat's cheered thee up.'

Tom grinned and touched his nose. 'All's very well wi' me. I'm sayin' nowt else.'

'Well, thoo looks good on it, whatever it is.'

All day, Tom worked with a skip in his step, and when nightfall came, he visited Jane again. He climbed up to the loft. William and Mary were below in the parlour with the children. He presumed they'd stay there and, anyway, he'd hear the ladder creak should anyone chance to come up.

His heart pounded as he lay beside Jane, and she loosened his breeches. She slid her hands down his belly and began to caress him with a touch as light as a butterfly. He fought the urge to throw himself on top of her; the bed would have made a noise. She kissed his face, neck and ears and, just as he thought he would burst, she managed to pull him closer without the bed tilting.

This time he entered her gently and she gasped with pleasure. He was dying to thrust in deep yet daren't risk it. If he were caught in the act of defiling William's young sister, there'd be such trouble. Somehow, he controlled himself and gained as much pleasure from her response. Her breathing came hot and fast in his ear. Suddenly, she grabbed his hair and whispered how she loved him. He was the happiest man alive.

From that day onwards, they met as often as they could, but in the first week of October, she had a prolonged coughing fit. Tom was alone with her in the loft and the amount of blood frightened him. He almost fell down the ladder in his panic to get help.

'It's Jane,' he called out as he reached the last rung.

'Hush – don't wake the children,' Mary warned.

William shot up the ladder to see for himself. He found his sister on her side with a bloodstained rag in her hand. She waved him away.

'I'll be alright soon,' she whispered. 'Don't worry.'

'This can't go on, Jane. Something has to change.' He sat on the edge of the bed for a while and stroked the damp hair from her eyes. She reminded him of her sister Anna. He'd lost her when she was only 19. It would be too much to lose Jane as well. When he returned to the parlour, he'd made his mind up.

'Jane can't stay in the loft. She's too ill.'

'Could she be moved to Uphall?' Tom asked.

William shrugged and pulled a face. He was thinking of his mother's reaction.

Tom pressed on. 'Jane could be tended better,' he argued. 'There's more maids an' there's 'er sister Dorothy. An' I can see 'er more often.'

William looked at his wife and she nodded in agreement.

The next day, William chose a good moment to speak to his mother. She was alone in the kitchen, kneading the bread.

'I've come to ask if Jane could be moved back here. It's too stuffy for her in the loft.'

She carried on stretching the dough and pressing it with the heel of her hand.

'No one else has caught her illness,' he added.

She sniffed and wiped floury hands on her apron. 'I'm not 'appy with it.'

'Remember Anna,' he dared to say. 'And remember Tom used to love her. Now he loves Jane.'

His mother remained unmoved. He watched her lift the dough and slam it down on the table. He knew she'd hardened her heart after Anna's death, had never grieved as others had. She needed time to come round. He waited. He was not going to leave the kitchen without an answer.

She sank her fingers deep into the dough and paused. 'Alright,' she mumbled at last. 'I'll see she 'as 'er own bed an' I'll keep 'er separate. Bring 'er this afternoon.'

When William carried his sister to the cart to take her to Uphall, he was surprised how light she was in his arms. Everyone, including his mother, was bound to see a great difference. On setting Jane down on the chair by the fire, he saw the concern on his mother's face. She obviously hadn't realised how weak and ill her daughter had become. When she held Jane in her arms and began to weep, he left the kitchen. It was about time his mother felt remorse. And it was the first time he'd seen his mother cry since Anna's death seven years ago.

Tom was stunned by the sudden change. At first, he rushed around in a desperate attempt to help and got in everyone's way. His chest was tight, he was breathless, and he couldn't sit still for a moment. His evening trysts were no longer possible, and with Jane so dangerously ill, his dreams of a shared life with her were going to be just that – dreams. His joy had been so short-lived. He had a vision of a large sack of grain being slashed with a knife. The precious, beautiful golden grain spilled out, lost in the dirt.

Francis Jordan, well aware of Tom's restless wanderings, thought it best to keep him occupied and sent him out to work each day as usual. One day, he and Dickon noticed how the lad kept stopping the plough to turn his head towards Uphall, as if gazing in that direction would help. Perhaps he was hoping someone would call for him.

Dickon took off his hat and scratched his head. 'The lad can't keep 'is mind off Jane. 'E loved Anna an' she died, an' now that Jane is so poorly, 'e thinks 'e's cursed. 'E thinks 'e's brought bad luck.'

Francis was sorry for Tom. 'I'll find 'im more work nearer Up'all. That might 'elp matters. Keep an eye on 'im, Dickon. We don't want to lose 'im.'

Tom prayed in church for Jane to recover. When that became a miracle beyond hope, he prayed she would not suffer as she grew weaker. Sarah Ezard had no new potions; she continued to prescribe her old herbal infusions to lower her temperature and ease the pain. Over and over again, Tom pleaded with God that Jane's death be gentle.

Ellen Smith visited Jane, guilty that she hadn't been more often. She found a girl who had wasted away, a girl that could hardly speak for fear of starting a coughing spasm. She placed a cool hand on Jane's forehead.

'I'm so sorry,' she said. 'Is there anythin' I can do?'

Jane, propped up on a pillow, gave the slightest shake of her head.

Ellen took one of Jane's hands, lifted it to her lips and kissed it.

Jane remembered how, years ago, she'd have given anything to have Ellen's kisses.

Ellen was also recalling the past and knew she'd been heartless. 'Will you forgive me?' she asked.

'I loved you too much,' Jane replied, her voice hoarse. 'It's my fault alone. There's nothing to forgive.' She coughed a little but controlled it and waved her hand limply to indicate no more need be said. They sat in silence while Ellen bathed Jane's forehead.

After a while, Tom arrived, and Ellen took her leave. He was determined to make Jane's last days as happy as possible.

He smiled as he sat beside the bed. ''Ow does tha feel today?'

'Not too bad, honest. No pain. Maybe a little cold, that's all.'

Though her cheeks were flushed, he re-tucked the blanket to keep her warm. She grew thinner by the day. Even her small chubby nose had a sharp edge. He could feel her bones beneath the covers and didn't wonder at what the maids believed. He'd heard them whispering that Jane must have been taken away at night to revel with the fairies and was wasting away through lack of sleep. That notion was preferable to another he'd heard; that Jane was bewitched at night, transformed into a horse and ridden to exhaustion. He couldn't believe such nonsense.

As he sat by her side and stroked her hand, he told her of the jobs he'd been doing that day. 'I've been 'elpin' grease an' mark our sheep, an' me an' Dickon 'ave been digging seaweed into top field. Tomorrow we'll think about sowin' winter wheat. Dickon always reckons it's best to sow when moon is waxin'.'

Her head sank deeper into the pillow, and it wasn't long before his soft murmurings of everyday tasks had soothed her to sleep.

William and Mary took turns to visit and allowed Francis to go with them, as he was missing his Aunt Jane. Young Mary wasn't invited; her grandmother did not want her chatter and clumsiness in the sick room. The vicar and his wife and Sarah Ezard also visited. Even Ben and Dickon called in. The visitors found that it was Jane's sister Dorothy and her mother who tended Jane the most, taking it in turns to stay up with her at night, a time when she was most vulnerable.

Often, in the hours before dawn, Jane lay awake and concentrated on the flickering candle, as if it were measuring the time she had left. She had ceased to worry and now accepted her fate with great calm. She loved Tom, her family and friends, and thanked God for the affection she saw returned in their eyes.

For a few days in a row, Jane seemed to be improving. After one such day, she fell into a deep sleep. It was her sister's turn to stay by her side through the night and, finding Jane so comfortable and peaceful, she fell asleep herself. Early the next morning, her mother woke her with a drink of hot milk. They assumed Jane was still asleep, but when they tried to rouse her, she was cold as ice.

'It's not thy fault, Dorothy,' her mother said with uncharacteristic pity. 'Jane 'as died in 'er sleep. See, there's no sign of 'er tossin' about. She can't 'ave woken at all. It's a blessin'. Stay 'ere while I tell rest o' family.'

When William was told at sunrise, he went straight outside to look for Tom. He thought it best if he broke it to him.

Tom was standing by the stable door. He guessed from William's face that there was bad news.

'I'm sorry, Tom. She died last night.'

Like one possessed, Tom crashed his fist against the door.

William stepped forward to hold him and instantly had to dodge a punch aimed in his direction. He gave Tom a well-directed right hook that laid him to the ground.

The lad sat on the wet earth holding his chin and then started to laugh. William hauled him to his feet and shook him. It was then that Tom's face crumpled. He sobbed as he collapsed against William's chest.

'I wasn't with 'er,' he cried. 'I never said goodbye.'

William held him tight and tried to comfort him. 'At least she died peacefully – in her sleep.'

'No one dies i' their sleep,' he shouted. Then he mumbled to himself, 'They just look as if they did. An' I wasn't there.' He tried to pull away, crying as he struggled. 'Let me go. Let me see 'er.'

'Not right now, Tom. Mother and Dorothy are doing what's necessary. By all means share the vigil. You're almost one of the family. You know, it must have been

Jane's heart. It must have grown weak – and couldn't beat any longer. There was nothing anyone could do.'

This was little consolation. 'Leave me be!' Tom growled. He wriggled free and ran off towards the church.

He went beyond the churchyard, sprinted past the gorse bushes on Reighton Hill and ran without stopping downhill towards Speeton ravine. He carried on running and tumbling in the early morning light, scrambling down until he reached the shore. Once there, he threw himself face down on the pale grey pebbles. He stretched out his hands, clutching at the cold stones, and sobbed until his chest ached. Suddenly, he stood up and pelted the stones at the sea; the calm sea that mocked him. Then he collapsed onto his knees and let his head droop. He grazed his forehead from side to side against the stones and then fell over curled into a ball. He hadn't slept much for weeks. Exhaustion overcame him and he fell asleep.

When he awoke, the sun had risen well above the sea. He felt its warmth on his back and rolled over to face the sky and the light. His body was loose and relaxed for the first time in days. His prayers had been answered; Jane, he now believed, had not suffered at the end. She'd died with God's grace, and he was grateful for the love they'd shared.

As he rose to stand, the enormity of his loss hit him. He swayed unsteadily. A life without Jane was unthinkable. How could he resign himself to that? Tomorrow, and all the days ahead, were empty. He sank onto his knees again and wept.

After a while, he wiped his face with his sleeve and stared at the horizon. He now realised how Dickon must have felt when he lost his wife. Dickon had carried on somehow. Dickon could maybe help him. He stood up, knowing there was a day's work ahead. Dickon and the others would be wondering where he was. He took one last look at the sea and turned his back on it. With fresh tears rolling down his cheeks, he made his way slowly back up the ravine.

Chapter 14

Tom continued to grieve for Jane in private. He haunted the places they'd walked together as if he might see her. The lonely walks along the cliffs gave no comfort and served, instead, to highlight his desperate longing. On his worst days, he had a deep, physical pain in his chest and stomach as he ached to have Jane once more. His body tensed, and hectic physical work gave no release. On his better days, he was lost and empty and wandered aimlessly. He knew he should follow Dickon's example, be strong and accept his loss. He must find a way to cope.

In late autumn, his memories of Jane, once sharp and painful, were transformed gradually into a gentler longing. He sensed Jane's presence in the warm southwesterly winds that blew leaves across his path. As winter approached, he lifted his head to the frosty air and let the first soft snowflakes land and melt on his cheeks. Her kisses had been as soft and light. He would never forget her or ever want to.

Dorothy Jordan watched her last remaining daughter at mealtimes. At 22 years of age, the young woman should be courting. Instead, she was still mourning her loss of John Dawson to another. What she needed was a distraction, preferably a young man. Perhaps Tom might try to court Dorothy next. Though he'd had such bad luck before, there was always the chance of being third time lucky.

Tom noticed how his mistress kept finding ways of putting Dorothy in his way. She either made her serve him supper or gave her jobs outside wherever he was working. At first, he thought this was a kindness. Dickon warned him otherwise.

'Watch out, Tom, there's summat afoot. I do believe our mistress 'as thee i' mind fo' Dorothy.'

'Nay, that can't be right an' it's too soon after Jane. I'm i' no mood fo' courtin'. Anyway, I can't believe Dorothy wants *me* – she only 'as eyes fo' John Dawson.'

To escape the Jordan matchmaking, Tom spent even more time with Dickon and the animals.

William and Mary never discussed Jane's illness and death. Mary kept busy from dawn till dusk – fetching water, cooking, cleaning clothes, seeing to the children, feeding the pig and chickens, milking the cow, spinning wool and then, at night, mending clothes and knitting. In the early winter evenings, the family sat close to the fire. Mary could see to sew by the firelight and William took to reading the Bible once more. He chose the Book of Job.

Young Mary sat on the floor and leant against his knee, her dog asleep between her legs, its warm head resting on her thigh. She listened attentively to her father.

'Wearisome nights are appointed to me,' he read aloud. 'When I lie down, I say, when shall I arise, and the night be gone? And I am full of tossings to and fro unto the dawning of the day. My days are swifter than a weaver's shuttle, and are spent without hope.'

Mary clung onto her father's leg and clutched at his breeches. She knew he was often tired, but he carried on.

'When I say, my bed shall comfort me, my couch shall ease my complaint; then thou scarest me with dreams, and terrifiest me through visions: so that my soul chooseth strangling, and death rather than life.'

She was too young to understand. Once, at night, she'd heard her father call out as if he was having nightmares. She was afraid he might die, and stroked Stina's ears and kissed her head for comfort.

'Father,' she cried, 'don't be sad!' She dug her nails into his leg and shook him.

He peered down and saw tears in her eyes. It was thoughtless to read such passages.

'I'm sorry,' he said. 'I'll read one last verse for the night. This one'll cheer you up.' He tickled her under the chin and smiled. 'This one is about the almighty power of God. Listen.'

He coughed to clear his throat. 'This power which alone spreadeth out the heavens, and treadeth upon the waves of the sea. Which maketh Arcturus, Orion, and Pleiades, and the chambers of the south.'

She grinned. He'd shown her those stars in the sky, and she knew their names.

In November, events far beyond the village occupied the adults and distracted them from the poor harvest and

Jane's death. George Gurwood, in his services, passed on information about riots and disorder in Lancashire and the Midlands.

'Our Church of England is in danger,' he reported. 'The Jacobites want a revolution and they may yet succeed. Our English commander, the Duke of Argyle, has warned that the rebels outnumber our forces in Scotland by at least a hundred to one. Now, after two months of raising men, the rebels have an army and they're marching south. They're coming down from the northwest.'

Below him in the pews, people shook their heads in dismay. The blacksmith stood up and waved his fist.

'We'll not 'ave this,' he shouted. 'If they come 'ere, we'll fight back.'

The men nodded but kept quiet and remained seated.

'Wait,' cried the vicar, 'the rebels, I hear, are coming down the other side of the country, down the northwest, not the east. However, I suggest that you able-bodied men could get together and practise military drills – just in case.'

'Aye,' answered the blacksmith as his wife pulled him back down. 'I'll see to it.'

Within days, groups of men, including the younger Jordan brothers, were drilling with broomsticks or with scythe blades fixed onto poles. News came through that, all over England, militia men were being called up, and anyone suspected of being a Jacobite was imprisoned. The next Sunday, after church, the men gathered at the forge.

'The stockades at 'Ull 'ave been repaired,' Phineas Wrench told them. 'An' there's trouble i' London

– mug-'ouse riots they call 'em. There's gangs o' young men on either side, 'Anoverians fightin' against Stuarts in ale-'ouses. An' one lot o' Jacobite lads smashed windows lit up specially fo' Prince o' Wales's birthday.' He expected his audience to be aroused and was surprised by their apathy.

'Well, let's 'ope they don't come 'ere,' Ben growled. 'They can stay i' London or stay i' Scotland an' northwest. I don't care as long as they don't come 'ere.'

Even the younger men mumbled in agreement.

Phineas was undeterred. 'I 'ave news fo' thee. I reckon we 'ave a Jacobite close by. That Scottish pedlar, Speckledy Golightly, is back i' Filey. She's back livin' wi' Stinky Skate. An' there's a rumour she were i' Preston when them Jacobites marched into town.'

Even that news made no difference. The men shuffled their feet. They'd never really suspected the woman though they'd never defended her. Also, they knew their womenfolk would be glad to see the pedlar and buy her wares again. One by one, they made their excuses to leave the forge.

William returned home and, as he sat down to dinner, he told Mary about Speckledy Golightly.

'I reckon she thinks she's safer here in the east,' he said. 'So far, we haven't had any trouble. She might have been in that battle in Preston. Maybe that's why she came back here.'

Mary hadn't forgotten the lucky coin given to her by the pedlar. She'd been pregnant with Francis at the time, and he was her first child to survive. 'I always felt guilty when she left like she did. We weren't fair. The woman was harmless enough.'

'Anyway, Mary, no doubt she'll be back in Reighton soon, and you can make amends.'

One damp and cold morning, Mary went as usual to fill her bucket at the well. She found half a dozen women standing round chatting. Huddled together with their shawls pulled across their chests, they gossiped about Speckledy Golightly. Mary ignored them and filled her bucket. All at once, Martha Wrench gestured with her head towards the lane.

'Talk o' the devil,' she muttered.

They turned and saw the pedlar. She was limping in their direction through the mist that still hung at the bottom of the village. One foot dragged and her back was bent. Mary didn't wait to see what the others would do. She hailed the woman.

Speckledy Golightly raised her head and drew the hood from her face. She recognised Mary and smiled at the welcome.

'Are ye well?' she asked. 'Had any moor bairns?'

'Yes,' answered Mary. 'Three boys now and a girl, all doing fine.'

The women nudged each other. They were eager to hear about the battle in Preston yet daren't ask. On seeing Mary and the pedlar on such good terms, they wanted to put aside their suspicions.

Mary saw their dilemma. She shivered. 'It's cold out here,' she said. 'Look, we've got our water – why don't we *all* go to my house and get warmed up?'

They'd never picked up their buckets so fast. They followed Mary and the pedlar in expectation of an exciting morning. After dumping their buckets by the front door, they took off their pattens and left them in the passageway. Mary led them into the kitchen, where Francis was looking after his young brothers.

'Leave the boys under the table,' she told him. 'They're safest playing there away from the fire and they seem happy enough.' Thank God, she thought, young Mary is at the vicarage. The last thing she wanted was for the girl to hear about Jacobites and then spread misheard rumours. She beckoned the pedlar to sit at the head of the table nearer the fire. The others sat on the benches at each side and shunted each other up, mindful not to kick the boys under their feet.

'So,' Mary addressed them, 'who fancies a drop of Ben's mead?' She fetched the bottle and the small mugs. 'I've just enough to go round.' As she poured out their drinks, she put her first question to Speckledy Golightly.

'We heard that thousands of Jacobites had marched south and got to Preston. Were you there?'

'Aye, ah'm afraid ah was.'

'But how did they happen to get so far into England?'

'Naebody stopped 'em.' The pedlar took a sip of mead and savoured it before swallowing. 'Ah was theer when they arrived an' the English dragoons just retreated. So did the local militia.'

'So what happened next?'

'Nae much at fost. The Jacobites settled in. They barricaded the streets an' eventually, when a force did turn up ti fight 'em, theer was carnage. Hundreds of English lay dead an' wounded… hundreds, just lyin' wheer they fell.'

'What about the Scots?'

'Och, they were fine. Hardly any were killed an' the English retreated once moor.'

The women were puzzled.

'So why didn't the Scots carry on marching south?' Mary asked.

'Ah didnae ken for sure. It was confusin'. Houses were burnt down an' ah got trapped at one end o' town wi' a group o' wounded rebels. Somebody set fire ti the buildings, maybe the English ti split up the enemy, but ah saw rebels had set fire ti places wheer the English were camped. It was the most frightenin' day o' ma life. Men were runnin' aboot shoutin' an' women an' children were screamin' – they didnae ken wheer ti run. We were feared the wind would spread the fires.'

The women stared wide-eyed. They lifted their mugs to their lips and sipped in unison, waiting for the next part of the story.

'So how did you escape?' Mary prompted.

'Ah didnae – not for a while anyways. Ah was still trapped theer along wi' rebels. Ah stayed theer all night, an' a sorry lot they were.' She nursed her mug in both hands and took another sip. Her hands shook and her eyes were wet with tears. After a pause, she set down her mug and stared unseeing at the fire.

'Theer was one bonny lad,' she resumed, 'can't have been moor than 15. He'd been wounded i' the stomach. Theer was nothin' we could do. He'd walked all the way from Inverness.'

She reached inside her coat and pulled out a crumpled blue cloth. When she smoothed it out, they could tell it was a hat and stained with blood.

'He asked me to return this ti Scotland. Made me promise. Ah couldnae say no, poor lad was dyin'.' She looked up at the women. 'See this bit o' white cloth sewn on, like a rose? That means it's a Jacobite bonnet.

If anyone finds ma with it, ah'll be thought a rebel. Ye must not tell a soul.'

For the second time, Mary thanked God her daughter wasn't around. Young Mary would have gabbled about it till the cows came home.

The pedlar sighed. 'Ye'd have pitied 'em if ye'd seen 'em. They'd marched miles ti get theer, many of 'em from the Highlands. They'd nae clothes or food an' were so tired an' shabby. Anyone would feel sorry for 'em.' She folded the bonnet and put it back inside her coat.

'What happened next?' Mary asked, still puzzled.

'Ah could tell they were only theer because o' their clan leaders. They'd follow 'em anywheer. But all night the clans argued an' squabbled. Some were for marchin' on ti London, others just wanted ti go back hame. Ah don't think they were that bothered aboot havin' a Catholic king.'

'So, did they go home?'

'Aye, a lot did. By mornin' ye could tell that many had crept away. By then though, they were surrounded. Word soon went roond that they might surrender, but that angered some o' the clans. They paraded up an' doon the streets threatenin' ti kill any who dared leave or surrender. Ah ken some *were* killed. Anyhow, it makes no differ.' She took another sip of mead.

'Next mornin', one o' the clan leaders did try ti surrender, but the English refused. They wouldn't accept it unless every single one o' the Highlanders surrendered. Ye can imagine some would never give up.' She bit her lip. 'They were slaughtered. Those that were left tried ti hide i' the kirk, or trooped inti marketplace ti gi' theirselves up. Proud men they were too. Such a shameful end.' She wiped away a tear. 'As ah left, the noblemen were being lined up o' one side.'

'Why was that?' asked Mary.

Speckledy Golightly shrugged. 'Ah'm not sure. Maybe they'd be sent ti different prisons. Maybe just the leaders will be executed fo' treason. Ah dinnae ken. Ah was glad ti leave that dreadful place. Fires were still burnin' an' theer was gore an' bits o' bodies i' the streets.' She shuddered as she recalled her walk out of the town. 'Swords an' sabres do such butchery.'

Mary glanced at the women round the table. Their eyes shone. They couldn't wait to go home and tell their families.

At suppertime, William heard only the bare facts; gory details had been omitted because of young Mary's presence. He suspected his wife harboured sympathy for the Highlanders.

'They're rebels plain and simple,' he argued. 'They need putting down.'

'But they weren't trained soldiers, and they walked such a long way for their clans.'

'Don't pity them, Mary. The rebellion's not over.'

Young Mary looked from one parent to the other. It was rare to see them so talkative.

In bed that night, when the children were asleep, William warned Mary of another large Jacobite army still in Scotland and undefeated. He turned to face her and whispered in her ear.

'They're dangerous men, the Scots. Phineas has been telling us about a man called Rob Roy MacGregor. He roams the countryside terrorising folk. He steals cattle and clothes and demands money. There's probably hundreds more like him in the Borders and the Highlands. You should fear them, not pity them.'

When he turned his back to her, she snuggled up behind him for warmth and comfort. He made the Highlands sound such a frightening place. As she fell asleep, she thought of the events in Preston. The Scottish clans, if they'd been of one mind, could so easily have marched south and taken London. Perhaps they'd try again.

Chapter 15

1716

The winter was one of the most severe for years. Folk stayed indoors and, when they had to venture out in the freezing weather, they bundled themselves in layers of clothes. Two full months of frost gave the Gurwood girls ample time to read, and Cecilia was the first to grab any newsletters that her father received. They made her feel in touch with London, its fashions and exciting events. One morning, as she sat with her mother and sisters crowded round the parlour fire, she smoothed out the creased newsletter on her lap and read to them.

'This is from…' She checked the date before continuing. 'It's from the 14th of January.'

They nodded, resigned to the knowledge that the news was weeks old.

'The Thames seems now a solid rock of ice,' Cecilia read. Then she scanned the page, deciding to choose the best parts.

'It is in a manner like a town; thousands of people cross it, and with wonder view the mountainous heaps of water that now lie congealed into ice. On Thursday, a great cook's shop was erected, and gentlemen went as frequently to dine there as at any ordinary one.'

Her sisters then heard of the numerous stalls and booths set out like streets on the frozen river, with butchers and bakers, oyster stalls, toyshops and all kinds of tradesmen – like at a fair. There was a steer roasted on a spit and people cooked over fires on the thick ice. The girls envied the people of London who could enjoy puppet plays and football games, who could go skating, play ninepins and watch cudgel fights. To be stuck indoors in Reighton of all places was both boring and unfair. When they complained to their father, he made them read psalms instead of the London news.

'You need a sense of perspective,' he told them. 'And don't forget, if you were in London, you'd hardly be able to breathe because of all the smoke.'

'At least we'd have some fun,' Cecilia grumbled.

'Your gowns would be coated in soot. The smoke from all those chimneys can't escape in the cold air. It just sits there.'

Cecilia folded her arms and sulked. He wasn't going to spoil her vision of London.

He ignored her and carried on. 'I've heard it's often so foggy that you can't even see to the end of the street. We're much better off here by the sea.'

Cecilia was not convinced.

George Gurwood hid from his daughters the other news he'd received. He would share it with his son though it did not make for pleasant reading. Once the women of the house were in bed, he sat by the dying fire with John, and they lit up their pipes.

'There's bad news from the north,' he said as he let the tobacco smoke seep from the side of his mouth. 'James Stuart has landed in Scotland and been crowned. And the pope has recognised him as the true king.'

'But he'll get no support, will he?' John asked as he struggled to get his pipe going.

'The good news is that he lost his treasure ship on the way over and, apparently, he has no troops or guns. The Scots would be mad to support him.'

'They are mad,' John replied through a haze of smoke.

'Don't forget, there's also folk in England who want rid of King George and the Whigs. There's many a secret Jacobite supporter. The town of Newcastle is against the Jacobites, yet the rest of Northumberland supports James Stuart.'

'What about Lancashire? I've heard about the battle at Preston.'

'Lancashire's riddled with papists. But at least the government's doing something about that. Those suspected of helping the rebellion will be put under house arrest. I reckon they'll soon lose their enthusiasm, especially if their property's taken.'

'We'll hope for the best then.' John's pipe was burning steadily now, and he leant back in his chair and yawned. 'I don't suppose they can do much without money or troops. Anyway, nothing's going to happen while this frost is on.'

With that comforting thought, they stared into the fire. The embers of the last sticks of gorse collapsed without a sound and disintegrated into ash. They finished their pipes in silence, put the lid on the fire and took their candles up to bed.

On Sunday, the congregation sat almost glued to their ice-cold pews and chuntered about the never-ending winter. George Gurwood chose to read Psalm 147.

'He giveth snow like wool: he scattereth the hoarfrost like ashes. He casteth forth his ice like morsels; who can stand before his cold? He sendeth out his word, and melteth them; he causeth his wind to blow, and the waters flow.'

Old Ben muttered under his breath. 'About damn time 'e did. I'm frozen stiff.' Then, to anyone within earshot, he added, 'It were that cold this mornin', chamber pot stuck to me arse.'

Young Mary heard him and giggled. Her nose, blue with cold, poked out from her thick woollen cloak. Her hands were warm inside a rabbit-skin muff, but she'd lost the feeling in her toes and bashed her feet up and down on the cobble floor to revive them. Like everyone else, she wanted the service to end so she could get back home and sit by the fire.

That night, the condensation froze once more on the inside of the windows. In the morning, William showed his daughter how to scratch her initials in the ice.

'My grandfather taught me how to write my name like this.' He drew a large W on the ice with his nail. 'He said that W was me – William. An M for Mary is just as easy to do – it's a W upside down.' He wondered if she'd find the experience of seeing her name in ice as powerful and magical a symbol as he'd done as a child. As he scratched the M, she gazed at it and then traced it slowly and solemnly with her finger.

'Mind,' he added, 'your finger's warm. If it melts the ice too much, you'll spoil your letter.'

She pulled her finger away and, moving closer so that her nose almost touched the window, she rubbed away a patch of ice and peered out. St Helen's Lane was a blur of white. No one walked by. It was silent, not a single bird or animal in sight.

Her father leant over to look and sighed; there was little outdoor work to be done in such weather.

'Will you be sledging down the hills again today?' he asked. When she nodded, he remarked, 'Your mother won't like it. Make sure you don't stay out too long. You'll only get wet and cold.'

'I'll come home when Francis starts crying.'

He smiled. 'That won't be long then. Enjoy yourself.'

He went to get his coat and boots, and she set to work to convince her brother he really did want to go out. She knew he preferred to stay in the kitchen by the fire and help Mother. Little William would have loved to go out with her; he was not allowed. She pestered Francis until he gave in. With reluctance, he donned extra clothes.

Their father had made them a small wooden sledge, big enough to take two children. Mary and Francis took it in turns to pull each other along the lane. The sledge glided smoothly over the frozen snow, but once they'd reached the end of the lane, they had a long, hard tramp up the hill.

At the top of Reighton Hill, they turned to look at Filey. The cliffs stood out so clear in the frosty air. The sun was shining, and the sea was a dark blue with three collier boats sailing on the horizon. Everything else was white. They gazed around. The gorse bushes cast long blue shadows and the branches of the trees were bowed down under the weight of snow.

This morning they had the hill to themselves. Mary took a deep breath and smiled as the cold air filled her lungs. She knew where the best runs were and went straight to her favourite place – a steep gap between clumps of gorse that led right down to the bottom. When the water was frozen on the meadow below, as it had been for over a month now, they had an extra long ride across the ice to the far end. They just had to make sure they swerved or stopped before they disappeared over the bank and into the ditch.

Mary sat at the front of the sledge. Francis sat behind and held her round the waist.

'Ready?' she asked.

Before he answered, she pushed off with her feet. They flew down the hill, the freezing air cutting into her cheeks. She loved it. The uneven ground, trodden by cattle, gave such a good bumpy ride. There was the thrill of the unexpected. Sometimes she or Francis lost their grip and were tossed into the air. Sometimes both of them were joggled off and they had to watch the sledge career down by itself. It was best when they both stayed on and their combined weight gave them a long, steady ride to the bottom of the hill, on and on over the ice with a satisfying scraping noise.

Whoever sat at the front had to shout 'Ditch!' to tell the other to brake hard with their legs. Francis could never decide if it was safer to be at the front or the back. If he was at the front, he could yell 'Ditch' as early as he liked – to be on the safe side – but Mary realised he called out too soon and then she deliberately delayed braking. Yet, if he sat at the back, he couldn't trust Mary to shout out in time. She was fearless and waited till the last moment. Many times, they'd skidded on the brink and missed hurtling into the ditch by inches. He couldn't win; Mary was excited by danger. After a near miss, she was keener than ever to get back to the top of the hill for another go.

Chapter 16

The children had been sledging for just over an hour when Francis complained of the cold. His woollen mittens were sodden and, when he pulled them off with his teeth, his fingers were red raw. Their rides down the hill had been better than he expected. His sister had been careful to avoid the ditch and he wanted to go home while their luck held out.

'Let's go now,' he pleaded when they climbed again to the top of the hill. 'I can't feel my fingers.'

'*My* hands are alright.'

'It's my feet as well. You know I've got chilblains on my toes. They really hurt.'

'One more ride and then we'll go. If you like, you can sit at the front.'

He sat on the sledge and lifted his feet to rest on the curved runners. His hands gripped the sides. At least he could see any dangers ahead and shout for her to brake.

She plonked herself behind him. 'Let's make this the best ride of all.' She gave a mighty push off with her feet. 'Wheee!'

They shot down the hill faster than ever, the snow so hard-packed it had turned to ice. Francis kept his eyes on the edge of the meadow. He would shout 'Stop' when they reached it. They bumped over the last ruts at the bottom.

'Stop!' he cried.

Mary ignored him.

'Stop!' he yelled louder. He knew he couldn't trust her. They careered on over the frozen expanse, heading straight for the ditch.

'Stop!' he screamed.

She stuck out both feet to brake and then, to veer away, she raised one foot and tried to ground the other deeper into the snow and ice. It was too late. The sledge caught the rim of the ditch and tipped. Francis was thrown off. He landed awkwardly on the other side, the fence preventing him going further.

Mary fell into the reeds by the bank. She laughed as she got up and brushed off the snow. 'That was the best, ever!' Then she wondered why Francis was not moving. He was lying on his side and crying.

'What's the matter? Can't you get up?'

'It's my arm. It won't move and it hurts.'

She clambered across and hauled him to his feet. He cried out and then stumbled, with her help, to the other side.

'You look funny,' she remarked. 'Are you going to be sick?'

'I don't think so.'

'I bet your arm has come loose. Remember Uncle Matthew at the wrestling? Sarah Ezard put his arm back. Do you want me to try?'

He stepped back. 'Don't touch me! I'm going home.'

'Alright, if that's what you want. But I bet I *could* fix your arm.'

She sighed and picked up the reins on the sledge.

Instead of going back up the hill, they made their way home across the frozen meadow. She dragged the sledge along and Francis trailed further behind. Every step jolted his arm.

By the time they reached home, he was trembling. He held his injured arm against his chest and did look as if he might be sick or else faint.

Mary left him at the front door. 'You go on in. I'll put the sledge away.' She intended to stay in the back garden and avoid trouble.

Francis went inside and stood in the kitchen doorway. The moment his mother turned to see him, he began to cry. 'I've hurt my arm,' he whimpered.

His mother could see at a glance that he'd probably broken it. She slipped his coat off, the good arm first, and sat him by the fire. When she pulled off his mittens, she saw that his fingers were red with chilblains.

'Oh, Francis, you shouldn't have gone out today. Let's get your boots off as well. Your grandmother would say to rub your feet with snow, but I'll wrap them in wool. You'll soon be warm again.'

As she handed him a mug of warm milk, she realised his sister was missing.

'Where's Mary?'

'Putting the sledge away.'

'I bet she is! She'll be hiding, that's what. She knows she's in trouble.'

She went to the back door and saw her daughter at the far end of the garden.

'You get yourself in the house this minute!'

Young Mary slouched back. There was no escape. When she was within reach, her mother clouted her across the head. Tears sprang to her eyes. It was so unfair. She was blamed for everything.

Her mother shoved her into the kitchen. 'Just look at your brother. You go too far. One day, you'll kill someone.'

'I won't.'

'Don't answer back. Get your wet clothes off and get to bed. When your father comes, he'll sort you out. It's plain I can't.'

Young Mary did as she was told. She was hungry and thirsty yet daren't ask for anything. She snuggled deep under the blankets and waited for her father. After dozing for a while, she heard the click of the door latch and her father's footsteps as he entered the kitchen. She lifted her head to hear what was said. It did appear that Francis's arm was broken. Her father didn't come in to see her. He went straight back out to get Sarah Ezard.

When Sarah arrived, young Mary got out of bed and tiptoed to the door. She opened it a fraction so she could see what went on. Sarah Ezard inspected Francis's arm and complained that she could have set the arm if he'd broken it in spring. When questioned, she explained that she needed comfrey roots to set bones, but the ground was frozen.

Her father stepped forwards. 'I could dig them up with a pickaxe. Just show me where they are.'

'Old Ben grows a large patch. 'E's nearest. 'E'll show thee where to dig. It won't be easy, mind. They grow ever so deep.'

Her father didn't waste time. He set off at once, leaving Sarah to comfort Francis in other ways.

Sarah took a small jar from her coat pocket. 'I 'ave summat 'ere fo' chilblains. Rub this on twice a day.' She removed the lid. 'Smell it, Francis – it's elderflowers an' pigs' lard. It'll soothe thee no end. An' it's better than what tha grandmother would recommend. She puts 'ot cinders in a chamber pot o' piss. When it bubbles, she dabs it on.'

Young Mary smiled to herself. She wished Francis had that remedy instead. She crept back to bed. Her father was a long time. When he returned, she peeped through the door again.

Sarah Ezard was given a pile of ugly black roots. She grated them and put the sludge into a pot to heat on the fire.

'Thoo's lucky it's not a proper break, Francis. I won't 'ave to 'urt thee. Thoo's young an' I think it's only cracked.'

Young Mary was relieved. Her parents might not be so cross. She saw Sarah tip the hot paste onto a piece of cloth and pack it round his forearm.

'When it cools, it'll set 'ard as rock. Tha knows, Francis, we used to call this plant "knitbone". Thoo'll soon be mended.'

Young Mary shot back to bed. Now that Francis was seen to, they'd come for her. She pulled the covers up high and pretended to be asleep. She heard her father open the door and walk towards her. He stood over the bed. She could hear him breathing. After a few moments, he left the room. She was hungry and thirsty. Tears of frustration wet her pillow as she realised her best day's sledging was spoilt.

William had his dinner and returned to Uphall. Preoccupied with his family, he didn't pay full attention to where he was walking. The foldyard was black with ice. As soon as he set foot on it, he slipped and fell flat on his back with a sickening thud. Both Dickon and Tom had seen it happen. They hurried over and helped him to the kitchen.

He saw the concern on his mother's face. 'I'm only bruised. I'll be fine. Just give me a few minutes and I'll be up and doing again.'

'Nay, tha face is white as a sheet. Thoo should be i' bed with an 'ot poultice.'

Dickon and Tom glanced at each other and shrugged. They weren't going to argue with their mistress. They backed out of the door and left William to his mother.

She rested her hands on her hips and glared at him. 'Now listen, Will, I've an old recipe for a good poultice. It won't take long to make up an' it'll take tha bruise out. Go an' lie down o' settle while we fetch blankets.' She shouted up the stairs to her daughter to fetch stuff from the beds.

He was soon warm and cosy under the rough woollen blankets, though he couldn't straighten his back. He closed his eyes and listened to his mother rummaging round the kitchen, talking to herself as she made the poultice.

After a short while, she nudged him. 'Thoo'll 'ave to turn over while I spread this o' tha back.'

'It stinks a bit,' he grumbled as he manoeuvred himself. 'What's in it?'

'That'll be vinegar. Don't complain.' She lifted up his shirt and spread it thickly on his lower back. Then she turned to her daughter.

'Dorothy, whenever poultice goes dry, tha must change it. I've mixed plenty up, but keep lid on to keep it moist.'

William succumbed to the treatment and began to relax. Once they'd left him alone, his pain eased, and he fell asleep.

When he awoke, he tried to move. It was impossible. He was stuck there like a sheep on its back. Now he wished he'd kept moving after his fall and not let his mother take charge. Perhaps she was glad he was stranded at Uphall.

'Thoo can't go out today, nor tomorrow neither,' she told him. 'I reckon tha should stay put for a few days.'

He had no option. 'Send word to Mary then. She has Francis to look after – he broke his arm this morning – and she'll worry when I'm not back for supper.'

There was nothing he could do. He resigned himself to being useless. The farm lads came and went. Some showed sympathy, others avoided him. He felt old before his time.

After two days of being imprisoned in the kitchen, he was determined to get up and go home. He braced himself and winced with pain as he dropped off the settle onto his knees. The floor was cold and hard, and his back would not straighten.

When his mother saw him crawling to the door, she was furious. 'Tha puddin' 'ead, get thassen back onto settle.' She could see he didn't look at all well. His face was drawn and grey. 'Thoo's no good to anyone i' this state.'

'Mother, just let me pull myself up. Once upright, I think I can walk home.'

He grabbed hold of the table leg and hoisted himself up, trying not to show how much it hurt. Then he stood still for a minute, hoping his back would unbend a little.

With great concentration, he put one foot before another and shuffled to the door.

'Pass me my hat and coat. I'm going home.'

'Thoo's a fool,' she answered as she passed him his thick winter coat. 'Make sure Mary sees to thee properly. Sarah Ezard 'as a good embrocation. Thoo needs summat!'

She held up an arm as he struggled with the door. 'Wait! Let one o' tha brothers go wi' thee. Someone'll be out there – Dickon or Tom if no one else.'

William nodded weakly and leant against the door while his mother went outside and shouted a few names across the yard. Dickon was nearest. He ambled over and let William use him like a staff. The two men made their way gingerly down the hill, avoiding the sheer ice in the middle of the road. At last, they reached William's house.

Mary had never seen him bent and in pain like an old man. Immediately, she made him lie down in bed and asked Dickon to fetch a remedy from Sarah Ezard.

When Dickon returned empty-handed, Mary wrung her hands. 'How can she not have anything?'

'She's run out of 'er usual stuff. An' seeing as it's winter, she can't get 'er ingredients. She can't get enough cream or eggs. She said tha could make a poultice o' linseed oil an' pancakes.'

Mary sighed and began to make the poultice.

'Oh, an' there's summat else tha can do – if there's any nettles about under snow, mix 'em in as well.'

Young Mary was sent out to search under the snow for nettles and came back with a good handful of crisp frozen leaves. She left them to thaw in the kitchen and watched them turn floppy. Disappointed, she had an idea.

'Mother, Ben uses his beeswax when *he* has a bruise. If you like, I could go and see him.'

Her mother was undecided for a moment. 'Oh, go on then. But wrap up warm, and don't be long. And *don't* wander off. I have enough to deal with right now, and I can't leave the boys to trudge through the snow searching for *you*.' As an afterthought, she added, 'And your father'll be waiting for you, won't he?'

The girl didn't need further prompting. Since her father had been ill at Uphall, she'd not been allowed anywhere in case she got lost or had an accident. She almost ran out of the house.

When young Mary arrived at Ben's cottage, he was in his garden stirring a pan over a blazing fire. She stood for a while, warming her hands. The pan stank of pine tar, so she asked what he was doing.

'I'm re-tarrin' knees o' me other breeches. Tha grandfather wants me to advise 'im on layin' new 'edges i' spring. I want to be ready.'

'Can I come and help lay hedges?'

'Nay, lass, it's man's work. Thoo'll be busy doin' tha learnin' at vicar's, an' tha should be 'elpin' tha mother out, not me. Anyways, what's up wi' tha father? I saw 'im earlier on wi' Dickon. 'E was all bent over.'

'He fell on the ice and hurt his back. That's what I've come for – your bruise mixture.'

''E must 'ave been badly a good bit, as I've not seen 'im around for a couple o' days. Wait 'ere an' don't go near the fire. I'll fetch linseed oil an' beeswax.'

Mary was tempted to stir the black mixture in the pot but kept her hands by her sides. When he returned, he placed a pot of wax near the fire and added oil and a bit of turpentine.

'We'll let it warm through a while. It won't take long to soften an' mix together. Then I'll put it in a jar for thee to take 'ome.'

'It smells like polish,' she said, wrinkling her nose. 'Grandmother uses something like that on her best chairs.'

'Aye, she would– it's good polish. It'll also get rid of a bruise. Rub it o' tha father's back an' 'e'll soon be better.'

After a few minutes, the wax had melted, and Ben poured the mixture into a small earthenware jar.

''Ere take this an', before thoo goes, tha can take tha father a walkin' staff too. 'E might need 'elp wi' walkin' again.' He went indoors and came out with a stout, well-worn hawthorn stick.

She tried it out. It was both smooth and knobbly at the same time.

'An' tell tha father to drink nettle tea every mornin' an' evenin'. It'll keep 'im young, eh, like me. Look!' He danced a jig round the fire but soon got out of breath.

She put the jar and stick down to give him a hug. His clothes smelled of tar. As she left, she turned and blew him a kiss.

When she got home, young Mary asked if she could be the one to rub in the ointment. Her mother gave in and warmed it first by the fire. Then she showed her daughter how and where to massage it. Soon, they had stained hands and they stank of polish.

Young Mary was conscientious and massaged her father's back four times a day. While he rested, she sat next to him and talked. The non-stop chatter about her adventures with Stina and old Ben always made him drowsy enough to sleep.

After another two days, he was able to walk about the house, taking care not to turn or bend suddenly and, by the end of the week, he was fit enough to walk to Uphall.

Young Mary missed her father's company and was bored once more. With Francis unable to do much with his broken arm, she was left to watch and see to her younger brothers. She begged to be allowed to go to the vicarage.

'I promise I'll find out about London and those rebels in Scotland.' She was counting on her mother's curiosity.

'Alright, off you go.'

Chapter 17

Everyone, except young Mary, was thoroughly tired of the white world of snow. Foxes had been seen lurking round the outbuildings desperate for food, and even buzzards had been seen overhead. It wasn't until the middle of February that the long-awaited thaw began.

Young Mary woke one morning to the steady drip of water from the eaves and, by the time she left to go to the vicarage, there was a narrow ditch of water around her house. The first thing she did on arrival was to stand over the parlour fire. As she let the bottom of her dress steam itself dry, Cecilia related the latest news.

'Dutch troops have landed to help us, and the Scots have moved further back north. Speckledy Golightly says she reckons the clans keep falling out with each other.'

Her father walked into the parlour carrying a pile of books. 'If you ask me, I think it's the Highland clans that can't get on with the Lowlanders. I've been reading about them. They lead completely different lives. The Lowlanders have nothing in common with the Highland lot. They're farmers and shopkeepers, they have trades. God knows how the others live. It's no wonder folk in the Lowlands and Borders are hesitant to support them.'

He put the books on the table. 'There now, enough of that. Time for your lesson.'

That afternoon, young Mary told her mother about the Jacobite army.

'What about their king though – James Stuart?' her mother asked. 'What's happened to him?'

Young Mary shrugged. 'Don't know. The vicar thinks he must've escaped – I think to France. He's going to give a special sermon on Sunday.' She imitated the vicar's deep voice. 'It's to praise God for the deliverance of the Church of England and the King.' She reverted to her normal voice. 'That's what he said anyway.'

'Amen to that. Speckledy Golightly won't be the only one relieved it's all over.'

Later that month, young Mary heard news of the captured Jacobite leaders. When she went into detail about the men being hung, drawn and quartered before being beheaded, Francis covered his ears. This didn't stop her.

'They stick their heads on a spike. I wish I could go to London.'

Her mother grabbed her by the arm and shook her. 'Shut up! We don't want to hear any more. *I* feel sorry for them. Listen, next time you're at the vicarage, you can find out what's to be done with those poor prisoners from the battle of Preston.'

The next day, when young Mary went to her lessons, she made a special effort to remember what she was told. She learnt the news by heart and, on the way home, repeated it over and over again, word for word. As soon as she stepped foot in the house, she went straight to her mother. She took a deep breath and recited it as fast as she could.

'The main rebels are kept in York, the rest in other prisons in the north. There's more than a thousand, and 400 are English.' She paused to take another breath. 'Some have been pardoned and some have been hung or shot. Many Highlanders have been sent to America, where they'll work as slaves.' She smiled. 'There – I've finished.'

Her mother was silent for a while and continued to stir the stew. 'Oh dear,' she remarked at last, 'I can't help thinking of all the families left without a father. The children and wives will suffer.' Almost to herself, she murmured, 'I wonder what your father will say.'

That evening at suppertime, while her mother was dishing up the broth, young Mary repeated the news.

Her father showed no sympathy. 'They had it coming to them. It's a shame we didn't catch James Stuart. That would really have put an end to them.'

Young Mary glanced at her mother, expecting her to say something, but she bit her lip and carried on passing round the bowls.

George Gurwood was impressed by young Mary's readiness to learn and decided to augment her education by teaching her to write.

'She's as keen as mustard,' he explained to her mother. 'She'll learn in no time.'

'Her grandmother says she's so sharp she'll cut herself.'

'Don't worry. I'll see that she keeps her feet on the ground and doesn't get above herself. Writing will give her more to do until spring comes.'

Young Mary was thrilled. At first, she was given a stick to use in a tray of sand so she could make mistakes and erase them. As she grew more proficient, she was given the quill that had belonged to Jane Gurwood and left behind on her marriage. From then on, handwriting became an obsession. She wanted every letter to be perfect and was determined to be as good as the Gurwood girls.

The vicar's daughters laughed at the way she stuck her tongue out when she concentrated, and thought her mad when she begged to take the quill home so she could practise there too.

William was concerned when his daughter came home with an old pewter inkwell. Writing could get messy, and he worried about the kitchen table. Luckily, he found the inkwell had a secure lid. All the same, he was dubious about his wife's response. He could tell that she wasn't at ease with the girl writing. Neither was Francis. Whatever young Mary did irritated them both.

William sat by his daughter each evening to watch her practise on blank leaves of paper cut from the vicar's books. He loved to see her curly head bowed over the page as she took such pains to copy the letters. They both ignored the deliberate crashing of pots around them and the noisy play of Francis, young William and John under their feet.

One night, when the children had gone to bed, he wanted to show his wife the progress young Mary had made. She stopped knitting to give a cursory glance at the writing and then sniffed.

'It'll be bad for her in the long run. It should be Francis that's learning it.'

'You know I've tried with him. He hasn't the same ability and, besides, he shows no interest.'

She began to knit again, faster than ever. 'He has more sense then. He knows he'll be spending his life in the fields. He need only sign his name. I don't see why our daughter needs to write at all.'

He didn't argue. There was some truth in what she said, but he couldn't stop young Mary now. The couple soon went to bed in silence, agreeing to disagree.

Francis hated to see his sister writing. Their father spent so much time with her, never him. One evening, while their father was in the loft mending the roof, he turned on her.

'Going to write recipes all your life, are you? That's all you'll be doing – or writing the price of eggs and butter at market.'

She ignored him. The feel of the quill between her fingers gave her such pleasure and she loved to see the ink flow onto the paper. She didn't care what he or anyone else thought. Writing made her happy.

William was delighted when she brought home a poem she'd copied out at the Gurwoods'. After supper, he asked her to read it out to them. He did not see his wife and Francis exchange looks and roll their eyes.

Young Mary got a stool to stand on and announced, 'It's called "The Creed". It's by Robert Herrick.' She began to read slowly, enunciating every syllable.

'I do believe that die I must,
And be returned from out my dust:
I do believe that when I rise,
Christ I'll see, with these same eyes.'

William was so proud he clapped his hands.

Francis turned his head and stared at the floor. He couldn't bear to see her smug looks or the delight on his father's face.

His mother put an arm round him. 'Never mind,' she whispered. 'Your day will come.'

In spring, Francis was expected to go out working with his father. He would be nine in the summer and, though resigned to leaving his mother and younger brothers, he found it hard to fit in at Uphall. His young uncles and the farm lads were so much bigger and stronger than he was, and he felt awkward around them. While he toiled outside in the unusually dry spring weather, he was annoyed that his sister still spent half her day at the Gurwoods'.

The vicar was not always at home. He had other parishes to visit and, whenever he was absent, Cecilia went to the bookshelves and chests and took whatever appealed to her. For years, she'd been reading the poetry and history books from her father's college days. One day, when the vicar was out, she introduced young Mary to a non-Christian work – Chapman's translation of *The Iliad*.

Whenever Cecilia opened any of the volumes, the leaves fell open at her father's favourite passages. It was obvious that, as a youth, her father had enjoyed the grisly descriptions of the battles and had been fascinated by the gods and their quarrels. Cecilia read out these passages.

Young Mary revelled in the tales of the heroes and never tired of hearing the same extracts until she knew them by heart. She loved the rhythm and the beauty of the words, especially the names of the gods and goddesses. Often, she whispered their names in bed, trying to recall each one in alphabetical order. Starting with Apollo, she was often asleep by the time she reached Mercury.

The battles in *The Iliad* gave her ideas. One afternoon, after hearing about warriors in shining armour and their fleet of ships, she rushed home, grabbed the ladder leant by the wall and laid it flat under the apple tree. The ladder was now her ship. She got young William to join in the game and gave him a broom for an oar.

'We must make an offering to the gods first, and then they'll fly down and help us. It has to be done properly though.' She fetched a pan of water and pretended it was wine. 'Will, go and fetch an oatcake. Mother won't say no to you. I'll make a pile of twigs for the fire.'

She pretended to slay an ox and lay it on the twigs. When William came back, she ordered him to throw the oatcake on top. Then she held the pan up high and poured out the water. At last, she stepped into the ladder.

'Come on in, Will, and sit down. Now we can set off.' But there was something missing. They didn't have a sail. She looked about for ideas. 'Wait while I fetch a sail.'

She ran to where the sacks were kept. 'This old one will have to do,' she mumbled to herself. She found the garden hoe and stuck the sack over the top of it. Then she stood the hoe in between the ladder rungs. It kept falling over. In frustration, she leant it against the tree.

'Right, now we can go.'

After a few pulls on the oars, she stopped and frowned. 'You know, William, the gods sometimes make things go badly wrong for you, but we'll have Juno and Minerva and Neptune on our side. If you see a cloud, it might be a god hiding from us. Or it might be a cloud sent to shield us.'

He was befuddled. His sister spoke so fast, and he never understood half of it. For a while, he was happy as they played at sailing. Suddenly, she leapt out of the 'ship' and informed him they must put on their armour and fight.

'I'll be Atrides. You be Paris. Get out and stand there.' She pushed him into place. 'Don't worry, I won't kill you. The goddess Venus will hide you and take you up in a cloud of gold. Then she'll set you down again ever so gently. You won't be hurt one bit. But listen – Atrides fights first – that's me, remember.'

She picked up the broom. 'Look, I'll throw my lance and it'll go right through your shield *and* your armour.'

She aimed at his stomach. 'There – I'll drive it through your guts.'

William stepped back in fear.

'You're fine! You would've died if Venus hadn't rescued you. Just be glad it's not Ulysses who's coming to get you. He attacks like a wild boar.'

She went down on all fours, pretending to be fierce. While she shook her head from side to side as if dripping saliva, she recited the rhyming couplet she'd learnt.

'He whets, with his lather-making jaws,
his crooked tusks for blood,
And, holding firm his usual haunts,
breaks through the deepen'd wood.'

William ran behind the apple tree. When he dared to peep round, his sister was standing and tapping one foot up and down.

'What next I wonder?' she murmured. Then it came to her. 'I know – Patroclus pulls a Trojan from his chariot. William, come here. You ride in a chariot and a lance gets you right through your jaw. That's what happened, you know. Come on, get away from the tree.'

'Don't want to.'

She took his hand and pulled him away. 'Stand there.'

He stood with his arms by his side as she once again aimed the broomstick, this time at his face.

'The lance gets stuck in your mouth. I'll pull you off your chariot now, like a fisherman landing a fish. Go on – come towards me and fall.'

He did as he was told. She stood over him, one foot on his chest, and pretended to withdraw the lance.

Their mother was watching from the kitchen window, unable to make out what her daughter was saying. She was intrigued by the antics and decided to go out and see as soon as she'd finished the baking. When she did finally venture into the garden, young Mary was still prancing about the grass waving a broom at William, darting towards him and then backing off.

'I'll get you Sarpedon,' the girl growled and pretended to throw the broom. 'There! Now you're wounded. Fall down, William, with the javelin stuck in your heart.' As she brandished the broom once more, she let go by accident and it caught him above the eye. He fell down of his own accord this time, clutching his face.

As if on cue, their mother stepped forward. She reached out, grabbed young Mary and swung her round.

'What on earth do you think you're doing?'

'We're playing.'

'I don't know what at! It looks terrible to me. I don't know why you have to play fighting games. And you've hurt William. See – the poor lad's shaking. You're scaring him. He can't even cry, he's that frightened.'

She knelt down beside him. 'There now,' she whispered, 'it's alright. Your sister was just being silly. It was only pretend.'

She spun round to her daughter. 'As for you,' she snapped, 'get inside *now*. You're staying in until your father comes home. *He'll* deal with you.'

Chapter 18

The next day, in the early evening, William went to the vicarage. George Gurwood chose to stroll in the garden rather than conduct a conversation in the crowded house. After discussing young Mary's writing, William explained her latest mischief and her confused ramblings about different gods.

'I'm sure you never meant any harm, but she takes it all so seriously.'

The vicar held up his hands and shook his head. 'I really had no idea.' He dreaded to think what went on behind his back. 'I'm so sorry, William. It must be Cecilia's doing. Leave it to me. It won't happen again. I'll see that Cecilia no longer reads unsupervised. And maybe I'll put a lock on my book cabinet.'

There were also repercussions in William's house. As a punishment, young Mary was made to stay at home and help her mother. She was also told to recite daily the first commandment – 'Thou shalt love the Lord thy God with all thy heart, and with all they soul, and with all thy mind.'

As usual, mother and daughter did not get on. Most young girls were a great help to their mothers, learning how to cook, wash and mend, and see to babies. Young Mary was different. She continued to be careless and clumsy and didn't take a bit of interest in the household chores. After four days, her mother could stand no more. She'd been showing the girl how to roll pastry.

'For goodness sake, leave it alone! You'll flatten it to death.' She pulled her away from the table, and the rolling pin fell to the floor.

'Why don't you go and see if old Ben needs any help. I can manage better here without you.'

Young Mary threw off her apron and whistled to Stina. Within minutes, she and the dog were at Ben's cottage. He was busy on hands and knees in the garden, making a willow fence. She knelt beside him and watched in silence as he flexed a long, thin withy and wove it in. With his bristly face close to hers, she thought his grey whiskers were like barley awns.

He sensed her intense gaze and gestured with his head. 'Over yon there's more o' these willow rods an' whips. Thoo could make thassen a den. There's nowt like it. Go on – run an' get some.'

She jumped up and began ferrying armfuls.

He pointed to a corner of the garden well away from the beehives. 'Over there, look. Make tha den over there. When thoo's got enough, I'll 'elp thee.'

After a while, he could see she was jiggling about, impatient to get started. He stood up slowly, stiff after being on his knees, and rubbed them before trying to walk.

She took hold of his hand. 'Come on, Ben. Let's go. Show me how to make a den.'

He stretched, keeping his hands on his lower back, and allowed her to lead him. 'Right,' he said, 'first we need some 'oles fo' rods to go in – this deep.' He bent down and snapped off a stick for her to use as a measure. 'Thoo can borrow me iron dibber to make the 'oles. I've finished with it fo' now. I'll do one to show thee.'

He pushed the dibber into the earth. 'Thoo must make the 'oles this far apart – one o' tha footsteps an' a bit more. Then choose a long, thick rod – this one'll do.'

With his knife, he sharpened the thick end. 'Then push it into 'ole like this.' He rammed it in at an angle. 'If tha makes a circle o' these an' does it like this, thoo'll 'ave a lovely den – like an upturned dish.'

Before he left to finish his fence, he prepared a dozen rods for her. The dog settled down to chew one of the sticks while she began to stake out the den.

Ben soon returned to show her how to weave the thin withies in and out of the rods.

'Once thoo's done that, tha can plug these gaps up with ivy an' grass.'

By the afternoon, she was sitting inside a small, shady den. She decided it was like a green beehive. The sun filtered through, making the ground dappled. She loved it so much she was desperate to share it and so ran home to fetch her brother, William. He was as good as having another dog. He did as he was told, and he'd follow her anywhere.

Once he was inside the den, he sat down obediently and stirred a pretend pot of broth. Young Mary squatted by the entrance, twisting ivy stems for the roof. She smiled and squinted into the sunlight. It was fun to make your own house. Already she had dreams of making the den a permanent home.

'Oh, William,' she said, stretching her arms wide. 'This time, right now, is good enough to sell in bottles.'

Throughout the spring, when they were free, young Mary and William played in the den. The weather stayed dry, and the dome retained its shape, getting stronger as they added more ivy and grass. They often stayed there for most of the afternoon, playing games in Ben's garden and eating anything he could give them. One day, Ben took them on a walk and pointed out pignut plants. He showed them how to dig them up.

'Thoo can eat these. Thoo'll never starve as long as there's pignuts.'

As they tasted the nutty tubers, he whispered, as if it was a great secret, 'It's manna to fairies an' elves.'

They stared at him in awe. No one else ever told them half as much.

Ben was too big for their den, but he liked to sit outside with them and tell riddles.

'What's wick at both ends an' dead i' middle?'

'Don't know.'

He grinned, revealing the gaps in his teeth. 'Why, it's a plough!'

Mary shook her head. 'I don't understand.'

'Why, there's two oxen at front pullin' an' there's tha father at back guidin' it, an' bit i' middle is dead wood an' iron.'

She frowned and pushed out her bottom lip, unimpressed.

'What's this then?' he asked. 'See if thoo can get this. An 'ouse full, an 'ole full an' tha can't catch a bowl full. What is it?'

'Don't know. Tell us.'

'Why, it's smoke!'

Mary frowned again. 'I've had enough of riddles. Show us your rabbit.'

He'd once shown them the trick of turning his neckerchief into the shape of a rabbit and making it disappear up his sleeve. Ben duly took off his neckerchief and folded it into a rabbit. He made it creep slow as a snail across his knee. The dog kept her eyes on it, ears pricked. Then – whoosh! In a flash, it went up his sleeve. The dog barked as the 'rabbit' shot out of sight. William leapt up and gave Ben a hug.

'This time, right now,' Mary announced, 'is so good you could put it in a pie.'

While young Mary was at Ben's, she didn't see as much of her father as she would have liked. Yet there was always suppertime. Before he went into the house, he sat on the step and let her pull off his boots. She yanked and tugged deliberately until she fell over, knowing he'd pick her up. Then she buried her nose in his shirt. He smelled of dried sweat, straw and tobacco. She couldn't decide which was best, the smell of her father or her dog, Stina. The dog was softer to nuzzle into and smelled of grass and fresh air – unless it had rolled in a dead bird or something.

One evening, as she sat on the step with her father, she put her arms round him and kissed him. She whispered in his ear. 'This time, right now, is so good you could put it in a poultice.'

At Easter, Francis Jordan and John Dawson were elected as churchwardens. Though John realised it was a sign of the villagers' respect, his wife Susannah was still treated as an unwanted stranger. It made no difference that she was quiet and unassuming. Their daughter Rebecca was turning out to be a fine girl and could now walk and talk, but Susannah kept her at home and the family avoided village gatherings. William's sister Dorothy was at the bottom of it. For her, the scandal was still fresh, and she made sure others were on her side. John's sister Ellen was still the only one to befriend Susannah. Her visits made the woman's life bearable.

When the hay in the meadow had been cut down in June, the women went daily to turn it over to dry. Susannah joined them for the first time with her daughter. The others kept their distance for fear of Dorothy Jordan's sharp tongue, but Ellen chose to work alongside her. She appreciated the woman's desire to work like the rest and wanted to make her welcome. First, they left their infants at the edge of the meadow.

'Stay 'ere wi' tha cousins,' Ellen instructed. 'There's young Mary an' Will to play with an' there's Francis 'ere to look after thee.'

At ease, having relieved themselves of the children, they looked forward to a day of tedding the hay and working in the sunshine with the other women.

Francis glowered at the three small new arrivals. It was not his choice to watch over the youngsters and keep them away from the hay and their mothers. He soon found it a hopeless task. He couldn't even control his own family. While he tended to his youngest brother, John, his sister and other brother ran off and played in the hay. At night, they'd be itching and sneezing, and he'd get the blame.

He shielded his eyes from the sun to see if his mother had noticed what was going on. She hadn't. She had her eyes on the ground, raking the hay in a line with the other women, and was laughing and chatting as she went. He hadn't realised how much she must have missed this outdoor work. No wonder she'd been such a crosspatch. Now, stuck with a group of children to guard, he could appreciate how hard it was to be a mother.

His grandfather Francis Jordan left his Uphall yard and strolled across the hilltop. He wanted to see how the tedding work was progressing in the meadow. From his high vantage point, he could see the wavering lines of white bonnets bobbing up and down like the floats of fishing nets on the sea. The murmur of women's voices accompanied the gentle swaying motion. The hay harvest was going well. The weather could not be better. It had been hot and dry for weeks and seemed likely to continue. His only worry was the lack of rain in the spring. It meant that the crops were on the small side and there was the fear of drought. The streams and the pond had almost dried up, and the two wells and the Jordan cistern were low. Still, he thought, they were much better off than others. He'd heard it hadn't rained in France since February.

In the summer, George Gurwood sensed young Mary's reluctance to be indoors. He'd heard all about her den, and she was torn between her lessons and Ben's garden. She did nothing but fidget and glance at the window where the sun streamed in. After a few mornings of fighting her restlessness, he gave in.

'Alright, you've done enough. We'll stop for now. Your reading and writing can be done when the weather breaks.'

Young Mary didn't need to be told twice. She jumped up from the table and ran to collect her dog from the garden.

Each morning, she now took her dog and her brother William on tours of the village, just as her Aunt Lizzie had taken her and Francis when they were little. They ran barefoot together, her plump legs pounding on the dry, dusty lanes, and he with his lopsided gait. They came to know the village through their feet as much as their eyes, nose and ears. The pond had shrunk, yet there was still mud around the edge. They stepped into it and loved to feel the warm clay ooze up between their toes. When they visited Bart Huskisson's shed afterwards, the sawdust stuck to their feet and made them smell of oak and pine.

One day, young Mary led William to the barley field. A gentle breeze ruffled the swathes. They stood watching the colours change from a soft grey to a sparkling green. It reminded her of a calm sea when the wind left cats' paws. William thought the waving barley was more like the fur on some enormous animal. He smiled at his sister, content with her company, for he'd learnt, at last, how to tread round the edges of the fields and avoid nettles and thistles. Now his sister was his best friend. Even better than the muddy pond and the barley field, she led him to the cliffs. There she helped him climb down the crumbling earth to reach the sands. They could stay there and play for hours unnoticed.

At Uphall, young Mary knew the best places to play and gave William his first close encounter with a calf. Its breath smelled sweet, and it had such soft and clean curly white hair on its forehead. After he'd stroked it for a while, she told him to put his hand near its mouth.

The calf thought he was offering a teat and licked it. All at once, his whole hand was sucked inside. He panicked as he felt the rasp of its long, muscular tongue. When she pulled him free, his hand was hot and slimy with saliva. To get his own back, he wiped his hand down her dress.

That made her stop and think. He wasn't usually so bold. Maybe he was getting too old to boss around.

The next day, Ben showed them the tiny green leafhopper that lives inside every bit of cuckoo spit. Unbeknown to his sister, William collected them and put them on top of her pease pudding supper – an excellent camouflage. By pure chance, and before she ate a spoonful, she caught sight of them moving. She stared at him open-mouthed as he giggled. From now on, she'd have to be more wary. Her little brother liked practical jokes.

Chapter 19

Young Mary was drawn to the sea despite her mother's disapproval of the time she spent there.

'You should help in the fields this fine weather. There's plenty to do. You shouldn't be scratting about on the beach or sitting on the cliffs daydreaming about ships.'

Young Mary ignored her and escaped many times to hide on the cliffs and wonder where the ships were going. Perhaps they were fetching cedars from Lebanon or bringing frankincense and myrrh. When there was a band of mist on the horizon, the ships looked as if they were sailing in the sky. And when the wind was in the right direction, she could hear orders being shouted about changes of sail. 'Only boys go to sea. Girls stay at home.' That's what her mother said.

Young Mary didn't believe her and asked at Uphall if girls could sail on ships. Her grandmother made a snorting noise like a pig.

'Lads are farmers an' mariners. Lasses cook an' mend an' 'ave bairns.'

It didn't seem fair. Boys could also be blacksmiths. Boys could be vicars and churchwardens. Boys could be anything they wanted. She'd heard of women who ran inns and had shops, but her mother said it was only when their husbands had died.

For days, young Mary imagined running away to Filey or Bridlington. She would dress as a boy and get on a ship. She even stole the clothes Francis had outgrown and hid them under her bed. She would cut her hair with the sheep shears and leave the house when there was a full moon. Then she'd walk across to Speeton and go down the coast.

One afternoon, she lay on her back by the cliff edge with William and her dog, going over her plans in detail. The sun was hot on her face. She shut one eye and saw the side of her nose. It was blurred and pink. She closed her other eye to see if there was any difference. Her nose jumped from one side to the other. Distracted, she forgot her ambitious plans, rolled onto her stomach and wrestled with the dog instead.

By August, young Mary often chose to go out with just her dog for company. That way she could think and dream without interruption. Her favourite place was the cliff top where she could lie and gaze at the bands of grey and white clouds above the sea. They looked like distant islands, places you could sail to. She recited the first two lines of a poem she'd heard at the Gurwoods'.

'My soul, there is a country far beyond the stars.' She sighed. Surely, somewhere, there was a beautiful place in the sky.

Another favourite haunt was Reighton Hill, where she could lie unseen among the gorse. There she could spend ages lulled by the heady scent of the flowers and watch the occasional cloud drift by. Sometimes, thistle wool from the meadow below wafted gently upwards on the rising warm currents of air. The only sound came from the gorse pods bursting open – a faint background crackling like raindrops on dry leaves. She lay beside her dog with one hand idly stroking Stina's ears while she pondered a life beyond Reighton.

One day, old Ben took young Mary and her brother down to the beach. He'd borrowed the mule from Uphall and had strapped on the panniers.

'We're off down Speeton ravine,' he told them. 'There's new buildin' goin' on an' I can earn money sellin' cobbles.'

The children had never been down that ravine before and, to Mary, the place was paradise. Most of Reighton was bleak and bare, but Speeton ravine was full of tall trees that closed overhead to make a canopy. Trickling to the bottom was a dark stream occasionally dammed by fallen, decaying branches. Birds flitted across the gap and unseen creatures scuttled in the undergrowth.

When Ben and the children emerged from the ravine, they found themselves on the open beach very close to the sea. While Ben loaded the mule with suitable cobbles, the children played in the stream, making a dam out of dead branches and driftwood. Young Mary noted this as a new place to be alone with her dog.

Another day, in late August, she set off just before dawn. She waded knee-deep through the ferns to find her way down the dark ravine to the sea. The stream, almost dry, made a constant soft tippling noise as it lost itself beneath the cobbles at the foot of the cliff. Though the sun had not yet risen, the sky was a blazing mass of pinks and reds. As she watched the deep orange globe rise above the sea, she imagined she was the first person in the world to see the dawn – like Adam in the Garden of Eden. 'Thank you,' she whispered to Apollo, her favourite god. She stayed a few moments more before hunger got the better of her and she hurried home for breakfast.

In September, the rain came at last. It was such a novelty that young Mary stood in the back doorway and gazed at a puddle that was almost perfectly round. As the raindrops fell into it, the ripples spread out in rings, colliding with each other. There was a pattern to them, and she began to time her breathing with the rhythm of the circles.

Her mother stood behind her, wondering what on earth went on in her daughter's head.

'Mary! Shut that door and get in. You've jobs to do and there's your knitting to finish.'

Young Mary traipsed back into the kitchen and picked up her knitting. She kept one eye on the weather, hoping the rain would stop. After a while, as if in answer to her prayers, the rain eased. She had an idea. Her mother never objected to a useful occupation, especially if it meant taking children out of her kitchen. She let drop her knitting.

'The rain's stopped now. Can I take William out brambling?'

As expected, her mother nodded. 'As long as you mind your clothes. Take the big basket and see William doesn't get juice all down himself.'

Young Mary led the way towards the ravine where she knew there were ripening brambles on one side. Once there, she gave William stern instructions.

'Listen. Don't grab at them. And don't pinch them with your fingers – just let them come off the stalk. Like this.' She demonstrated. 'They'll come off when they're ready.'

As they gathered the berries and filled up the basket, she reminded him constantly, 'Don't squash them! Gently does it.'

He couldn't help squeezing them, and the brambles burst between his fingers. By the time the basket was full, his hands, shirt and breeches were stained purple. His hands were scratched by thorns and, since he'd been gathering most of his brambles from underneath, he'd also been nettled.

When they got home, their mother took one look at him and ripped off his clothes. She was furious. Her face reddened and spit flew from her mouth. 'I should have known better! Why is it whenever you go with your sister, there's trouble?' She threw the clothes down in disgust. 'These will have to go in to soak straight away. And now I'll have to fetch more water. It's one thing after another with you two. Wait here while I go – and *don't move*!'

When she returned, she made them scrub their hands and nails in the cold water. The wash had little effect and the children steered clear of their mother until she banged a hot bramble pie on the table.

Young Mary glanced at William. She gave him a sly kick and winked. 'Mmmm, it smells delicious.'

'Yes,' he answered with a colluding smirk. 'It smells nice.'

Their mother sighed as she dished it out.

As the days grew shorter, young Mary took advantage of any fine weather. On calm, sunny days, she strolled along the cliffs so she could stand and gaze at the glittering blue sea. By October though, Bempton Cliffs were often half hidden by a grey mist, and sombre clouds appeared on the horizon.

On her way home, she always visited old Ben and sat by the fire while he told her stories. One tale was about Knox Well. She heard how, hundreds of years ago, two men had fallen in and drowned. Ben said they still haunted the place. Afterwards, whenever the cold east wind blew across the top of Reighton Hill, young Mary thought of the poor drowned ghosts and wondered if the men were ever pulled out.

One morning, as she and William wandered among the gorse bushes on the hill, they stumbled across a tree with a large hollowed-out trunk. They climbed in with the dog to shelter from the wind and curled up together to keep warm. Young Mary shivered with fright as she realised they must be close to Knox Well. Soon, every noise was either a tree spirit or a ghost come to get them. She whispered prayers to Apollo. Only then did she pluck up courage to leave the safety of the tree and go home.

Later that day, the children were walking through the boggy part of the lower meadow when they were alarmed by a toad-like creature, as big as a kitten. It leapt up suddenly out of the tall grass and then disappeared. Ben had once told them about Marmaduke Constable, who'd died after swallowing a toad. It had eaten his heart. They panicked and put their hands over their mouths – just in case. Young Mary's head was full of unanswered questions.

'Do you think the Knox Well ghosts have turned into toads? And, William, do you think you really die if you swallow one?'

He had no idea.

The very next day, Ben sat them by the fire and informed them he'd seen fairies.

'Aye, they were dancin' one summer's mornin' at dawn – wearin' such bright clothes, all colours tha could think of.'

They held their breath and opened their eyes so wide it hurt.

'An' listen, if thoo 'appens to feel a gush o' warm air risin' from a crack i' ground, I tell thee it's warmth comin' from their bodies.' He added with a wink, 'Some folks 'ave even 'ad a whiff of 'em.'

The children could hardly believe it and left Ben's cottage in a daze.

When young Mary saw a dragonfly hover over the pond and then fly towards her, she thought it must be a fairy. It landed on her foot. Its wings were so delicate and transparent, and she thought nothing could ever match the brilliant blue of its body. Thinking she'd entered a world of magic, she whispered reverently, asking it to make her mother less cross.

When she heard the gossip that John Dawson's wife was with child again, she put it down to magic – to something brought about by the fairies.

There was no magic as far as her Aunt Dorothy was concerned.

Chapter 20

Young Dorothy Jordan sulked for days. She still hoped that Susannah would get sick of Reighton and leave. Now, with yet another child on the way, the woman was bound to stay, and John Dawson would never be hers.

The rest of the village was secretly pleased for Susannah. Sarah Ezard, in particular, had nothing but good to say.

'That Susannah means well,' she told the women as they drew water and filled their pails. 'She did 'er fair share o' work at 'arvest, an' remember way she toiled all day i' sun, down i' yon meadow.'

Martha Wrench agreed. 'Aye, an' I'm glad she's joinin' in wi' knittin' circles. It's thanks to Ellen Smith. She's been a good friend to 'er, made 'er feel part o' village.'

'Aye, that's true, though best not say owt to Dorothy Jordan. We'd all best mind our tongues.'

Unbeknown to the Jordans, the village mothers clubbed together to give Susannah small gifts both for her and the coming child. Sarah Ezard gave her a petticoat with a splinter of witch elm sewn into it.

'This'll 'elp thee when thoo goes into labour.'

Susannah was very grateful. Being superstitious, she aimed to help her pregnancy by appeasing any local spirits. She rammed small pieces of cloth into the forks of trees and left powdered beef and apples in out-of-the-way places. Knowing that young Mary could write, she invited her into the house to write out charms. She then folded them up into tiny squares, hid one in a bottle and placed one above the door and one above the window.

Young Mary was inspired to write a charm for her own house. She took great pains and wrote in a minute hand, 'Remove the evil from this house', and then she rolled it into a tube to hide above the front door. She saw good and evil forces all around her and lived in dread of disturbing or angering the 'evil ones'. From now on, she and her young brother spat on the ground if they passed a stranger or an old woman on their walks round the village.

'Don't look them in the eye,' she warned William. 'They can't give you a funny look if you turn away.'

Old Ben had told her of a witch in Scarborough who'd given a little girl violent fits just by giving her a funny look once at the fair. Thanks to Ben, she was wary of taking elder twigs into the house in case they brought in a witch or the Devil himself. A hare racing across an open field might not be a hare at all but someone transformed. She even began to wonder about Sarah Ezard and took a guilty pleasure in spying on her.

One day, young Mary saw Sarah bury cream in her garden and heard her chant strange rhymes to her herb-cutting knife. Perhaps Sarah was a witch.

If young Mary's fire at home did not burn well, or else burned without giving any heat, she blamed the spirits and asked her parents to burn ash logs to drive away the Devil. If the milk turned sour, she blamed it on the boggarts. Each dark corner of the house and each tree and outbuilding now hid a hobgoblin of some kind. She was sure she'd heard one rattling its chains in the Uphall stable. She'd seen her mother leave a bowl of milk out each night. She'd assumed it was for the cats, but when she saw the milkmaid at Uphall do the same, she was told it was for 'the hob'.

'They're 'elpful imps,' the maid explained. 'They'll do tha work durin' night. We mustn't upset 'em though. They soon get cross an' then they'll leave tha farm forever. If there's no food for 'em, they'll stamp an' say 'emten, 'amten, 'ere will I never more tread nor stampen.'

The one place young Mary was sure to be safe was the church. One late afternoon at the very end of October, young Mary led William up the hill to the church to search for newts.

'They're easy to catch,' she said. 'They look dead, but they're not.'

She pushed open the heavy door, and then listened to make sure no one else was there. They stepped down onto the church floor, onto the smooth, worn cobblestones. Although the place was always cool and damp, today there was a strange coldness in the air.

Young Mary trod slowly up the rush-strewn aisle towards the chancel, making no noise as she went. William tiptoed behind her. All at once, she stopped. She sensed she was being watched. She put a finger to her lips to warn William to be quiet and peered around the dark church.

Very little afternoon daylight came through the lancet windows in the south wall. It was difficult to see into the far corners. The church was as silent as a tomb, and as cold. There didn't seem to be anyone else about, so, thinking they were alone, she walked on, pausing to check each pew for newts. She also stopped frequently to turn her head and see who or what might be behind her.

Neither of them spoke, and William was infected by his sister's unease. She was unusually cautious. He stepped up behind her and tugged her sleeve. She turned to face him and saw the fear in his eyes. The hair rose on the back of her neck. There was something not right about the church that afternoon.

'I don't think we should get newts today,' she whispered. 'I don't think we should be here.' She had the strangest feeling that something was going on that wasn't for her eyes, that there was a preparation being made for an important event – for older folk, not for children. The more she thought about it, the more she was convinced that they really were being watched and were definitely not welcome in the church.

She grabbed William's hand. 'Come on, we'd better go. This isn't for us.'

They walked quickly and quietly out of the church, and she closed the door behind them. She stood for a moment in the churchyard, relieved to be in the warmer air outside. The experience had unnerved her, and she needed comfort and reassurance.

'Let's not go home yet, William. Let's go to Ben's. Come on, Will, let's run.'

She set off at speed. It was good to escape the church and she was halfway down the hill before she stopped and waited for William to catch up. As soon as he reached her, she ran off again, this time holding his hand to hurry him.

'What's up?' Ben asked as they tumbled through his doorway, out of breath.

'We've been in the church,' she gasped.

'Not today?'

'Yes, but we weren't long.'

'Thoo shouldn't be i' church today, nor tonight neither.'

'Why?'

'It's All 'Allows' Eve. It's when dead leave their graves an' walk among the livin'. It's last chance fo' departed souls to get revenge o' their enemies before they move on.'

Young Mary's eyes prickled with fear.

'It was all wrong in there,' she whispered. 'Ben, it wasn't friendly. We were scared. It felt like we weren't wanted – like at Uphall when Gran's busy. She never wants me when she's getting ready for Christmas.'

'Well, maybe summat was going on – summat serious.'

She began to cry. 'I used to like looking for newts.'

'There'll be other times to get newts. Come 'ere.' He gave her a gentle hug. 'Thoo'd best not tell tha father though,' he added as he let her go. 'It's nowt but old stuff I've been tellin' thee. No one celebrates 'Allows' Eve anymore, 'aven't done since God knows when.' He paused to think, unsure of his own beliefs. 'I wonder, just 'cos folk no longer 'ave bonfires to drive off evil, it doesn't mean spirits won't still be about.'

He walked over to his window and peered out. 'Maybe it's an omen,' he muttered to himself. He turned to face the children. 'Or maybe thoo's just 'ad tha first brush wi' folk on other side. Who knows?'

Young Mary was very quiet for the next few days. She feared being tainted by whatever it was she'd felt that afternoon in church and took whatever precautions she could to distance herself from it. She copied out verses from the psalms and prayed hard each night. When she found a crow's feather, she stuck it in the middle of the ploughed fallow field and made a wish. She also made a habit of collecting birds' feathers and putting them under everyone's mattress, even under Stina. That way, she believed, no one in her family could die.

Chapter 21

In November, the families settled into their winter routines. The women gathered to make pickles and to gossip while the children collected sticks and hunted down any mice that had invaded their homes. Once the muck had been shovelled out of the cowsheds and the animals fed for the day, the men had the ploughing to finish for the year. After that, tools would be repaired and everything put away– the ploughs, the carts, the barrows and ladders. By mid-month, the lads at Uphall were restless, already anticipating the fun of the Hunmanby Hiring Fair. Also, John Dawson's wife felt her baby quicken for the first time.

'It's like bubbles slidin' about,' she told Ellen as they knitted by the kitchen fire. Her daughter was playing at their feet with a ball of wool and a rag doll. 'Come 'ere, Rebecca. See if thoo can feel bairn movin'.'

Rebecca put her hands over her mother's stomach.

'Can thoo feel it quiver?'

The girl shook her head.

'Try me,' Ellen offered. 'My bairn's bigger. I've only a couple o' months to go.'

Rebecca hesitated and then stroked the hard mound under Ellen's gown.

Ellen smiled. 'If it's a girl, I'll call 'er Susannah.'

'An' if *I* 'ave a girl, I'll call 'er Ellen.'

'Let's 'ope we both 'ave 'ealthy bairns – whatever they are.'

Days before the Hiring Fair, the weather turned frosty. It rained early in the evening and then the temperature plummeted. By dawn, black ice covered the pathways and yards. John Dawson left home in the morning before it was even light, intending to keep a close eye on the Uphall lads. His wife and daughter stayed in bed.

Susannah rose at last to liven up the fire and make the porridge. She went to the outhouse for more gorse and failed to notice the ice on the doorstep. As soon as she put her weight on the step, she skidded off, fell sideways and bashed her head against the wall. She remembered her daughter was still in bed, and then fainted. The back door closed by itself.

Rebecca lay in bed for a while, unconcerned, and then struggled out of the covers and called for her mother. Soon, she was toddling around the house in tears.

Outside, Susannah regained consciousness. With just a woollen shawl round her, she was chilled to the bone and her back was stiff. She was shivering, her teeth knocking together so much she thought they'd break. Taking a deep breath, she managed to pull herself up by holding onto the doorpost. Then she was aware of something hot trickling down her leg. At first, she thought she'd wet herself, but it was blood, and it was fresh and bright red.

Her heart thumped as she staggered indoors, bent double and clutching her stomach. She found her daughter sitting in the middle of the kitchen sobbing so hard she was choking. Heartbroken, Susannah went down on her knees to hold her and calm her down.

'There, there,' she crooned, 'Mother's 'ere. Everythin's alright. I'll warm up a drink o' milk for us.'

As she limped to the fire, the contractions began. She was afraid the baby would come before its time and so lay down on the bed in the parlour and tried to relax. Her daughter curled up next to her and took hold of her mother's hair, twisting it round her finger for comfort.

Susannah concentrated on breathing, on slowing it down to steady her heartbeat. She shut her eyes and attempted to think of other things. Yet still the contractions came. They were regular and there was no stopping them. Realising that there was no way out of it, that she was definitely in labour, she knew she needed help. She rolled off the bed, still holding her stomach, stood up and shuffled to the front door. There she stood and shouted.

Cecilia Gurwood heard the cries on her way back to the vicarage. 'Susannah, whatever's the matter?'

'Me bairn's comin'. Get Sarah Ezard.' She winced as another cramp doubled her up and she cried out in pain.

Cecilia didn't waste any time. She hitched up her gown in both hands and rushed to Sarah's cottage.

Within minutes, the two women returned and heard about the fall and the exposure to cold. Sarah feared the worst when she saw Susannah's ashen face and the blue shadows under her eyes. When she felt her pulse, it was fast and uneven, and the poor woman was hardly aware of her surroundings. Her eyes were glazed as she stared at the roof beams, and she groaned whenever her womb contracted.

Sarah calculated the baby couldn't be more than four months old at the most. This meant that, when the baby came, it would not be lying in the correct position for birth. The last thing she wanted was for Rebecca, not yet two years old, to witness what could well be a frightening and messy ordeal. When Susannah's contractions grew more frequent, Sarah took Rebecca aside and wrapped her in a blanket. She found the rag doll that had fallen on the floor and put it in the girl's hands. As Cecilia was standing idle, Sarah told her to take the girl into the kitchen and keep her there.

With the girl out of the way, Sarah concentrated on the mother. Susannah was breathing in shallow gasps, and she looked terrified. When Sarah tried to check her pulse again, Susannah thrashed on the bed and dug her nails into the back of Sarah's hand. She wouldn't let go and both women cried out.

Rebecca, sitting on Cecilia's knee in the kitchen, heard the noise and sucked her thumb as she nestled further into the blanket. Cecilia hugged her tight and began to rock her. They both heard one last unearthly scream and then there was silence.

In the parlour, Sarah was faced with the whole lot coming out at once – not just the baby, but also the placenta, the water and a large amount of blood. Susannah was still. She lay with her eyes closed, exhausted.

Cecilia walked in with Rebecca. Sarah waved an arm to direct them away from the bloody mess while, with her other hand, she covered it up with a sheet. She did not know yet whether the baby was alive or not.

Ignoring everything else, she attended to the mother, who still had her eyes closed and was struggling to catch her breath. She knew she ought to check the mess on the bed to make sure everything had come away cleanly. When she lifted the sheet a little, she saw the remains were ragged. This was not good news.

To help expel more, Sarah pressed down on Susannah's womb. Fresh blood oozed out, followed by several large dark red lumps. She hoped that everything had now come out. Tomorrow, she'd dose her with ergot and that should bring out any stubborn bits and pieces. For now, though, Susannah was still bleeding.

All at once, Cecilia saw a tiny hand poking out. She spun Rebecca away, approached the bed and held up a corner of the sheet. There was a tiny, fully formed baby. It was no bigger than a newly born pup, but it was purple and wizened like an old man. It lay there with its eyes closed, not moving or crying. Its whole body was covered in soft hair like an animal and the skin on its head was so thin she could see the veins beneath.

Sarah grabbed the baby and laid it in the palm of her hand. Instinctively, she rubbed its back with her ring finger. The baby's thumb was in its mouth, so she removed it to help it breathe. It was no good. The baby boy was far too small to survive. He'd never lived beyond the womb, had never taken a single breath. She turned to Cecilia and shook her head.

'I'll stay wi' Susannah an' 'elp 'er grieve. Could thoo go wi' Rebecca an' get a message to John at Up'all? 'E needs to know what's 'appened.'

Cecilia nodded, relieved to get away. After wrapping Rebecca in an extra blanket, she carried her up the hill and wondered how to tell the Jordans. God alone knew how they'd take the news. Would they show compassion? John Dawson would not be able to go home for a while, not until his wife was better, and someone would have to look after both him and his daughter.

Dorothy Jordan was swift with her answer.

'We're not 'avin' 'em 'ere. Rebecca an' John can go an' live wi' Smiths. An' Smiths can pay for any medicine.'

On her way back down the hill, Cecilia reflected on the Jordan family's lack of sympathy for John and his family. Would they never forgive and forget? As she re-entered the parlour, she saw there was no change in Susannah's condition.

Sarah waved her away. 'Thoo'll 'ave to wait i' kitchen again wi' Rebecca. I think there must be summat else still to come out.'

As soon as she was alone again with Susannah, Sarah pushed her hand right up inside, until she could feel the neck of the womb. She couldn't find anything there so reckoned it was just a matter of time before things were expelled. It might take days, maybe even a week. She washed mother and baby and cleared up the mess as best she could.

Susannah knew that she'd lost her child. She held him for a while and then fell back against the pillow. 'I only want to sleep,' she murmured through her tears. The cramps continued, however, and she got no rest.

Ellen Smith arrived in the afternoon to relieve Cecilia. She sat awkwardly by the bed stroking Susannah's fair hair, now dark with sweat.

'I'm sorry I can't stay an' look after thee, but I will take Rebecca. She'll be fine wi' me.' She got up and walked Rebecca to the door.

Sarah called her back. 'Wait! Go into kitchen. We need to talk.'

When Sarah had closed the kitchen door, she began. 'Listen, Ellen, I need someone to 'elp me. I can't stay 'ere all day an' night, neither can Cecilia.'

'Why not ask young Dorothy Jordan?'

'Thoo must be mad,' Sarah snapped.

'Yes,' agreed Cecilia, 'it's a ridiculous proposition.'

'No – think about it. God forbid anythin' should 'appen to Susannah – but if... well... *if*, then John'll need a new wife, won't 'e?'

Cecilia shrugged, unconvinced. 'I suppose it could work out for the best,' she conceded. As she left the cottage, she turned and added, 'John could hardly ignore Dorothy if she helped out. I'll see what the Jordans have to say.'

Chapter 22

Cecilia stood in the Uphall kitchen and told the two Dorothy Jordans about Susannah's situation. When she then made the suggestion as to who might care for her, both Dorothy Jordans were lost for words. They couldn't spit or curse in the presence of the vicar's daughter and stood in shocked silence. Young Dorothy soon saw the possible advantages. She winked at her mother.

'I must go and help. It's the Christian thing to do. I'll go straightaway.'

Her mother shook her head. 'Wonders will never cease.'

As Dorothy made her way to the Dawsons' cottage, she had second thoughts. She'd never befriended the woman, had been her enemy more like. She'd avoided even looking at her. Susannah's prominent nose said it all – the way she'd nosed her way into Reighton and taken John from her.

The uncharitable thoughts vanished when she saw a pale Susannah shivering in bed. Struck with pity, she beckoned Sarah into the kitchen to find out how things stood.

Sarah explained the problems that Susannah faced – the bleeding and the stillborn child. She gave instructions as to how Dorothy should clean and feed her.

'I'll fetch some meadowsweet i' case o' fever, an' mugwort fo' thee to boil up as a tonic. Thoo mustn't leave 'er.'

After a few days, when there were no signs of improvement, Sarah Ezard feared the worst. Susannah was still bleeding and expelling large clots and, whenever her womb was pressed, she cried out. Such things did happen, but Susannah developed a fever and complained of a deep, sickening ache in her womb, as if badly bruised. When she became delirious and fought off the bedclothes, Sarah wondered if she'd caught a chill from being out in the cold. The bruised feeling could be due to Susannah falling on the doorstep.

Sarah remained puzzled until one morning she arrived and was met by a foul stench, like meat that had gone off. She inspected Susannah and found that, instead of red blood, there was a yellowish discharge, and it stank.

Dorothy was burning rosemary on the fire to rid Susannah of her fever and disguise the smell. She apologised to Sarah.

'I don't know how it happened. I woke up this morning and the room stank to high heaven.'

'It's not *thy* fault. Summat's very wrong wi' Susannah. Summat inside 'er 'as gone rotten, an' it 'asn't all come out. I've got summat at 'ome though. I'll fetch it to rid place o' this smell.'

Sarah held a cloth over her nose while she cleaned the top of Susannah's thighs. Her patient was oblivious to what went on, lost in her own hell of fierce, burning heat followed by icy chills.

The meadowsweet had not worked, so Sarah prescribed an apple-bark remedy. She returned later in the day with it plus a bottle of lavender water. She gave instructions to Dorothy.

'Use this lavender as a cleanser. It'll also 'elp purify air i' parlour. An' I've left a pail o' limewater out back – thoo must wet cloths in it an' drape 'em round parlour. That should take stench away.'

John Dawson had been told to stay well away. His wife's illness was a woman's ailment, and he was not required. He missed her and so did his daughter, who cried herself to sleep each night. It was days before she settled into the new routines and could enjoy having a girl and boy a little older than herself as playmates. It helped that the Smiths' farm was much livelier and busier than her own home.

When John heard that his wife was growing weaker and not eating, he asked if he could visit. It was one thing to be excluded after a child had been born, and quite another when your wife might be dying. He didn't mind so much the loss of the baby, though it was bitter news to hear it had been a boy.

Sarah advised him to come alone and not bring Rebecca. She forewarned him of Susannah's condition and explained the reason for the smell. Before he arrived, Dorothy and Sarah sprinkled herbs among the rushes on the floor and put more lavender water to warm near the fire.

In spite of the efforts made, John was still taken aback by the sickening odour. He tried to ignore it and approached the bed. Susannah barely recognised him. Nevertheless, he sat beside her and spoke softly.

'Thoo'll soon be right, an' I promise we'll all look after thee better.' He took hold of her hand and was alarmed to find her skin so cold. He began to warm it between both his hands. 'Don't worry about Rebecca. She's doin' well.' He wondered what else he could tell her. 'She's learnin' all sorts o' tricks from Ellen's bairns.' He couldn't think of anything more to say.

Beads of sweat appeared on her face, so he wiped her forehead with one of the damp cloths by the bed. He turned to Sarah and Dorothy for help, but they had little to offer.

'We've done our best, John,' Dorothy whispered with genuine tears in her eyes. 'Susannah's in God's hands now.'

He knelt by the bed and began to pray. The two women said the Lord's Prayer.

That night, when Dorothy saw that Susannah's breathing had become laboured, she sent for Sarah and John and also George Gurwood. More candles were lit, and Bible passages were read as they waited for the inevitable. Susannah was no longer conscious. She was so thin that the bedcovers were almost flat.

John wrung his hands when he saw the cold dew on her face, knowing it was a sign of approaching death. He reflected on her life. She'd not had much luck, what with only one daughter and two stillbirths. He hoped fervently that she hadn't regretted seducing him that day at the fair or marrying him. Apart from him and their daughter, she'd led a lonely life for most of the time. She'd never complained.

A short while before midnight, Susannah's eyes blinked open. Though everything was blurred, she knew who was present by their voices. When she closed her eyes again, they thought she was asleep, but she could hear everything spoken and knew she was dying. Strangely, she felt quite aloof. She was tired. The effort of breathing was too much. She just wanted peace. John was holding her hand too tight. It was a distraction, keeping her in this world when she was ready for the next. She didn't have the strength to pull her hand away. Now he was pressing and playing with her fingers. Aware of his distress, her last thoughts were for his future. She prayed that he would re-marry. Dorothy Jordan could be his wife at last and be a mother to Rebecca.

She lost consciousness again. In the early hours of the morning, she died.

John wanted to be alone with his thoughts and pray by her side. He sent the others away and kept a vigil until it grew light. At dawn, he let Sarah and Dorothy back in to wash the body and lay it out. He thought to bring Rebecca to see her mother once Susannah was laid out on the table, clean and without the smell.

Dorothy Jordan avoided his eye. It hurt to see him grieving, though she now had a glimmer of hope. It was obvious he needed a wife and someone to rear his daughter. He could not manage alone. She'd not forgotten that St Agnes Eve many years ago when she'd been granted a vision of her future husband. Yes, she would step in and be the one – but not too soon. Best to keep a respectable distance and allow him time to mourn. Christmas was now less than a month away. There'd better not be any other women with designs on him.

Chapter 23

Susannah's brief funeral was remarkably well attended. Even the Jordans turned out, every one of them, in spite of the arctic wind screaming across the churchyard. For John, it was some consolation to see so many people. His one regret was that they'd not shown as much respect for Susannah while she lived.

As for Dorothy Jordan, she was disappointed to hear that John planned to stay with the Smiths for the remainder of the year. Apparently, Rebecca was settled there, and despite Dorothy's protestations, he would not change his mind. She did get to see him once a day when he had his midday meal at Uphall. This wasn't enough, and she wondered if he'd even be with her for the Christmas holiday.

The day before Christmas, Dorothy grew more hopeful. Uphall was busy with the traditional preparations and there was excitement in the air. She helped her mother prepare a large amount of grain for the frumenty and spent ages cleaning and cooking to allow more free time later, preferably spent with John.

Young Mary was supposed to be helping her mother, but she escaped as usual with an excuse to go and see

Ben. Her dog trotted behind. When she arrived, he was sprinkling spices into a pan of mead.

He was not surprised to find her standing there with Stina, both looking ready for mischief.

'Now then, trouble, keep out o' way while I warm this up.'

He pulled the poker from the fire and stuck the red-hot end in the mead. Immediately, it hissed and bubbled.

'That should do trick. Thoo can 'ave a taste if tha wants. It's best on a cold day like this.'

He poured it into a wooden bowl. The mixture of cloves, nutmeg and cinnamon was pleasant and made her nose tickle, but when she took a sip, she didn't like it and spat it out.

He chuckled. 'It's too strong fo' thee, which is just as well. We can't 'ave thee crawlin' 'ome drunk!'

He held the bowl in both hands to warm them. Then he leant over and breathed in the spicy aroma. Suddenly, he tilted the bowl to his lips and drank it down in a few gulps.

'That's better,' he said as he patted his stomach. 'That's what I calls a good poker mead. Now, come an' sit by fire.' He lowered his voice to a whisper. 'I've summat to tell thee.'

When she was comfortable with the dog lying at her feet, he spoke as if confiding a secret. 'I know what 'appens i' cattle sheds o' Kesmas Eve. Towards midnight, listen, our cattle turn to face east – an' they kneel in honour o' Jesus.'

She was amazed. Her eyes glittered in the firelight as she imagined the scene and wondered if she could go and see. It was exciting to be with Ben. He had so many things to tell her.

'You're my favourite person,' she said, snuggling up to him, 'apart from Father – and Stina, but she's a dog.' Then she remembered why she was there. 'Ben, have you any spare holly and ivy or mistletoe for us?'

'Well now, seein' as it's Kesmas Eve, I can't let tha go 'ome without summat. Come into garden.'

She followed him up and down the hedge and in and out of the apple trees while he cut down various pieces. By the time he'd finished, she had to borrow his sledge to drag the greenery home.

Her mother was pleased for once and sent her straightaway to the church with the surplus. 'Make yourself useful. You can help the Gurwoods decorate the pews. And take your dog – I don't want her under my feet.'

Young Mary found all seven of the Gurwood girls at the church. Their brother John was also there, come home especially for Christmas. When she staggered in carrying an enormous armful of ivy, the younger girls cheered.

Cecilia and John were not so pleased. The dog would be a nuisance in church and young Mary wasn't always a helpful addition.

'Oh, thank you.' Cecilia tried to sound grateful. 'Perhaps you can help our Mary and Priscilla trail the long pieces on the backs of the pews. Leave the plaiting to us though and *don't* touch the altar. *I'll* deal with that.'

The three girls worked well enough at first but soon competed over the ivy stems. The dog saw them fighting over a long, leafy tendril and joined in. She wouldn't let go and shook it like a rat. The girls tugged on the other end and dragged the dog with them, knocking off the ivy they'd already hung on the pews.

'Get that dog out of here!' shouted Cecilia. 'We'll never get done at this rate.'

Young Mary bit her lip and scowled as she hauled Stina to the porch. There she tied her to the boot-scraper with an ivy stem.

'Stay!' She kissed the dog's head. 'I won't be long.'

It was late afternoon before the church was decorated to Cecilia's standards. John lit extra candles to see the effect. Young Mary stood in awe. The wood of the pews glowed golden against the dark green leaves, and bright red holly berries hung like stars above the altar. He blew out the candles and the magic disappeared.

It was dark when young Mary untied her dog and walked back down the hill. She imagined, or at least hoped, that her mother would have the food ready. When she arrived, her father and Uncle Thomas had just carried in the Yule log. They were busy trying to get it alight from the wood left over from last year. She joined her brothers standing by the fire. They watched the two men kneel down and blow on the charred remains.

Her father turned to face her. 'Where've *you* been?'

'Putting ivy in the church – with the Gurwoods.'

'Oh, good lass. You'll be ready for the frumenty then. It must be even colder in the church than outside.'

'Father, can I go to Uphall tonight to see the cattle?'

'Why do you want to do that? You can see them any day.'

'Ben says they kneel for Jesus.'

Her brother snorted and began to giggle. Her mother intervened. 'Ben says. Ben says. What doesn't Ben say? Your mother was right, William, when she said Ben says owt but 'is prayers. Instead of being with Ben, your daughter should've been helping me get ready for Christmas. It's been hard enough with the boys under my feet.'

Young Mary ignored the look on Francis's face. She could tell he wanted to go too though he'd never admit it. She also ignored her mother's frowns. She cast her eyes down and whispered mournfully.

'Can't I go then, Father?'

He paused, knowing he'd give in. 'We'll see. Maybe Dickon won't mind standing in the shed with you. I can't see anyone else bothering.'

'That means I can then.'

Her mother noted the smug smile. She sniffed and bent down to check the pan of wheat that was drying by the fire. All at once, she spun round and wagged her finger.

'Just make sure, young lady, you're back home in plenty of time for the frumenty and for lighting the Yule candle.' She glared at the men. 'William, it'll be *your* fault if she's late.'

As soon as the Yule log was kindled to his satisfaction, William allowed his daughter to go to Uphall with Thomas to see the cattle. She was carried on his shoulders all the way up the hill. He jiggled her up and down, swung the lantern about and sang 'The Holly and the Ivy'. Her cheeks burned with the cold, and she could smell snow in the air. He dumped her by the cattle shed, told her to wait there in the dark, and went to fetch Dickon.

Alone in the blackest of nights, she was thrilled to be the only one in her family to see the cattle kneel. Then Francis would be sorry he laughed and sorry he hadn't come too. As she waited, her feet grew cold. She stamped them on the frozen ground and gazed at the sky. It was such a deep black that stars were everywhere. She wondered which one had led the wise men. Certainly, one of the stars was brighter than the rest and twinkled more in the frosty air. Lost in thought, she didn't hear Dickon creep up behind her. He waved the lantern in her face and made her jump.

'Come to see cattle kneel, eh?'

'Yes, Ben told me. He said they do it for Jesus – on Christmas Eve.'

'Well, I can't promise they'll do it while we watch, but come into shed an' tha can stay for a bit.'

It was a lot warmer inside than out in the yard. The cows' flanks were steaming, and the air was full of their hot, damp breath. She knelt down on a patch of clean straw while Dickon hung the lantern on a nail. Thinking it might help, she began to hum the carol 'I Saw Three Ships'. The cattle continued to stand. The cold seeped into her knees, so she got up again and stood to one side to wait.

Dickon also stood patiently, thinking how long he should allow before suggesting they give up. The cattle lowed and shifted on their feet, occasionally peering round at the two of them. None showed any sign of facing the east or kneeling. It was getting colder, and Dickon saw she was shivering. He knew she was losing heart.

'Look, maybe cattle won't kneel while we're 'ere. Maybe they don't like bein' gawped at, eh?'

She nodded while her eyes pricked with tears. She didn't want to go home and say nothing had happened. Francis would smirk.

Before they left the shed, Dickon stroked one of the cows and, unseen by Mary, pushed his knee behind its leg. The cow's leg buckled. It stumbled forward and then stood firm again.

'Never mind,' Dickon murmured as he opened the door, 'there's always next year.'

He led her by the lantern to the Uphall door and shouted for Thomas to take her back home. When Thomas came, all smiles, Dickon put a finger to his lips and shook his head. Thomas understood the girl's disappointment and hoisted her up gently for another shoulder ride home. As he marched out of the yard, swinging the lantern before him, she shouted back.

'Thank you, Dickon, for trying.'

No carols were sung this time as they made slow progress down the hill. Thomas put her down outside the door and followed her in. The family were seated at the table with the Yule candle in the middle ready to be lit. He sensed they were late and guided her forwards.

'About time,' grumbled her mother. 'Thomas – you'll sit and eat with us, won't you?'

He sat down and began talking to William about the new farm lads and about how they were settling in. No one mentioned the disappointment over the cattle.

To avoid Francis's questioning gaze, young Mary bent down to hug Stina. Then she took off her coat and slipped quietly into her place at the table. There she stared at the Yule candle, and at the pepper-cake and cheese laid out on a large plate. A tear was about to roll down her cheek, so she brushed it away. When she swallowed, there was a lump in her throat.

Everyone ignored her. William was about to light the special candle. They held their breath, afraid to cause a draught with any sudden movement. Only when the candle flame was secure did William take a piece of cheese and cake and pass the plate round. They ate in solemn silence.

Mary left the table to bring the frumenty to boil. When she finally spooned in the sugar and nutmeg and poured it out, they relaxed at last and knew Christmas was almost here. The thick, milky drink warmed and filled their stomachs. As the pepper-cake and cheese were passed round once more, they heard a distant gun shot.

'That's your grandfather at Uphall,' William announced. 'He's shooting in the Christmas.'

Almost at once, the front door blew open and a gust of wind made the Yule candle sputter. They stared at the precarious flame as it flickered and then went out. The adults knew what it meant. Mary turned cold, as if a claw-like hand had clutched her ribs. William, not normally given to superstition, went pale. He tried to laugh it off.

'It's only the wind. It happens often enough this time of year.'

'Aye,' agreed Thomas, 'only a gust of wind. I can't have shut the door properly.'

Mary and William glanced round at their family. They were thinking which one of them would not be here next Christmas.

Part Two

A Family Adrift

Chapter 24

1717

Dorothy Jordan's hopes of seeing John Dawson over Christmas came to nothing. He stayed at the Smiths' the whole time, finding solace in the company of his sister and her family. When the crescent of the new moon became visible after sunset in January, Dorothy went outside with a lantern and her Christmas present – a silk kerchief. It had never been washed and so she believed that, if she looked through it, then the number of moons visible would equal the number of years until she married.

Ignoring the cold northern breeze that turned her nose red, she held the silk over her eyes and peered through. Her heart leapt when she saw just the one moon. She hardly dared hope she'd be married a year from now. But it had to be John Dawson. No one else would do and she knew a way to find out. She walked across the yard and stopped at the gate to the field. After setting down the lantern, she stood on the bottom spar and dangled her arms over the top. The sky was black, dusted with stars. Gazing at the moon, she recited dreamily.

'All hail to thee moon, all hail to thee,
I prythee, good moon, reveal to me
This night who my husband shall be.'

She retired to bed early in high hopes, and in the morning, she recalled her dream. *Yes*, she whispered to herself. *Yes, yes, yes. I've dreamed of John Dawson.*

It was only when the New Year's ploughing began, however, that Dorothy saw John regularly again. She overheard him in the kitchen talking to William about the future, expressing his desire to move back to the cottage with his young daughter.

'I can't rely o' me sister an' 'er family forever,' he said, 'an' I don't want to. An' I don't want Rebecca gettin' over fond o' livin' wi' Smiths.'

'I understand,' William sympathised, 'though it won't be easy looking after Rebecca on your own.'

Dorothy had an idea. She waited for the chance to talk to her brother alone and waylaid him as he crossed the yard. She pulled him back by his coat sleeve.

'Do you think *I* could look after Rebecca every day? Here at Uphall?' Before he could answer, she blurted out her plan. 'You see, that way, John can still live in his own home. He can bring Rebecca here every morning when he comes to work, and he can take her back home again in the evening.'

William gave a wry smile. 'Hmm, I'll suggest it to John.' As he left his sister, he hoped that John would be firm and not be bamboozled by Dorothy.

Days later, in the middle of January, John Dawson moved back to his cottage. Circumstances had assisted him; John's sister was about to have her third child and she wanted the men out of the way. A week later, Ellen gave birth to a girl and, as promised, named her new daughter Susannah, in memory of John's wife.

At Uphall, Dorothy Jordan attempted to befriend John's young daughter. The girl was brought there every day except Sunday, and Dorothy found it wasn't easy. For one thing, the girl already had a large nose, just like her mother's. It didn't exactly endear the child. A further annoyance was that Rebecca missed the Smith children and whined for their company. She was bored and lonely at Uphall and Dorothy found little to entertain her.

William suggested she take the girl to his house sometimes. There, she could play with his young sons. 'Mary won't mind, honest. You'll find she's more patient these days.'

Since Christmas, it was true that Mary Jordan had been kinder, more tolerant. She'd told no one about the Yule candle going out. She hoped that, if not mentioned, the bad omen might not count. However, it preyed on the minds of both parents. They now placed more store on the shared family mealtimes and took greater pleasure in their children. Mary even began to show more affection for her daughter.

Despite the kindness shown by her mother, young Mary was wary of the change. Each evening, she chose to sit by the fire with her father while he read parts of the Book of Job. She never tired of hearing the descriptions of gigantic creatures.

'Read me about the leviathan again,' she begged.

He soon found the chapter she wanted. 'I will not conceal his parts,' he read, 'nor his power, nor his comely proportion.'

'No, read the next bit – about smoke and fire.'

He moved his finger down the verses. 'Out of his nostrils goeth smoke, as out of a seething pot or cauldron. His breath kindleth coals, and a flame goeth out of his mouth.'

'Yes, that's it. Now read all of it.'

Her mother sighed, having heard that chapter many times. William was so good with their daughter and had such patience. She knew her daughter needed plenty to occupy her mind when they were stuck indoors, but during the dark days of winter, she often felt insufficient. Young Mary did sit and sew at times or take up her knitting, and she did help with the cooking – when there was nothing else to do. Yet, whenever Mary saw her daughter's foot tapping up and down, she knew the girl was desperate to be outside doing something else.

One morning towards the end of January, William announced at breakfast that there'd been a hard frost overnight.

'Look out of the window,' he told his daughter. 'See for yourself.'

She scraped away a circle of ice and gazed at the garden, white with hoar frost. The apple tree was transformed into a fairy castle and the hedge was draped in silvery cobwebs. After much pestering, her mother gave in. Yes, she could take her dog out for a while. Young Mary rammed straw into her boots to keep her feet warm and then grabbed her cloak. Stina took that to mean a walk and stood alert by the door, wagging her tail.

Once out in the lane, young Mary took a deep breath. It was so good to be in the fresh cold air. The bottom of Reighton lay under a milky mist, yet as she walked further up the hill, she emerged to find the sky was blue. The dog snuffled among the frosty grass, scenting rabbits or foxes, and ran on ahead to the top of the hill and the field beyond the church.

Young Mary had been told on innumerable occasions *not* to play alone up there. That made the place more enticing. And, she argued, she was not alone; her dog was there. The place could be quite forbidding though. Thick patches of gorse dotted the hills and there were unexpected hollows full of tangled briars. You could wander the hills for hours thinking you knew where you were, only to find you'd gone round in a circle. You could get lost, especially if it was dusk or if a mist came creeping in from the sea. Ben often put rabbit snares up there – another reason to stay away. Young Mary knew this but still followed wherever the dog led.

She remembered the Knox Well ghost story and dreaded feeling an icy hand reach out. When she saw a dark shadow, she feared it meant bad luck or even death. Putting such thoughts behind her, she let Stina roam at will, following whatever scents were found. All morning they capered about, not noticing the change in the weather. When Mary became aware of the darkening sky, it was too late.

The sun had disappeared behind a thick mist, and she couldn't tell which way was the church or the sea. She called to the dog and squatted down under an overhang of gorse. There she could shelter from the wet air. She now noticed her overskirt was torn and her boots sodden. She'd be in big trouble when she got home. Why did such a good day have to end like this? And she hadn't thought to bring any food. Even a cold potato would have been welcome. She wiped away a tear with the back of her hand and left her cheek smeared with mud. When Stina licked her chin, she wrapped her arms around the dog for comfort. The fur was wet though, and they both shivered.

It wasn't long before Stina started to whimper, impatient to be off again, but Mary didn't know which way to go. She decided it was no good staying there in the cold, so she got up to see where the dog would lead. Maybe Stina would know the way home.

'Come on,' she coaxed, 'you take us home.' The dog set off. 'There's a good lass – take us home.'

The mist was so thick she couldn't see more than a few yards. She slipped down into chalky hollows and had to put her hands into thistles to scramble back out. Her face was bloodied, scratched by the gorse and, in the early twilight brought by the mist, the bushes were like animals ready to pounce.

At home, her mother had begun to worry. The mist was thicker at the bottom of St Helen's Lane, and she had no idea where her daughter might be. She just hoped there was someone about who had taken her in.

William came home in the afternoon, unable to work any longer in the mist. He was surprised to find young Mary still out. Knowing what she was like, he said he'd go to Ben's – see if she was there. He soon returned, anxious that neither Ben nor anyone else had seen young Mary or her dog all day.

'I'll go back to Uphall and search there.'

Mary now felt guilty about letting the girl out in the first place. William would never forgive her if any harm befell their daughter.

'I'll stay here with the boys then and keep the broth hot. When you find her, she'll need warming up.'

William ran to Uphall. Finding no sign of her there, his mouth went dry. It was now getting dark. In a panic, he made his brothers and Tom and Dickon search the sheds and go across the fields shouting her name. When there was still no sign anywhere of her or the dog, he knew they'd have to search in every direction with lanterns and torches.

Tom went round the village asking everyone to help, and a crowd gathered at Uphall for instructions. Everyone knew what young Mary was like and, while they sympathised with William's urgency, they were aggrieved to be going out in the cold.

'There's a fever goin' round village,' Sarah Ezard warned. 'It gives folks a bad throat. Last thing we want is to catch a chill.'

This time, Elizabeth Storey persuaded her husband to stay indoors. She feared for Robert's father, frailer than ever, and didn't relish being left alone with him.

Young Mary and her dog had stopped wandering around in circles. They now sat side by side, sheltered in a deep hollow under the gorse. Stina pushed her nose under Mary's hand, asking to be stroked. Both of them were wet through, chilled to the bone. Mary thought she heard her name being shouted and guessed she was dreaming. The cold and the dark were making her sleepy. She put her arms round the dog and leant her cheek against Stina's back. The dog was shivering even more than she was.

Groups of men with torches began to fan out across the hill from the church. They shouted the girl's and the dog's name as they went. Treading cautiously, they peered under every clump of gorse. Stina heard her name called and leapt up. She didn't run off but stayed there and barked for attention.

William ran across the hill with his lantern and spotted Mary's red cloak through the gorse. He crawled in and pulled her out. She was a sorry sight. The mist made her hair stick up in all directions and her face and clothes were muddied. She flung her arms round his neck, curled her legs round his waist and clung on like a limpet. He shouted to let the others know she'd been found.

'Thank God,' he whispered and kissed her wet hair. As he carried her home, the dog slunk at his side with her tail between her legs. The other searchers trudged home behind them, grumbling about the girl and the cold.

As soon as they were indoors, William took off his daughter's wet cloak and boots. He sat her by the fire and Mary fetched a bowl of broth. The girl shivered so violently she couldn't hold the spoon, so her parents stripped her down to her winter bodice. Even that felt damp. Mary unlaced it and William wrapped his daughter in a thick blanket.

Young Mary managed to stammer, 'Is Sssstina alright?'

'She's fine,' William replied. 'Look, she's here steaming by the fire.'

Mary remembered what to do to prevent a chill. She needed grated horseradish yet had no fresh roots in the house. Instead, she put a spoonful of horseradish sauce into a cloth and secured it round young Mary's neck. She also put a clove of garlic under the blanket.

William watched, unconvinced of such measures. He decided to fetch something from Sarah Ezard. He soon returned with a small clay pot.

'Sarah says it's got rosemary mixed in with ewes' kidney fat.' He prised off the lid and sniffed the greasy paste. 'It's quite nice – nothing to complain about. Open up the blanket a bit so I can rub it on her chest.'

'Here, give it me. Your hands are too cold and rough. *I'll* do it. You see to the boys.'

Young Mary's brothers were seated at the table with their broth, spooning it in while staring at their parents. Francis wanted to complain about the kitchen smelling of wet dog but kept his peace. It was unnerving to see his sister so quiet and his parents so worried.

Chapter 25

For the next few days, young Mary was kept wrapped in blankets and given beef tea to drink. William had the idea of letting her sleep in his bed, tucked in between him and Mary for warmth. This arrangement didn't last long. She was feverish and tossed and turned all night, making the three of them irritable the next day. Then she complained of a sore throat. William thought it wise to keep her away from the others, so moved her bed further away.

When word got out that the girl had a sore throat, Sarah Ezard came to warn of a difficult time ahead.

'I've been all over village seein' to folks an' their throats.' She carried on talking as she leant over young Mary and felt her forehead and pulse. 'Milkmaid at Up'all was first to get ill. Little Dorothy Janton's got it now. She's not even two yet, poor lass. She's *very* poorly. This throat business, it's mostly young'uns an' old folk who get it.'

She stood up and took a sniff from her bottle of vinegar. 'I don't think there's a single family without someone ill.'

'Do you think the village is bewitched?' Mary dared to ask.

Sarah shrugged and took another sniff of vinegar. 'I can't think who'd cast such a bad spell.'

'No, though I've heard you can stick pins and needles in a piece of cloth then put it on the embers of a fire and –'

'I know,' Sarah interrupted, 'an' then thoo thrusts in a dagger, an' next person to enter thy 'ouse is the witch.' She shook her head. 'Don't do it, Mary. Listen, thoo's not thinkin' straight an' it's a good job William isn't 'ere. Why, tha sister Elizabeth might be next one to visit. Then what?'

Mary chewed her nails. 'But our daughter's not getting any better. It must be witchcraft.'

'Listen,' Sarah relented, 'in another day, moon'll be full. I can take some o' thy blood an' mix it wi' salt an' burn it. That'll injure any witch an' stop 'er tricks.'

Mary considered this. Such a remedy might be too late.

'Or,' Sarah continued, 'thoo can get young Mary's nail clippin's an' some strands of 'er 'air an' boil 'em over a clear fire.'

'No, William's bound to find out. I'd love to try it, but he'd never forgive me.'

'Well then, I'll leave thee wi' this ointment. This should work.' She handed over a small stoneware pot. 'It's full o' goodness – mutton fat an' butter an' beeswax. Spread it on a cloth and lay it right across 'er throat. Keep it covered an' change it twice a day. If that doesn't work, thoo can make up a poultice o' flour an' dry mustard. I'll come again tomorrow an' see 'ow she is.'

Mary's sister Elizabeth wanted to help look after young Mary, but her husband forbade it. He argued that his aged father was weak enough without having to fight the new illness sweeping the village. Elizabeth spent her days and nights caring for her father-in-law, who was now definitely failing. Despite her efforts, his breathing grew laboured, and Elizabeth stood by, helpless.

Robert bullied his father to eat and drink and got Ben to remove the pith from a young elder shoot. The straw worked well enough, but soon old Roger Storey fought all attempts and closed his lips tight whenever it came near. Robert saw the stubborn glare in his father's eyes that amounted to hatred, and yet still he persisted. He refused to believe that his father was dying.

Elizabeth knew. Sarah Ezard knew. The vicar's wife Susanna came daily to see how her father was doing and she knew the signs too. The whole village knew, yet Robert continued to believe that his father might recover.

Elizabeth held out more hope for young Mary; the girl had always been full of energy and had such a strong will. However, when she went round to visit, she was shocked. She found the girl sitting up in bed, persuading her brother to find pigeon feathers.

'William, I want you to put them under my mattress,' she whispered hoarsely. 'Stuff them in if you can. Then I won't die.'

Young William nodded and brought her his lucky rabbit's tail. 'Here – you have it. I've no one to play with now.' He stroked the tail and pressed the soft fur to his cheek one last time before passing it over. 'Francis is no fun. John just sits by the fire – he doesn't even talk properly. Mother says he might not – ever.'

'Would you take Stina out for a walk?' she asked. 'I don't want to spoil her life.'

Elizabeth stepped forward and offered to take both William and the dog for a walk. When she tried, Stina was reluctant to leave the house without her young mistress. They dragged her to the door, where she stood her ground and turned her head, ears pricked, waiting for Mary to go with them.

Ben came to visit and sat by young Mary's bed. He told her about his plans for the beehives, how they'd both be looking out for new swarms come spring.

'Ben, tell the bees I'm sorry – I'll help soon.'

'Aye, I'll 'ave a word with 'em.' He spoke of her den and how they could rebuild it, make it even better. He promised to carve another bird for her, maybe a seagull if she liked.

'This time,' he promised, 'it'll 'ave proper wings an' thoo'll see all its feathers.'

She smiled and nodded, but she just wanted her sore throat to stop.

Before he left, he gave her a bottle of homemade cough mixture. 'I've only used virgin honey, mind. It might soothe tha throat a bit. Oh, an' before I forget, I saw Dickon. 'E's orderin' thoo to get better. 'E says 'e needs thy 'elp to oil 'is leather traces. 'E can't do 'em on 'is own. An' them Gurwood lasses asked to come. Priscilla an' Mary miss thee, but they 'ave to stay away – i' case they catch summat.'

Young Mary showed no improvement and, within days, developed an itchy rash on her neck that spread to her chest. Though her cheeks were flushed, she was very pale around the mouth.

'You look as if you've been in the sun,' young William remarked. 'You look funny. Your skin's all bumpy. You've got goose pimples.'

'Go away,' she croaked. 'Leave me.'

She had a splitting headache, couldn't keep warm and was in no mood for his banter. Each side of her neck had become tender, and her throat was now so sore she dreaded to swallow. When she did, she gripped the sides of the bed ready for the sharp pain. She also had pains in her stomach. The last thing she needed was to be sick; she didn't think she could bear that, not with her throat being so sore. When her mother made her drink, she found, to her relief, that it was less painful to swallow a large amount of water than a tiny amount of saliva.

Sarah Ezard came again. On inspection, she found young Mary's tonsils and the back of her throat had a white coating, as did her tongue. She went to the kitchen and made up a fresh poultice; there was little else she could do. As she left the house, she spoke to Mary.

'If she gets worse, send fo' laudanum. Ten drops i' water should 'elp 'er sleep. If not, try 15 drops.'

That night, young Mary couldn't sleep. Each time she swallowed, it was like a knife in her throat, and she felt so hot. By midnight, she couldn't stop crying and nothing would soothe her. She called out weakly for anything to help her, any medicine. William, in desperation, went to Sarah Ezard's and came back with the laudanum. Ten drops were given and, although it pained her to drink it, she did fall into a fitful sleep.

William and his wife went back to bed. A few hours later, they awoke to young Mary's cries. They found her burning up, so Mary got a bowl of water and a cloth to cool her down. Helpless, William went to the back door for some fresh air. The sky was just beginning to lighten, and a white frost silvered the trees. The ice-cold air was like a slap in the face as he realised the real danger of losing his daughter. Today, he'd stay at home. Ploughing could go on without him.

At breakfast time, he gave young Mary more laudanum – enough to calm her without sending her to sleep. She lay like a limp rag, so unlike his lively, energetic girl.

'Would you like me to read to you?' he volunteered, thinking she might enjoy her favourite parts of the Bible.

'My tongue's sore. My throat hurts,' she rasped.

'I know, I know. Try not to talk. Put your tongue out. Let's see it.'

Her brother William was there in a moment, curious to see for himself. He flinched. Her tongue, once white and furry, had peeled and was now red and swollen.

'Ugh, Mary, your tongue's like raw meat.'

She rolled her eyes. She couldn't care less.

'Where's Stina?' she whispered.

'Here, look, by your bed, as usual,' her father answered. 'Are you sure you don't want me to read to you? I'm going to be here all day.'

She managed a weak smile and nodded. 'Job,' she whispered more faintly. 'The bit about that thing like a bull.'

'I know,' he said and fetched the Bible. He sat on her bed and found the verses she wanted. 'Are you ready? Close your eyes and imagine that bull you liked at Argam – the one you hoped to set free. Remember?' He read the passage very slowly to make it last.

'He moveth his tail like a cedar: the sinews of his stones are wrapped together. His bones are as strong pieces of brass; his bones are like bars of iron.'

'I want that bull free.' She spoke so forcefully it made her wince.

'Try not to talk.'

'It must be free, in the sun.' She pulled herself up to sit.

Her brothers clustered round, wondering at her sudden surge of life. At that point, her mother came in from the kitchen and feared the worst.

'Oh Lord, what's happening?'

Francis informed her. 'She's going on about that bull at Argam. She wants to set it loose. She's mad. Anyway, I'm off to work even if Father isn't.'

No one spoke again until Francis left, and the door shut behind him. Young William turned to his father. He wanted to please his sister and make her happy again.

'*Can* the bull be set loose?'

His father turned his head so that young Mary couldn't see. He winked while putting a finger to his lips. Then he turned back to his daughter and stroked her damp hair away from her forehead.

'We'll do our best. Listen, Mary, that bull will be out in the field before long. It'll soon feel the sun warm on its great shoulders. It'll soon be wading in the pond again.'

She fell back and closed her eyes.

'I'll leave you to have a little sleep. Would you like me to read to you later?'

'*The Iliad*,' she murmured, half asleep, still with her eyes shut.

Her mother shook her head. 'No, William. Only the Bible should be read.'

He ignored her. 'Alright, lass, *The Iliad* it will be. I'll fetch it from the Gurwoods.'

Mary spun on her heels and stomped back to the kitchen.

George Gurwood was not in when William called round. When Cecilia heard what he'd come for, she went straight to the bookshelf despite the book being forbidden. She was about to pass it to William when her father returned and caught them. William explained the reason for wanting it, but the vicar was adamant.

'No more of *The Iliad* for young Mary. Remember how she filled her head with those gods. She had them everywhere, in the trees and in the clouds, deciding who to help and who to harm. I'm sorry, William, we can't have that. It's not Christian.'

He put the book on a higher shelf and took down *The Pilgrim's Progress*. 'She liked this, and it might light her way. Listen, I'll find suitable passages for you to read. They might help you too.'

When William returned, he found that his daughter had visitors. Elizabeth had taken time off from tending her father-in-law and had brought a piece of red cloth to tie round young Mary's neck. Ben was also there and complaining of Elizabeth's 'cure'.

'Nay, that won't do owt. What thoo wants is a piece o' fat bacon. Tie that to 'er neck wi' left leg of a stockin'. That does trick. Better still, I've brought summat fo' young lass to gargle.'

He held up a bottle. 'This mornin' I poured boilin' water onto some sage leaves an' let it cool, then put in a bit o' vinegar an' honey. It'll be sweet to taste an' it'll soothe 'er throat.'

To Ben's disappointment, she couldn't gargle – it hurt too much. Her throat was closing up and she was still feverish and complaining of a headache. William and Mary didn't know what else to do except fetch Sarah Ezard again.

When Sarah arrived, she advised Mary to bathe her daughter's forehead and temples with hot water and mint. 'An' roast a potato,' she ordered. 'Wrap it in a bit o' cloth an' put it on 'er throat – as 'ot as she can bear, mind. It's steam that cures throats.'

William frowned. The house was too full of people offering different, dubious advice. Still, he felt stupid walking in with a book, as if that was of any use. He sighed on seeing their concerned faces.

'Thank you for your help, but I'd like it if we could be left alone for now. Young Mary needs rest more than anything else.'

Not wishing to be inhospitable, Mary ushered everyone else into the kitchen for a drink. She was glad of their help. They had far more practical ideas than any William could offer. A book wasn't going to cure anyone.

As soon as the visitors had left the parlour, William moved the dog aside and sat on the bed. Stina nuzzled his hand, expecting to be stroked; she was pining and had gone off her food. William took his daughter's hand out of the covers and rested it on the dog's head. When Stina began to lick it, young Mary smiled at last.

For most of the day, young Mary slipped in and out of a laudanum-induced sleep, not even wanting her father to read to her. She was content to hold onto the dog's ear and fondle it.

By suppertime, when Francis returned home from work, young Mary was restless and had trouble breathing. William, frightened at the change in her, couldn't eat his supper. When she'd had more laudanum and had relaxed, he went out for a walk. He needed to be alone.

The moon was still large in a cloudless sky though it was on the wane. As he marched towards the sea, he prayed hard for his daughter to live and be well. His words adjusted themselves to the rhythm of his stride.

'Please, O Lord, please don't take her. Please, I beg you. Please don't take her. I'll never ask for more. Please, just this. Let her live. Only this – let her live.'

He clenched his fists as he walked, repeating the same prayer over and over again, either out loud or in his head. He reached the cliff edge and gazed out across the moonlit sea. Everything except him was untroubled and calm. He recalled the words from Mark's gospel. 'If thou canst believe, all things are possible to him that believeth.'

He raised his voice and shouted to the sea and the moon, 'Lord, I believe. Help thou my unbelief.'

After a while, he took a deep breath and then walked back home with a firmer tread. Though more confident, his legs were trembling.

At home, his daughter lay in her lonely nightmare, time measured by breathing and swallowing, both tasks proving more difficult and painful. The laudanum made her pupils dilate and her eyes were wide with fear. William held her hand. Though her pulse was fast, he dared to believe that, if she could get through this night, she'd be over the worst.

Mary had put the other children to bed, yet they lay awake, aware of their parents' distress. They hated to see their sister so poorly and held their blankets up to their eyes, not daring to move. Although there was no fire in the parlour, Mary brought a chair in and sat down with her knitting. She couldn't forget the heart-stopping sight of the Yule candle going out. She also knew the moon was waning – another bad sign.

William was about to fetch the vicar, but Mary told him that they were too late – he'd been called out already to both Roger Storey and little Dorothy Janton. There was no help for young Mary, only laudanum to ease the pain. William couldn't bear to sit idle so opened *The Pilgrim's Progress*. The bookmarked passages were about Mount Sion, the heavenly Jerusalem. He shuddered at the vicar's choice.

Sitting on the bed with the book heavy in his lap, he peered at the text in the candlelight. Tears blurred his vision.

Young Mary touched his arm. 'Read.' Her voice was so faint he could hardly hear.

He tried to read with a steady voice, to sound calm and hopeful.

'It's about heaven.' He cleared his throat and swallowed with difficulty.

'It's the Paradise of God, wherein you shall see the tree of life and eat of the never-fading fruits thereof.' He paused, knowing what he had to read next and didn't trust his voice. He swallowed hard again before continuing.

'And when you come there, you shall have white robes given you, and your walk and talk shall be every day with the King, even all the days of eternity. There you shall not see again...' He stopped to collect himself. 'Sorrow, sickness, affliction and death.'

Young Mary heard her father's voice though it came and went in waves. She nudged his arm for him to read on.

Much as he tried to control himself, tears ran down his face. In a broken voice, he resumed.

'There you shall enjoy your friends again that are gone thither before you, and there you shall with joy receive even every one that follows into the holy place after you.'

Young Mary jerked suddenly and raised herself on one elbow. She stared around in panic.

'Whatever's the matter? Mary? What is it?'

'Stina,' she breathed.

'She's still here, still keeping an eye on you. There,' he put her hand on Stina's head, 'you hold onto her ear.'

He realised she must be wondering if her dog would follow her to heaven. He had no idea. Did animals go to heaven? Certainly, they were not baptised. If only the vicar had been there to ask. She was waiting for an answer, her eyes pleading.

He leant closer and gave her a hug. Then he looked her straight in the eye to make sure she heard him and understood.

'You love this dog like one of the family, don't you? You love Stina and I know she loves you – very much. So... yes! She'll go to heaven one day.'

Young Mary sank back down on her pillow and closed her eyes, instantly peaceful.

William decided to finish reading the passage, although he wasn't sure she could hear him. It was about God bringing you home at the end.

'He shall come with the sound of trumpet in the clouds, as upon the wings of the wind, you shall come with Him.'

It was the last thing she ever heard.

Chapter 26

When William realised young Mary had died, he sat paralysed, unable to take his eyes from her. Mary put down her knitting and approached the bed warily. As soon as she understood, her knees buckled, and she collapsed to the floor. Neither of them spoke or moved until Mary prised her daughter's hand gently from the dog's ear. Instantly, William leapt up. He spun round with a wild look and saw Francis, wide awake, peeping out from his bedclothes.

'You!' he yelled. 'See to your mother.' He then strode blindly out of the house, charged along the lane and up the hill. On reaching the church, he crossed behind it and headed to the gorse above the cliffs. Alone there, he stopped and fell to his knees in the wet grass. He wrenched at the turf, snatched handfuls and swayed with the effort. In the east, the sky was beginning to lighten over the sea. He bellowed at the horizon.

'Why? Why?'

How could God take young Mary and dare leave him behind? He might as well take him too. The sky was unresponsive. Behind him, it was dirty and grey as an unwashed shirt. In front, there was a faint yellow smudge. He could not bear to see the sunrise. He turned to face west again, only to have the church in view, and spat on the ground. There was nowhere to turn. He'd gone out without his coat and now shivered with cold. Empty and sick to his very bones, he stumbled to his feet. With legs that hardly belonged to him, he made his way back to St Helen's Lane, to the house that was no longer a home.

He found his wife already washing young Mary. The boys were up and dressed and stood staring, helpless. Stina was still lying by the bed, her head between her paws, alert to any sounds from her mistress.

When Mary saw William so wild and dishevelled, she was afraid he'd lost his mind – even more so when he pulled her from the body.

'*I'll* wash her,' he growled. 'No one else is to touch her.'

Mary backed away. It was best not to thwart him. 'Come on,' she ordered the boys, 'get into the kitchen. I'll make your breakfast.'

They followed her, eager for some normal routine.

After breakfast, Francis went round the village to tell people. He returned with Sarah Ezard, who, on learning about his father's strange behaviour, was intent on laying the body out properly. On seeing William kneeling by the bed and washing his daughter's arms with such care, she thought it best if she brought the vicar.

When she arrived at the vicarage, Sarah learnt that the vicar had been up all night, his time spent between the Janton girl and his father-in-law, Roger Storey. The old man still held onto life, but the young girl had died.

When George heard of young Mary's death, he rammed his fist against the door. 'I should have been there! I'm so sorry.' It was one of the few times in his life when he was at a loss for words. He stood in the doorway with Sarah, gazing beyond her at the cottages opposite.

'Young Mary's given me so much pleasure these last years. I can't imagine Reighton without her. My daughters'll miss her. Oh, Sarah, it doesn't bear thinking what this will do to William.'

Instead of having his breakfast, he went straight back with Sarah to William's house. They found him sitting on the girl's bed, staring into space. William didn't notice the vicar's presence, not even when George touched his arm. His body was rigid as a post. George sat beside him on the bed and waited. After a while, he quoted from Matthew's gospel.

'Come unto me, all ye that labour and are heavy laden, and I will give you rest.' There was no response. 'I'm so sorry, William. Please let me help you.'

William shuddered as if woken from a deep sleep. He turned and howled a confession.

'I loved her too much. It's my fault. It's my pride that's killed her.' He broke down, folded his arms and doubled up as if punched in the stomach. When George put an arm round him, he shrugged it off. Though his chest heaved as he sobbed, he refused to be comforted.

It was some time before William could be persuaded to leave the room and follow George into the kitchen. There he sat at the table, unaware of those around him, his chest so tight he could hardly breathe.

His sons blinked nervously and avoided his eye. Their father was a stranger. Their mother put food and drink before them, and then went into the parlour with Sarah to deal with her daughter's body.

George Gurwood left the house. There was little he could say right now. William was in no state to listen.

The boys watched their mother return carrying the mattress from young Mary's bed.

'Sarah says to burn it,' she muttered, 'in case of further infection.' William didn't hear what she said.

Unable to resist a bonfire, the boys followed their mother into the garden. Francis helped her get it alight and they stood in silence as the flames leapt up. Young William ran indoors and came back clutching the lucky rabbit's tail. With tears in his eyes, he flung it onto the fire.

Ben did not know about young Mary. When Francis called with the news, Ben was at Robert Storey's house. He aimed to see his lifelong friend Roger for what could be the last time. He sat quietly by the bed and stroked his hand. It gave him something to do and it might offer comfort. Roger, he feared, didn't know he was there.

When his friend grew restless and beads of cold sweat broke out on his forehead, Elizabeth asked Ben to leave. Roger needed to rest. She knew her father-in-law did not have long to live and hoped he would have a peaceful end. With that in mind, she gave him a strong opiate.

Robert sat by the bed for the rest of the day. Calmed by the drug, his father lay still, breathing more easily and yet so slowly. Robert listened to each long intake of breath and then waited, for what seemed ages, to hear his father breathe out again. After each exhalation,

Robert was anxious. He now knew that one of these long breaths would be the last. Unsure whether his father could still hear, he recited Psalm 23, just in case. As he reached the end, his voice gave way, choked by tears. He was sure that goodness and mercy had followed his father all the days of his life, and that he would dwell in the house of the Lord forever. He was sure yet went on his knees and prayed.

It was late in the afternoon, with the rushlights giving a meagre light to the room, that Robert heard the last breath. In sudden grief, he threw himself onto the bed across his father's chest. The hard bones creaked beneath him. The body was so frail and brittle, more skeleton than flesh, and nothing like the father who'd cared for him as a boy.

Suddenly, his father's body lurched as if come to life. Robert leapt back in alarm and then all was still again. The sudden spasm after death left him shaking. Was he meant to take it as a sign? But of what – a goodbye, a thank you, a warning? Or a reassurance of a life hereafter? He couldn't fathom it. He only knew he'd lost his father.

When Elizabeth came in, he was praying by the bed with screwed up eyes, tears sliding down his cheeks. A tall, strong man, he wept like a child. She knelt by him and leant her body against his so he'd feel her presence. It was obvious he was struggling to come to terms with death, and she had no idea what crises of faith he might have in his grief. She prayed for him, knowing no other way to help. He'd never discuss his problems. She so wanted to touch his soul and soothe his pain. Her tears arose from her aching love for Robert and the gulf that lay between them.

During the day, Elizabeth heard news of the other deaths. It was what they'd been taught – the Lord gives, and the Lord takes away. As George Gurwood often pointed out, we are all part of the intricate web of life where threads are broken and renewed evermore. Death and birth both had their season and yet, Elizabeth thought, those affected the most found little consolation.

Young Mary's funeral was to be the same day as little Dorothy Janton's. Mary made sure that her husband and sons were clean and in their Sunday best, but apart from such practicalities, she could not help them. William was too shocked to care, and the boys grieved privately and said nothing. As they left the house to go to church, young William put his sister's dog on a rope and held his younger brother's hand. It was February 2nd and wintry rain blew straight into their faces as they made their way along the lane. Francis held his mother's hand and hunched his shoulders to keep warm.

William walked numbly in front of them, just behind the coffin carried by his father and brothers. The repeated three tolls of the church bell were blunt nails driven into his heart. When they faced east again to enter the churchyard, the rain had turned to sleet. He welcomed the sharp slap of the ice – a different pain to offset the ache in his chest. He followed the coffin down the aisle and stumbled inside a pew. Mary pushed him along, seated the boys on the outside and took hold of his hand. He was trembling and staring at his shaking knees. Throughout the short service, he barely noted a word. He paid more attention once they were outdoors again for the final committal.

In the graveyard, Ben stood shivering with a box tucked under his arm. His chin was rough and sore where he'd shaved, and thin wisps of wet white hair were plastered to his cheeks. He was as miserable as his surroundings. The church walls were dark and damp, the graveyard sodden, and the two piles of earth beside the small open graves had turned to mud. There were no flowers since only the gorse was in bloom; Mary had wanted no reminders of gorse.

The Jordan family huddled in a large group. William's mother, tight-lipped as ever, kept her thoughts to herself. While vindicated by his upbringing of young Mary, she hated to see her eldest son so haggard and drawn. His eyes were red-rimmed and bloodshot and, judging by the blue shadows beneath, he hadn't slept in days.

George Gurwood read out the customary passage. 'For now, we see through a glass, darkly: but then face to face, now I know in part; but then shall I know even as also I am known.'

Until then, the dog had stood obediently. As soon as young Mary was lifted from the coffin and lowered into the ground, Stina pulled forward on her rope. Francis yanked her back and made her sit. The dog had seen young Mary's white face at the top of the shroud and now, with ears pricked, wanted to be with her mistress.

Ben stepped forward with his box and opened the lid. He'd brought the items as he and William had planned. There was young Mary's hazelwood bowl and her applewood spoon and cup. Despite this being a pagan idea, George Gurwood allowed them to be placed in the grave. Ben knelt down on the sodden grass and leant forward to see the girl's face.

'I've whispered to the bees,' he said and dropped her belongings gently onto the shroud.

As the grave was filled in, the dog pulled to be free once more. When they left the churchyard, she had to be dragged all the way home.

Chapter 27

The next morning, Robert Storey's father was buried. The passing away of old Roger Storey was not unexpected. The death, however, so soon after the two young girls, cast a deep shadow over the village. For Ben and Sarah Ezard, it signalled that their generation was on its way out.

Ben sat stiffly at the back of the church. He saw William and his family shuffle in with their heads bowed. They didn't look fit to be out. Neither did Robert Storey as he followed the coffin to the front. Ben glanced sideways at Sarah Ezard sitting next to him. He heaved a sigh. Yes, all attachments brought suffering with them. There was no way out. Even his love of the mule had caused pain. He recalled the people he'd seen buried already. The vicar would tell him to put his trust in the immortal, never-changing face of God. Well, he'd try. He stuffed his cold hands under his armpits for warmth. The vicar had mounted the pulpit to begin.

'God is our refuge and strength, a very present help in trouble. Therefore, we will not fear. Therefore, we do not lose heart.'

The words went over Ben's head. He'd heard the same so many times.

'Though outwardly we are wasting away,' George Gurwood continued, 'yet inwardly we are being renewed day by day. For our light and momentary troubles are achieving for us an eternal glory that far outweighs them all. So we fix our eyes not on what is seen, but on what is unseen. For what is seen is temporary, but what is unseen is eternal.'

Ben could see the back of Robert Storey's bent head and wondered if he still had as much faith. He knew that William was faltering after losing his daughter. At least Roger Storey had lived a full, long life and it was natural for him to die. Ben tried to think of other things while the vicar finished the service – jobs for the future, like making more beehives. Even such plans led him to think of young Mary.

When the congregation followed the coffin into the churchyard, the weather was still bitterly cold. The vicar kept the final committal brief as a northeasterly breeze blew straight in from the sea. He stood by the grave and kept a tight hold of his surplice while his voice was carried away by the wind.

'I have fought a good fight; I have finished my course; I have kept the faith. Henceforth there is laid up for me a crown of righteousness, which the Lord, the righteous judge, shall give me that day.'

As Robert Storey dropped the first soil into the grave, the vicar added, 'A good name is better than precious ointment; and the day of death than the day of one's birth.'

Ben met Sarah Ezard's gaze. They were of one mind. It would be them one day. When everyone moved off, she slotted her arm through his. As they left the churchyard, they saw that young Mary's dog was back again, sitting by her grave.

For days after the funerals, William worked as best he could in the daytime, and went to Ben's cottage each evening. Somehow, he couldn't bear to be in his own house without his daughter. Instead, he sat with Ben by a meagre fire and drank beakers of mead. The alcohol relaxed him, and they spoke freely about young Mary, recalling her funny antics and the things she'd said.

'I remember,' Ben chuckled, 'I caught 'er one day at bottom o' me garden an' she were pourin' summat over young William's 'ead. When I went to see, she said it were mead an' she were makin' 'im a king. She were anointin' 'im. I soon put a stop to it – a waste o' good mead.'

William smiled. 'She came home once from the Gurwoods' like a cat that had got the cream. She told us that George had called her a shitey Norma.'

Ben frowned. He hadn't heard this story and was puzzled.

'So I went and asked them what it was all about. Apparently, she'd climbed up a tree to rescue their cat. George had told her she was a knight in shining armour.'

Ben laughed. It was as if young Mary was still there.

Like the dog, William could not accept that she really had gone forever. At home, no one spoke of her, and no one mentioned her at Uphall. People were very careful around him, avoiding conversation.

His denial of young Mary's death put a greater distance between him and his wife. She began to fear for his sanity and, since he was absent in the evenings, she treated their eldest son, Francis, as the head of the family. The boy was only nine and assumed the extra responsibility very seriously. He would no longer play with his younger brothers, and he was often too tired anyway after a day of ploughing.

Young Mary's dog gave up the graveyard vigil after three days, coaxed away by Ben. He led Stina home and told young William that he must take more care of the dog, must take her for walks as his sister had done. Although not quite five years old, the boy took Stina out each day whatever the weather. He did it for his sister's sake. He missed her more than his other brothers and walked out so often and so far with the dog that his limp became more pronounced. His spine, malformed since a baby, made him walk with a rolling gait, like a mariner. Anyone new to the village always made comments.

His mother tried in vain to curb his long walks, still guilty at allowing her daughter out in bad weather. She was fighting a losing battle. The family was getting out of hand. There were days when her husband was alert and full of plans, and then he'd lapse suddenly into a morbid state, and sit as if drugged and not move. Each day was such a struggle. The fact that she'd missed her monthly bleeding again, she put down to worry, to not eating and to lack of sleep. When she missed for the third month in a row, she decided to do the nettle test. It was a simple procedure, the hardest part being to find a green nettle at that time of year.

The next day she did find a nettle and put it straightaway in her urine. She covered it tightly and left it overnight. To her dismay, the nettle was full of red spots in the morning. Somehow, she'd have to break the news to William that she was with child once more. She didn't know if a baby daughter would help or make things worse.

William's refusal to grieve with his family was affecting his health. One morning, as he went into the kitchen for breakfast, his chest tightened, and the walls spun round him. He fought for breath and collapsed onto the reeds spread sparsely over the floor. Even those reminded him of young Mary. Her homemade reed families had been all over the place. Everything in the house had a connection. He didn't know if he could stand the pain anymore.

Mary struggled to get him onto the bench and there he sat the whole morning with his head in his hands.

On another occasion, William went into the kitchen for breakfast and couldn't stand the sight of the dog. He grumbled something about Stina being alive and not his daughter. He glared with such evil intent that the boys shooed her into the garden. Then, when he forced down his porridge, he still glowered at everyone.

At mealtimes, his sons were afraid. They stared down at their food or at the grain of the table, anything to avoid their father's eyes.

William's body weighed heavy when he left for work. The hill was a struggle. Without warning, darkness would descend in waves and leave him weak. He found it hard to breathe. He felt sick. As he steered the clumsy plough, a great weight rested on his shoulders. Memories of young Mary pressed in from all sides and yet she was absent. How could his heart still beat when she was no longer there? How could one breath succeed another? One morning, he stopped ploughing right in the middle of a furrow. He gazed down at his hands lying uselessly at his side. They, like the rest of his body, were alien to him. He turned to the wintry sky and cried out the words of a psalm he now knew so well.

'My God, my God, why hast thou forsaken me? Why art thou so far from helping me, and from the words of my roaring? I cry in the daytime, but thou hearest not. I am poured out like water, and all my bones are out of joint: my heart is like wax; it is melted in the midst of my bowels.' He let his head droop onto his chest.

The ploughboy holding the oxen waited and watched, not knowing what to do. No one knew how to deal with William.

At Uphall, they noticed that William now had a habit of shaking his head, as if trying to rid himself of an annoying fly buzzing round. Sometimes, he suddenly screwed up his eyes. Tears squeezed out and he'd wipe them away with his coat sleeve. Although he worked hard, he was not the same man. At times, he was weak as a kitten.

Villagers began to avoid him since he trudged about with his jaw clamped shut, his lips thin and tight. He wasn't the first to lose a child, wouldn't be the last either.

George Gurwood wasn't the only one to wonder why William's faith brought no consolation. He went round to sit with him one evening and apologised for not coming more often – it was a difficult time of year, the roads being so bad and him having to see to his other parishes.

Mary offered him a drink and he settled down by the fire opposite William. The boys were about to go to bed, so Mary hurried them into the parlour, leaving the two men alone.

'I'm so sorry, William,' George began. 'Can you find comfort in the Bible?'

William shrugged. 'I know plenty by heart. I'm trying. I cry out to God for help.' He shook his head. 'Look at me – do I look like a man who's had an answer? No.' He stared into the fire. 'There's nothing, nothing.'

'Your grief is raw, William. Help will come, trust me.' When William didn't reply, he offered advice. 'If and when you read your Bible, read the Book of Job if nothing else.'

William nodded. He knew the vicar meant well.

George stood up, ready to depart. He was wise enough not to push William too far. 'My wife and daughters join me each night in prayer for you and your family. We're all thinking of you.'

William didn't look up. 'Thank you,' he whispered. He stayed gazing into the fire while George let himself out. He put his head in his hands. People were kind.

When William worked in the fields, Dickon did his best to distract him with problems over the harrowing and spring sowing, but he also was not himself. The winter funerals reminded him of the loss of his wife. He now lived more in the past than the present and had trouble remembering his tasks for the day. The one time he looked happy was when he sat in the stable oiling the leather straps. Then he talked about the old days or about how young Mary used to sit and chat to him.

Tom and the other farm lads tried to cover for Dickon; this was difficult since they were also covering for William. They had no idea how long it would be before he was himself again. And, like William, they had no idea that Mary was with child again.

Chapter 28

Mary left it until late March before she told William of her pregnancy. Her sister Elizabeth called at the house, eager to find out how he'd taken the news. She found Mary busy baking oatcakes on the stone.

'Well, what did he say?'

Mary sighed and pushed stray hairs back under her cap. 'He said nothing, nothing at all.' She turned the oatcakes over. 'He's acting strange, Lizzie. He looked right through me, then blinked a few times. I think he was trying to take it in, but then he turned his back on me – as usual. He went out to spend the rest of the evening at Ben's.'

'Does he still go every night?'

'Not *every* night. But when he stays here, he just sits by the fire with his Bible. He doesn't open it. He just stares at the fire.'

Elizabeth was sorry but didn't know how to help.

'He doesn't speak to me or the boys,' Mary added, 'not even to Francis, who's been out all day, poor lad, harrowing and sowing with him.'

'I could get Robert to come and talk to him. He's grieving too.'

Mary did not think for a moment that Robert could help, and yet two nights later, she let him into the house. He took off his coat and hat and sat opposite William by the kitchen fire. The boys were fast asleep in the parlour and Mary settled down at the kitchen table to darn stockings. She intended to keep out of the conversation and was afraid Robert might make things worse.

After a long silence, broken only by the ashes settling in the fire, Robert began a well-prepared speech. Most of his words were taken from his favourite book of the moment, *Holy Living*.

'William,' he said softly, 'we're like men playing a game of chance but, you know, the chance is not in our power. We can only play the game. When we lose, we must manage it as best we can.'

Although William gave no sign that he was listening, Robert was confident and continued.

'Or think of ourselves as mariners. We can't avoid the storms, yet we can avoid a shipwreck. We can take sanctuary in our faith and cast out anchors for our souls.'

William did not lift his eyes from the fire. He mumbled the well-known words of a psalm, words that echoed in his head every day.

'Thou hast lifted me up and cast me down. My days are like a shadow that declineth and I am withered like grass.'

'But thou art the same and thy years shall have no end.' Robert knew the psalm equally well.

William went silent again.

Undeterred, Robert tried another analogy. 'Think of our life as a play, with God as the master of the scenes. We cannot choose which part we shall act. All we can do is strive to act the part as best we can, and if it pleases God, then so be it.' He leant forward to touch William's shoulder. 'To be content throughout our accidents brings great peace of spirit. It removes the sting.'

William leapt up and knocked away Robert's arm. He stood over the fire, clenching and unclenching his fists. How he wanted to punch him and take that smug look off his face. He could not begin to explain the knife-sharp pain that was cutting his body and soul in two. That man had never lost a child. With tearful, bloodshot eyes, he spat out an answer.

'Your father is dead. A long life he had.' He thrust a finger into Robert's chest. 'Wait till *you* have a daughter. Wait till *you* –' He bit his lip. Elizabeth was barren. She'd never give Robert a child. He slumped back down on the stool and held his head in his hands.

Robert continued undaunted. 'You know time will heal, William, and good may come of evil. Trust God to govern his own world as he pleases. Bear your sorrow with patience.'

William glared sullenly at the fire.

'Your impatience and grief just entangles you – like the fluttering of a bird in a net. You cannot escape. You must suffer, yes, but get through it, bear it out. It's better to be composed and patient than be so troubled and suffer even more.'

William groaned. 'I cry and God does not listen. He hides his face when I'm in trouble. I call for help and no help comes. My days are consumed like smoke, and my bones are burned as a hearth.'

Robert sighed. He wondered how best to get through to him, which argument to try next.

'But think, William, how your daughter is better off now. Her soul was in a pure state and she's in heaven. You should be grateful you were blessed with such a daughter.'

William lifted his head and wiped his eyes.

Robert sensed he was making progress at last. 'And, since she's safe in heaven, it's an ill expression of your love that you weep for her good fortune. You should take your thoughts back to those days before young Mary was born and be like you were then. There's no difference.'

Robert didn't know what hit him. He regained consciousness a minute later. Flat out on the floor, he gazed up into Mary's concerned face.

'It's alright,' she whispered, 'William's gone. You're lucky it wasn't worse. He's just bruised your jaw. I think you'd better get home to Elizabeth and not come back.' She helped him to his feet. 'William isn't ready. I'm not sure he ever will be.'

She guided him out of the door and watched him until his lantern was out of sight down the lane. She didn't know where William had gone but assumed he'd return soon.

William strode quickly in his anger towards the cliff top. By the time he got there, the night air had cooled his temper somewhat. He was desperate for solace and spoke the words of another psalm as he stared bleary-eyed at the dark sea.

'Save me, O God, for the waters are come into my soul. I sink in deep mire, where there is no standing. I am come into deep waters, where the floods overflow me.' He paused for a moment and then shouted, 'I am weary of my crying; my throat is dried; mine eyes fail while I wait for my God.'

He found no answer from the sea or the sky, and the cold unfeeling moon, half hidden by cloud, seemed to mock him. Then he noticed a light flickering out at sea. For a moment, he thought it was a sign. No, he reckoned it was most likely free traders bringing in goods. They signalled to the cliffs somewhere to the north, though he didn't see the answering light.

As he turned away, he realised how accurate the whole of that psalm was. It's true, he thought, I have become a stranger unto my brethren. My family don't know me anymore. I don't know myself. Ashamed, he cried out once more.

'O God, thou knowest my foolishness, and my sins are not hid from thee.' Only God knew the full extent of his love for young Mary – and his pride. Only God could therefore help him. He raised his eyes as more clouds swept across the moon.

'O God, hide not thy face from thy servant, for I am in trouble. Hear me speedily. Draw nigh into my soul and redeem it.'

He turned to the west in despair. If the evening star, Venus, had been visible, William would still have paid no heed. He'd already turned up his collar and begun to stride back home.

William's strange behaviour and deep grief had forced Mary to put aside her own sense of loss. Now she felt so alone, even in the company of her sons. That spring, she could do the cleaning and washing without young Mary in the way, yet it was a miserable exchange. She knew she'd never appreciated her daughter – a girl so full of life she couldn't sit still.

Mary often had a desperate urge to get out of the house. At such times, she'd leave the boys with Elizabeth or Ben and go to an especially quiet place on the hill. Sometimes, she took the dog. The day after Robert's visit, she couldn't bear to be in the kitchen any longer. She left the two boys with Elizabeth and headed towards Knox Well with Stina. She aimed towards a certain dead tree that stood further away, nearer the sea.

The tree was bent, blown backwards by the northeast winds, and had been struck many times by lightning. No one ever went there. She sat down behind it out of sight, leaning her back against the remains of the charred trunk. The dog lay beside her, resting her one white paw across Mary's leg. Only then did Mary feel free to cry. She put her face against the rough bark and sobbed until the ache in her chest relaxed a little. Like William, she cried out for an answer. Why? Why? It was always the same – there was no answer, no reason, just the cold, hard bark against her cheek. The tree was dead. It was stupid to expect help.

In despair, she turned to lean her cheek the other way and noticed three bright green shoots at the base of the trunk. They were so small and fragile, yet they glistened in the spring sunshine. She leant over to kiss them and wept to see them so new and fresh, so beautiful. For a while, she sat with one arm around the tree, nursing it like a child. It had weathered the east coast storms, had lost its branches and was hollow after the lightning strikes. Yet it was not dead. It was alive, like her. Both were anchored helplessly in one place, struggling to survive, but they were both definitely alive. She put a hand over her belly and was, for the first time, grateful for the new life growing there.

The sun shone over Filey Bay and made the sea sparkle. She thought how lovely the cliffs looked near Filey Brigg with their smooth bands of lavender and brown sloping down to the water. She made a decision. She would come to the tree more often and renew this feeling of peace and hope. She smiled to think that Robert Storey would probably not approve, and neither would George Gurwood. They'd think that visiting an old tree should not contend with going to church or reading the Bible.

'What do you think, Stina?'

The dog sprang to attention, keen to walk again.

She stroked Stina's head and gazed into her soft brown eyes. 'You're right, I needn't tell anyone.'

She stood up and stretched her arms wide to encompass the sea and sky. 'Come on, Stina, it's time to go home.'

Chapter 29

Throughout the spring, William worked hard to keep his mind occupied. He was torn between the desire to remember his daughter and the need to forget her to avoid more pain. Every little thing still reminded him. As he laid his shoulder into the plough and heaved forward, the clods sliced away cleanly. Why couldn't everything in life be as simple and straightforward as ploughing? Why couldn't he talk to his wife and explain how he felt? He couldn't look her in the eye, let alone find the words. At least it was better to be out of doors than stuck inside with the family.

As he ploughed and trod forwards with a reassuring rhythm, he recalled words from the Book of Job. 'For thou shalt be in league with the stones of the field; and the beasts of the field shall be at peace with thee.' For a moment he was calmed, and then his grief returned. He gritted his teeth, leant harder into the plough and repeated to himself, 'My skin is black upon me, and my bones are burned with heat.' At the end of the furrow, he wiped away his tears with a dirty hand and left his face streaked with mud.

Unlike William, Mary *was* stuck indoors most of the time and was surrounded in the kitchen by the things young Mary had used – or damaged. As she kneaded the bread or rolled the pastry, she fought back the tears. Her youngest son John was always pulling on her apron and wanting attention. She could not grieve in peace.

One day, after wiping the flour off her hands for the umpteenth time so she could see to John, she decided to confront William. Certainly, their life was different, but it must carry on. She'd noticed that he'd begun to read the Bible more now that the evenings were lighter. He'd open it at random and search among obscure chapters, though for what she didn't know. That night, once the children were in bed, she plucked up courage and made a suggestion.

'William, why don't you just read the Book of Job?'

His reply was immediate and angry. 'I already know it, don't I? Know it back to front, inside out, know it by heart. It's in me. It *is* me.' He grabbed his hair in both fists and groaned.

Mary wished she'd kept her mouth shut. Neither spoke for the rest of the evening.

At the end of April there was, at last, a welcome event in the village; the vicar's son John was to be married in Reighton Church. He'd been working as a clerk in Bridlington for almost three years and had courted the daughter of one of the clients. To his father's surprise, the couple chose to live in Reighton rather than the busy town, and John had asked to take over one of the church's cottages. In future, rather than work indoors for someone else, John hoped to oversee the glebe land and make it more profitable.

On the morning of the wedding, the bride caused quite a stir at the church. The Gurwood girls gasped as she made her entrance. Cecilia was shocked as well as envious.

'She has a hooped petticoat!' she hissed.

They took full note of her matching green camlet gown, silk petticoat and light green stockings. Her dark hair was drawn up in a high bun with ringlets hanging loose on each side, and she wore a beautiful lace hood over the top. On her feet were heeled shoes with pointed toes and tiny silver buckles.

Whispers went round the congregation. Robert Storey averted his gaze. The woman's clothes were vain, and the hooped look was unnatural. If it was windy outside, the gown might even blow up and reveal her ankles.

The bride was obviously not used to walking with a domed gown, so her intended elegance and social superiority was lost somewhat.

Ben's eyesight was failing, though not enough to miss such a treat. 'Good God!' he cried as he nudged Sarah Ezard. He gestured with his thumb and began to chuckle at the sight of the bride swaying awkwardly down the aisle. 'Wearin' that 'oop under 'er gown, it reminds me of a funnel – upside down, like.'

He spoke too loudly, and others overheard. There was a commotion as children giggled and their parents tried to silence them. Cecilia, at the front of the church, turned to face them and frowned. Determined that nothing would spoil her brother's wedding, she turned to the front again. It was time to give her full attention to John, for there he was, watching the approach of his bride.

Cecilia was so proud of him in his new clothes. He looked a real gentleman. In a long dark brown collarless coat, he contrasted well with the bride in green. As well as a new pair of breeches, he wore fine Shetland stockings with heart and diamond patterns, and his black leather shoes had tall wooden heels painted red. The cuffs of his coat were undone to reveal the white ruffles on his shirt sleeves, and he left his coat open on purpose to show off the matching waistcoat. This was also unbuttoned to display the fine embroidery on his shirt opening. A narrow red cravat completed the picture.

At the back of the church, Ben had also noticed the cravat. 'What's wrong with old style o' cravat?' he grumbled to Sarah. 'An 'angin' cravat is better than all them fancy chitterlin's on 'is shirt. Why, 'ow's 'e goin' to keep that shirt clean?'

'I bet 'is wife'll wish that shirt front could come off an' wash. She'll rue the day 'e spent money on such showy chitterlin's – an' them white gloves. Who does 'e think 'e is?'

The clothes were remarkable enough, but John also had a new dark brown wig, and he carried a fancy cane.

George Gurwood sensed the atmosphere in the church. Although proud of his son, he disliked ostentation and aimed to keep the ceremony short and simple. He didn't like the hoop fashions either, never had, and just hoped that John's wife would not influence his daughters too much.

Once outside the church again, even Ben and Sarah had to admit the young couple looked handsome in the spring sunshine. It was unfortunate that clouds gathered and threatened a sudden shower. George hustled the crowd to the vicarage.

'Aye, let's be quick,' shouted Sarah, grabbing hold of Ben's arm. 'If it rains before they get 'ome, it'll be a life o' misery for 'em.'

They hurried to the churchyard gate where Dickon was standing patiently, holding on to a live cockerel.

'Now then,' Sarah said to him, 'I'm glad to see someone stickin' to our old ways.'

Dickon rushed on ahead, making the cock squawk as much as he could. On reaching the vicarage, he stood his ground in the doorway. He managed to pull off his hat and set it by his feet. Then he yelled for everyone to hear.

'I'll not move an' take this cock away till it's fed.'

Now anyone who passed him had to drop bride money into the hat.

The house wasn't big enough for all the guests so most stayed outside, where a barrel of ale was set up by the wall. No one minded the brief April shower. The vicar winked at William and beckoned him inside. He brought out a bottle of the best brandy and stood it on the table. Matthew Smith and other leading yeomen were already sitting there waiting. They were in no doubt over where it had come from and savoured it the more for being taxfree.

William saw Matthew whisper in George's ear but didn't catch all that was said. It was probably about Matthew being elected as the next constable. The vicar raised his eyebrows and Matthew grinned. There was something afoot, maybe to do with smuggled goods.

William didn't really care, but he did appreciate the brandy.

The Gurwood girls and their mother bustled in and out offering bridal cake and warm posset. Their one regret was that their grandfather had not lived to see this day. During a quieter moment, Cecilia borrowed the bride's ring. She pulled her sisters to one side, stood them in a line and pushed a piece of bridal cake through it.

'Now,' she instructed, 'each of you must take your turn and eat a crumb of cake as it comes through the ring. It's what you have to do if you want to be married soon. Come on, it's me first.'

William's brother Thomas, now almost 19, watched them from a corner of the room and gave Milcah a knowing wink. When she blushed, he decided he would ask her later for a dance.

John Gurwood had invited his new friends from Bridlington. Since they all played fiddles, it was the first wedding he'd attended when he'd not had to play the music. Now he could relax and dance with Dorothy, his wife. He didn't have to worry about his sisters either; the village had plenty of single young men, and he knew that each Jordan boy had one of his sisters in mind.

He led his wife into the street, where Thomas was already dancing with Milcah. The couple looked as if they'd be together for the rest of the day. Before long, Samuel and Richard Jordan were asking his sisters, Elizabeth and Margaret, to dance. No doubt they'd end up courting the girls. And, to his and everyone's surprise, John Dawson had finally asked Dorothy Jordan to dance. So, all was well in Reighton, he thought, as he took hold of his wife and spun her about.

George Gurwood leant against the doorpost and smiled as he watched the dancing. He could see how his daughters had a civilising influence on the Jordans. The boys used to stomp and make as much noise as they could. Now they asked politely for a dance and tried their hardest not to tread on the girls' toes.

After a while, the older people left the street to the youngsters. Robert Storey manoeuvred his wife away in disgust.

'You know I don't approve of this mixture of ale and dancing. It brings temptation. It only ends in groping and kissing in corners.'

Elizabeth sighed and followed him home. She turned round for one last look at the dancing and noticed that William and Mary were also leaving. No doubt the family was in no mood for fun without young Mary. One thing worried her – William was swaying like a drunkard. For her sister's sake, she hoped the brandy would not become a habit.

Chapter 30

Often, for a brief moment, William forgot his grief. It was usually when he awoke at dawn and heard the birds singing. Then he'd remember and, like a shutter slammed over a window, he was plunged into the dark. Another bleak day stretched suddenly before him. He found that the aching space in the centre of his body did not diminish no matter how much mead or ale he drank. He needed stronger stuff and knew where to get it. Smuggling went on just north of Reighton; it became all too easy to lay his hands on a bottle of brandy.

For a while, only his wife and Ben noticed that his drinking habits had changed. They smelled the brandy on his breath, and both suffered from his moods and violent outbursts. At home, he cuffed the boys across the head for no reason, and it wasn't long before they cringed when they heard him at the door.

The eldest boy, Francis, though he'd always been annoyed by his sister, now wished more than ever that she was still here. The atmosphere in the home was cold and fearful and his youngest brother, poor John, knew nothing different. Francis hated to hear his parents arguing and his father crying. There had been a time, he thought, when Ben and Dickon would have helped matters, but the two old men were not themselves either these days. He wondered if his uncle Matthew could help in any way and spoke to his mother about it.

She was in the garden bringing the dry washing off the hedge. Heavy with child, she looked tired and shrugged at the suggestion. 'What can your uncle do that I can't?'

'He's a constable now,' argued Francis, helping her to carry a sheet. 'He must know people. Someone might be able to help Father. It's worth trying.'

'I suppose so. Here, take this sheet off me. I'll get the rest. You know,' she said as she untangled more sheets from the hedge and dropped them in the basket, 'I don't see your uncle Matthew much these days. He's that busy with his own affairs and his family – quite the gentleman now, always after more land.'

Francis took her hand and pleaded. 'Just try it, eh? Please, Mother.'

'Well, maybe once the harvest is over and the baby's here, then we'll see. We'll have more time then to think ahead.'

The new baby, Richard, was born at the end of September when most of the harvest was in. For the next month, William spent more time in Ben's cottage than at Uphall, and didn't care that he had another son, even if a healthy one.

At the christening, William's mother made only one comment. 'It's a restless bairn that's born when birds are thinkin' o' leavin'.'

William couldn't care less. After the service, he took the baby home to Mary and then returned promptly to Ben's.

For Mary, the month without William was almost happy. As she fed the baby, she listened to the birds singing in the morning and late afternoon. It was as if they were praising the last days of summer and embracing the quiet peace of autumn. Elsewhere, women were busy conserving fruit and pickling onions, but her house was quiet and tranquil. She and the boys appreciated the calm as well as the extra food brought in by neighbours. They began to dread the return of their father.

At the harvest supper in October, William drank half a bottle of brandy before he began on the ale. This was noted by everyone, including Matthew. Since Mary was absent from the supper, Matthew decided to call on her. He was ashamed he'd neglected his sister and, with William drinking so much, he felt obliged to act. He left the noise of the barn and wandered down the hill to St Helen's Lane.

Mary was surprised to see him. 'Hello, are you my brother or someone I've imagined?'

'Mary, I'm sorry I haven't seen you much. I've been so busy, what with the new land and being a constable. And then there's the children – you know how they take up your time.'

'Oh, don't think anything of it. Come on in and have a sit down.' As he followed her down the passage to the kitchen, she added, 'Elizabeth comes to see me. She's a great help.'

'Yes, I'm sure she is, but it's not you – it's William I've really come about.'

Mary lowered her eyes, ashamed of what he might say.

Matthew made himself comfortable by the fire and then began. 'He used to be so strong and level-headed, was my best friend, my adviser even. It's wrong of me, I know; I haven't spoken properly to him for ages. Perhaps I might visit him one night – sit for a while with him – see if I can help.'

'You'll be lucky to catch him at home. He's never in. You can try though. No harm in trying, I suppose.'

'I'll do that then. We can't have him making an ass of himself and making you miserable.' He reached over, lifted up her chin and kissed her forehead. 'Cheer up, little sister, something will be done.' He rose to leave. 'I'll let you go to bed now. The new baby must be tiring.' With that, he left the house to return to the harvest supper.

He strolled back up the hill with the seed of an idea growing at the back of his mind. He had to admit it was a selfish scheme he was devising, one that would benefit himself rather than William. As a leading landowner and now also a constable, he had dealings with the financial backers of the smuggling trade – all important gentlemen of the area. He was one link in the chain and thought William could be included. It would give William a distraction, keep him more occupied during the winter. Mary might not be pleased, and he did have a twinge of guilt about that, though it was momentary and soon put out of mind.

Matthew waited a couple of days and caught William one night as he was finishing his supper. He offered to walk with him to Ben's.

'I have a proposition to put to you. We can talk it over as we go.'

Mary and Francis wondered what it could be about, but Matthew gave no clues. The two men ignored them and left the house.

Matthew waited until they were at the end of the lane and past the pond before he stopped to talk. 'I know of a job that you might be able to do. It's mostly during the winter when work is slack.'

'Don't know as I need any more work.' William was sullen and kept his eyes on the ground.

'You'd need to use your best horse, perhaps have a pistol as well, and you'd be paid £25 a year, with an allowance for the horse.'

William was curious. He gave a sidelong glance. 'Why would I need a pistol?'

'I've heard they're engaging more customs officers along this coast.'

William couldn't believe what he was hearing and spluttered, 'You don't seriously expect me to stop the free trading! Why, you yourself – *you* buy your tobacco and brandy cheap. Ben gets it. We *all* buy goods cheap where we can. Why would I stop that? And for five guineas a quarter?' He ignored Matthew's steady, unruffled gaze. 'Why, even George Gurwood gets the odd bit of French lace for his girls, and the brandy. Everyone takes advantage. Everyone.' There was nothing more to say.

It was getting dark, and Matthew looked ahead towards Ben's cottage, where a light shone from the window. He waited patiently for William to come round to a different way of thinking. After poking the toe of his boot around in the dry dust of the lane, he grinned at William and winked. William, he reckoned, was beginning to get the idea.

'You see,' Matthew explained, 'as a riding officer, you'd be patrolling a *long* stretch of coast, probably the whole bay from Filey and on to Flamborough, and then inland, and not just to Hunmanby. That's a *lot* of ground to cover to prevent smuggling.' He tapped his nose and winked again. 'A *lot* of ground.'

William wasn't sure he wanted to be that involved. It could be a dangerous game to be a customs officer and only pretend to halt the free trade.

'I can't see what I'd get out of it,' he replied. Already though, he had visions of bottles of brandy. 'I'll think about it.'

'Don't take too long. Scarborough Customs want this sorting before winter sets in.' Matthew smiled and rubbed his chin. 'I've a feeling that employing one more riding officer is not going to affect things much, eh?'

They walked on to Ben's, saying no more about it. After a couple of hours smoking his pipe and supping warm mead, William was more at ease with the idea.

As Matthew carried a lantern and escorted William back home, it was agreed that they'd ride to Scarborough together the next week, and William could be sworn in as a customs officer.

'Don't worry, William. I'll put up the necessary surety and, since I'm a constable and know a few gentlemen, your post is bound to be accepted.'

'Have you no qualms at all?'

'No. Listen, William, even if you're obliged to "catch" the odd free trader, the local magistrates are going to be lenient. Trust me. Just be sensible in any deals you might strike with the Hunmanby gang – then everyone's satisfied.'

Mary was appalled when William returned from Scarborough, showed her the pistol and announced his intentions. She'd heard rumours of the free traders and their violent ways if thwarted and wondered if William was up to the task. She also wondered about her brother's motives. What with the new baby and William's drinking and violent moods, the last thing the family needed was a pistol in the house.

November proved very windy, making it difficult for any smuggling to be organised with the Dutch sailing luggers. William had leisurely rides here and there, knowing that nothing much was going on. What he did do was frequent the inns in Hunmanby and make it known that he liked a drop of good brandy. As he hoped, certain interested locals suspected his loyalty to the crown and discussed among themselves how to bribe him when the weather changed and a run could be planned.

Sauntering around Hunmanby, through the market and round the backs of the inns, William guessed that almost everyone would be involved in the free trading. No one in his right mind would pay top prices for tobacco, lace and brandy when he could get them much cheaper tax free.

What William didn't know was the extent of the profits to be had. He had no idea until he overheard a conversation at The Swan Inn. A group of men who worked at the tannery had drunk a few pints too many and were talking about prices on the continent. In between gulps from their quart tankards and sucks at their pipes, they tried to outdo each other. William was all ears.

'Tea can be bought i' Netherlands for as little as six pence a pound.'

'Aye,' interrupted another amid a cloud of pipe smoke, 'an' then it's sold 'ere fo' three shillin' a pound.'

'Or more!' A man butted in with a face pitted with smallpox scars.

'Aye,' agreed the first man, 'an' what's good about it – it's light an' easy to carry.'

The pockmarked man had more to say. 'There's not a bad profit o' tobacco neither. I 'eard it can be bought o' continent fo' three pence a pound an' sold 'ere for a shillin'.'

'Aye, maybe,' the first man mumbled, 'but what about Geneva, eh?'

'Oh, aye,' the rest answered as one.

'I' some parts it's smuggled more than brandy an' wine. It's maybe bought for a shillin' a gallon an' resold at owt from four to six shillin'.'

The men gave each other knowing looks and changed the subject. They didn't want William to know that the gin was especially profitable, bought well over-proof and then diluted.

William also had no idea of the people behind the organised runs. He realised that wealth was needed, as were contacts abroad, but it didn't do to dwell on such things. Perhaps the less he knew the better. He had to hand in his journal from time to time, so he couldn't get away with doing nothing. If he kept an eye open, he'd know when to intervene and when to steer clear. Unfortunately, he reckoned, some smuggled goods would have to be seized.

As he left the inn and strolled around the busy market, he couldn't help thinking how isolated he was now as a customs officer. He began to speculate on the chain of command in Hunmanby. Running from top to bottom, the smuggling must involve folk like Richard Osbaldeston at the Hall or Charles Stutville at the Old Manor House, or maybe both of them, though they were still rivals. William settled for the greater wealth of the Osbaldestons and thought it of interest that the Hall was having expensive rebuilding done to the east wing; he'd heard rumours that it was to be three storeys high and with cellars beneath. He'd have to be very careful if such highly placed people were involved. Matthew, he guessed, knew more than he was telling, but William never thought for a moment that his boyhood friend and brother-in-law would put him in danger.

Chapter 31

1717-18

The stormy weather continued into December and lasted right until Christmas. William rode the cliffs routinely and spent many evenings in the inns at Hunmanby. As far as he could tell, there was no smuggling going on at all. The seas were high and crashed into the cliffs well before each high tide. There was no way a boat could land and unload and, even if any goods were left anchored offshore, they'd have been wrecked or washed up further down the coast. His one consolation was that he was active and often away in Hunmanby, where he could better forget young Mary. It was now almost a year since she'd died.

At home, Mary prepared as usual for Christmas, yet the bustle and the young boys' excitement made her daughter's absence more noticeable. On Christmas Eve the weather worsened, and a gale hit the coast. Even at the bottom of Reighton, Mary could hear the tidal surge beat against the cliffs and then suck the gravel and stones back for another onslaught. In the evening, the wind grew stronger and there was a constant background roar from the sea. While Mary boiled the frumenty, hailstones battered the house.

William, sullen and reluctant, fought his way back to Reighton against the gale and, instead of going home, called at Ben's for a drink. The mead did nothing to improve his temper. When Ben finally sent him home, William was in a foul mood, angry at everything. He kicked at loose stones in the lane with such a force they could have broken a window.

He barged into the kitchen to find Mary and Francis moving the baby into the parlour out of his way. His two other sons were cowering in a corner. Frowning at them, he saw that the table was set for the Christmas Eve supper. Without a word of greeting, he took off his coat and prised off his riding boots.

Mary returned from the parlour and stood the Yule candle in the middle of the table. She could see that the boys were hungry and eager to start on the savoury cakes and cheese, but they had to wait for their father. They sat in silence, heads bowed, and sneaked glances at their parents.

William hadn't even sat down and seemed reluctant to start the Christmas ritual. He didn't move until he was handed a lighted spill for the candle.

Francis noticed his mother's hand shake as she passed the spill. It had not been half as windy last year and yet the candle had still gone out, and his sister had died. He was afraid the candle would sputter and go out again. Out of sight, beneath the table, he crossed his fingers.

His mother said a silent prayer and then shot a glance at him. 'Francis, quick, go and put more rags up against the door. The candle must not go out this Christmas.'

The door rattled in the wind and there was a cold draught no matter where Francis stuffed the cloth. Even the walls shook with the force of the wind. They watched as the candle flame flickered for a while and then became stable. At last, Mary dared to relax and offer the food round.

William put a piece of cheese in his mouth and then couldn't eat it. Instead, he let it rest on his tongue. He had no heart for celebrations on this first Christmas without young Mary, and his mind went back to previous times. He became so absorbed in remembering young Mary getting her puppy that he was oblivious to his surroundings. When his father fired the gun at Uphall to herald in Christmas Day, the sound of the shot broke his dream. It was a cruel shock to be forced so abruptly back to the present. He glared at the candle. How he hated the thing.

All night the storm raged and the weather suited William's mood. Even the next day the wind was so strong that many preferred to stay in their own homes rather than attend the church service. William could not bring himself to go. He didn't want to spend the day at Uphall either.

Mary could understand his reasons yet regretted it for the boys' sake; they'd miss the Christmas dinner and any fun and games. Now they'd have to make do with a fry up of sausage and onions. No one complained when she dished up the food, but she noticed tears in young William's eyes and Francis glowered, tight-lipped. John, as usual, stared wide-eyed, unable to understand why everyone was so quiet.

At night, there was a severe thunderstorm with more hail. The whole family went to bed early without any games and couldn't sleep for the noise of the wind tugging at the thatch. The sea was still roaring in the distance.

On Boxing Day morning, the wind abated at last, only to restart with rain and sleet in the afternoon. The family remained cooped up together. Mary tried her hardest to keep the boys away from William while he sat in the kitchen all day staring at the fire.

Two days after Christmas, the weather cleared, and the sun came out. As soon as the seas had calmed down, William recommenced his patrols. One day, he sensed a change in the atmosphere at Hunmanby and especially in The Swan. There was tension in the air despite the usual clatter of pots and the coarse jokes, so he decided to be more vigilant on the cliffs.

That night he tucked his pistol into his coat pocket and rode northwards towards Filey. He hadn't gone far when he spotted a lugger out at sea. It was heading for the shore. A lantern was waved briefly from the boat and there was an answering flicker from the cliffs. William waited and watched. A couple of fishing cobles emerged from the darkness and approached the larger boat. He couldn't see clearly what was happening and heard no noise, though he suspected that kegs were being offloaded. He needed to get closer but didn't want to be seen. A lone horseman riding on the cliff top would stand out against the sky, so he dismounted and left his horse tied to the gorse. It wasn't long before the cobles turned to the shore and the lugger disappeared into the night. He crouched down and edged forwards.

As he neared Butcher Haven, the cobles ran up the beach. He stopped dead, unable to grasp the sheer scale of the run. The place was crowded with black figures. Men of all shapes and sizes flowed back and forth in the dark. In moments, the cobles were unloaded and the goods, whatever they were, had disappeared into the gap in the cliffs. He had to admire the speed and efficiency of the operation. Hardly a sound had been made. He couldn't see any faces or recognise anyone by their movements. It was hopeless. What could he report? And, as a lone customs officer, he was so vulnerable.

He waited a while before going back for his horse, but once he was astride again, he grew more confident and had an idea. Instead of going home, he decided to return to Butcher Haven and follow the tracks. However, as soon as he reached the gap in the cliffs, he saw that any tell-tale marks had been cleared away. All he could see in the dim moonlight were the scrapings of a gorse bush dragged round and about the beach. The men must have gone up the ravine and then on to Hunmanby or Filey, and he hadn't a clue where they hid their stuff.

Now cold and fed up, he returned to his horse and rode home. In a week or so, it would be time to start ploughing again and then he wouldn't have the time or energy for such futile pursuits.

Before Plough Monday, two more smuggling runs were organised. Whoever was in charge knew that the best chance of getting labourers was before the farm work restarted. He, or they, also knew that William had been asking questions and had been nosing around the Hunmanby inns and outbuildings.

Suspecting something was afoot, William decided to spend an afternoon at The Swan. He hoped to hear of the next smuggling run and settled down in the inglenook with his pipe and a drink. The landlord kept the fire going and always seemed on hand to refill his tankard. Various men came and went, one or two befriending him and giving him a plug of tobacco. After a while, and many pints later, he was less alert. He couldn't catch what people said and began to lose interest and feel sorry for himself.

He drained another tankard of ale and stared into the fire. How he hated his idle days of winter, stuck indoors without young Mary. He hated being at home. His eldest son irritated him, and the other boys were no consolation. Ben wasn't such good company either these days; he missed young Mary and was getting more ill-tempered by the day. Ben grumbled about his arthritis – or was it rheumatism, William wasn't sure – and all he wanted to discuss were his aches, pains, and Sarah Ezard's remedies. William shook his head at the memory of his last visit. Ben swore by his beeswax embrocation.

'An' if that doesn't work,' he'd boasted, 'I just rub a rotten apple o' me knees.' He'd chuntered that Sarah had advised heat – 'bags of 'ot moist bran or a poultice o' steamin' cabbage leaves.'

And if they didn't work, she'd told Ben to 'make a pad o' grated 'orseradish, or wrap 'is joints in a vinegar-soaked bandage.'

What a pair! And both of them drank nettle tea twice a day. William smiled to himself; at least they agreed on something. But, in truth, he was sick of hearing Ben's nonsense. He was in need of better distractions. An afternoon spent drinking amid the warm fug of The Swan Inn should have helped.

It grew dark outside, and candles were lit. William found it difficult to keep his eyes open. His tankard was heavy in his hand again – it never seemed to empty. As he was thinking that perhaps the landlord had drugged him, he dozed off. The tankard fell to the floor, spilling ale into the sawdust.

The landlord winked at the man sitting in the opposite corner. Everything was going to plan. The miller had already set his sails to signal the run was on, and farm labourers had gone down to Butcher Haven with horses and donkeys and an assortment of sledges.

Kegs were soon lifted from the cobles beached on the shoreline. So confident were the men that half the goods were stored in The Swan Inn's hayloft right above William's horse.

William sobered up enough at dawn to go home. As he rode with a thick head slowly towards Reighton, he changed direction. He thought he should take a look at Butcher Haven, for surely something had happened there during the night. It was not like him to fall into such a deep sleep after a few pints. The landlord had made a fool of him.

He rode through the cold mist to the top of the cliff and peered down. The smugglers hadn't even bothered to hide their tracks. The tide was out, and the patch of sand below was covered in footprints and ruts. Now he knew the full extent of his isolation as a customs officer. He spat and cursed his life. He was getting nothing from the smuggling and his scant pay as an officer did not make up for the shame of being duped. He turned his horse homewards, his damp coat now stinking of The Swan Inn – stale sweat, tobacco, candle wax and ale. It also reeked of greasy mutton and onions. He almost puked.

As soon as he got home, Mary hung his coat outside. His hair and his clothes stank so much that the boys held their noses over the breakfast table. Francis was disgusted. He couldn't bear to look at his father and prayed the ploughing would start. Then, at least, his father would have to work as a farmer again.

William had other intentions. He was determined to assert himself and make sure that the next run of smuggled goods would be to his advantage or else. He hadn't yet figured out the 'or else'.

Chapter 32

1718

Less than a week later, William sensed a tense atmosphere in Hunmanby once more. He spent time in The Buck and The Black Horse as well as The Swan. Everyone knew who he was, and folk either avoided him or were overly polite. He planned to curb his drinking and ride out a few evenings in succession. Then he might find out where the goods were stored.

That night, the breeze was from the southwest and there were few clouds to hide the moon. William had a good chance of recognising someone if there was a smuggling run. He rode out with his coat collar up and his hat pulled down. Though bitterly cold, he took a grim pleasure in the misery of the ride; it paid for the guilt he still felt. He'd been too proud of young Mary and loved her far too much.

His horse walked on, the silence broken only by the creak of the saddle leather and the wind whistling through the dead grass. High over the sea, there was a shower of falling stars. He thought once more of his daughter. It was in January, a year ago, that she'd become ill. He gripped the reins tight and forced himself to think of smugglers instead. Tonight must be the night that made a difference.

He left his horse tied to a bush on the cliffs as before and went on foot to Butcher Haven. He waited at the cliff edge till he was cold to the bone, but his hunch was sound – a lugger was loitering in the bay.

Before long, a single coble rowed alongside the larger boat. Now William just had to wait for the coble to land. He could already see a few men on the beach standing beside tree poles, ready to roll the boat further up the beach. Men appeared from the dark cliff to unload, and William did nothing but observe. This time, though, he'd be quicker to follow them.

He ran back along the cliff, bent double so as not to be seen. Then he scrambled onto his horse and turned it inland. He aimed to be ahead of them on the moor in the hope of seeing the carriers before they entered Hunmanby. They'd make slow progress with their packhorses and sledges. It would mean another long wait in the cold.

He soon reached the Filey road. He dismounted and led his horse out of sight, hoping it would make no sound when the other horses passed by. Crouching low in the wet grass, he waited patiently and took out his pistol. His fingers were so numb with cold he doubted he could load it, let alone fire it. He pulled his gloves off with his teeth and managed to unscrew the barrel. His hands trembled as he filled the chamber with powder and cursed when it spilt over his breeches. Feeling around his pocket for a lead ball, he then placed one in the top of the chamber. He screwed the barrel back and grew more confident. He was ready. All he need do now was wait.

The long minutes spent crouched in the wet grass sapped his courage. He soon became more apprehensive. Just as he was thinking of giving up and going home, he heard the dull thump of wooden kegs knocking against each other. He threw himself full length to avoid being seen. One by one, the sledges and packhorses went by. No one spoke and no one noticed him.

When they were out of sight, William got up. He was stiff and his breeches were wet through. At least he now knew the route they took, but he thought he deserved more for his night's pains. He knew he should have gone home while he was still safe yet decided to wait a while then mount his horse and head on after them.

When he judged to have waited long enough, William took the road to Hunmanby. He expected to see men and horses in the distance ahead, so he was taken totally by surprise when he saw a man on horseback trotting straight out of the dark towards him. There was nowhere to hide. The man saw him and stopped. William also stopped and then urged his horse forwards at a slow walk, trying to stay calm but with one hand feeling for his pistol. When he was a yard or two away, he asked the man to identify himself.

'Who wants to know?' came the hoarse reply.

'William Jordan, customs officer.'

'Then go to hell!'

The horse in front had large saddlebags on each side. William asked the man what he kept in them.

'None o' thy business. Damn thy eyes an' clear off out o' me way.'

William gulped. 'In the name of the King, I order you to dismount and give proof of your business.'

The man was defiant. 'I'll dismount when thoo does. Not before.'

William slid off his horse and the man did likewise. They stood facing each other, William at some disadvantage in height. He didn't know the man, didn't recognise his voice, and was unsure how best to proceed. If there was a fight, he'd come off worse. Yet there was always his pistol – so long as the man wasn't armed too.

As he glanced at the saddlebags, William eased the pistol from his pocket. Suddenly, a whip slashed across his face. He winced in pain and dropped the pistol. As he bent to retrieve it, he was kicked hard in the groin. He crumpled to the ground, his eyes bulging.

The man picked up the fallen pistol and held it to William's head. 'Thoo'll be dealin' wi' me again if tha dares follow me. Leave well alone.' He kept the pistol and slapped William's horse on its rear. When it had galloped off, he remounted his own horse and went on his way, confident that William Jordan would not bother him again.

William groaned and got up off his knees. He stood for a while with his legs apart until the pain subsided. Then he limped away in the direction of home. His horse had not gone far. It stood shivering by an overgrown hedge. William couldn't face sitting in a saddle, so rather than remount, he led the horse all the way back to Reighton. He had plenty of time to rue the loss of the precious pistol. That would take some explaining in his journal and, no doubt, the cost would be deducted from his pay. He was cold, wet and miserable. His plans had been a complete waste of time.

By the time he descended into Reighton, he'd recovered enough to grumble about the injustice. He must not let the experience defeat him. He could still plan something and get his own back. He'd had a good look at the man when the moon emerged from the clouds, had seen his large bulbous nose and stubbly chin close up. One of the man's eyes was wide and staring while the other was closed up. William guessed it was most likely tobacco in those saddlebags and was determined to find that man again. As he'd never seen him before, he suspected he might be from Flamborough or Bridlington. He'd search both places for him and get information. He would get his revenge.

William still had almost a week before ploughing began. He spent them not checking and preparing the ploughs as he should, but traipsing round the alehouses and markets of Flamborough, Sewerby and Bridlington. In The Dog and Duck at Flamborough, he enquired about purchasing tobacco. Though they didn't know he was a customs man, they were a close-knit bunch, tight as limpets, and reluctant to divulge anything. Outside, in the square, he met various men, though never the right one. It was the same at Sewerby.

On the Saturday, he rode to Bridlington. He started at the quay and meandered around the harbour and sheds. His last chance was in the town, at the market. He was beginning to lose heart. The north wind whipped down the street and swirled through the alleyways. He headed to the bottom end, to the butchers' stalls, where sawdust flew in his eyes. There were too many inns to visit in one day, so he concentrated on The North Star and The Nag's Head. He was quite adept now at finding out where to buy cheap tobacco and he was unknown there as a customs officer. He was told to try The Seven Stars and ask for Beale.

William walked further along the High Street and stepped down into the dark room of the inn. It was so thick with pipe smoke he could hardly see the fireplace. After being served, he stood as near as he could to the fire. There he entered into the usual conversation about tobacco, the quality and the prices. As he finished his drink, he mentioned the name of Beale.

'Aye,' remarked an old man sitting on a side bench. 'Thoo might find 'im o' South Back Lane. 'E 'as a woman there. I reckon 'e'll be there or thereabouts.'

William bought another pint and drank it slowly, not wanting to arouse suspicion. Then he said an amicable farewell and left. Once outside, he took a deep breath of the cold January air. He clenched his fists, determined to be bold, and then marched off down the alley towards a lane behind the High Street. Before he even got to the end, he saw the very man he was looking for. There was no mistaking that bulbous nose and the odd eyes.

Beale stepped out from a doorway and almost bumped into William. He hardly had time to recognise the customs officer before he was flattened.

All William's pent-up grief and anger went into that punch. The man lay dazed on the ground, half-propped up by the door with a trickle of blood and spittle on his chin. William was shocked at what he'd done. He'd been reckless and didn't know what to do next. Suddenly, he heard footsteps behind him, and his arms were pinned back. He panicked and struggled, but two men spun him round and thrust him against the wall. His cheeks scraped against the rough bricks.

'What the devil's goin' on?' one shouted. 'What's up, eh?'

William didn't reply.

The men eyed Beale with concern. 'What's up, John? Is 'e givin' thee trouble?'

'Aye.' John Beale used the door as his support and got to his feet. He wiped his mouth and glared at William. ''E jumped o' me fo' no reason. It'll be last time 'e does.' He took a closer look at William. ''Ere, I've seen 'im before. 'E's up to no good. An' I know 'is name – William Jordan. 'E's a customs officer, damn 'im.'

'We'll report 'im. Go on, Zak, go an' find our constable. 'E'll be i' Green Dragon – bound to be at this time o' day.'

With Zak gone, William saw his chance to escape. He thought the remaining man was no match for him, being rather portly, and John Beale was still leaning on the door, unsteady on his legs. William relaxed so that the man holding him let go a little. Without warning, he elbowed the man hard in the stomach and ran out onto South Back Lane. He then nipped up another alley to get back to The North Star, where his horse was stabled. There were no footsteps behind him.

He rode quickly out of town and headed for home. Every now and then he checked over his shoulder to see he wasn't followed. He smiled to himself. A little revenge was better than none. Probably he'd hear no more of the matter. He wouldn't tell Matthew what had happened, and he'd invent something to put in the official journal. His cheeks were grazed, but for now, he just wanted to forget customs and smuggling and do a day's simple, honest ploughing.

William's mood improved with the January work in the fields. At home, he listened to his wife and to his eldest son, and he patted the dog's head. Even his youngest sons dared to approach him, and he let them sit on his knee. It was as if he was recovering from a bad dream.

Mary was not convinced that this change would last but took the opportunity to talk about his sister. That night in bed, they spooned together for warmth. He had an arm wrapped round her, his face pressed up to the back of her head.

'Did you know a date's been fixed for Dorothy's wedding?' she murmured.

'No. It's about time John Dawson did the right thing. She's waited long enough. When's it to be then?'

'The 28ᵗʰ – of this month.' She knew this coincided with the anniversary of young Mary's death. Perhaps the wedding date was deliberate, to provide a distraction. She sensed the sudden tension in William's body. He didn't reply.

'William, I do think it's good, don't you, to think of the future rather than the past?' She heard him sigh. Still, he said nothing.

'Since I've a new and healthy baby, I've been asked to prepare the wedding bed. They think I'll bring Dorothy good fortune.'

William relaxed a little. 'Well,' he whispered, 'at least we know John can provide children. She deserves to be happy. First, she loses him to some stranger and then she even looks after his daughter. Years of devotion! I thought she'd never get him to the altar.'

Mary turned her head and kissed him. 'A wedding is just what we need.'

Dorothy's mother knew how much the wedding meant to her one remaining daughter and spent days preparing food. She asked Martha Wrench to make buttered ale and a beer flavoured with rosemary, and she asked the Gurwood girls to decorate the church with extra rosemary. The girls were also to gather rushes and strew them before the couple on their way into church.

Dorothy sewed a new blue dress for herself and made a matching one for John's daughter, Rebecca. Though not yet three years old, she was to be a bridesmaid. The bride-to-be recalled how, years ago, she'd seen John Dawson's face in a vision on St Agnes Eve. Now, at last, in spite of everyone and everything, she was going to be his wife. It had been worth it in the end – those terrible weeks spent tending Dickon's wife in her illness, then seeing to Dickon, then her sister Jane and even John's wife and daughter. Yes, John must have been won over by her unselfish compassion. Yet Dorothy remained cautious and daren't trust her luck. The day before the wedding, she pulled her mother aside.

'Listen, I don't want waking up in the morning by anything but birds singing. Think on, I want a peaceful married life. And I don't want any pigs running out in front of me. I want good luck – nothing else.'

Her mother understood. That afternoon, she took even more time and effort in making the syllabub. It almost finished her off. Her husband put out a hand to stop her.

'Put that birch whisk down. Leave it fo' one o' maids to do.'

'Nay, I'll do it meself. It must 'ave a good froth an' I won't stop till it's right.' She carried on whisking for a few more minutes and then leaned over the table, almost fainting.

'Alright,' she conceded, 'thoo can get maid to cover it and put it i' milk'ouse fo' the night.'

That same day, late in the afternoon, Matthew Smith called unexpectedly at William's house. He carried an official-looking letter. Instead of handing it over, he placed it on the kitchen table as if it was unclean and he didn't want to be responsible.

'What's this?' William asked.

'I'm sorry, I can't say. But I did my best, believe me. They won't always pay heed to a local constable.'

The boys, who had been playing on the floor, stopped their game and stared at the two men. William broke the seal and held it to the firelight. He soon got the gist of it and was appalled.

Mary saw his face go white. She put down her knitting. 'What is it, William?'

'I've got to appear at the next quarter sessions, at Easter.'

Chapter 33

The letter didn't make any sense to Mary. 'William, you've done nothing wrong – or have you?' When William didn't reply, she attacked Matthew. '*You* tell me – what's this all about? Do *you* know?' Matthew looked embarrassed, so she turned back to William. 'You'd better read it out – immediately!'

'I'll explain later,' he mumbled, 'but if you must know what it says exactly, then I'll read it.'

'Go on then. Let's hear it.'

'It's a condition that I…' he held the letter closer and read aloud, 'appear at the next general quarter sessions to be holden for these parts and in the meantime to keep the peace towards all His Majesty's liege people and especially towards John Beale of Burlington.' He threw it on the table. 'It's signed Richard Osbaldeston.'

Mary put her hands on her hips and shook her head. 'I'm no wiser.' She frowned and turned on her brother. 'I bet *you* know about this, don't you! *You* tell me what's happened.'

He shrugged and avoided her eye, guessing it was to do with a smuggling confrontation and therefore partly his fault. Before he could think of a suitable answer, she'd thrown herself onto the stool by the crib, leant her head against the oak panel hood and begun to cry.

'There's the wedding tomorrow,' she moaned. 'What will people think!'

Francis sidled up and put an arm round his mother's shoulder. He stroked her arm up and down while he glowered at his father.

William glanced at Matthew and gestured towards the door with his head. 'I'll deal with this,' he cautioned. 'You'd best go now.'

As soon as Matthew had left the house, William explained to Mary everything that had happened. He was still trembling at the thought of the summons.

'I should have known it would be like this,' he concluded. 'They're all in it up to their eyeballs – free traders, magistrates, God knows who else. They protect their own. I should have known better.'

'Please, William, leave all this customs officer business. Leave it and do what you're best at – farming.' She leapt from the stool and took hold of his hand. 'Look – there's your sister's wedding tomorrow. Let's put this letter out of our minds for the day. We'll think about it again after.'

He nodded miserably and resigned himself to a day of forced merriment.

The next day, the weather was sunny though still very wintry. William led his family to church and seated them in their pew. The sight of his sister in blue should have raised his spirits. She was the happiest he'd ever seen. Festivals and feast days, however, no longer held any pleasure; they were more like drudgery. He resented John Dawson's youthful vigour and gazed with a jaundiced eye at the little bridesmaid tottering up the aisle, her bunch of rosemary as big as she was. He closed his ears to the 'Aw' exclamations from the women. The cold church reminded him of death and funerals rather than weddings, and his black mood would not shift.

Mary did her best. She gave the boys handfuls of grain to throw over the couple as they came out of church, and she crumbled up a cake to throw over Dorothy. She even coaxed Francis into joining the lads' race to Uphall.

'Go on, Francis. Run with your young uncles. It's not far and you might win. See, there's your uncles waiting to start. We'll be at the barn waiting to see you run in.'

Thomas, Samuel and Richard Jordan were eager to set off, each believing they could win the ribbon from their sister. Francis was the youngest. When almost everyone except the racers had left the churchyard, he stood in line with his uncles, each one a gawky lad in their teens. He didn't stand a chance against them.

As soon as they set off, Thomas shot ahead. He was the eldest and nine years older than Francis. He was also the best sprinter. When he reached the barn first, he wasn't even out of breath.

Old Ben clapped his hands and smiled. He delighted in seeing the next generation growing up. 'I reckon thoo'll be winnin' many more such ribbons before tha gets wed, Thomas. I've never seen anyone run so fast, not for many a year.'

Thomas grinned and swaggered into the barn amid more applause. He was quite aware that he was the best looking of his brothers; they still had spotty faces. Folk cheered as he collected his ribbon and then he made a lot of unnecessary fuss when removing his sister's garter. Still full of himself, he fastened the ribbon to his hat, strode towards Milcah Gurwood and bowed elegantly. She was the only girl he'd ever fancied.

William watched without interest. He should have seated the family with his parents and brothers at the big table, but he chose to sit with Robert Storey and Elizabeth. He knew Mary wouldn't object; the boys loved their aunt Elizabeth, and she would help nurse the baby.

Robert's sober and puritanical nature suited William's mood. While others became bolder with drink and began to sing and dance, the two men ate little and drank less. They both saw how John Dawson was uncomfortable as the centre of attention with his new bride.

'He's a good lad,' Robert commented. 'He's overcome a lot since coming to Reighton. He's learnt to read, and he made a useful churchwarden.'

'Dorothy'll sort him out. If I know my sister, she'll soon be in charge. Just look at her – now she's got John, she thinks she's Queen of Uphall.'

At that moment, Dorothy bustled John off the bench to take her for a dance.

William elbowed Robert. 'See what I mean?'

Robert nodded and paid more attention to the dancers. 'Look there,' he gestured with his head, 'those Gurwood girls certainly have a calming effect on your brothers.'

William saw his three brothers concentrating on their steps. Samuel even had his tongue out. He noticed his mother watching with her eyes fixed lovingly on the youngest, Richard. He sighed; that boy was always going to be Mother's favourite. No doubt, seeing the size of his feet, he was also going to be the tallest.

When the music stopped, he watched Milcah Gurwood approach Ben. He listened to their conversation with mild interest.

'Please, Ben, would you mind peeling this apple for me? Peel it in one long piece.'

'Oh, aye, an' I know why. Thoo wants to see tha sweet'eart's name, eh?'

She blushed while Ben went carefully round the apple with his knife.

'There,' he announced as he passed her the coiled skin. 'Go steady.'

As she tossed it over her shoulder, her sisters gathered round to see. The peel broke in mid-air and the girls gasped in disappointment. When Milcah turned to look, the peel was in two pieces on the floor. She studied them from all angles and came to a decision.

'That bit could be a kind of a T and that one is like a J, don't you think?'

Her sisters were not convinced. Neither was William. He didn't believe in such daft superstitions. To save any argument, John Gurwood struck up another dance tune on his fiddle and the girls resumed their usual Jordan partners. Those sisters without a Jordan their own age were content to dance with any son of a yeoman.

Ben and Sarah Ezard supped more ale, convinced that it relieved their aching joints. When the youngsters twirled by, Ben leant heavily against Sarah. The dancers made him dizzy, and he was much the worse for the drink.

'I couldn't see an 'ole through a ladder,' he confessed, 'an' I'm full o' roast beef an' goose.' Yet still he called for more food and drink.

Sarah wondered where he put it and watched him stagger to the top table to propose a toast.

He shouted breathlessly between hiccups. ''Ere's to us – all of us. Me an' all. May we never want nowt, none of us, nor me neither.' He took a swig from his jug and then collapsed across the table.

William nudged Robert. 'Come on, let's help him.' Glad of an excuse to leave the celebrations, they left their bench to carry Ben home.

Mary and Elizabeth had no option but to follow them with the children.

Much later that night, and even early the next morning, the various couples went to bed, some too drunk to do anything, others too tired. When the newly-weds got home, they put little Rebecca in her truckle bed and left a candle lit while they undressed. It was freezing cold, and they didn't waste time.

Dorothy was breathless with excitement. It was seven long years since she'd seen John Dawson as a hero at the ploughing match and fallen in love. That day, his shirt had been wet with sweat and revealed each of his muscles. His hair was still as thick and black; it had always reminded her of the curly heads of young cattle. As she pulled him down towards her, she could hardly believe she'd got him at last, all to herself, this broad-shouldered young bullock of a man. That he was also thoughtful and respected for his work made her happiness complete.

Matthew Smith was not too drunk that night to enjoy his wife and hoped she might conceive her fourth child in just six years. Before he fell asleep, he reflected on his good fortune. He was doing rather well with his new contacts as a constable; they allowed him to amass a small fortune, some of it through free trading. He couldn't understand why William was not taking more advantage of his position as a riding officer. While his own purchases and sales of land made the future look promising, William attracted trouble. In spite of another twinge of guilt, Matthew fell into a deep, untroubled sleep.

At the bottom of the village in St Helen's Lane, William and Mary put the children to bed and then climbed into their own bed. Mary was thinking to comfort him, to ease his troubles. She curled up behind his back and wrapped an arm round him. Suddenly, he turned to face her and then threw himself on top. He pulled up her nightgown and thrust into her violently, without care and without pleasure. She suffered in silence, thinking it so unfair to use her body in this way. If only he'd talk about his feelings. If only he'd ask for help, she'd give it. But he never did.

She lay with her head to one side and stared with weary eyes into the dark. She hadn't forgotten it was a year ago that they'd lost their daughter. And now, on top of that, she had to worry about the Beverley sessions.

Chapter 34

The next morning, Francis watched warily from the window as his father went into the garden. He saw him sit on the chopping log and grab the dog to stop her running away. As his father fondled the dog's trembling head, Francis wondered what mood he was in; he might be gentle, even tearful, yet the next minute he could be angry, bitter or violent. He hoped the dog would free itself soon – just in case.

Francis had always known he was not the son his father wanted. For one thing, he found it hard to read and write and he'd never been as interested in the Bible as his sister had. He'd never understood her weird obsession with the printed word. All he could do was help his mother and brothers whenever he could and avoid his father if possible. His thoughts were interrupted as the dog was pushed away and his father jumped to his feet. It was time to go ploughing. Francis resigned himself to another long day.

Father and son walked in silence to Uphall and then on to the southern field where the ploughs stood ready. There they separated to work the different field portions. William leant into his plough with a heavy heart. Thick clods stuck to the bottom of his boots and welled up round the sides, making each step more difficult. Though he slipped often and lurched from side to side, he plodded on. He could not rid himself of the desolation that crept up on him, the thought that young Mary would not be waiting at the end of the furrow. She would not be waving to him from the hill or bringing his dinner. Worse still, she would not be there when he returned home.

When everyone else had finished for the day, William worked on until it was too dark to see. He finally gave up and trudged home. The moment he lifted the door sneck, grief hit him again like a huge wave surging up a beach.

Mary watched him traipse in, his head down. She knew what it meant. They would eat their supper in silence and then he'd sit by the fire with the Bible. Before long, he'd sigh and get up, put his coat back on and go to Ben's or wherever he went these nights. She'd almost ceased to care.

After supper, William did go to Ben's, to talk for a while about young Mary. They sat as usual almost on top of the fire and drank mead. Ben recalled the way she crinkled up her nose and giggled; he missed her more now that spring was on its way. She'd been such a funny stick. His life was dull without her and her odd ideas. He gazed into the fire.

'I often expect to see 'er,' he mumbled dreamily. 'I often think I'll see 'er come boundin' into garden with 'er dog.'

She'd always disturbed his tasks but had filled his days with life and hope. He knew that William suffered the most and was perhaps over-working to compensate for his loss. If William didn't watch out, he'd be making himself ill.

'Don't work so 'ard, William,' Ben advised as he poured out more mead. 'Don't fight an' rail against things. Each season brings its own work.'

William didn't interrupt. Although Ben sounded like Robert Storey, he wasn't annoyed.

'I know thoo can chop an' saw wood i' winter,' Ben went on. 'It keeps thoo warm an' builds up tha wood pile. An' I know ploughin' 'as started, but *I* say rest i' winter. Stay close to tha fire an' fam'ly. Most outdoor jobs can wait. Thoo should rest easy an' wait fo' spring.'

William sighed and stretched his legs before the fire. Ben, no doubt, would have more to say.

'An', William, when dawn begins to break earlier an' earlier, why then thoo'll 'ave a spurt o' new life an' energy to match it. Then summer suns'll warm tha muscles an' gladden thee. *Then* thoo can work outdoors, an' never stop.'

William took Ben's advice to heart. He waited with more patience for the year to unfold and provide different chores to distract him. When spring came, he worked hard and took comfort from the harrowing and sowing, but at the back of his mind, the Easter quarter sessions at Beverley were looming.

The day before William's journey to Beverley, his mother drew him aside. Her face was lined with worry.

'Take heed, William,' she warned, clutching his sleeve. 'I remember me mother tellin' me they 'ave plagues i' Beverley. She said it always broke out there. So, thoo watch out! Mind tha takes a bottle o' vinegar.'

He promised, though he'd no intention of doing so.

The next morning, he rushed his breakfast, eager to start. Matthew would accompany him. They'd stay the night and attend the sessions the day after. With his mouth still full of porridge, he ruffled the boys' hair and then took the hot potato offered from Mary's apron.

'This'll keep you warm on the way. And mind you don't go too fast – there'll be lots of ruts.' She wanted to tell him not to stop at any alehouses but thought better of it.

William buttoned up his coat. 'Don't you worry. I'll be back late tomorrow.'

She followed him to the door. Leaning forward, she lifted the sneck for him. 'William – please be careful.'

He shrugged and gave her a quick peck on the cheek. Then he clapped his hat on and strode through the early morning mist to Uphall.

Dickon had the best horse ready, its nostrils steaming as it tossed its head. He had to hold the reins tight, as it was skittish, keen to be off. Tom came to give William a leg up just as Matthew entered the yard.

Dickon eyed up the new arrival. 'That's a fine mount thoo's got, Matthew,' he remarked. 'An' thoo looks fit to be one o' gentry.'

William slotted his other foot into the stirrup and stared at Matthew. He had to agree with Dickon; Matthew was dressed like a gentleman and even wore a wig. His grey frock coat with side skirts was arranged round him in neat pleats, and he wore a fancy red cravat folded round his neck. In preparation for the ride, he'd put goatskin gaiters over his shoes and had tilted his hat down at the front so as not to crush the wig.

William sighed and glanced down at his own usual travelling attire. He did not pretend to be anything other than a yeoman farmer with his fustian breeches tucked into riding boots and his best greatcoat with the brass buttons. His one concession to this special trip was to knot his best kerchief round his neck, the red one embroidered by Mary with green leaves.

'Come on,' he said, 'let's get going. I trust you know the way.'

Matthew nodded. 'I've been a few times to Beverley. We'll follow the roads and maybe stop at Great Driffield. We should be there early this afternoon.'

The initial journey was cold. The sun remained a small, pale yellow circle beyond the mist that did not clear until late in the morning. Then the sky turned blue, and the sun sparkled on the dewy grass. As they reached Rudston and continued onto Kilham, Matthew kept standing up in his stirrups to take better note of the winter wheat.

'William, look at the height of that wheat sprouting. I reckon it's more sheltered here. The trouble with Reighton – it's too open to the weather, to the northeast winds.'

William was not in the mood for discussion. He was anxious about attending the sessions, about staying overnight in a town he'd never visited. And Matthew, dressed as he was, would make him feel even more out of place.

Matthew rode on for a while in silence. It had seemed a good idea at the time to involve William as a riding officer. He never thought William would get involved with John Beale of all people. Putting aside a growing sense of guilt, he attempted another topic of conversation.

'What do you think, William? Is it better to have lambs at Candlemas so they'll be tougher if they survive, or would you choose to have them born in the middle of March or even in April? There's new grass for them if they're born later.'

William didn't care; it was the shepherd's problem, not his. His let his head droop to his chest and showed no interest in his surroundings.

To Matthew, the morning was perfect. The grass was bright green, and the blackthorn was in blossom. Pheasants called from the copses and rooks circled the trees, making nests. His horse, on a loose rein, could be trusted not to stumble and he twisted this way and that in his saddle to enjoy views in all directions. He turned again to William and tried to lift his spirits.

'Come on, I'm sure it won't be so bad at the sessions. I reckon the justices'll be quick. They'll want the business over with so they can have a good dinner. Believe me – you'll be out of that Sessions House in no time.'

William ignored him and stared ahead. They were on high ground now, northeast of Driffield, and he could see for miles. Sowing and manuring was going on in the fields. In the distance, men were busy repairing fences, no doubt keen to finish before May Day.

'We'll turn off here,' Matthew said, pointing to a grassy lane on his left. 'It'll take us into town.' He watched William take a potato from his coat pocket and start to eat it. 'Don't you want to stop in Driffield then for pie and beer?'

William shook his head. Once he'd swallowed his mouthful of potato, he explained. 'I'd rather get to

Beverley. It might be busy. We might not find anywhere to sleep.'

'You wouldn't say that if you'd seen Beverley. The place is full of inns and alehouses – and there's stabling everywhere. You'll see.'

'I'd still prefer to keep moving.'

Matthew was disappointed. Though he'd looked forward to a brief stop in Driffield, he appreciated William's reluctance.

'Alright,' he agreed, 'we won't even go into town. We'll head straight on to Beverley. But, I want you to promise me we'll go round the shops when we get there,' he added and held up a finger. 'I need a new pair of gloves and maybe more shoes.'

William's heart sank. He hated shops.

Matthew saw the disgust on his face. 'Well, I bet you'd like to see the pipes and tobacco, eh?'

'I might,' William conceded and tipped his hat down over his eyes.

As they made their way downhill towards Driffield, the sun was now directly in front of them. The low bright light made it difficult to pick their way through the ruts. What had begun as a ride down a pleasant green lane soon became a trek through mucky puddles. Recent rain had filled each hole and the horses often sank up to their knees and hocks. By the time they left the lane and re-joined the main road, the horses were filthy and both men's breeches were spattered with mud. This quietened Matthew down somewhat, and as they drew nearer to Beverley, he shut up altogether.

Unbeknown to William, Matthew was also concerned as to where they could sleep the night. He'd have preferred to stay at The Blue Bell but guessed it was beyond William's means. Besides, William would probably feel uncomfortable since the justices and sheriffs stayed there as well as the wealthier merchants.

'We're almost there,' he announced with feigned confidence. 'This is Molescroft. I wonder if they suffer from a lot of moles here. Lift your head up, William – you can see the minster of Beverley.'

William raised his head. In the distance, he could see a church. Beyond that was an even finer building gleaming in the sunshine. He wished he'd come for different reasons, or that he had young Mary sitting in front of him on the horse, her bonnet bobbing as they went. He could almost sense the warmth from her body. She'd have loved the journey and been so excited to see Beverley. Everything was so pointless now, and the smoke rising steadily from the numerous buildings was depressing. He gulped at the thought of appearing in court.

'Cheer up, William. Look over there.' Matthew pointed to his left, where a large moated house stood back from the road. 'That's a fine place.'

As they approached Beverley, the open fields on each side gave way to cottages and closes. Matthew gestured to the roofs.

'You see there? Those houses have pantiles. They're much better than thatch, don't you think? They won't catch fire and spread.'

William couldn't care less, although the nearer they got to the North Bar, even he was impressed by the larger houses. He could hardly credit the number of chimneys on some of them. His wife would never believe him. He counted as many as a dozen on one.

The entrance through the Bar was just as amazing. A bridge took them over a deep ditch half-full of water, and then they confronted a massive structure of two towers built from fancy red brick. They trotted through the archway and emerged into a different world.

The sudden bustle and noise came as a shock after their quiet ride. It was like a crowded market day. There were so many men coming and going, horses and carriages, men with wheelbarrows and carts, women and lads rushing about and, William noted with alarm, so many men wore wigs – even the tradesmen. There were large inns on both sides of the road and a particularly grand house near the church. A breeze wafted the familiar yeasty smell from malt houses. There was also an over-riding stench, one he knew so well from Hunmanby.

'There must be a tanners' yard close by,' he reckoned. 'It reeks of rotten meat and dog muck.'

Matthew put a gloved hand to his nose. He was more interested in the kind of inn they might choose. The nearest one, The King's Arms, was likely to be full, and he'd already decided against The Blue Bell. Moving on past the church, he turned his horse down Hengate.

'We'll try The White Horse. I had dinner there once. Look, the mud's dried on our breeches. We can brush it off before we go in.'

They passed the front door and went to the yard and stables behind. The ostler met them and explained they'd be lucky to find a room, but he'd stable the horses. They brushed off the mud splashes and William stood waiting while Matthew removed his gaiters. Then he ducked his head and followed Matthew through the back door and along a narrow flagged passage. It was dark and the smell of onions and roast beef made him hungry. Loud voices and a clattering of tankards came from somewhere ahead. Suddenly, they were in a room full of pipe smoke. There were women as well as men, either sitting at small tables or standing together in a crowd. Matthew elbowed his way through, seeking the landlord.

A serving youth heard him asking for help. 'Tha wants a room?' he shouted through the haze.

'There are two of us,' Matthew shouted back. 'Only for one night – and dinner, supper and breakfast.'

The youth made his way through, pushing people aside as if they were curtains.

'All rooms are taken,' he said, 'but if tha doesn't mind the noise an' smell, there's a shared room over by kitchens an' facin' yard.'

Matthew shrugged and glanced at William. 'We'll probably not find anything better.'

'I don't mind,' mumbled William. 'Tell him it'll do.'

Matthew turned back to the man. 'Alright, and we've left a couple of horses in the stables.'

'See our landlord an' pay in advance if tha doesn't mind. Dinner's in an hour, unless tha just wants bread an' cheese or cold meat.'

'We'll wait for dinner.'

As soon as the youth had gone, William turned on Matthew. 'Why on earth do we have to wait? I'm hungry now.'

'Listen, it's the only hot meal we'll get here, so we're having it. I'll pay for it. Anyway, I want to see the shops first.'

William groaned.

Matthew ignored him. 'Collect your riding crop as we go.'

'Why? We're not riding anywhere.'

'No, but I want folk to think you are. Look – you're wearing riding boots in town – nobody except farmers do that unless you've just arrived on horseback and not had time to change.'

William could hardly believe Matthew was so ashamed of him. 'I *am* a farmer,' he grumbled, 'same as you.'

'Look, we're in Beverley now. Do as I say.'

As Matthew went to pay the landlord, William gritted his teeth and collected his crop.

Chapter 35

William trailed after Matthew, first up Hengate and then into the market area. The acrid smell of urine and animal dung was worse there – a stench that overpowered the bakeries and malt kilns. Suddenly, Matthew caught sight of a glover's shop and headed in that direction. William followed reluctantly to the small window that displayed a variety of leather gloves. He was not interested in the slightest.

'What kind do you want?' he asked in a low monotone.

Matthew gave a broad smile with his lips tight. 'Now that would take all the pleasure away. Let's go in and see.' He stepped through the door and checked to make sure William was behind.

Straightaway, the proprietor stopped work at his bench and rushed forward to serve them. He was wearing a similar wig to Matthew and looked as pleased as a dog with two tails.

'Good day,' said Matthew as William edged further into the background, 'I need new gloves for myself, maybe for my wife too.'

'Please, take your time,' replied the man, waving his arm towards different shelves. 'I have short wrist-length ones, long gauntlets, and I also have fingerless. There are riding gloves and hedging mitts – gloves for all kinds of work.' He eyed Matthew more closely and added, 'If it pleases you, sir, I also have some made from the finest Cordova Spanish leather.' Pulling out a drawer, he showed Matthew the gloves and invited him to feel the quality. 'See how supple and soft they are. And rain won't spoil them.'

Matthew was impressed. 'You feel them, William.'

'No – I can see from here what they're like.' He was wishing himself miles away, preferably out in the open air and doing a day's hard work.

Matthew handed back the gloves. 'Perhaps I'd like wrist-length ones, in pale kid leather, maybe with a little embroidery or fancy stitching.'

William rolled his eyes. Matthew was aping the gentry, trying to show that he didn't work with his hands and get them dirty.

The man pulled out another drawer and brought a lamp closer for Matthew to see. 'Take a look at these, sir.' He lifted out a pair and laid them delicately on the counter. They were cream-coloured with dark blue arrowhead stitches. 'The edges are trimmed with silk. I can tell you're a discerning man and these will certainly complement your fine lace cuffs.'

William couldn't believe anyone would be so gullible.

Matthew tried them on. He flexed his fingers and held his hands at arm's length to admire the full effect.

'Fancy that,' crooned the shopkeeper, 'the blue matches your eyes.'

Matthew thought the man presumptuous, but since he was in a good mood, he smiled and waved the gloves at William. He said he'd take them and didn't even ask the price.

William frowned and wondered if Matthew's money came from a lucrative smuggling deal.

Ignoring the grimace on William's face, Matthew asked about gloves for women.

'Ah,' whispered the man as if in a conspiracy, 'I do have a pair of real chicken skin gloves for your wife to wear at night. They keep the hands soft and white.' He winked and passed Matthew a walnut shell. 'Go on, sir, open it. You won't believe it, but the gloves are so thin that they fit inside.'

Even William was curious and moved closer. He peered over Matthew's shoulder and watched him tip out the gloves. They were so fine you could almost see through them. No wonder the man was so delighted to show them.

'Many ladies wear these for just a week or so and then buy new ones.'

Matthew thought better of the idea. 'Perhaps they're not for my wife.'

'Well then,' the man continued, 'now that the ladies are wearing shorter sleeves, maybe these will suit.' He took pairs of elbow-length kid leather gloves from a shelf. Most were blue or yellow and some were almost white. All were embroidered with flowers.

Matthew turned to William. 'What do you think? Which colour do you think Ellen will like?'

'*I* don't know. *You* decide. You know her best.'

Matthew took his time. It was silent in the shop apart from an apprentice cutting leather in the backroom. William was hungry and heard his stomach rumble. Finally, the choice was made.

'I'll take the yellow ones. They're cheerful enough.'

William thought that was the end of it, but his hopes were dashed instantly by the shopkeeper.

'Would you prefer them scented or plain?' he asked.

Even Matthew was puzzled.

The shopkeeper explained. 'A great many ladies don't appreciate the smell of animal skin. I can rub them inside with cinnamon or cloves. It's your choice, sir.'

'Perhaps cinnamon then. Cloves remind me of toothache.'

The man nodded and took the gloves to the backroom to be scented and wrapped. Matthew stood by the counter and drummed his fingers while he waited. He avoided William's eye.

Soon, the man returned with the package and handed over the bill. William wanted to see how much it all cost, but Matthew stuffed it into his pocket and, with his back turned, paid the man. As they closed the door behind them, William complained.

'Don't forget I'm hungry, and I'm worried we'll be late now for dinner.'

'Alright, we'll go straight back. We'll have time to see more shops later.'

When they arrived at the inn, they found the main room allocated for dinner already packed with people. There was no room left to sit round the table and men were already helping themselves to slices from the huge joint of roast beef. William's face dropped. They'd paid for dinner, yet he didn't know how they'd eat it.

The landlord saw the look on his face and strode over.

'There's no need to worry, gentlemen. You're both welcome to fill a plate and join my family in the kitchen.' He brought them a couple of plates. 'Take as much bread and meat as you want and have some pease pudding to go with it. Over there you'll find honey sauce. Do you want drinks bringing through?'

'Yes, that'll be fine,' said Matthew. 'We'll have quarts of your mild beer.'

The landlord left them to fill their plates, not an easy task as they leant over people's heads or tried to squeeze between them. Matthew found it much harder with his parcel of gloves tucked under one arm.

When they couldn't fit any more food onto their plates, they carried them to the side table where an old man was fiddling with the tap on a cask. Matthew made sure the man poked the hops out before filling their tankards.

'Follow me,' grunted the man, a tankard in each hand. 'Kitchen's this way.'

He led them down a dark and narrow passage, turned a corner and rammed open a door with his foot. Stepping down into the kitchen, a blast of heat rose towards them. Copper saucepans gleamed in the firelight and sides of bacon hung from hooks in the blackened beams. The walls had racks stacked with pewter plates, and there were shelves full of pickle jars. At a table to one side, the landlord's family was sitting eating their dinner. Girls shunted each other along the bench to make room for the newcomers and smiled as William and Matthew sat down.

Soon, the landlord joined them and began polite conversation about the weather and the new houses being built in town. He didn't ask them the purpose of their stay. Since it wasn't a market day and the sessions were due to start, he assumed they'd come to attend. Maybe they were witnesses in a case. It wasn't his business to pry.

William and Matthew concentrated on their food, preferring not to say much. Neither was quite used to the faster speech of Beverley, and they didn't catch everything the landlord and his daughters were saying.

As soon as their plates were empty, they mopped up the sauce and meat juices with the last bit of bread. One of the girls saw that they'd finished. She jumped up and swapped their plates for dishes of dumplings with treacle.

William had not expected such a treat. The girl smiled and passed him a spoon. Though full of beef and bread, he could hardly wait to taste the soft dumpling sitting like an island in a sea of warm syrup. As he spooned in the last dribbles, he thought he'd never eaten so much except on Christmas day at Uphall. Then he began to feel uncomfortable. It could be the heat from the fires or the amount of food and beer in his belly. He wiped the sweat from his forehead and wished he'd worn shoes for the journey, like Matthew. He couldn't wait to pull off his leather riding boots.

Matthew nudged him. 'Come on, William. We've finished dinner and we're not in Beverley every day. Remember – there are more shops I want to see.'

'Can't we stay here and rest instead, and maybe smoke a pipe or two?' William pleaded.

'We'll do that later. Come on, let's get out in the fresh air.'

William thought 'fresh' was an exaggeration; the stale urine used by the dyers and the stink of the nearby middens made him think he was carrying a dung heap round with him. He mumbled his thanks to the landlord and followed Matthew out of the back door and into the stable yard.

The sunlight was so bright after the dark kitchen. William tipped his hat lower and trod sullenly behind. He was led back into the market area and then up and down both sides of the square.

'What in God's name are you looking for?' he demanded.

'A shoe shop.'

'But we've already passed a few.'

'No, it's a particular one I want. I've heard of a Robert Banks. He's said to have more choice than most.'

William resigned himself to a long afternoon. He traipsed after Matthew, who, despite seeking out Banks the shoemaker, also loitered at the tailors and breech makers and even the wigmaker.

'Here it is,' Matthew announced at last. 'We'll see what he has to offer.'

When they stepped inside, they were immediately accosted by a man they presumed was Banks. He was small, dressed in black and, as William had come to expect, he wore a wig.

'Good day,' said Matthew. 'I'm not after bespoke shoes, as I won't be returning to Beverley. What do you have ready-made?'

Robert Banks estimated the rough size of Matthew's feet and then fetched a few samples. 'These are our best, sir – for walking in town.'

Matthew thought the shoes were almost identical. Each one was black, had a high wooden heel, a square toe and a long tongue running up the ankle. The only difference was in the tiny buckles, dainty and made in plain steel or brass designs. He was given time to inspect them.

'Try a few on, sir,' urged Banks. 'The buckles can be removed. You can exchange them according to your attire. Those in your hands are calfskin – the others are Spanish leather. I'm afraid I can't take credit. I take cash only from January to July.'

Matthew tried on each pair. Two of the pairs fitted well. 'What do you think, William?'

'Oh, don't ask me. They all look the same.'

Matthew walked around the shop in both pairs before making his decision.

'Alright, I'll take these with the steel buckle and, since I'm giving cash, I expect a reduction in price.'

'They would normally cost 60d. I can let you have them for 50.'

'If you add an extra pair of buckles.'

'You bargain hard, sir.'

William wondered who would give in. The shop was quiet, hardly over-run with customers. Amazed at himself, he intervened and asked politely,

'April's a slack time for trade in shoes, is it?'

Robert Banks coughed to hide his discomfort.

'It is, isn't it?' William repeated and winked at Matthew.

'Very well,' agreed Banks, '50d and extra buckles.'

Wonderful, thought William, as he watched Matthew pay up and take the wrapped items. When the door closed behind them, William let out a deep sigh and smiled. 'Now we go back to The White Horse. No more shops.'

'But what about tobacco?' Matthew asked. 'And maybe a new pipe or two?'

'Damn the tobacco. The landlord can give us some.'

'Alright,' Matthew conceded, 'but it's your fault if there's only poor stuff.'

Trudging back through the square, they noticed the shopkeepers and tradesmen were already closing the shutters over their windows. Women were walking home with food in their aprons, chatting as they went, while others were filling pails with water. William paused to watch, impressed by the wells. They were built of red bricks, waist high, and so easy to use. Each one was provided with a strong pulley and bucket. Now that he was more comfortable in the cooler early evening air, he was beginning to see Beverley in a better light. When they reached the Market Cross, he even stopped to admire it. He'd never seen anything quite like it, with its tall white pillars and coats of arms.

Matthew pointed to one of the shields. 'That's the Royal Coat of Arms.'

'I could guess that much,' William replied.

'Fine, but I bet you don't know that one.'

William looked more closely at where Matthew was pointing. There was an oval shield with blue stripes and a blackbird in one corner. In the middle was a red glove held palm up, or maybe it was meant to be a bloody hand. Who could be sure? He shrugged.

'That's the Hotham coat of arms. You'll be seeing Sir Charles Hotham at the sessions tomorrow.'

William swallowed hard. He hoped it was a red glove.

Matthew pointed to another shield. 'I'm not sure about that one.'

William saw that it was painted gold with a blue surround. In the middle was a blue chevron with something like two golden Vs or candlesticks. There was also a golden bird, maybe a dove.

'Why have candlesticks on your shield?' he asked.

'You dolt. Those aren't candlesticks. I don't know whose coat of arms it is, but I do know they're not candlesticks. They're arrowheads pointing down. Look, you can see the barbs.'

William peered again. They still didn't look like arrowheads.

'You should know those arms,' Matthew said, pointing to the last shield. 'We saw that one as we came into Beverley, above the arch.'

'It's obvious. It's Beverley's arms,' William replied. 'Anyone can see that – there's a beaver on top. I've seen enough coats of arms now. Let's go.'

The wind had dropped, and the smells no longer bothered him. He lifted his head and sniffed. Now he could just smell horses, straw and oats, all homely, comforting aromas. Close by, a group of stray dogs were rummaging about. Two hounds stood over a large bone. Their hackles were up, their feet planted ready for a fight. Suddenly they crouched low, their black lips pulled back. A growl rose from deep in their throats.

'Do you want a bet?' asked Matthew. 'I'll wager tonight's tobacco on the black one.'

'Fine, I think you're wrong though. The scruffy grey's like a gypsy dog. I bet it'll win.'

Without further warning, the dogs sprang at each other, and the other dogs backed away to give room. Well-matched, the two dogs leapt high, trying to get the first bite. They landed and rolled over and over in the muck, snapping their jaws. Then, as quickly as it had started, the fight ended. The black dog yelped and cowered under the grey.

William smirked. 'What did I tell you? Always back a gypsy dog.'

The other dogs returned to sniff around the pavement as if nothing had happened. The grey dog, still with its hackles up, carried the bone away triumphant. The black one wandered off to sit and lick a bloodied paw.

'Since it's a pleasant evening,' Matthew asked, 'do you fancy sitting outside the inn for a pipe?'

William nodded. For once, Matthew had made a welcome suggestion. As they re-entered Hengate, they were pleased to see the bench outside the inn was vacant.

'You stay here,' said Matthew, 'while I get our tobacco. You've brought your pipe, I trust?'

'Yes. It's in my pocket.'

'Good. I won't be long.'

William leant his back against the wall and listened to the blackbirds singing from the many gardens nearby; the sound reminded him of Reighton. He let his gaze wander. The top of the church tower was just visible above the rooftops. Of more interest was the new house opposite. It had two storeys, a pantile roof and more than one chimney. The brickwork was unusual – a bond he'd not noticed before. That was something he could report back to his father, that and the number of chimneys in Beverley. It was certainly a wealthy place. No doubt Matthew had been taking a good note of the buildings. He wouldn't be surprised if the Smith family had ambitions for a grander home in Reighton.

He watched idly as shutters were closed over the windows of the inn. For all its fine buildings, Beverley must have trouble at night. As he ruminated on the advantages and disadvantages of living in a town, Matthew returned with the promised tobacco. He'd also bought a new pipe.

'The longer stem'll give me a cooler smoke,' he explained.

William smiled to himself. He thought the pipe wouldn't last long; it would snap in half in no time.

Matthew sat down heavily on the bench, opened up the pouch and held it out for William. 'Smell that – best Virginia, or so I'm told. We'll fill our pipes, go in and light them at the fire, then come back out here and sit.'

Within minutes, they were lounging with outstretched legs watching the shadows lengthen in the street. For a while they smoked in silence, lost in their own thoughts. Matthew was still puzzling over the fact that William had been in Bridlington when he assaulted John Beale.

'How come you had that fight?' he asked.

William took his pipe from his mouth. 'He's a free trader. He attacked me near Hunmanby, kicked me hard where it hurts most. *And* he took my pistol.'

Matthew frowned. 'Ah, that's not so good. We don't want John Beale armed with a pistol. I wouldn't trust him. But what I don't understand is why you went after him in Bridlington.'

'He was selling cheap tobacco there.'

'Yes, but you were commissioned in Scarborough. Anything further south than Flamborough Head isn't your concern.' He clicked his tongue. 'You're going to be in trouble tomorrow.'

Chapter 36

Matthew finished his pipe and tapped it out against the bench. 'The landlord says he has some snuff. Do you fancy a sniff? It'll clear your head – you need to be alert tomorrow.' Before William could answer, Matthew jumped up and shot back inside. He soon returned with a folded piece of paper.

'I didn't pay much for this,' he lied as he sat down again. He opened the paper carefully so as not to spill any powder. 'I'll take a pinch first.' He sniffed a bit up each nostril and then inhaled deeply. Almost straightaway, he sneezed.

William thought it a waste of money, but Matthew egged him on.

'Go on, have a go. Take a good sniff, mind. It's supposed to cure headaches and keep you calm.'

William copied Matthew and took a deep breath. Like Matthew, he also sneezed. It certainly cleared his head. 'I think I'll stick to smoking a pipe. It lasts longer. What are we going to do now – go back inside and have a few drinks?'

'I don't think that's wise to stay up drinking tonight. We'd best get our supper, then go to bed early.'

Matthew found the landlord still busy with customers. He explained what he wanted, and a platter of cheeses and bread was brought to them. The landlord suggested they sit by the fire. Others were already there spearing cheese onto toasting forks. Matthew smiled to see William so eager to sample the different cheeses. It was as if he'd never had one in his life.

'Try this white one, Matthew. It's dense but see how it crumbles. Mind that one – it's hard and has a sour edge. It melts well though.' He had an opinion on every one he tried.

As they enjoyed their supper and washed it down with a pint of small beer, other customers drank heavily. There was much loud talk and thumping of tables. Matthew thought it wise to leave before it became too boisterous.

'We've had enough supper. Come on, William, we'll piss in that pot in the corner and tell the landlord we're ready to retire.'

One of the daughters soon brought a lamp and led them up the well-worn wooden stairs to the chamber above the kitchen. She set a candle on the table, lit it and said water would be brought for them in the morning.

'And, since thoo's first to retire, tha can choose tha beds. Oh, an' we 'ave a barber 'ere if tha needs i' mornin'.' With that, she left them.

There were eight identical beds, crammed closely together. William preferred to be by the window, so they took the two nearest. The first thing William did was lie on the bed and get Matthew to pull off his boots.

'Oh, that's better!' He stretched out and wiggled his toes, glorying in the relief. 'Thank you, Matthew, for coming with me.'

'It's my pleasure,' Matthew answered as he undressed. 'It's good to have an excuse to come here. And you never know,' he added with a smile, 'there may be time to buy more things tomorrow.' For once, William didn't object. 'And we'd better use the barber first thing in the morning. *You* must look smart for the courtroom.'

They both got under the covers and lay on their backs surveying the walls and ceiling. In the candlelight, they could just make out the moral maxims pasted on the back of the door.

'That's daft sticking those two together,' Matthew decided. 'Strike while the iron's hot, and then right below that it says a fool's bolt is soon shot.'

William read out one that he thought very apt to Matthew and the shopkeepers. 'Crows will not peck a man till he be dead, but flatterers will devour a man being alive.' He read another about a sinner being the Devil's miller, always grinding. Such words did not auger a restful sleep. He knew he'd sinned in attacking John Beale and would pay for it the next day.

In spite of his worries and the noise beneath, William dozed off. He was soon woken by the door opening and a group of men clomping past. By their flickering candle, William saw the men collapse onto the beds. They didn't bother to undress or even take off their shoes. Before he could relax and fall asleep again, the men were snoring. Nothing William could do would muffle the sound. He tried fingers in his ears; this only made his arms ache and, besides, as soon as he felt drowsy, his fingers fell out. To his annoyance, Matthew was fast asleep and snoring; if anything, even louder than the rest.

He realised he must have slept a little when he was alerted suddenly to the clopping of hooves in the yard outside. It was barely daybreak, yet as he peered out of the window, the stable yard below was full of lads coming and going with barrows and buckets. There was no point trying to sleep anymore. From the kitchen beneath came raised voices and the crash of pans. Another day at the inn had obviously begun. He now started to worry again about the quarter sessions, and wished he'd slept better. Instead of lying in bed fretting, he got up and put on his breeches. Matthew was still asleep, so he gave him a shake.

'Come on,' he whispered. 'Get dressed and we can have the barber before anyone else.'

Matthew was up and dressed before he realised how early it was. Then he threw down his cravat and hissed, 'For pity's sake, William! You're not going to work. We don't have to be at the sessions till later. You clod-head!'

William had no answer. It was true, he knew nothing of the town's ways. He knew only about ploughing and sowing and reaping.

'At least you can help me fasten my cravat. There's a tiny button at the back.'

William fumbled with fingers too big for the job. He presumed it was Matthew's wife who'd fastened it yesterday.

With the cravat in place, they opened the door as quietly as they could and crept downstairs to the kitchen. They bumped into the chambermaid, about to take the water upstairs.

'Oh, sirs. Thoo gave me a shock.' She put down the jug. 'Now thoo's 'ere, tha might as well get washed i' yard.'

'And we'd like to see the barber' Matthew suggested, 'before breakfast.'

Within minutes, they were sitting outside the kitchen door having their stubble shaved. William began to feel better about the day. The morning was fresh and cold, the weak sun sending slanting shadows across the yard. The barber was quick and efficient and, though he charged a shilling, William was not too upset by the cost.

'At least the razor was nice and sharp – much better than the one we have to share at Uphall.' He rubbed his hand over his chin. His face was never so smooth and clean when he shaved himself.

More ready for the day ahead, he followed Matthew back into the kitchen for breakfast. A girl stood over a fire with a pan of sizzling black pudding and sausage. Another girl was frying scallops of ham in dripping.

'Go an' sit i' parlour,' she said, turning her head. 'Breakfast'll be brought through.'

They ordered a pot of small beer each and sat at a table and waited. Bread and cheese were put before them as well as boiled beef. They were disappointed; the fried food they'd seen and smelled in the kitchen was not for them.

When they'd finished their breakfast, Matthew told the landlord they'd be back later in the day to collect the horses.

'Time to go,' he said to William. 'Come on. It'll be pleasant to walk through town on such a fine morning.'

William lost heart as soon as he put foot outside the front door. Rushing along the street was a group of young men. Each one was smartly dressed and wore a wig.

'Powdered pups,' he muttered under his breath, and was obliged to walk behind them all the way to the Sessions House. He kept his head down as he went through the market area and up the High Street. He ignored every inn, alehouse and shop, paying attention only when he caught sight of the pillory on its platform. A bellman in a red coat was strolling up and down calling out the names of properties to let or to sell; he also reminded folk that the sessions were to start today.

Matthew took William's elbow and ushered him towards Registrar Square. They walked across the open space, past the impressive new Registrar's Office and then faced the old timbered Guildhall where the sessions would be held. More men wearing wigs were entering the place. Matthew urged William forward and almost pushed him through the carved oak door beneath its stone surround.

William's mouth went dry as he was directed to the Great Hall through a wide oak door on his left. He entered a huge space, like a great barn, the difference being the King's Arms displayed at the front. Shafts of sunlight streaked through the high windows on one side but did not dispel the general gloom of the dark timbers and black furniture. It was also colder inside than out, and the room smelled musty like a damp church. He and Matthew were jostled to the back of the hall, which was already full of people huddled together on long benches.

As soon as William sat down, the man next to him poked him and pointed to the large door to his left.

'If it goes badly for us, we'll end up goin' through yon door.'

William was none the wiser.

A man in front overheard and twisted his head round. He had large protruding eyes and a thin, wide mouth. William thought he looked like a frog.

'It's the prison through there,' the man announced with a leer.

The man next to William grinned. With small, pointed teeth and a sharp, lean face, he reminded William of a weasel. To make sure he wasn't going mad and seeing everyone as an animal, William stared at Matthew.

'What's the matter?' Matthew asked. 'Are you alright?'

William nodded. He couldn't explain. A couple of officials were now taking their seats. With their off-white wigs and long faces, they resembled sheep. Tables were piled high with papers, various clerks busy shuffling them into order, and the side benches on each side of the hall were now filling up with well-dressed men. There was a raised area with a table at the front, no doubt reserved for the justices of the peace.

'Those men at the side are the jurors,' whispered Matthew. 'Don't look so miserable. Put a better face on, and if you plead guilty, you won't even have to be tried.'

'Well, I am guilty,' William mumbled. 'What am I supposed to look like?'

'Shush,' Matthew whispered again as everyone rose to stand. 'The judge and JPs are coming in. That's Sir Charles Hotham.'

A man in a full-bottomed white wig and a black pleated gown walked solemnly to the front and up the steps. William knew the next man to appear – Richard Osbaldeston of Hunmanby. Other JPs followed wearing shorter wigs.

Now that the door was closed, it grew stuffy and, despite the lack of any heating in the room, William began to feel too hot in his coat and boots. He glanced around at the mixture of folk squeezed together on the backbenches. John Beale was there with his ugly, bulbous nose and, like William, he'd bothered to shave. It didn't look as if he'd brought any witnesses with him, but no doubt the Bridlington constable was present and would speak up for Beale.

There was a flurry of movement as the Clerk of Peace took a sheaf of papers to the front, and the crier stood and proclaimed the sessions had started. There was a speech about the JPs and juries, and then the clerk collected more documents.

Matthew whispered to William. 'I trust our Osbaldeston gave orders for your case to the clerk in good time. Cases are heard in the order received.'

Those summoned for jury service had their names called out and were sworn in. At last, Sir Charles Hotham read out the articles of charge. As well as William's particular charge of an offence against a person, there were other misdemeanours – drunkenness, profane swearing, a few petty thefts and the sale of bad meat.

One by one, the cases were heard. The JPs were brief, and William had the impression they were not that interested, especially the nearer it grew to dinnertime. When it was his turn, the clerk read out the charge.

'In January last, William Jordan of Reighton did assault John Beale of Bridlington in public, in Bridlington, and without provocation.'

John Beale and William stood up. The constable also stood and, on behalf of the absent witnesses, presented his case.

'I can confirm that, in Bridlington, in January, William Jordan punched Mr Beale in the face. It was completely unprovoked.' Knowing that William worked for the customs and would therefore prove unpopular with his audience, he sneered as he spoke. 'I must add that William Jordan is a customs officer.' There were the expected jeers. 'I must also add that William Jordan, though a customs officer, is employed by Scarborough and *not* Bridlington, where the offence took place.' At this, there were murmurs of disapproval from all quarters.

Richard Osbaldeston intervened. 'You suggest he was over-stepping his authority?'

'He had been asking questions as to where he could buy cheap tobacco.'

'And you surmise he was acting as a customs officer, and not simply as a man eager to fill his pipe?' There was laughter from the benches.

The constable was not deterred. 'I do believe he thought John Beale guilty of selling free trade tobacco.'

Sir Charles Hotham added his opinion. 'Whether or not this is the case, there is no excuse for assault. William Jordan – how do you plead?'

William's legs were shaking and his mouth dry as he croaked an answer. 'Guilty.'

'Do you have any witnesses, or anyone to speak in your defence?'

Matthew coughed and rose to his feet. He nodded towards Osbaldeston and bowed towards Sir Charles Hotham.

'William Jordan is my brother-in-law and life-long friend. I speak in his defence also as the parish constable of Reighton. While I cannot condone the assault, he has suffered greatly this past year. The death of his only daughter may have led him to be overzealous in his post. He is not a violent man, and the incident took place almost exactly a year since his daughter died. He has been overwrought with grief.'

Sir Charles Hotham listened with interest, though he continued to frown. 'William Jordan,' he asked, 'is this correct – you were not sworn in as a customs officer in Bridlington?'

'No,' William answered, 'it was in Scarborough.'

'Then you had no reason to be conducting enquiries in Bridlington. You have acted outside the boundaries of your office.'

Richard Osbaldeston exchanged glances with Matthew. He then whispered something to Sir Charles Hotham and the JPs on his other side. They all nodded in agreement.

Sir Charles Hotham gave his verdict. 'William Jordan, for assault, a fine of 40 shillings.'

Matthew nudged William. 'It's over. Sit down.'

William's heart was still thumping and his legs shaking as he slumped to the bench.

Matthew put a hand on William's knee and gave it a squeeze. 'That wasn't so bad, was it? Don't worry about the fine. I'll sort it out.'

John Beale was grinning, and so was the constable. Not for the first time, William wondered if everyone, from top to bottom, was involved in free trading. Most likely, Matthew had connections with Richard Osbaldeston, and a 40-shilling fine was nothing in their greater schemes. The fine would be paid, and he'd have to sign to say he'd keep the peace from now on.

Other cases were heard, and people acquitted or fined. William paid little heed. The room was stifling and increasingly noisy, the sound of guffaws and angry tirades coming and going as his ears blocked and cleared. Just when he thought he could bear it no longer, Sir Charles Hotham declared the sessions would adjourn for dinner.

As soon as the JPs and clerks had left, William was shoved off the bench and herded with the crowd through the door.

It was such a relief to be outside again. He gazed at the sky, still blue with clouds scudding from the west, and longed to be back in Reighton.

'Matthew,' he pleaded, 'please, please let's collect the horses and ride home.'

For once, Matthew agreed.

They strolled back to The White Horse in silence. They'd both decided, without admitting it, that things would never be the same between them. Just before they mounted their horses, Matthew shook William's hand. There was something sad and final in the gesture.

Chapter 37

Both William and Matthew were subdued on the journey back to Reighton. William was full of unasked questions. He wondered how long he could function as a customs officer if his own brother-in-law and the local gentry were so involved in free trading. Matthew was riding slightly ahead of him. William had to admire the bay gelding; it had a strong rear, good enough for jumping, yet was also gentle and sure-footed. His own nag was older and dun-coloured. He sighed and patted his horse's neck as if to say, 'never mind – you can get me home just as well as Matthew's mount'.

As they passed through the extensive ancient parkland of Leconfield with its mighty trees, William scowled. Matthew looked as though he belonged in such a landscape. It wasn't only Matthew's fine clothes; it was the way he sat on his horse and the way he tilted his head as if he owned the very air he breathed. There'd always be the wealthy and the poor, William reflected, and the yeomen inbetween. That didn't mean he couldn't improve his lot. He made up his mind there and then to stop being such a fool. He wouldn't resign his post. In future, though, he'd make more effort to benefit from the illicit trade like everyone else.

By the time they arrived back home, William was more content, even relaxed. He greeted Mary and reassured her straightaway.

'It's alright. I've been fined, but your brother is seeing to that, and no one thinks the worse of me.'

'Thank the Lord!' she cried as she helped him take off his boots. As soon as she'd poured him a drink, the boys clustered round. Mary took the opportunity to tell him some news herself.

'The vicar called round today. He'll be pleased to hear you're back safe and sound. He says you're to be a churchwarden this year.'

William was surprised. Maybe it was to make him feel part of village life again. Whatever the reason, he must not betray the vicar's trust. He would put the past behind him.

'The vicar was in a good humour,' Mary continued. 'He's just found out his son's wife is with child. He hopes the baby might be born at Christmas.'

William was reminded instantly of young Mary's birth, also in December. He glanced at Mary and could tell she remembered too.

She gave a half smile. 'We wish the Gurwood family well, don't we?'

'We do.' He returned her weak smile. Yes, he would share others' good fortune. And from now on, he would try to be more optimistic about his own future.

The weather that year was kind. The early summer brought many fine days with enough rain for the crops to grow strong and healthy. As a result, William concentrated on farming rather than the customs work. He made sure his children worked outdoors and kept them busy with various menial jobs.

Young William preferred to be at the blacksmith's and pump the bellows on dull, rainy days, but whenever it was fine, he wandered barefoot in the pasture to see the cows didn't stray. And, whenever he could, he took Stina with him. The dog now saw him as her master.

Each day, young William took his brother John to collect sticks for the fire. They'd sit together in the garden and tie the sticks into faggots. John was just four years old, small for his age and not in breeches yet. Since he was only capable of stick gathering and bird scaring, young William found him boring. Compared with his sister, John was no fun at all. When he could, William ran off with the dog and left John to cope by himself.

Villagers noticed how often John was neglected and told Mary.

Young William returned home with Stina one suppertime and could tell, the moment he walked in, that he was in trouble. Even the dog slunk into a corner. His mother took hold of his ear and dragged him further into the kitchen.

'You haven't been looking after John, have you?' she demanded.

'Who told you?' William grumbled.

'Never you mind who.'

'I bet it was Francis, or one of the Gurwood lasses.'

'I'm not saying. It doesn't matter who. You were told to stay with John. He can't be left alone – you know that.'

'I'm fed up of seeing to him. He's slow. He –' His mother clattered him across the head. This didn't stop him. 'He hardly talks!' William shouted back. 'He just stares at folk!'

'Don't you say another word! From now on, you're not to leave him. And you can go to bed without your supper.'

Young William sulked for days. He wanted more fun and excitement. He especially enjoyed the game of conquering and so, one morning, he took John out to collect snails. He watched his brother stroke each one and kiss it before placing it in the bag. Then he told John to pick one out and hold it still. William pressed another snail against it. He pressed harder and harder until the shell in John's hand cracked.

John stared at the broken snail between his fingers and began to cry.

'I've won,' cried William. 'Pick up another. Go on, John, choose another. You might win this time.'

John shook his head.

'Here – have this one. *This* looks a strong one. Here, take it. Take it, you donkey.'

John picked up the snail with delicate fingers and stroked it.

'Don't be daft. It's a shell. It can't feel anything. Hold it up so I can test it against mine.'

John held the snail out in front. He closed his eyes as William pressed a snail hard against it. He heard the crack.

'*You've* won *this* time,' said William. 'Open your eyes. See – I told you it was strong. Have another go.'

'Want to go home,' John whispered and wiped a tear from his cheek.

'Alright, you baby, we'll go home.'

As they walked back, William thought of a practical joke he could play on his brother. John would believe anything, and it was so easy to scare him.

The next day was very warm, and young William knew there'd be lots of crane flies at the back by the milkhouse window. He collected as many as he could and put them in a muslin bag. Then, when no one was about, he went to the meal chest in the kitchen, lifted the lid and tipped the creatures inside.

'John!' he whispered. 'Come over here. There's a present for you in the meal chest – a nice surprise. You'll love it. Wait till Mother's in the garden. Don't let *her* see.'

They waited until they were alone in the kitchen. John went to the chest where it stood in a dark corner. His eyes were wide with excitement. He struggled with the large lid but managed to prise it up. As he put his head in, a cloud of wings and legs flew into his face. He slammed the lid shut and screamed as if being murdered.

William took fright and ran out the front door.

Their mother heard the noise and rushed in to find John shaking with fear and surrounded by crane flies. She knelt down and held him close, rubbing his back and kissing his head. It was a while before he stopped shaking. Then she relaxed her hold and stood him away from her.

'It was William, wasn't it?' she asked. He sniffed in response. 'Well, he's made himself scarce. Good riddance, eh? You stay in with me today and help me make butter. You can watch Richard for me – stop him putting things in his mouth.'

John sniffed again and had one last shudder. Then he gave his mother a wonderful smile that transformed his face.

She pulled him towards her and hugged him again. If only the rest of the family were so easy to please.

That night, young William was told off by both his parents. It wasn't the trick so much as who he'd played it on. He sulked and wouldn't say sorry.

The next day, he was sent out on his own to tend the cows in the lower pasture. When the cows looked peaceful and unlikely to wander off, he went to sit on the hill in the shade of a gorse bush. It was a hot summer's day, and the flies were bothersome. For a while, he watched butterflies settle on the flowers. He yawned, picked up a stick and poked around the dry soil under the gorse. Then he sighed and watched the butterflies again. He was so bored.

He got to his feet and strolled among the flowers. A butterfly was feeding. He paused to watch its long tongue curl down between the petals. He grabbed it by its wings and held it up to see. When he let it go, his fingers were dusted with a fine yellow powder. He caught different butterflies and moths to see what colour they'd leave and, when he tired of that, he pulled their legs off. Then, out of curiosity, he tore one wing off to see what happened. It wasn't that much fun. He was bored again.

Unbeknown to him, he was being observed. Further up the hill, Milcah Gurwood was picking wild flowers with her two youngest sisters. She knew straight away that it was young William by his lopsided gait, and she could see that he was being cruel. As a daughter of the vicar, she believed she had a right to reprimand the six-year-old boy. Besides, she'd be 20 this year, and her sisters' presence would give added weight. Determined to have a word, she marched her sisters down the hill and stood between him and the sun so that he had to shield his eyes.

'What *do* you think you're doing, William?' she asked.

He shrugged. He didn't know what to say. He hadn't really thought. He just did things.

'It's cruel,' she persisted. 'Can't you see how you're hurting them?'

He hadn't reckoned on that and shrugged again. It was just something he could do, and he'd been bored. The three girls were very pretty standing before him in the sunshine – Milcah especially, with her cheeks flushed in anger and her eyes all dark and shiny. The girls were so clean and tidy in their colourful dresses and white bonnets. Like his father and brothers, he wore the same dull clothes day in, day out, while these Gurwood girls were like wild flowers. Overwhelmed and ashamed, he stared down at his bare dirty feet, at the caked soil between his toes.

Milcah saw his discomfort. 'We won't tell your mother – or anyone else. But please, William,' she pleaded as she took hold of his grubby hand, 'please don't hurt the butterflies again. They've done no harm to you.'

He nodded and yanked his hand away. He was sorry, not for what he'd done, but for the Gurwood girls seeing him in a bad light. They were even being kind to him. He heaved an enormous sigh.

'I've got to go and watch the cows,' he mumbled, and wandered off back to the pasture with his head low.

The Gurwood sisters went back to picking their flowers, pleased to have prevented further cruelty. Milcah gazed at young William in the distance.

'In future, I'm going to keep an eye on that boy.'

Chapter 38

Smuggling went on at Butcher Haven throughout the summer, though it was somewhat haphazard and piecemeal, never a large run. William came to an agreement with the two tanners at Hunmanby that, each time, they'd leave him brandy and tobacco. He could collect the stuff from their stable. It was hidden in the hay above a horse that was known to rear and kick without warning. Whenever William was expected, they'd move the horse. He entered fictitious events into his journal and, to show he was being conscientious, rode twice to Scarborough to hand in a pack of smuggled tobacco. Things were running smoothly, and everyone was satisfied.

Mary informed him that the Gurwood girls were now wearing French lace on their dresses, and that Sarah Ezard was using expensive soap.

'And Matthew's family is drinking tea.'

At harvest time, the smuggling ceased. There was a shortage of men for a safe landing of goods, and runs would not begin until the autumn. The harvest was plentiful, and the fine weather continued well into October. Lofts were brimming with good-quality hay, and the barns were full of sheaves waiting to be threshed. Apples were stored and, at Uphall, the women worked for weeks to bottle fruits and store food for the winter ahead. George Gurwood received his tithes and, as was customary, provided a supper for the leading yeomen. This year, he gave them brandy to drink.

When word came of a typhus outbreak in Hornsea, the villagers were not too concerned. They reckoned they'd be safe enough; after all, they did live miles away to the north. Yet, when it grew colder suddenly at the end of October, the older folk grew apprehensive.

Ben chuntered about the weather and complained to Sarah Ezard. 'It's me big toe an' me knees – they're worse when it's cold an' damp.' He didn't like to admit it, but he was also having trouble with his eyesight. He could no longer work by candlelight. Even outside in the daytime, the sun dazzled him and hurt his eyes. When he walked out with the mule, he fretted that he'd not be able to look after her much more. Fearful of the future, he admitted to Sarah that things were blurred, as if he was peering through a mist.

She inspected his eyes and saw how they'd grown a milky film. 'Oh, Ben, thoo should 'ave spoken sooner. I'll go now an' fetch thee some eye lotion.'

On her return, she put the bottle on his table. 'It's made from eyebright flowers – nowt to worry about. Let me dab a bit o' this clean feather an' I'll dribble it in.'

Though his eyes were blurred, he could see she struggled with the cork on the bottle and her hands shook as she held aloft the feather dripping with lotion. He feared he'd get an eyeful of feather, but she managed to drip the liquid skilfully into each eye.

'There, that should do it,' she said. 'For a bit o' relief, thoo could make thassen a poultice o' rotten apples. Leastways it's right time o' year. Listen, I'll be gatherin' club moss when there's a new moon. I'll come back soon an' I'll 'ave summat better fo' thee.'

'An' 'ow's thoo doin' these days?' he asked. 'Thoo's old like me.'

'It's me 'ands – me fingers more like,' she confessed. 'Thoo's right, I'm gettin' old like rest of us. Cold weather makes me 'ands stiff. I can't get me fingers movin' of a mornin'.'

''Ere, take this, Sarah, in exchange fo' tha medicine.' He pushed a jar of honey across the table. 'Us old folk 'ad best take care, eh?'

On the eve of the auspicious new moon, the weather turned colder, and it rained. In the evening, the sky cleared. Sarah Ezard stood in her doorway staring at the stars and reckoned there'd be a frost in the morning. She didn't look forward to walking out gathering plants with ice on them, though she'd do it for Ben's sake.

She went back indoors and climbed into bed, wearing sheepskin mittens to keep her hands warm. Despite the ache and stiffness, she knew she must keep her fingers supple.

The next day, at sunrise, she washed her hands, stood outside her cottage and held up her knife to the invisible new moon in the east. Then she chanted the usual words.

'As Christ 'ealed the issue o' blood,
Do thou cut what thou cuttest good.'

The moss grew in profusion down Speeton ravine. Once there, she knelt down and used the special knife to cut off plenty of stems. She wrapped them in a white cloth and filled a bottle with fresh water from the stream. Her hands were numb with cold as she trudged back home. There'd be trouble with her fingers that night; she'd need her own medicines to help her sleep.

As soon as she got home, she stoked up the fire and put the bottled water on to boil. She dropped in the moss stems and, after a while, strained the liquid for Ben's eyes into another bottle. As an afterthought, she mixed a few of the strained stems with butter to make an eye ointment. If it was to be potent, she should add the milk from a young cow. That meant another walk out and she thought she'd done enough for one day. At 70 years old, she reckoned it no shame to have a sleep by the fire now and again. 'Let young'uns run about an' do most o' work,' she mumbled to herself.

The young farm servants at Uphall were not running about or working very hard. The ones who'd decided to move on at the next hirings were lazy and oblivious to reprimands. A popular way to show their derision was to drop their breeches and wave their bare behinds. The Jordan brothers were afraid the Gurwood girls would see, and afraid they might have to fight the lads to knock sense into them. Bullock Jack and Muston George were the worst ones, always picking on someone.

Young William heard from his brother Francis how the lads competed in forcing each other over a wall – preferably the one with the dung heap on the other side. Without his parents knowing, he took John to Uphall to see.

The two young brothers hid by the side of the barn. They watched in awe as Bullock Jack and Muston George set upon another lad and sent him flying into the wall, knocking the wind out of him. Then, with almost the same continuous movement, they tipped the lad over and into the stinking, putrid dung.

'Good God!' cried William. 'That was something, wasn't it, John? See the way they did that!'

John stared vacantly, showing no emotion. It didn't make any sense to him. He could never understand why his brother got excited about such things or why he wanted to watch. He tugged at William's sleeve.

'Go home now. Want to go home.'

'You dolt! You always want to go just when it's getting good.' He sighed. 'Come on then, before you start bluthering.'

The next day, when the two brothers were out together gathering sticks from under the trees near Uphall, William sneaked off and left John by himself. He hoped to see more wrestling.

John carried on collecting sticks, putting them methodically in the sack. It was a while before he realised he was on his own. When William did not return, he left the sack and walked over to Uphall, reaching the shed where a sick ewe was kept. He heard laughter from inside and peeped in to see.

A group of hired lads were holding the sheep. One stood astride the ewe's neck and held its head while the other two kept its body still. Another lad had his breeches down. He saw John out of his eye corner and shouted.

'Now then – we're just givin' sheep 'er medicine.' The others laughed.

John watched without understanding. Something wasn't right, yet he remained puzzled. He shrugged and wandered off to seek his brother. He met William at the end of the yard carrying the sack of sticks.

'John – I told you to stay near the trees! Can't you ever stay put?' Then he noticed John's pale face. 'What's up? You don't look very well.' Now guilty at leaving him, he asked more gently, 'Are you alright? You know, you shouldn't wander off.'

John took William's hand. 'Go home now.' He felt sick and miserable and had no way of describing or explaining what he'd seen.

That night, John couldn't sleep and fidgeted so much that his mother thought he might have worms. In the morning, she fetched wormseed and treacle from Sarah Ezard. On Sarah's advice, she treated all the boys. John could not have been more unpopular. Mary had no sympathy for the older boys, but she pitied poor John. He was like the runt of a litter and needed more love and attention.

Sarah Ezard could not hide her arthritis for much longer. She was afraid folk would notice her crab-like hands when she handed over her medicines. She could just about manage to gather herbs and make decoctions, though had trouble grinding powders and filling narrow-necked bottles. Greater problems could arise if she was called upon as a midwife.

Matthew Smith's wife Ellen went into labour on Bonfire Night. She had three children already, each one delivered with no trouble; it was as if she was made for childbearing. Matthew was instructed not to fetch Sarah until Ellen was well into her labour. She paced about the chamber breathing heavily whenever a contraction came, expecting the birth to be over soon. After another couple of hours, she began to worry. This time was different.

'Matthew, leave me now an' fetch Sarah – I think summat's wrong.'

Matthew put on his coat and boots but did not leave before saying his mind. He argued that he could afford a proper surgeon; for five guineas, she could have the best help, all the new instruments if it proved a difficult birth.

She shook her head and protested. 'What – an' 'ave bairn pulled out by a hook? Never. Besides, Sarah's brought most o' village into this world. I trust 'er.'

He suggested fetching Barbara Nicholson from Hunmanby, or a married couple from Filey, all licensed midwives.

Ellen was adamant. 'Thoo can't go ridin' to 'Unmanby or Filey i' dark – so there's an end to it. Just fetch Sarah.' Ellen couldn't be bothered to argue. She winced as the next contraction took hold. 'Matthew!' she bellowed. 'Fetch 'er!'

He took a lantern and left, knowing he'd not see his wife properly again for weeks.

When Sarah saw it was Matthew at the door, she expected to be aiding another straightforward delivery. However, in the light from the lantern, his face was anxious, even angry.

''As summat 'appened?' she asked.

'No, not yet. Listen – I wanted Ellen to have a male surgeon, not a midwife. But she insists she wants you. May God forgive me – and you – if anything goes wrong.'

Sarah set off with her bag. She was confident in her knowledge and experience and yet worried about her hands, afraid they might let her down at a critical moment. She tried to appear confident and optimistic.

'They say, "Good nut year, good baby year." I'm sure Ellen'll give thee another fine bairn.' When he didn't reply, she justified her role as midwife. 'It's i' Bible, Matthew – God found favour with us midwives. We 'ave authority from God to deliver bairns. Why, us midwives even 'ad special 'ouses built.'

He didn't answer and they reached the house in silence. Matthew opened the door and pushed her in. Then he left to fetch his mother and Susanna Gurwood. He would spend the rest of the evening with the vicar rather than drink ale and watch the dancing round a dying bonfire.

While Matthew stretched his legs out before the vicarage fire and drank mulled wine, his wife was doubled up in pain. There was no sign yet of the baby wanting to come. Sarah Ezard wasted no time in giving Ellen a dose of deadly nightshade and henbane. The labour was not progressing as it should, but at least the medicine should slow Ellen's heartbeats and relax her muscles. She frowned and sat by a candle to consult her little book.

Ellen watched Sarah unhook the book from her belt and open it. The pages were well thumbed. She prayed that Sarah knew what to do.

When the other women arrived and opened the door, the smell of bonfire smoke filled the chamber. Sarah reckoned it would be a memorable night one way or another. Without putting her hand up inside Ellen, she couldn't tell whether the baby's head or its bottom was presenting first. Although she moved her hands over and around Ellen's womb, her fingers no longer had their magic touch – they were as stiff and awkward as carrots. She spoke cheerfully to hide her alarm.

'Ellen, thoo 'as a lazy bairn. It doesn't want to come out yet.' If her fingers had been more flexible, she might have massaged Ellen's 'privities', as she called them. The contractions would be stimulated, grow stronger and the labour would speed up. She'd never been keen on that method though, preferring a calm, unhurried approach.

Ellen screamed suddenly. 'I want to push! Let me squat an' push. I'm sure bairn's ready.'

'Nay lass, not yet. I've a better idea. Lie o' tha back across bed an' dangle tha legs over edge. An' don't push. Wait till I tell thee.'

When Ellen was in position, Sarah gave instructions to the women. 'Take 'old of a leg each, stretch 'em apart an' 'old tight. Now, don't worry, Ellen – I need to take a peep inside.'

Sarah went down on her knees. On inspection, she saw what appeared to be a baby's bottom appearing. She prayed to God she could do what was necessary. Using both hands, she tried to ease the bottom out, all the time fearing the cord might be trapped. The baby could not be delivered as it was. It would have to be turned.

'Listen, Ellen, I'm goin' to go up inside thee to turn bairn around a bit. Sorry, but it'll 'urt an' I want thee to pant, not push. Alright?'

Ellen nodded and began to pant in readiness.

Under her apron, Sarah rubbed her hands together, both to warm them and unbend the fingers that were the most crooked. Taking a deep breath, she put her hand up inside. She could feel the baby's bent limbs and struggled for what seemed ages before finally hooking her fingers over the legs. Slowly, she managed to ease them out. Part of the cord was visible, purple and still pulsing. That was a relief.

'Ellen, when next pain comes, push a bit.'

Ellen obeyed, and the baby came out but only as far as the shoulders. There it stuck.

'It's a girl, Ellen,' Sarah announced. 'Don't push anymore, not just yet. I'll 'elp thee deliver 'er. Wait while I grab a cloth.' She was relieved that it was a girl since girls' heads were usually smaller than boys'. Grateful for such mercies, she wrapped a piece of linen round the baby's body to get a better grip. Then she hooked a finger under one of the arms and managed to turn the baby a little so that one shoulder appeared.

'Push a bit more now, Ellen. That's right – both shoulders are out.'

There was just the head left. Sarah was trembling with the effort and the fear of failure. Sweat was dripping off both her and Ellen. Matthew's mother mopped their brows while Susanna Gurwood held Ellen's hand and tried to comfort her.

'Now, Ellen,' Sarah instructed, 'I want thee to push 'ard. Push as if tha life depended on it. Push *really* 'ard.'

Ellen breathed in, grimaced and began to bear down. She ground her teeth together as she used all her strength. She grunted like an animal with her last effort and left nail marks in the back of Susanna's hands.

Suddenly, the head came out and it was over. Sarah was as relieved as Ellen. The baby had a blue tinge, so she held her upside down by the ankles and slapped her until she cried. After the cord had been cut and tied, Matthew's mother pressed a shilling into Sarah's damp palm.

'I thank thee,' said Sarah. 'I hope tha doesn't mind me leaving thee to wash bairn. I'm tired an' it's gettin' late.' It was an excuse. She didn't want them to see her crippled hands. She borrowed a lantern and smiled as she left. On her way home, she vowed it would be her last delivery.

Chapter 39

A week later, Matthew's new daughter was christened. Everyone was there on time and sitting in their usual places – everyone except the gentry and the Smiths. The box pew for the Cockerell family was predictably vacant since the gentry, if they were to attend at all, would arrive late. Yet the Jordans were surprised to see the Smiths' pew also empty.

Dorothy Jordan whispered to her husband, 'I can smell beeswax polish. Someone's been busy. An' we don't normally 'ave so many candles. It's not as if it were a Sunday.'

He leant towards her and breathed in her ear, 'William says Matthew wanted even more candles. Vicar told him it were too popish.' Both were wondering why the Smiths were so late to arrive. Were they hoping to make an entrance?

The eight Gurwood girls were seated with their mother close to the Smiths' pew and kept their eyes on the floor. They wished to avoid the glances of the young men, including the Jordan boys, who would keep craning their necks to ogle them. Their mother turned her head and frowned to discourage such behaviour in church. At least, she thought, my girls' presence stops the boys fidgeting and searching under the pews for newts.

All eyes were on Matthew Smith when he entered the church. 'Oh, no!' Mary hissed to William. 'Look what he's wearing!' She giggled at his legs; her brother was wearing black plush breeches.

William was amazed to see Matthew in a short, dark bob wig and with a red cloak thrown over an expensive woollen coat. He even wore white gloves. As Matthew stepped into his pew, William caught a glimpse of a fancy white shirt and patterned silk waistcoat.

'That's too obvious,' William snapped, 'aping the gentry like that.'

'Talk of the devil...' Mary nudged him. Thomas Cockerell, lord of the manor, was now striding in with his family and was wearing similar clothes. 'My brother certainly has ambitions.'

As the vicar welcomed everyone and began a brief introductory service, William reflected on his own simple but clean white shirt and his old grey coat. He did not envy Matthew so much as wonder at the difference between them. He peered across the aisle at him sitting so proudly with his three daughters and one son. Most people, he reckoned, would have preferred sons to daughters and yet, when he glanced at his own boys, he had to acknowledge that his eldest was not robust, his next son walked lopsided, and poor John was tuppence short of a shilling. As for the baby, Richard, hc had yet to survive his first year.

George Gurwood signalled for the family and godparents to gather round the font. As a churchwarden, William attended and walked beside Mary, who'd been chosen as one of the godparents. He disliked having to stand still in the stuffy church and resigned himself to the full-length baptism that Matthew had requested. Mary's childless sister Elizabeth was another godparent, and the girl was to be named after her. To William's surprise, the other godparent was none other than Thomas Cockerell.

Matthew held the baby tightly swaddled and wrapped in a white shawl. As soon as she woke up and began to work her lips in hunger, he passed her to Elizabeth.

'Dearly beloved,' the vicar began, 'ye have brought this child here to be baptised; ye have prayed that our Lord Jesus Christ would vouchsafe to receive her, to release her of her sins, to sanctify her with the Holy Ghost, to give her the kingdom of heaven, and everlasting life.' Various responses were given and then George Gurwood prayed and sanctified the water.

Elizabeth prayed that the baby keep quiet. The tiny girl's eyes were screwed up as if she was ready to bawl the place down.

The vicar noticed the problem and speeded up. 'Grant that this child, now to be baptised therein, may receive the fullness of thy grace, and ever remain in the number of thy faithful and elect children; through Jesus Christ our Lord.' Then, rather gingerly, he took the baby from Elizabeth and held her over the font. 'Name this child.'

'Elizabeth,' the group responded, and the vicar poured water over the baby's head. This was the moment for the girl to emit a high-pitched wail. The vicar shouted above the racket.

'I baptise thee in the name of the Father, and of the Son, and of the Holy Ghost.' He made the sign of the cross on the girl's forehead, almost threw her back to Elizabeth and proceeded to say prayers of thanksgiving. The baby squalled throughout.

At last, the whole congregation knelt for the Lord's Prayer. More prayers were uttered and then everyone stood again to pray for the godparents.

William thought it would never end – either the prayers or the wailing. He wondered if George Gurwood was adding extra prayers and ritual because Thomas Cockerell was present.

Afterwards, folk gathered in the churchyard to offer their respects. The baby quietened down in the cold air, and the women crowded round to see who she looked like. Sarah Ezard thought the girl had Ellen's eyebrows and mouth. 'She's goin' to be a beauty, like 'er mother.' When the others agreed, she showed off the tea caddy she'd been given by Thomas Cockerell; it was made of wood, shaped like a squat bottle and was full of tea. Until then, she'd never received much for her services. Remembering her vow, she trusted that John Gurwood would make other arrangements for his wife; she was due her first child next month.

John Gurwood's wife was from Bridlington. She'd always planned to have a proper licensed midwife and so, as soon as the very first signs of labour began, John left her with his mother and rode to Bridlington to fetch Eleanor Hodgson. It was the morning of Christmas Eve. John set off, wrapped up warm against the cold but sunny day and, on his father's advice, he wound cloths round the horse's legs to prevent cuts from the frozen puddles.

On his way back to Reighton with Mrs Hodgson, the weather changed. A northwesterly wind sprang up and occasional showers of sleet lashed their faces. Nothing deterred the woman. Huddled in thick clothes and a riding cape, she rode confidently next to John and never stopped talking. She made sure he knew how expensive her licence was and what he was getting for his money. Then she rattled off her usual well-worn patter.

'Tha knows I've sworn not, in any wise, to neither use nor exercise any manner o' witchcraft. No, nor charm nor sorcery nor invocation.' She paused for breath. 'Nor any other prayers that may stand against God's laws an' King's.'

'Very good,' answered John, already tired of hearing her voice.

'An' I shall not give any counsel, nor minister any 'erb, medicine, nor potion, nor owt else to a woman bein' wi' child whereby she would destroy or cast out that child before 'er time.' She paused for breath again.

He took his chance and shouted against the sleet flying into his face. 'That's hardly necessary in this case, is it? I'm asking you to deliver a child that is wanted and ready to be born.'

'Well, I've more to say.'

'Look – I've heard enough already. You can stop now.' But she would not be curtailed.

'If any child be dead-born, I must see it buried i' such a secret place as neither hog nor dog nor any other beast may come unto it.'

'God forbid. You've said more than enough.'

'An' I will not suffer any such dead child to be cast into a midden nor any other inconvenient place.'

'Utter one more word,' John warned, 'and I'll take you back to Bridlington. We have a woman in the village that's as good as you.' And a lot quieter and more considerate, he thought.

'Thoo'll 'ave to pay me if tha takes me back.'

His nerves were on edge. It was his first child, and he was afraid for his wife. 'If you stop talking, we'll get there sooner. And when we get to Reighton, you just do your job well and you'll be paid.'

'Fine!' she answered. 'Fine! I'll say nowt else. Nowt shall pass me lips.'

He could still hear her mumbling and grumbling under her hood all the way to Reighton.

As soon as they reached his cottage, he helped the woman off her horse and led her through the door towards the parlour.

'Mother,' he shouted, 'the midwife's here.' He watched Mrs Hodgson waddle in carrying her bag of God-knows-what. He blew out his cheeks with relief. His mother could deal with the woman now and he'd escape to the vicarage.

As John sat by the fire singing carols and drinking frumenty with his father and sisters, his wife gave birth to a healthy son. The boy was to be named George after his grandfather. The midwife stayed the night and then demanded to be ridden back to Bridlington on Christmas Day. John paid the full fee and, although the last thing he wanted was a ride to Bridlington, he thought it better to get rid of the woman than have her hanging on over Christmas.

'Just do me one courtesy,' he asked her, 'try and be quiet. It's a sunny day and I have a healthy son – don't spoil the day with your prattle.'

'Fine!' she replied. 'Fine! That's fine by me, but don't ask me to come 'ere again. Reighton's a miserable 'ole. I wouldn't come back if tha paid me treble.'

Chapter 40

1719

The winter was turning out milder than expected. The animals had enough good-quality fodder, and folk managed their supplies well. The smuggling that went on provided the village with luxuries, and William found that he had more than enough brandy and tobacco.

In January, when William went to Bridlington on market day, he decided that, when he'd offloaded his surplus illicit goods, he'd spend the money on woollen cloth for the family's clothes.

With all good intentions, he entered The Green Dragon and duly sold his tobacco. Neither John Beale nor the local constable was present. There was a strong aroma of mulled wine and rum drifting from the fireplace, and a warm haze hung above the men in the main room. William was reluctant to go back out into the cold, so he lingered and ordered a dog's nose, one of his favourite tipples. A noggin of gin was added to his mug of beer, and he looked around for the group of men in the smuggling trade. When one called him over, he strolled across to join them in a side room.

'We've already appointed our officer for today,' the leader explained. 'He's ordered our bottles, so why not spend some time with us – thoo knows tha likes a good drink or two – or three.'

William smiled and unbuttoned his coat, glad of the company. The month of January was always going to be difficult, it being two years since his daughter had died. The hurt of that loss never left him. Lively conversation coupled with drink and bravado was a good distraction. He sat at their table and put his money in the hat going round. Soon, they were served with pewter cups and three bottles, and their cups filled to the brim with Dutch gin.

'William, propose our first toast, there's a good man.'

'To a dark night and a gentle tide.' They drank to that, and toasts then followed to various local heroes of the free trade. When that bottle was empty, they opened the West Indian rum. Conversation meandered into horseracing and other pleasures. This led to toasts to favourite horses and then to local whores until the rum bottle was empty. Last of all came the bottle of port.

William burped. He wished he didn't have such a long ride home, but he didn't refuse either. His cup was filled, and he drank to whatever toast was proposed.

'To one-eyed constables – may they only see 'alf o' what goes on.'

'An' 'ere's to a revenue ship with a leaky bottom.'

'Aye an' torn, flappin' sails.'

William's sight was becoming blurred. He thought he'd better take his leave. 'I've a long ride ahead,' he mumbled in excuse.

'Nay, William, 'ave one more drink before tha goes. Landlord's made us lemon punch.'

William shook his head and stood up. The room was spinning, and he was unsteady on his feet.

The men would not take no for an answer. 'If thoo won't 'ave punch, then we'll get thee a brandy an' 'ot water. That'll warm thee up for tha ride back to Reighton.'

'Aye,' another agreed, 'an' get landlord to add a bit o' gin. Then thoo'll be right.'

William sat down again.

As soon as he'd finished his cup of punch, he struggled to get up. He swayed and grabbed the edge of the table for support. The door seemed a long way off. Somehow, he managed to stagger through the mist of pipe smoke and call for his horse. He opened the door, leant against the post and gulped in the cold air.

When his horse was led to him, he handed over his last few pennies and had a leg up onto the saddle. He slumped over the mane, and the horse, knowing its way home, set off at a brisk trot.

The ride was too quick for William's comfort. If he slipped off, he doubted he'd be able to remount. On the way back to Reighton, he had the vague recurring thought – he'd done it again, had spent all his money on drink and had nothing to show for his trip. Trusting his horse, he let himself doze, but each time they had to go through a deep rut, he was jolted awake. The one time he did fall off, he didn't hurt himself. He slid off so slowly that he landed with a soft thump like an overloaded sack. The horse waited with great patience while he fought to remount.

It was late afternoon and getting dark when William finally reached Reighton. He left his horse at Uphall and tottered down the hill. No longer warm and mellow from the drink, he was irritable and cold. By the time he reached his house, he was in a foul temper.

Mary and the boys were dreading a late return, for they knew he'd have been drinking. He'd be in a vile temper and find fault with everyone and everything. They'd learnt the hard way to leave him alone. Mary watched his arrival from the garden, saw him spit in the road and trudge with his shoulders hunched. She ran inside to warn the children.

'Quick, lads, your father's back. Get into bed. Pretend you're asleep.'

'But we haven't had our supper,' Francis complained.

'Do as you're told. Don't argue or you'll be sorry.' The boys heard the front door slam shut as they rushed into the parlour. Francis took young Richard into his own bed and hid him under the blanket. Young William and John pulled out the truckle bed and dived into it.

John thought it was a game. 'When do we say "boo"?'

'Shush, John. Be quiet. It's not funny,' Francis warned. 'Pretend you're asleep. That's the game. Don't move.'

'Like dead fishes?' John asked in a voice muffled by the hairy blanket.

'Yes. Whoever wins gets a gingerbread biscuit.' That shut him up.

They held their breath as their parents argued in the kitchen. Pots were thrown and knives and spoons clattered onto the floor. There was a dull thud and the dog yelped.

Young William wanted to leap out and get Stina. He couldn't believe they'd forgotten to get her.

'Francis,' he hissed. 'Go and get the dog.'

'No. You go if you're that worried.'

'I think I'd better.' He put his hand over John's mouth. 'John, be quiet and don't you move. You're still in the game.'

John lay rigid, making a very good impression of a dead fish.

Francis was having second thoughts. 'No, Will, I didn't mean you to go. Don't do it. Stina can look after herself. She can bite if need be – or run away.'

'She won't though. She's a good dog. I'm going to get her.' He tiptoed to the door and opened it a fraction so he could see what was going on.

His father had his hands round his mother's hair. Her bonnet hung loose round her neck, and he was dragging her towards the fire. The dog was cowering under the table. Unseen, young William shot in and joined the dog. He put his hand beneath Stina's collar and tried to pull her away, but she wouldn't budge.

'Stina, come on,' he whispered urgently, afraid for both of them. The dog dug its claws into the earthen floor and refused to move. They were trapped and now his mother was crying. He couldn't bear to hear and put his hands over his ears. Suddenly, his stomach churned, and he thought he'd be sick. There was nothing for it; he had to do something.

He found himself rolling out from under the table. He threw himself at his father's legs. He had no plan – he just wanted it all to stop.

His father lurched when he felt the weight round his shins. He let go of Mary and stared down in surprise. When he tried to move, his son held on tight. Then he burst out laughing.

Mary stepped away and forced a smile. She smoothed down her clothes and stuffed her hair back under her bonnet, trying to look as if nothing had happened.

Young William still held on.

'You rapscallion, you,' his father murmured with tears now filling his eyes. When his legs were free, he sank down onto the bench, put his head in his hands and sobbed.

Mary and the boy glanced at each other. She bit her lip, ashamed he'd seen his father in this state.

'Go back to bed, Will,' she said softly. 'I'll be fine now. I'll bring you something to eat. And I'll make sure the dog is fed.' She guessed her husband's behaviour was due as much to the loss of young Mary as to the drink. If he wouldn't talk about it though, there was little she could do. He'd be guilty now about hurting her and upsetting his son. When he cried like this, he looked so vulnerable.

The whole village knew about William Jordan's problem. Folk chuntered about the state he got into, glad it was none of their business. The women pitied Mary and the boys. George Gurwood was reluctant to interfere, but his wife and daughters persuaded him to act. After all, it was shameful with William still a churchwarden.

The vicar timed his visit carefully. He went to William's house on a Sunday evening when the children were in bed. His wife came too and invited Mary to the vicarage to see the new quilt the girls were making.

When the two men were alone, they sat opposite each other at the kitchen table. William took out his tobacco and they filled their pipes, ready to enjoy a quiet time without the women. Neither spoke for a while, sucking at their pipes and listening to the wood settling in the grate.

George wondered if he should start by talking about the weather. It was already late in January, and they'd had very little snow. For him, the winter was proving quite relaxing, yet he sensed the tension in William. He knew that this time two years ago, young Mary had been fighting for her life. William would be remembering each detail afresh.

'We need a drink to go with our pipes,' William said and fetched a jug of beer. He held the poker in the fire, waited until it was hot and then dipped it in the jug. The beer hissed and he poured it into two tankards.

'Here's to us.' He drank half of his straightaway, wiping his mouth afterwards on his shirtsleeve.

George waited for his beer to cool. He warmed his hands round the tankard for a while before speaking his mind.

'I've been meaning to ask you, and don't think I'm criticising, but... do you really need to drink so often?' William didn't answer. 'You never used to. It's just a thought.' William still didn't reply. George put a hand on his arm. 'Perhaps I could help you in some way.'

There was a long pause. William sniffed and still didn't answer. They heard the wind getting up outside, blowing leaves and twigs against the window. George sipped his beer and waited.

William drained the rest of his tankard and went to refill it. He took his time walking back and then sat down as if exhausted. Staring into his beer so that he didn't have to look the vicar in the eye, he tried to explain.

'I don't know as you'll understand, but I feel different when I'm drinking. I feel free. I can forget for a while.' He raised his eyes. 'You know what I mean?'

George nodded in full sympathy.

'It's two years now.' William's eyes welled with tears, and he swallowed hard. 'I can't help myself. When I'm with the others, drinking, we have a laugh, we joke, we take bets.' He wiped away the tears with his hand and then shouted, 'And – I'm away from here!' He waved his arms about and then, remembering the boys were asleep in bed, he lowered his voice. 'I can't forget, especially here. How can I? The drink helps.'

'You should be here at home though, not out with your drinking partners. Your family needs you.'

William's sombre mood turned to anger. 'Don't you tell me where I need to be and who with! When I want to drink, I'll drink.' He lifted his tankard, drained it without stopping and then banged it down empty on the table. 'There! I'll do what I like!'

His anger didn't last. George had not judged him. There was no reason to shout. He was angrier with himself. The good times at the inns never made up for the bad evening and day that followed. He was always so tired and sick the day after, of little use to anyone. No wonder his family kept their distance.

'I'm sorry, George, I didn't mean to shout at you. And I am sorry for hurting Mary and the boys. I am, truly, believe me.' He leant over the table and grabbed George's arm. 'Believe me! I am so sorry. I'll do better. I will. I promise.'

George was not sure that William was capable of change. He knew of other cases where men could not leave drink alone no matter how hard they tried or how sorry they were.

'I believe you do want to change. Listen, William, come and see me any time if you're low in spirits. Sorry!' He put his hands up and grinned. 'I didn't mean if you're short of brandy!'

William laughed and shook his head. 'I don't know – there can't be many vicars like you.'

They shook hands and parted on good terms. William realised what a privilege it was to have George Gurwood in the village. He wouldn't have swapped him for anyone. As he sat waiting for Mary's return, he thought seriously about what he'd promised. At the same time, he was imagining a tot of brandy sliding hot down his throat and warming his belly.

Chapter 41

Two weeks later, William faced his first test of keeping sober. He rode to Bridlington with his spare tobacco and left his horse at The Green Dragon as usual. Instead of going in, he walked to The Black Lion on the High Street, had just the one tankard of beer and sold half his tobacco. There he overheard talk of the new anti-smuggling act that had come into force. The man serving drinks was holding forth to an attentive audience.

'From now on,' he announced as he passed over a bottle, 'any ship less than 50 ton can be forced into port. That's if it's carryin' brandy, an' it's hoverin' around within two leagues o' coast – without *proper* cause.'

William wasn't too concerned. There were so few revenue ships, and they had such a large area to patrol. Besides, even if caught, the smugglers would only lose their ship and cargo. They'd not be hanged for it, and the men who put up the money would compensate them. The boats carrying the goods from Holland would be at greater risk as they hung around waiting for a signal from the cliffs. William shrugged. Nothing would change. He finished his beer and left the inn.

It was late morning, and he was hungry, so he decided to walk on to The Bull and Sun, have a pie there and sell the rest of the tobacco. As he left the High Street and crossed the road to Church Green, the north wind sent flurries of snow. He turned up his collar and pressed his hat down. It was a miserable day with nothing but cold beer in his belly.

Once inside The Bull and Sun, he chose to sit in the kitchen rather than the parlour. There was a good fire going and the boiled hams and cheeses on the shelves looked inviting. He ordered bread and cheese and, reluctantly, another beer, though he longed for something stronger. Sitting on a high-backed settle by the hearth, he warmed his hands. When he'd eaten, he prised off his boots and held his stockinged feet up to the blazing coals.

By this time, more men were piling in for their midday meal. William watched them jostle and swear as they settled down to their pies and pasties. A couple of shopkeepers in long aprons moved him along the seat to make room. They ordered a jug of mild beer and asked the landlord for tobacco. As William put his boots back on, he nudged the man next to him.

'I have tobacco.' He took out a pack from inside his coat and held it to the man's nose. 'It's best quality. Try it, then maybe you'll want to buy it.'

'Don't mind if I do. 'Ere, Jack, thoo 'ave a sniff an' all.' Eager to try a different tobacco, they tamped it down and lit spills from the roaring fire. Then they leant back and sucked rapidly to get their pipes alight. They smacked their lips and reflected as the smoke rose around them.

The elder of the two gave nothing away. He intended to drive a hard bargain when he bought it. He puffed away quietly. When he did speak at last, he was slow and deliberate.

'To be fair,' he said as he took a gentle sip at his pipe, 'there i'n't much to choose between this an' landlord's.'

Jack wasn't so sure. 'Aye, but this baccy's more moist. It don't rip tha throat out like some others.'

'Per'aps.' The older man nodded, most unwilling to praise William's tobacco. 'See 'ere, Jack, if thoo'd just buy a new pipe an' not keep that old broken off nose-warmer, then thoo'd talk more sense. That pipe o' thine is so short thoo'll singe the 'airs up tha nose.'

'There's nowt wrong wi' me favourite stubby. Anyways, I can see this baccy's a better colour. Look – it's golden. T'other one o' landlord's is pale – lost all its colour.'

'Well... I don't know as much.' The man was not giving an inch. He leant back on the settle and scratched his ear.

William decided to speed up the deal. 'It's cheaper the more you buy. You can resell it in your shops and make a decent profit.'

Jack was delighted but left it to the other to negotiate a price. It didn't take long. Soon, William was rid of the rest of his tobacco and had a pouch full of cash. To close the deal, he bought them another beer and, although he'd already eaten, he asked for a whole cheese to be brought too.

When the cheese arrived, they were handed spoons. They soon realised why – it was to scoop away the maggots. William didn't fancy it, though the men were not deterred by the wriggling cheese. They tucked in as if it was a rare treat.

When they'd finished their drinks, William ordered rum punch. He was beginning to feel loose, friendly to everyone. Those around him sensed a good drinker and encouraged him with toasts. Before long, a crowd of men of varied character and occupation had gathered round. The kitchen table was moved nearer the hearth and the men sat round it, hoping to spend the whole afternoon there. They expected to have a fine time. Away from home and with plenty to drink, they could curse and make jokes, and be free to say whatever they liked.

The drinking became competitive. More punch was bought, and each cup filled to the brim. To refuse was to lose face. They tried to outdo each other with stories of past drinking bouts.

'Remember that man what 'ad a bet 'e could sup a dozen pints o' cider an' brandy in 'alf an hour?'

'Aye,' they yelled.

'But 'e dropped dead,' someone reminded them.

'Aye,' they mumbled, recalling the event with mixed emotions. They drank to his memory.

It wasn't long before the talk grew argumentative, and toasts became more personal and political.

'A toast to Germany,' one shouted. 'May King George never come back.' Everyone repeated it, drained their cups and banged them upside down on the table.

'I wish we'd never 'ad 'im for a king,' grumbled another.

'Aye, an' none of 'is German women neither.'

'Women? Is that what thoo calls 'em? A maypole, one of 'em looks like – she's that tall an' scrawny an' dressed up showy.'

'T'other one's fat as fat. I' London they calls pair of 'em Elephant an' Castle.'

The men laughed, including William. Like them, he was unhappy at having a king who couldn't be bothered to learn English and who preferred to live in Hanover. Now that he thought about it, he was angry at the taxes as well, at having to finance the national debt. The fact that the King gave money and fine presents to his German courtiers incensed him further. He stood up, swaying a little.

'Fill up your cups,' he commanded. 'I have a toast.' They refilled and waited with glittering eyes. 'To King George – the sour little turnip – may he rot in hell and all his cronies with him.'

'Aye, may George rot,' they echoed and drained their cups.

By this time, men in the parlour had heard the raised voices. A few were now standing in the kitchen doorway watching and listening. Two of them were well-dressed and looked out of place. They did not approve.

'Should we intervene?' asked one.

'No,' said the other. 'Wait. They might say more – him in particular.' He gestured with his head towards William. 'I've seen him before – at The Green Dragon, passing on tobacco. His name's Jordan. He's definitely not one of *our*s.'

'You want to report him, get him dealt with?'

'Let's wait. He's drunk as a wheelbarrow. Give him enough rope and he'll hang himself.'

William obliged. He was pot-valiant and ready to say anything.

'That king of ours,' he bellowed, 'that so-called king...' He paused to wipe his mouth and burp. 'That king can't even treat his wife right, let alone his subjects.

I hear he's locked her away in a castle. She can't even see her own children – or her father.'

The men around him nodded and muttered among themselves.

'And what's more,' William shouted, 'he even dares to employ two Turks in his bedchamber.' He gazed around to see their response. 'Think on – not even a true Englishman in his bedchamber! Two bloody Turks forever at his side, to dress him, warm his shirts *and* watch him piss. Turks!' He spat on the ground in disgust.

This was news to some of them and they wondered why the King would choose Turks.

William enlightened them and passed on rumours he'd heard at other inns and alehouses. He lowered his voice.

'I've heard he has these Turks to satisfy his filthy, unnatural lusts.'

The gentlemen in the doorway had heard enough. They left and went straight to the local constable, described William and registered a complaint.

After two weeks, William received a letter, his second summons to the quarter sessions at Beverley. This time he was charged with 'speaking dangerous, malicious and reflecting words of the King.'

Mary was embarrassed. 'What on earth have you been saying?' He couldn't remember. She told her brother Matthew, showed him the letter and asked him to accompany William when the time came.

Matthew read the names on the letter and knew immediately that it was more to do with competition between the free traders. He handed the letter back to Mary and apologised.

'I'm afraid I can't help him this time, and it'll be a 40-shilling fine if he doesn't attend. Listen, all I can do is try to persuade him to be more discreet in future and not flaunt his extra tobacco so much. And he must get control of his drinking habits and his temper.'

Mary chewed a fingernail. 'It's a long time till Easter and the next sessions.' She took a deep breath. 'I don't know if William can stay out of trouble that long.'

Chapter 42

Mary took the unprecedented step of going to Uphall when William was out in the fields. She loitered in the yard, waiting for his father to appear and hoping to avoid his mother. It wasn't long before Francis and Dickon left the kitchen and headed towards the stable. In a few strides she was at their side and held Francis's arm.

'Please can I speak with you?' she asked.

'What's up, lass?'

'I'd like you to keep William from going to Bridlington. You know why he's got a summons?'

'Aye, 'e's a damn fool. All this so-called customs officer work will ruin 'im.'

'So, I thought... if you kept him busier here, then he wouldn't have time to... you know...'

Francis and Dickon glanced at each other. Neither of them had ever had a problem with drink. Dickon wandered off, mumbling something about ploughing the fallow field.

'Aye,' agreed Francis. 'I'll see to it. I'll make sure William's fully occupied wi' ploughin' an' sowin' right till Easter.'

'Thank you.' She gave a tight-lipped smile and added, 'Matthew's not going with him this time. I suggested he take Robert Storey.'

'Robert?!' he spluttered.

'That was William's reaction. I think he'd rather take Francis. He'll be 12 this summer and I know it would be good for him to see Beverley and all that but...' She shook her head. 'I don't want him to see his father at the courthouse.'

'It might do the lad good to see what 'appens when tha breaks the law.'

'We'll see. Maybe I can persuade him to take someone else.'

The night before William's journey to Beverley, he dreamed he was in a burrow deep underground, safe and far away from prying eyes. When he awoke, he continued to feel protected. Mary and the boys were still asleep, so he eased himself from the bed and went outside to wash. A few stars were still visible as he groped his way in the dark towards the bucket of water. He dipped his head right in and then shook his hair. Shivering with the cold and the thought of the day ahead, he recalled this time last year.

Matthew had arrived at Uphall dressed like a gentleman and looking forward to the trip. William sighed, reflecting once more on the difference between them. He shook his head again to rid himself of the annoying sense that he was Matthew's inferior. Such thoughts were not helpful. He went into the kitchen and blew on the fire, added a faggot of gorse and set a pan of water to boil.

He appreciated that Mary had put out his best shirt and breeches the night before. She'd also cleaned his riding boots, brushed his coat and polished the buttons. Now he just needed to have a shave without cutting himself. As he sharpened the razor on the strap, it occurred to him, quite matter-of-factly, that he could cut his throat and have done with it all. In his heart, he knew he never would, but the thought was there.

When Mary woke up, she forgot for a moment what day it was. Then, realising, she woke Francis, dressed as fast as she could and set about making their porridge. While William and Francis ate their breakfast, she rushed around for extra clothes to keep them warm.

'Don't fuss,' William complained. 'It won't be that cold once the sun comes up.'

She handed the woollens to Francis. 'Be careful,' she warned. 'Listen to your father and do as he says. I'll enjoy hearing about Beverley tomorrow when you get back.'

The sky was lightening in the east as father and son trudged in silence up the hill to Uphall. Dickon was standing waiting with the horse. William mounted, but when Dickon prepared to give Francis a leg up to sit behind, the boy balked.

He looked up at his father and mumbled, 'I'm not coming.'

'What?'

'I'll stay behind with Mother.'

'But I thought you were keen to come with me. I thought you wanted to see Beverley.'

'I've changed my mind.'

'Well...' William blew out his cheeks. He was speechless. He'd have jumped at the chance of going somewhere new when he was that age. Young William wouldn't have backed out; it was a pity he was too young. And young Mary, she'd have loved to go with him.

'Well,' he repeated. He sighed and stared at Dickon, who was equally shocked. 'I suppose I'll go on my own then. I'll see you both tomorrow… I hope. You'd better wish me luck – I think I'll need it.'

'Aye,' said Dickon, 'let's 'ope it turns out alright and tha can come 'ome again.' He gave the horse a gentle slap on the rump. As it set off, he ruffled the boy's hair. 'An' thoo'd best get on 'ome an' explain to tha mother.' He wondered if the lad had an ulterior motive for staying in Reighton that day. Maybe there was a lass he was after.

For a while, William enjoyed the peace of the early morning ride. There was no Matthew forever chatting about lambs and comparing the crops. This time he could listen to the birds and appreciate the dawn light spreading over the rolling hills. Though a stiff breeze blew behind him from the sea, there wasn't a cloud in the sky.

By the time he reached Driffield, he was talking to his horse. It was a pleasure not to have any smart answers coming back. He stopped at an alehouse by the road and had just the one beer with a hot mutton pasty. After watering the horse, he set off again.

The rest of the journey was less pleasant. The further he travelled from home and the nearer he got to Beverley, the less confident he became. Leconfield reminded him of Matthew and his rising fortunes. It was there he'd made the decision to stop being such a fool and benefit more from the smuggling. Now it seemed that this decision had only led to more trouble.

He began to worry more about the possible consequences of his drunken words against the King. What on earth had he said that could be thought of as 'dangerous' or 'malicious'? He couldn't remember any of it exactly and could only hope it wasn't treasonable. Perhaps Richard Osbaldeston would be present as a JP and be lenient as before.

William knew that men with previous convictions were often given severe punishments. What if he *had* said something that amounted to treason? It didn't bear thinking about. No, he couldn't have said anything to imply he'd harm the King. A public flogging might be expected, not a hanging. That would be bad enough, but at least it would happen in Beverley where none of his family or acquaintances would see. He'd seen a man once, roped to the back of a cart and whipped up and down Bridlington High Street; he flinched at the memory. Perhaps he'd be put in the pillory, stripped to the waist and pelted with rotten fruit and old bricks. No, he reasoned, he was a yeoman and would pay the fine; it was just the poor who were whipped and shamed in public. He clung to that frail hope and spurred on his horse. The sooner he got there, the sooner it would all be over and done with.

When he entered the North Bar at Beverley, William found the smells much as before – the same sharp tang of the tanneries and the same yeasty smell of the breweries. This time he was prepared for the sight of so many men in wigs and fine clothes and was determined to ignore them. He rode straight to The White Horse down Hengate and asked for a bed above the kitchen with dinner and breakfast. It was then that he missed Matthew. He couldn't help but feel a country blockhead again surrounded by the fast-talking customers.

The dinner was already set out in the main room – a beef and kidney stew that smelled so rich his mouth began to water. As he piled his dish with meat and dumplings, he thought Mary would be interested in the seasonings. He could identify pepper, thyme and horseradish and yet was sure there were many more. After eating far too much and washing it down with a quart of beer, he slumped into a large chair in the corner. There he stayed with his hands resting over a tight belly and soon drifted off to sleep.

When he woke, the inn was candlelit. He looked around and saw that the stew was still on the table, no doubt replenished. The smell now hit the back of his throat and made him queasy. He heaved himself from the chair and asked the time. Though it wasn't late, he decided to retire early.

One of the landlord's daughters, the same girl as last year, showed him to the chamber above the kitchen. She didn't remember him.

'I was here this time last year,' he told her. 'I won't need the barber, thank you, just water for a wash in the morning.'

He undressed to his shirt and lay on the bed staring at the rafters. Apart from eating too much, he was satisfied with his day. The other beds were empty, and within minutes of blowing out the candle, he was asleep again.

Hours later, he was dreaming of heavy rain pouring off the thatch of his house. He awoke to find a large man pissing noisily into the chamber pot. The same man then let out a huge fart before getting into bed. Last year it was the snoring that had kept him awake. No doubt there was plenty of time for that too. He turned over, put his head under the pillow and tried to get back to sleep.

When it grew light, William was the first one up and dressed. He washed in the water left by the chambermaid outside the door and went down for breakfast. All he could face was porridge. He just wanted to get to the sessions, deal with whatever might happen and go home.

As he trudged through the town, smoke from the cottage chimneys hung low and suited his sombre mood. The way to the Guildhall was full of folk going in the same direction. Jostled along, he noted fine new buildings, but there were also the same dilapidated dwellings tucked closely together on the streets and up the passages. When he arrived, he was not too surprised to find the courtroom already packed.

He shoved his way onto a crowded bench and waited. The room was already stuffy and the man next to him stank to high heaven; his breath could have felled an ox. William grew impatient. He gritted his teeth and tapped his boots on the floor. The preliminaries went on forever. Men in wigs fiddling and faffing with piles of papers – it never ended. He prayed that his case be heard soon. No doubt, as Matthew had said, the justices would want to enjoy an early dinner. True to form, half a dozen misdemeanours were dealt with in a very cursory fashion. Then his name was called.

His mouth went dry as he stood to hear the charge. Although he expected most of the people present would agree with his views on King George, no one would dare defend him openly.

'Richard Stavely and Richard Conyston,' the clerk announced, 'please stand and give evidence against William Jordan of Reighton.'

Mr Stavely began. 'We were in The Bull and Sun in Bridlington on February 17th. We were drawn to the kitchen by the noise coming from a group of men drinking toasts.' He pointed to William. 'This man was the leader, and he was well into his cups. He began to speak ill of the King.' There was a shuffling of feet and murmurs ran through the chamber.

'Silence!' shouted the clerk.

Richard Osbaldeston, JP, interrupted. 'Let the gentleman speak. We wish to know the exact nature of the ill words spoken.'

Richard Stavely cleared his throat and hesitated. 'It was about the King employing Turks in his bedchamber.' There was complete silence in the packed room.

'And?' prompted the JPs.

'Well... he implied the King was satisfying his...' He lowered his voice. 'His abominable lusts.' There were gasps from those who heard.

'What did you say?' demanded Richard Osbaldeston. The JP to his left whispered in his ear. 'Ah...' There was a frantic interchange of whispers between the justices. They kept staring at William. Men around him were passing on what they thought they'd heard.

'Silence!' repeated the clerk.

Richard Osbaldeston, embarrassed by the way the case was progressing, wanted a swift conclusion. 'William Jordan, your presence here seems to be an annual event. How do you plead this time?'

'It was the drink. I don't remember what I said.'

'Do you plead guilty to drunkenness?'

'Yes.'

'Then we fine you three shillings and four pence for your drunken behaviour and a further 10 shillings for keeping disorderly company.'

William couldn't believe he'd got off so lightly. He was about to sit down when Sir Charles Hotham, chief magistrate, intervened.

'Wait one moment,' he said. 'Such words as you, William Jordan, have spoken in the presence of two witnesses may be deemed seditious. If so, further punishment will be in order.' He conferred with the other JPs. There was obviously some disagreement.

William glanced from one to the other, trying to gauge their reactions.

At last, Richard Osbaldeston nodded his head. 'Constable,' he pronounced, 'take the man away to the House of Correction. We'll decide later on the exact form of punishment.'

William found himself pushed along to the edge of the room where the constable stood waiting with chains.

'Please, that's not necessary,' William implored as his wrists were bound regardless. He was marched through the door that led directly outside to an adjacent building. A large man, whom he presumed was the gaoler, stepped towards them and took hold of the chains.

'Pay or strip,' the gaoler said.

'What?'

'Pay or strip,' he repeated. 'Gimme a shilling an' tha can keep tha clothes.'

With his hands bound together, William fumbled to find a shilling.

The gaoler pocketed it and began unlocking the door. He pushed it open, thrust William inside and slammed the heavy door shut.

William sensed he was not alone. It was dark and the air was foul. The only light came from the tiny metal grill in the door. As his eyes grew accustomed to the gloom, he realised why the place reeked – it was full of people, even women and children. Whichever way he moved, he bumped into someone who swore at him. He had little choice but to move wherever shoved. He soon found himself cornered beside the night tub. It had not been emptied and overflowed at the slightest knock. The straw on the floor soaked up most of the liquid, but it stank worse than the manure at Uphall. If and when he tired of standing, he'd have to sit there in the piss and the muck.

While the JPs were pleased to have finished their morning business early and sat down to dinner, William was fretting about his possible punishment. In a panic, he thought of floggings. He'd be whipped 'upon his naked shoulders till the blood comes'. That was what they pronounced at such times. The pillory might be a better option; he'd only be there for an hour. Sitting in misery in the piss-damp straw, he then realised that, if he *was* put in the pillory, he'd have to wait and stay locked up until market day. Mary would worry when he didn't return home. His eyes filled with tears. How could he have been such a drunken fool to end up like this?

Chapter 43

The JPs discussed William Jordan's punishment over their soup course. They were divided. Sir Charles Hotham dabbed his mouth with a white napkin and argued for the pillory.

'It has always been the accepted outcome for sedition.'

'Yes,' agreed Sir Richard Osbaldeston, 'but are his words seditious? Do they really intend harm to the King? While his words are malicious and certainly scandalous, do they incite rebellion? I don't think so. He's no Catholic, no Jacobite sympathiser. I know a bit about him. He's the brother-in-law of an acquaintance of mine – Matthew Smith.'

Sir Charles wavered for a moment. 'You may be right, though the man needs to be taught a lesson.' He finished his soup and signalled for the dish to be removed. 'I still suggest a spell in the pillory.'

Sir Richard coughed politely before replying. 'There's another reason not to put him in the pillory.' He lowered his voice so that the servants wouldn't hear. 'Many folk, as you well know, will agree with the man's opinions of the King. If we put him in the pillory, I can't guarantee there won't be flowers thrown at him instead of stones. There might even be a collection going round for him. That sort of thing has happened before.'

The other JPs recalled the incident and agreed. They paused while the rest of the soup dishes were removed, and a different wine served.

'What about a private punishment then?' Sir Charles ventured as his glass was filled. 'How about a flogging behind closed doors?'

Sir Richard shook his head. 'I think such a punishment too severe. A fine is enough.'

Sir Charles raised his eyebrows and helped himself to slices of beef and pickled cabbage.

Sir Richard continued. 'And we shouldn't keep him locked up much longer. He has a long ride home. His family will be expecting him.'

'Then get the flogging done while we have dinner.'

'Word of it might get out though. I still think it unwise to make this case too important. Enough attention has been given already in open court.'

Sir Charles shrugged and finished his wine. He flicked his empty glass for it to be refilled. Then he moved on to the pigeon pie.

As glasses were topped up, Sir Richard had another idea. 'If you're all in agreement, I will act as his surety.'

Such a proposal was most unusual. They'd think him mad. He stared at his plate of food, hardly touched, and added, 'Believe me – I think William Jordan will have learnt his lesson.'

Sir Charles bridled. 'Alright,' he snorted, 'I'll agree with you this time, but he's your responsibility.'

When William heard the prison door open and his name called, his heart pounded so violently he thought he'd be sick. He pushed himself up from the floor and wormed his way through the other prisoners.

The gaoler took one look at William's white face and wide eyes. 'I've come to take thee. It's *thy* turn. It's a floggin' fo' thee.'

William's legs began to shake.

'Nay, I'm only jestin'.'

William clenched his fists. He wanted to punch the man, knock that silly grin off his face. Instead, he concentrated on putting one foot in front of the other.

As he was led out into the fresh air, the gaoler added, 'Thoo must 'ave friends in 'igh places. Sign tha name o' this paper 'ere an' tha can get off 'ome.'

Shaken by his experience, William left the town as fast as possible. His clothes stank, his nerves were in shreds and his legs were still trembling as he rode out of Molescroft. It was already mid-afternoon, and he worried about reaching home before nightfall. As he rode on, the sun disappeared behind threatening clouds. The sky darkened and the temperature dropped. Suddenly, a hailstorm pelted down.

William raised his collar and hunched further into his coat. The horse slowed to a walk and let its head droop. In the fields, the sheep and early lambs huddled miserably by the hedges. As the hailstones pounded round him, he thought of home and the emptiness there without his daughter. Young Mary was never far from his thoughts. Grief swallowed him up and tears fell down his cheeks. His life wasn't worth living. He'd sunk to the level of a drunkard and a wife beater. Today he could have been flogged. What in God's name was he doing? He lifted his head to the elements and cried out for help.

Almost as soon as the hailstorm had begun, it ended. The sun streaked through the dark clouds, its brilliant rays illuminating the fields. Immediately, he was aware of the freshness after the storm. With a sense of well-being and relief, he breathed in deeply the smell of wet grass and earth.

He turned his face to the sun and wondered if young Mary was looking down on him. He smiled and stroked the horse's neck. The leather saddle between his thighs was now warm and comfortable, the reins sure in his hands. He could almost feel the blood coursing through his veins. He was reborn like the spring. Then, scanning the country around, he realised he was in Leconfield, the place where he'd made a big decision last year. His life had to change. *He* had to change. As he viewed the lush green pastures, now in full sunshine, he knew the time had come. As if in response, a faint rainbow appeared in the north. He was no Paul on the road to Damascus, but from now on, he *would* be a better citizen and a better husband and father.

William arrived back in Reighton as dusk fell. He was hungry and thirsty, and the horse quivered from exertion. Dickon and Tom ran out to greet him, only to be appalled at the state of the horse.

'I'm sorry,' said William, 'I needed to get back home. Just deal with him as best you can.' He slid from the saddle and walked stiffly down the hill as the first stars appeared.

William's sons were already in bed, dreading their father's return. When they heard the front door open, they crept further under the covers.

'Will he have brought us a present?' John asked, muffled by the blanket.

'No, don't be daft,' Francis snapped. 'Get your head down and keep quiet.'

Mary had been sitting knitting by the fire. She tensed and stood up in readiness. As William entered the kitchen, she tried to gauge his mood. Had he been drinking? She watched him take off his hat and coat and throw them in a corner.

'How did it go?' she dared to ask.

'I got a 13-shilling fine. I think Osbaldeston had a hand in it or else it might have been worse. Get me a drink and something to eat. I'm exhausted.' He sat down at the table and stared at his trembling hands.

When Mary walked past him, she caught a whiff of pigsties and manure. 'Oh, William – there's such a stink!'

'I can't smell anything,' he replied innocently. He'd hoped the long ride home would have cleared away the lingering prison odours.

'It's coming from you. It's your hair and clothes.'

He decided to tell the truth. It was better that than Mary think he'd soiled himself on the way home. 'Don't go worrying, but I had to spend a few hours in the gaol.'

She put a hand over her mouth in horror. 'Oh, William, you might not have come home at all.'

'Well, I'm here and I'm fine – apart from the smell. You'll have to give my coat and breeches a good clean. And maybe, before bed, you'd better check my hair for lice.'

Mary made him wash his hands and then, once he'd eaten his bread and cheese, they spent the rest of the evening together drinking mulled beer. They chatted quietly about the latest addition to the Jordan family. William's sister Dorothy had given birth to a girl and was now safely past her first month.

'And she managed without Sarah Ezard,' said Mary. 'Your mother swore it was as easy as shelling peas.'

William was relaxed and in a good mood as he spoke of his sister's happiness and her future with John Dawson.

Mary was tempted to ask, 'Did you happen to bring a present for them from Beverley?'

'No, I'm sorry. I should have thought.' He took hold of her hand. 'Listen, I just drank small beer while in Beverley. I'm not a saint and I can't do everything, but I will try harder. Believe me.'

She leant over the table, kissed his cheek and laughed. 'You still stink.'

For the rest of the spring, William drank nothing stronger than beer. He kept himself busy ploughing and sowing; there was the manure to dump in the fields for spreading as well as the ditches to scour and roofs to repair. He had more to do now since Dickon was getting unreliable – often forgetting which jobs to do or else doing them twice.

Dickon could only supervise Tom as the lad mended hedges and made new fences and hurdles; he knew what to do, but his hands were so swollen and clumsy they let him down.

Old Ben couldn't do much either and, though his eyesight was worsening, he wanted to be useful. He spent many days at William and Mary's house where he could mind the youngest boy while Mary worked in the milkhouse or garden. In return, he had a hot meal.

As the days were warm and dry, William's older boys could work outdoors. John scared birds off the field all day without even getting bored. Young William did a bit of weeding and bird scaring, though without the patience shown by his brother. As for Francis, he was expected to work longer hours with his father and uncles.

In the midst of what seemed like a normal late spring and early summer, news came of a Spanish invasion. Folk heard of it after the event when George Gurwood gave thanks in church for the deliverance of England.

'The Lord,' he explained, 'sent a mighty storm to confound the wicked Spanish. He raised such a wind that the seas were like mountains. He dispersed every ship so that not one landed on our English shores. Let us give thanks to the Lord. Amen.'

Old Ben turned his grizzled cheeks to Sarah Ezard. 'Them Scots,' he snarled, 'are nowt but traitors. They're i' league wi' Spanish – can't trust 'em. Let's 'ope there's an end now to all this trouble wi' Catholics.'

Francis took an interest in the latest Jacobite rebellion and often went to the vicarage after supper for news. He had an ulterior motive – Milcah Gurwood. She was 20 years old; Francis was almost 12. He knew he should have fancied Mary, who was his own age, or Priscilla, who was just two years his senior, and yet, out of the seven available girls, he could only love Milcah.

The young woman soon realised that she was the reason for Francis's visits. It should have been Thomas Jordan instead who called round; she danced with

Thomas at festivals and weddings. It was ridiculous, though also flattering, to have such a young lad follow you with his eyes.

One evening, Francis came home late. He was worn out, sticky and sweaty after a hard day in the fields. Instead of sitting in the kitchen, he went straight into the garden, stripped off his shirt and scooped water from the bucket over his head, chest and arms. He avoided his mother's suspicious glance as he put on his Sunday shirt. When he left the house, he caught his mother shake her head and smile.

His heart beat fast as he strode up the hill. When he reached the vicarage, he combed down his wet hair with his fingers and knocked on the door, hoping Milcah would answer it.

The door opened and he was in heaven. He followed Milcah into the parlour, feasting his eyes on her narrow waist. She walked as if gliding above the floor. Compared with her sisters and the other girls in the village, she was so graceful and calm. He swore he'd adore her always, no matter what, even if he could never have her for himself.

As Milcah entered the parlour, her sisters stifled their giggles. Francis looked so gangly and uncomfortable, as if he'd grown too big for his clothes. Determined not to hurt or embarrass him, Milcah sat down and began a conversation, one that would give him a chance to join in.

'I hear that Tom has to help Dickon out a lot more at Uphall.'

'Yes,' he answered politely, 'Tom does all sorts now.' He gave a nervous cough. 'Dickon knows everything about horses and cattle, but he's not up to it anymore.'

'He can advise Tom though, tell him what to do?'

'Oh yes.'

There was a long pause. The girls cast glances at each other. Cecilia gazed at the ceiling.

Milcah tried again. 'The barley's coming on well in the top field.'

'Yes.'

'Does your grandfather think there'll be a good yield this year?'

'I don't know.'

At this point, Cecilia and the other sisters began to talk amongst themselves, ignoring Francis completely.

Milcah stood up. 'I expect, Francis, you wanted to see my father and hear news of the Jacobites. I'm sorry he's not here. Come another day. You're more than welcome.'

That night, in bed, he imagined coming to her rescue. He'd arrive on a white horse to save her from disaster. He'd reach down and pick her up. She'd sit in front of him, and they'd gallop off together. The dream didn't go any further. It was the rescue that was important and the holding of hands and then... nothing. The next night, he envisioned a soft kiss on the forehead in gratitude for his bravery. Later that week, he dreamt of kissing her hand as they paid farewell. He played out these scenarios in his head so often that he was afraid he might cause embarrassment – one day he might really give her a kiss.

By midsummer, Francis was visiting the Gurwoods every evening. As he left home after supper, he told his parents that he wanted to hear the latest news.

'Spanish troops have managed to land in Scotland,' he reported. 'The vicar says they'll be joining forces with the Highlanders.'

'Go on then,' urged his mother, smiling to herself, 'get off to the vicarage and find out what you can.'

He returned an hour later. The moment his foot was inside the door, his mother interrogated him. 'So, Francis, what have you got to tell us?'

He'd run all the way home, rehearsing what to say. He flopped down at the table out of breath.

'The Spanish did join up with Highlanders and they set up base in a castle. Three of our Royal Navy ships sailed up to it.' He paused for breath. 'And they bombarded it till they surrendered.'

'That's good news then. Here, have your drink.'

'It's not the end. There were still a lot of Scots. Let me remember… George Keith, the 10th Earl of somewhere or other led them. Anyway, we had an army and they met to fight at Glen Shiel. We beat them with a mortar and an infantry attack.'

She watched him finish his drink in one go. 'Is that the end of the fighting then?'

'It could be,' he said as he wiped his mouth. 'The rebels fled. The vicar doesn't think there'll be any more trouble.' He frowned with such a serious expression. 'You know those Highlanders may be wild and fierce, but they don't have the guns and equipment that we have.'

Mary tried hard not to smile. Francis looked so funny talking like that in his outgrown breeches.

In the summer, other news came to the vicarage of more interest to a household full of women and girls. Francis wondered what was so fascinating about the Calico Riots. Though he preferred news of rebels and battles, he listened intently to the conversations. The girls told him that silk and wool weavers in Norwich and Colchester were rioting against the calico printers.

'You see,' Milcah explained, 'the weavers feel threatened by the imports of calico. It's cheaper and it's printed in bright colours.'

The Gurwood family was split on the issue. George took the side of the English weavers. 'You can't blame them for protecting their industry. Those calicoes are coming from India. We should be supporting our own woollen industry. Why, we have sheep in plenty in England. We should be wearing wool.'

'But, Father,' protested Cecilia, 'the prints are so much better, especially when it's hot like this summer.'

'Yes,' Susanna agreed, 'and it's said they dry quickly. The colours are brighter, and they don't run. We want to wear them.'

'It's unpatriotic,' he replied.

'They're cheaper too,' Cecilia argued. 'Why shouldn't we be able to buy cheaper petticoats and curtains? We can't afford to wear silk, can we, so why can't we have prints instead?'

Francis glanced from one to the other, amazed at how the girls dared to argue with their father.

The vicar was adamant. 'You should support our English workers and our wool trade,' he repeated. 'It's irresponsible not to.'

Cecilia stood up and began pacing the room. 'Why shouldn't we be free to buy what we want?' she cried, waving her arms. 'If we like the prints, and they're in fashion, we should be free to buy them.'

'Listen, if you ask me,' answered her father, 'I think they're cheap and tawdry. All those colours! It's barbaric, that's what it is. And you women,' he pointed at them, 'you're slaves to fashion – you're capricious. And if the prints are that cheap, you'll have the poorer classes wearing them as well, and then where will we be?'

Francis felt the girls' eyes turn to him as if he might side with them. He wanted desperately to agree with the girls yet didn't want to offend the vicar. He blushed and stared at the floor.

Cecilia went to the table and picked up the Weekly Journal. 'It's not just the riots – it's what the weavers are doing to women.' She found the page she was looking for. 'Listen, it says here that women who wear calicoes are being attacked. They're frightened into fits and have miscarriages. In London, the weavers have thrown stuff onto women wearing Indian linen – not just water and ink but even acid.' She tossed the journal back onto the table. 'How can that be right?'

Her father was losing patience. 'If you read on, Cecilia, you'll find that the Lord Mayor has had the men arrested. He doesn't condone the violence.'

'But clothes have been ripped off women's backs,' Cecilia carried on regardless. 'They call it "unrigging". Weavers have torn up any calico gowns they can find – they've *stolen* them from women. It's *most* unfair.' She stamped her foot and her eyes filled with tears.

Francis was out of his depth and hoped no one would ask his opinion. He glanced at the door, thinking to escape.

Milcah sensed his discomfort and intervened. 'Perhaps the government might put a higher tax on the prints. Then people will still buy woollen gowns and the linen prints too if they can afford them. No one need suffer.'

Her sisters sighed. Trust Milcah to find a compromise and put an end to an enjoyable argument. The last word came from their mother.

'All I can say is that in this heat, even I would wear a calico print.' The girls burst out laughing.

George held his hand up as if to surrender. 'There's only thee and me, Francis, against these women. What can we poor men do?'

Francis grinned, pleased to be accepted by the vicar on equal terms. He imagined buying Milcah a beautiful calico print and presenting it to her on bended knee.

That night, he dreamed she was dressed in a gown of printed red and blue flowers with interwoven green leaves on a pure white background. Her shiny hair tumbled from beneath her bonnet as she leant towards him and whispered, 'Thank you, you've saved my life.'

Chapter 44

The summer months were extremely hot – ideal weather for calico prints. William and the boys grew dark as gypsies from the hours spent outside and the older folk could not remember a summer like it. At night, many lay on their beds with their windows wide open to catch a breeze. If they did manage to sleep, they awoke in the morning clammy and uncomfortable; they were never refreshed. The sun shone from a cloudless sky, and with the heat came a drought. The cistern at Uphall dried up and water had to be fetched once more from Knox Well. Streams carried a thin trickle, the pond shrank to a filthy puddle, and there was a continuous queue at St Helen's Well. Cracks widened in the fields so deep the children caught their feet in them. As for the crops, they were stunted; the barley grew no higher than William's knees, and the peas and beans shrivelled.

Though most people looked healthy enough, disturbing news came of a plague that was sweeping through the country. Francis reported to his family what he'd heard at the vicarage.

'So far, it's just affecting the cities and market towns.'

His father was reassured. 'We'll be safe then so long as we avoid the markets.'

'The plague's already in Hornsea though,' Francis added, 'and in London, people are dying after they've only been ill for three days. The vicar says it's either the spotted fever or smallpox. Everyone's blaming the hot summer.'

His father couldn't deny the effects of the weather.

On Francis's next visit to the vicarage, Cecilia was reading aloud from a book on husbandry and the weather.

'Listen, Francis, it explains why a prevailing south wind is so bad for your health.' She ran a finger slowly across the page as she read. 'It dejects the appetite, it brings pestilential diseases, increases rheums. Men are more dull and slow than at other times.'

That was so true, he thought. Even his brother William had stopped charging about with the dog, and Dickon hardly left the cool of the stable. Folk went about their jobs at half the pace.

Cecilia gave a cheeky grin before continuing. 'On the other hand, a north wind makes men more cheerful and begets a better appetite for…' She hesitated.

He wondered what she was going to say.

She winked at him. 'An appetite for meat.'

He knew she'd made that up and felt his face redden.

In the next Sunday sermon, George Gurwood suggested that the hot weather might be due to moral laxity. 'To regain God's favour, we must take care to live as good Christians and obey the Ten Commandments.'

Yet the heat continued whatever folk did or didn't do.

The ones who suffered most were the elderly, the women and the very young. Ben was full of ideas when it came to making garments for cold and wet weather but was at a loss when faced with unremitting heat. He did have a large straw hat to shade his head, yet his clothes, like those of most people his age, were thick and heavy and quite unsuitable. Most evenings he slept outside on a wooden hurdle, and in the daytime, he hobbled to the sea to feel the onshore breeze.

In July, John Gurwood's wife found out that she was with child again. She was queasy enough without the heat conspiring to spoil her appetite. She stayed inside the cottage where it was cooler with her six-month-old son and soon looked pale and fragile.

In John Dawson's cottage, the new mother, Dorothy, spent her time feeding and washing her baby girl. At times, she was so fed up with being indoors that she carried the baby to the beach, also taking along her four-year-old stepdaughter, Rebecca. It was cooler down there, and she and Rebecca could walk in the sea barefoot. She was convinced the baby was suffering from heat exhaustion, so one day when they were alone, she unwound the baby's swaddling bands. She laid the damp strips of cloth to dry on a rock and dandled the child in the pool beneath. From then on, her walks to the beach became a daily ritual.

The sea began to draw folk who'd never given it a thought before. Many were tempted to go wading in the water. Sarah Ezard and Ben thought it worth the steep scramble down the ravine to have cold waves swirl around their feet and legs. The problem was that by the time they'd hauled themselves back up the cliff, they were hot and sweaty again.

William's sons went down to the sea at noon, and then again before supper, taking the dog with them. Old Ben stood watching them one day from the top of the cliff and wished he were 70 years younger. The boys stripped off their clothes, left them on a rock and ran straight into the sea yelling and screaming. He noticed that John didn't go in far, preferring to run alongside the waves as they broke. Francis was content to stay immersed and cool down while William wasn't still for a moment. He dived through the waves and leapt about, making as much noise and splash as he could. All the while, the dog stood at the edge and barked. Ben guessed it was the best summer the boys would ever have.

It was the worst summer for the farmers. Each day, the swallows flew high, indicating yet another dry day. The hay harvest was secured, yet the grass was of poor quality. As for the oats, they were so small they could not be harvested properly; instead, they were scythed down and raked together for animal fodder. A difficult winter lay ahead.

In October, William and the other leading yeomen were invited to the vicarage for the tithe feast. He didn't expect much this year, with it being such a scant harvest, yet was appreciative that George Gurwood, out of sympathy, had not even insisted on his full tithe of 24 stooks. William dressed as if it was Sunday and called for his father. Together they walked across the road and knocked on the door. Cecilia opened it and led them to the parlour, where they found Matthew deep in conversation with George. There seemed to be some disagreement between them, and William overheard the name 'Osbaldeston'.

As soon as the vicar saw him standing there, he changed the subject. 'So, Matthew, the land certainly does need improving. What do you think, William?'

'Yes, it can always do with more manure. Father's forever telling me, aren't you?'

'Aye, that's right. I reckon, next storm we 'ave with an east wind, we get down o' beach an' gather up all seaweed washed up.'

Matthew nodded. 'We'll do that. It takes a lot of organising, but it's worth the effort.'

Stephen Jefferson and Richard Maltby were about to step in with their opinions when the Gurwood girls entered with the food. The men were amazed at being treated to roast beef. There was also boiled beef and grated horseradish and what appeared to be an enormous bramble pie. Cecilia and Milcah returned with a bowl of apples and a platter of cheeses.

'We're pleased to see you all,' Milcah announced. 'Enjoy your food.' She curtsied as she left.

'Yes,' echoed George, 'I thank you for coming. It's not been an easy year, but when we work together, we can survive. Go on now, help yourselves. My wife's made this fruit punch and I can tell you it's very potent. Take a cup each and start.'

As the other yeomen stepped to the table, George held on to William's arm and whispered in his ear. 'I'll open a bottle of my best French claret. That punch is full of brandy, so maybe it's best you leave it be. It would only give you a headache in the morning.'

William was grateful; George was a discreet and thoughtful friend. It was also generous of him to provide such a lavish meal in the circumstances. As William grew to enjoy the wine with slices of beef, another bottle was opened. When the men had finished eating at last, George passed round his tobacco. Stephen Jefferson and Richard Maltby moved to the fire to light up their pipes, and William and the others followed suit. Full of good food and drink, they relaxed and stretched out their legs to enjoy the moment.

Outside, in the front garden and the street, the tenant farmers were treated to half a barrel of Martha Wrench's ale. They were also given apples and cheese. As usual, the free drink made a few of them argumentative. Before long, they were fighting. Cecilia peeped through the window, eager to watch. Her mother pulled her back.

'Get away from that window! It's none of our business. And on *no* account are you to go out there. Do you hear me? We stay put in the kitchen till they've all gone home.'

Cecilia nodded, but when her mother wasn't looking, she edged nearer the window. It was interesting to see how the men behaved without their wives present. They were singing now, lolling against each other. They weren't fit to fight anymore. The yeomen in the parlour were very quiet. She could hear low, murmured conversations and guessed the men would be gone soon.

William and his father were the first to leave. They stood up and thanked the vicar for his generosity. George walked with them to the door and shook their hands solemnly, an unusual gesture. He seemed sad. William reckoned it was because of the poor harvest and yet the handshake was like a formal goodbye. The vicar was unlikely to leave Reighton; he'd married here, and his family had been born here. Shrugging off his unease, William stepped through the bodies of the drunken, sleepy men in the garden. He saw his father safely to Uphall and then ambled home. The autumn air was refreshing. The wine had agreed with him, and he looked forward to being in bed with Mary.

Mary had already retired. She heard William come in and undress in the dark. She could tell by his movements that he wasn't drunk. That was something at least. The bed sank to one side as he got in. When he leant over, she could smell wine on his breath.

'Did you have a good time?'

'Mmm, very good. Roast beef. And the night isn't over yet.'

He heaved himself onto her and began kissing her neck and nibbling her ear. She surrendered to the pleasure and, since he was sober, didn't discourage him. Afterwards, he shrank out of her and was soon fast asleep and snoring, his full weight still on top. She rolled him off and lay awake on her back. October, she reflected, had often been the month she'd been caught out. It had meant another child born in summer. She prayed there'd be no consequences this time.

Chapter 45

By late October, Mary's worst fears were realised. The last thing she needed was another child to feed. Determined to lose it, she panicked and jumped up and down, then bent over double a few times. Then she chopped wood, stretching the heavy axe high over her shoulder before crashing it down onto the logs. She took long, strenuous walks carrying Richard, and carried buckets of water for people. When these ploys failed, she consulted Sarah Ezard.

Mary broke down in tears when she tried to explain. Sarah understood and took pity. She sat her down and put an arm round her.

'Oh, Mary, thoo's 'ad enough trouble an' enough bairns. I do 'ave an enema tha can try. An' I think thoo should drink a fennel an' rue tea ev'ry day. That should 'elp.'

Two weeks later, Mary returned, still pregnant, and asked for strong laxatives as a final solution. She soon wished she hadn't. The white bryony had violent results. Her family had no idea what she was trying to do and were horrified when she daren't leave the chamber pot for more than a few minutes. They stayed well clear, afraid of catching the flux.

After an exhausting day of being purged, Mary felt she had nothing left, either in her bowels or in her resolve. She decided with reluctance that if there was a child still there, then it must be God's will and he or she deserved to live.

The following week, when she'd recovered her strength, Mary broke the news of her pregnancy to her sister, Elizabeth. No one else knew, apart from Sarah Ezard, and Mary was fearful of her reaction.

'I'm expecting the baby next year – in early summer.'

Elizabeth was silent for a moment and then sighed. 'You don't need any more babies. It's so unfair.'

'I'm sorry, Elizabeth, I really am.'

'Alright, but enough is enough. I'm going to find out why I've never had a child. I don't know if it's me or Robert at fault. I'm going to find out – before it's too late.'

'How are you going to do that?'

'I'm not sure, but Cecilia Gurwood knows of some flowerpot test.'

Mary raised her eyebrows. 'Cecilia seems to have a surprising amount of knowledge for an unmarried woman.'

Elizabeth waited for an opportunity to speak with Cecilia alone. She found her by the vicarage stable feeding bits of apple to the horse. After chatting about the surprising success of the apple crop this year, she explained her purpose and enquired about the plant pot test.

'I think I know what you're referring to,' Cecilia answered. 'I read about it in one of my father's medical books. You have to get two handfuls of barley. You soak them separately, one in your urine and the other in your husband's. Have you got that?'

'Yes, I'm listening. Go on.'

'Then plant each lot of barley in a separate pot and water them with the same urine – yours or Robert's. Make sure you don't mix them up. Then whichever barley grows the quickest is the more fertile. It's that simple.'

'And what if neither grows much?'

'Then I'm afraid you're both barren.'

Elizabeth went home to try it, knowing she'd have a long wait for the results. Impatient, she attempted to seduce Robert. She'd also heard from Cecilia that doing it the way animals did was a recommended way to get with child.

That night, at bedtime, Elizabeth stood before Robert and smiled. Then she turned her back on him, bent over and lifted her petticoat slowly to reveal her bare bottom.

He was shocked at first and then aroused. All at once, repulsed and ashamed by his body's response, he crashed out of the house and went for a three-mile walk along the moonlit roads.

Left alone, Elizabeth threw herself on the bed and sobbed. It would be ages now before he even touched her.

When the barley didn't grow in either of the pots, she realised that, at almost 40 years old, she'd better resign herself to being childless.

Sarah Ezard heard from Mary about Elizabeth's last-ditch attempt. She called to see her, making sure Robert was out.

'Listen, Elizabeth, I'm goin' to boil up some wild carrot. I've seen it growin' by chalk pits. I'll mix it wi' wine an' send thee a bottle. If thoo's lucky, tha might still get wi' child – even at thy age.'

'No, don't bother, Sarah. It's too late. I'm past it now and I don't care anymore. Please don't give me any more hope. I'll devote myself to helping my sister instead.'

'Fine, I understand. It can't be easy for Mary living in a house full of boys.'

Mary found it more than tiring to rear four young boys. They drove her to distraction the way they competed with each other over every little thing. Mealtimes were the worst; they were so eager to get second helpings that they stuffed their food in and almost choked. At night, young William often shoved John out of bed to give himself more room, and she'd find the poor boy asleep on the floor the next morning. Despite his limp, William was the strongest and picked fights with Francis as soon as look at him. They kicked and punched each other with vicious intent. Mary despaired of ever having any peace.

One morning, even the youngest, Richard, caused an upset. It started innocently enough when he and John were waiting for their breakfast. They were playing together under the table. Richard had a pewter tankard in his hand, and without warning, he swung it straight into John's mouth. There was a sickening crack, a cry and then silence. Instantly, Mary left stirring the porridge and peered under the table. John was sitting in shock with bright red blood bubbling from his mouth.

'Oh Lord, what's happened?' she cried. John's eyes were full of tears, but he made no sound. Richard still had hold of the tankard. He stared at the blood and bits of broken teeth in John's lap and began to crawl away.

'Richard – did you hit him?' Just as she was about to grab him and give him a shake, John held up his hand. He managed to speak in between spitting blood.

'He didn't mean it. Don't hurt him.'

'Oh John,' she said softly. 'Let me clean you up and see the damage.'

Once she'd wiped his chin and dabbed his mouth, she sat him on her knee to inspect his teeth. 'It's only your baby ones. New ones will grow through.' Then, turning to Richard, she raised her voice. 'And you'd better not hit him when he's got his next teeth. That's all poor John'll have then.' She wagged her finger at him. 'Bad boy!'

When she returned to her task, the porridge was stuck to the bottom of the pan. She wondered how she found the time to get anything done these days. If it wasn't one thing with the boys, it was another.

That same night, William came home with sad news. 'Tom's decided to leave us.'

'What?' Mary stopped cleaning Richard's bottom. 'I don't understand. He's your most reliable and trustworthy lad.'

'Well, he's going at the November hirings. He said it's been four years since Jane died and he's grieved long enough. He's sorry to leave, but he's made up his mind. He intends to make a new start elsewhere.'

Mary finished dealing with Richard, wondering why children chose to mess themselves near mealtimes. She washed her hands and served the supper. They ate in silence, subdued by the news about Tom. It was hard to imagine Reighton, let alone Uphall, without him, and life for Dickon would never be the same. And who would take proper care of the mule? Ben shouldn't be asked – he was getting far too old.

As the nights drew in and Mary's boys spent longer indoors, Elizabeth suggested that they might spend time each day at the Gurwoods'. The vicar would be happy to teach them.

'Francis,' she reasoned, 'will always be keen to go – because of you know who – and young William will be afraid he's missing out if he doesn't go too. John can stay at home, and you can both enjoy a bit of peace and quiet away from the others.'

It was soon arranged, and three times a week, the two boys went to the vicarage. George Gurwood chose Bible readings for the most part, and while William listened with half an ear, Francis paid full attention. He wanted to know the Bible better so that he could join in the discussion that always ended the lessons.

When the story of Ruth was chosen one night, Milcah asked to read the first chapter. Even William took note of it, as it began with a famine in the land – something his grandfather often spoke about. While William enjoyed the verses about barley harvests and reaping and gleaning, different verses enchanted Francis. He'd heard them before, though never quite like this. His beloved spoke the verses softly and with humility. She was just as he imagined Ruth to have been – loyal, kind and gentle, though stubborn when it came to questions of the heart. He felt the words were for him alone, and later in bed that night, he recalled the gentle rhythms and beauty of her voice.

'Intreat me not to leave thee, or to return from following after thee: for whither thou goest, I will go; and where thou lodgest, I will lodge: thy people shall be my people, and thy God, my God: where thou diest, will I die, and there will I be buried: the Lord do so to me, and more also, if ought but death part thee and me.'

He whispered the words again as he fell asleep. They gave him great comfort, as did the other Bible readings. They distracted him from the fear that his father had begun drinking again. The poor harvest had led to an increase in smuggling. His father was now out most nights of the week doing whatever he did and, sometimes, his clothes stank of brandy.

Chapter 46

In autumn, William had plenty of repair jobs to keep him occupied in the daytime. Even so, his thoughts often wandered to young Mary. As he prepared the wood to repair the barn at Uphall, he hoped that grief might be like sawing through wood – there were only so many pushes and pulls of the saw before you were through. Perhaps there were only so many tears to be shed before the grief would lessen. At least the weeks passed quickly with his time spent patrolling the cliffs and visiting the inns. And the brandy helped keep out the cold.

Mary continued to send her two eldest boys to the vicarage. They needed a dependable father figure as well as moral guidance. She assumed they read the Bible, yet whenever the vicar was away, Cecilia took charge and found something quite different to read – Nathaniel Crouch's *Admirable Curiosities, Rarities and Wonders*. Young William was thrilled by the gorier tales and loved to relate them to John as soon as he got home. One afternoon, he crawled under the table where John was playing with Richard.

'Listen to this, John.' He spoke in a low tone so that his mother wouldn't hear. 'Folk were in church when a thunderbolt and a ball of fire came through the window right in the middle of the sermon. The vicar wasn't hurt,' he whispered with great drama, 'but one woman had the flesh torn off her back – almost to the very bones.' When John's eyes widened further, William added, 'And a man had his brains thrown on the floor. Yes – and his hair was stuck to the pillar behind him!'

John retched.

William smiled, pleased with the effect he'd caused. 'Francis is like you. He can't stomach the stories either – says he can't get them out of his head. And he doesn't like Milcah to hear such things. He's like a fond lass himself.'

One choice of reading that appealed to both Francis and young William was George Meriton's *Yorkshire Dialogue* – a long poem about a farmer who grumbled a lot. The boys thought it was like their grandfather at Uphall – like when the farmer's tools were never there when he wanted them. Cecilia amused them; she had a knack of mimicking their grandfather.

'Can nothing lig, that's lighter than a stone?
We shall 'ave nowt left soon, all will be gone.
Our land is tough, an' full o' strong wickens,
Cat whins, an' seevy furs, an' many breckins.
    It's nowt but gore, it ploshes under feet;
We shall find trouble enough when we come to it.'

The boys giggled. 'That's him to a T,' Francis admitted.

'You sound just like him,' William agreed. Grandfather chunters just like that and Grandmother's as bad.'

'In the poem,' said Cecilia, 'the wife complains to her husband.' She tried to imitate Dorothy Jordan. 'Thoo'll not let me be merry long I'm sure, fo' there's allus summat wrong.' When the boys laughed again, she added, 'I do believe I heard those exact words from your grandmother at the last harvest supper.' They had to agree.

Francis liked the part where the old couple go to bed and blend their feet together for warmth, and both enjoyed the verses about the cat getting the bacon. What amused them the most was that no one in the farmer's family bothered in the slightest about the meat being trailed along the mucky floor.

There was one verse Cecilia thought to omit. It referred to courting habits. In the end, she couldn't resist.

'Thou knows young women will,
To get a lively lad, use all their skill.
He kissed me first, did grope my breast and then
Went lower down...'

Milcah stopped her. 'That's enough, Cecilia.' She could see Francis squirming in his chair and blushing.

William was most disappointed. When they went home, he repeated the verse to John, though the words were wasted on the boy – another disappointment.

Milcah mentioned Cecilia's choice of reading matter to her father, but he had other things on his mind. He was losing patience with the vicar at Hunmanby and his father, Sir Richard Osbaldeston. One Sunday, he returned from giving a service at Grindale. He stood in front of the kitchen fire to warm his hands and then, since his daughters were occupied in the parlour, he complained to his wife.

'It's all very well us sending money for the upkeep of Hunmanby Church, but on top of that we have to pay for their fence too. It's not as if our own church doesn't need repairs.' He turned to warm his back. 'I was only telling the churchwardens yesterday – our porch looks so rickety it might be better pulled down and rebuilt.'

She passed him a mug of mulled wine and tried to appease him. 'There's not a lot you can do. It's the way of things. Reighton's never been seen as more than a chapel of ease for the mother church.'

He took the mug in both hands and sat down at the table. After staring into space for a while, he sighed. 'Hunmanby's now demanding payment of the skin pennies. And it's backdated,' he added. 'It amounts to over two shillings.' He held up a hand to stop her interrupting. 'It's not the money, it's the principle.'

She sat down opposite him. 'I've always thought it mean, and I bet the Osbaldestons are making it worse.' As she watched him sip his wine, she remembered earlier times. 'It's not like the old days when the Stutvilles had the manor. Now Hunmanby market's not up to much and both families live to outdo each other.'

'You're right there,' he agreed. 'Their latest row's over the common land. It's been brewing for seven years or more. It's no surprise it's coming to a head.'

'That moor,' she replied, waving her arm vaguely towards the window, 'it's always been for folk to keep their beasts – and gather fuel.'

'Yes, and now that Osbaldeston has his warren up there, folk say they can't go about their business because of all the rabbits. They run in herds. There's even a warrener employed – he lives on the moor in a lodge built specially.

As he finished his wine, he mused on where the Osbaldestons lived. He'd seen their Tudor hall with its Queen Anne front and lavish stone dressings. It stood on high ground overlooking the town with a forecourt and terraced gardens – all very impressive.

'Those Osbaldestons, they're full of ambition,' he said at last. 'Rumour has it that Sir Richard's daughter Mary might be marrying the High Sheriff, Lord Robert Mitford.'

'I can well believe it. Sir Richard gets what Sir Richard wants. I bet he's already used devious methods to buy his fields and properties. He has tenants everywhere now.'

George sighed once more. 'I don't know what can be done. Charles Stutville got 30 people to support his complaint against the warren and still nothing happened. I must say my piece though about the skin pennies.'

When George Gurwood attempted to contact the vicar of Hunmanby, Dr Richard Osbaldeston refused to see him. The assistant minister dealt with him instead. George returned home thinking his visit was fruitless.

A week after he'd complained, George received the shock notification that he was to be appointed as vicar of Rudston as from November 12th. He was to continue to give the services at Speeton, Grindale and Burton Fleming – quite a task. A new curate for Reighton would be instituted officially on January 5th. He waited a day before breaking the news to his family.

'I have something very important to tell you,' he announced as they sat together for supper. He avoided his wife's gaze and looked instead at his daughters, but his eyes kept returning to her. 'I've been appointed to Rudston.'

They stared at him. It didn't make any sense.

'I'll be leaving soon, though you don't need to join me till later.'

His wife went pale. She clutched the edge of the table and stood up. 'Why? For God's sake, why? Don't tell me you haven't been happy here in Reighton all these years. Our children were born here. This is our home!' She began to cry.

Cecilia saw the wild glint in her mother's eyes and took hold of her arm. 'Sit down, Mother, please. Let Father explain.' She pulled her mother back down onto the chair.

George swallowed with difficulty. His wife was taking the news even worse than expected. 'Susanna, think of it as a promotion – and there are advantages.'

'What advantages?' she snapped.

He cleared his throat. 'Well, for a start, the vicarage in Rudston is new. It's only ten years old – chalk-built.' He tried to ignore her tight-lipped glare and carried on. 'It has three rooms on the ground floor and two chambers. And there are even garrets. And there's a chalk barn with three bays and a stable.'

The girls clapped their hands. Their eyes glistened at the prospect of the move. Cecilia spoke up first. 'Mother, we'll have *so* much more room – think of it.'

Susanna raised her hand, about to slap her daughter. She thought better of it and pretended to adjust her cap.

'Yes,' George agreed, 'we'll be more comfortable, much better off.' He thought of the study he would have. Maybe there was even a lockup cabinet so he could keep his books from prying eyes.

'When can we go?' asked Cecilia.

'You can join me in the spring when the roads improve. Then you can travel with our belongings.'

Susanna was speechless. The whole family seemed set against her.

Milcah was quiet and did not join in the excitement. She didn't like change and she was attached to many people in the village, especially the Jordans. She leant towards her mother and held her trembling fingers. There was nothing either one could do.

In the garden the next day, Susanna was alone with Milcah. She strolled arm in arm with her daughter and stopped by the old plum tree. It was a calm day at the end of October. The air was clear and still, the leaves on the trees turning red. Gazing around the garden she'd tended for so many years, she confided in the one person in the family who might understand.

'I'm too old, Milcah, to be shifted and start again in a new place. I couldn't sleep last night. I spent the whole night praying for guidance.' She looked back at the house. 'Your father's been very good to me all these years and I've come to the conclusion... I must not fail to support him as he's supported us. It's my duty to follow him.' She turned to Milcah. 'With you, though, it's different.' She rubbed her daughter's arm. 'I could try to find a way for you to stay here – if that's what you want.'

Chapter 47

1719-20

On the day before his last Sunday service, George Gurwood took a stroll around the churchyard, touching the cold, damp walls lovingly as he passed. He entered and stood for a moment by the font and recalled his children's baptisms. The whole of his married life had been spent in Reighton. He'd even become attached to the over-crowded vicarage. Each room held such memories – the births of his children in the upstairs chamber, teaching them to read and write on the kitchen table, his wife and daughters making quilts together in the parlour. He recalled William's young daughter, her mind like a windmill. Whenever she came for a lesson, she was so full of ideas and was never still for a moment. It was all in the past now. He stroked the carving on the font and then braced himself to go round the village and say his farewells.

First he called on Robert Storey. He'd always suspected he'd never quite come up to expectations and hoped Robert wouldn't think too badly of him.

Elizabeth opened the door, glad to see him. 'Come in. Robert's in the kitchen reading his Bible.' As she led him down the passage, she added, 'I know you two have had your differences, but you must part as friends. Here you are. I'll leave you to talk alone.'

Robert raised his head. 'Ah, it's you. Take a seat.'

George settled down opposite him. 'Robert, I am sorry to be leaving Reighton. I hope you'll remember me with affection.' When Robert didn't answer, he carried on regardless. 'You know, I have no regrets about my life here. I've walked the tightrope like you between the flesh and the spirit.' He saw Robert stiffen and cast his eyes down to the Bible. 'Robert, we both do what we think is right. We can but pray that we've both acquitted ourselves well and will do so in the future.'

'Amen to that!' Robert stood up to say goodbye. Already he was looking forward to the new vicar, who might show a better example to the young and not be such an ordinary man with ordinary passions. He shook George's hand. 'I expect you'll prosper in your new parish. I'll keep an eye on Susanna and the girls until they can join you in Rudston and, until I hear otherwise, I'll carry on supervising the glebe land.'

George was surprised that the visit was so short. He left the kitchen and made an excuse to Elizabeth. 'I can't stay longer, I'm afraid. I have others to visit.' As she let him out of the door, he smiled. 'God bless you. Be kind and understanding with Robert. We both know he means well.'

His next call was to William and Mary. He knocked on their door and walked straight in, knowing he'd be welcome. To his surprise, Mary flung her arms round him and gave him a hug.

The boys, seated at the table, stared in silence. It was so unlike their mother. William was equally astonished.

'I know,' said George, when Mary released him, 'it's hard for me too, hard to leave those we're fond of.'

William leapt up and filled a couple of tankards with warm beer. He set them on the table.

'No, thank you, William, I haven't time. I've a sermon to prepare. I wanted to tell you what a good family you have here. Take care of them! They're great lads and, if you spend time with them, they'll reward you later when they're grown. I'll be going then. Look after yourself, Mary – and be good, you boys. Do what your parents tell you.'

William went to the door to let the vicar out and then decided to walk him to the end of the lane. He wondered if George had known about the move to Rudston at the tithe supper. He didn't mention it and they sauntered along in quiet companionship. William was the first to speak. 'I will try and be a better father.'

'Yes, and you need to take extra care with Francis,' George advised. 'That lad has more about him, and he's taken quite a fancy to Milcah. I hope she doesn't break his heart. I wouldn't like to think any daughter of mine would egg on a young lad – I don't think she will, mind.'

'He'll be fine, I'll watch him.' William stopped at the lane end and shook the vicar's hand. 'I wish you all the best for your new life in Rudston. God knows I'll miss you.' He then turned and took his time walking back. He wondered how often in the future he'd get the chance to speak with him.

The last house that George visited was that of his son. John was sitting by the fire with his young boy, who had just begun to say his first words; his wife was standing ironing. She was about five months with child, and it was beginning to show. George wiped his eye. He was not going to see the children grow up. He took the boy from John and sat him on his knee, jiggling him up and down till he giggled. 'I'm going to miss this.'

'But, Father, you'll get the chance to see us whenever you give a service at Speeton. And Rudston's not so far away. I'm sure we'll see each other from time to time.'

'Yes, you're right,' George replied though he doubted it. He'd be kept very busy in and around Rudston. He stood up and handed the boy back, apologising that he couldn't stay longer. Turning to Dorothy, he added, 'I hope all goes well with your new baby. It'll be before spring by the look of you. Susanna will be eager to help while she can. She won't be joining me till Easter you know, so don't be shy to ask.' He embraced his son, kissed his daughter-in-law on the cheek and gazed at the boy one last time.

'Goodbye, little Georgie. May God watch over you.'

He returned to the vicarage to plan his last sermon. The moment he arrived, he went into the parlour and asked for some peace and quiet. Then, as soon as the women had removed themselves to the kitchen, he took down his worn copy of *Marcus Aurelius* and re-read his favourite passages. Although tomorrow's service would have the usual scripture readings, he wanted to convey the stoicism that was so appealing in the little book. He hoped his parishioners would accept the fact of his leaving without unnecessary sadness. There was no point in struggling against the unavoidable. They were surely aware of his disagreements with the Osbaldestons and his need to move away.

After reading a few pages, he closed the book and shut his eyes. The sermon need not be written down. It would be more like a few last pieces of advice, and he'd remember what to say in the morning. The day's farewells had been tiring; within minutes he was asleep, and the book fell to the floor.

Despite the cold November morning, the whole village turned out for the Sunday service. William and his family walked through the mist enveloping the lower streets and emerged to find the church bathed in pale sunlight. They entered and, even though extra candles had been lit, a solemn atmosphere pervaded. There were no murmured conversations. Folk just tipped their heads in acknowledgement of each other and then stared at the altar, waiting for their vicar.

George Gurwood stepped into the pulpit. He gave a broad smile, determined to be cheerful and give them courage for the future.

'I expect you to be here in such numbers next Sunday to welcome your new vicar. As you know, John Sumpton won't be moving here yet, though I'm sure he'll help you when he can. He has to ride over from Filey. I know that's not far, yet I trust you'll understand if he's not always on time.'

Sarah Ezard and Ben rolled their eyes. Neither relished waiting in church in the middle of winter.

George conducted the usual service for early November and, when it was time for the sermon, he made a point of shutting the great Bible.

'We have heard the word of God, now hear the word of man. And I will be brief – you can trust me on that. It's a cold day and my wife has a beef joint turning on the fire. Like you, I wish to be warm and comfortable. I also have Speeton to visit later. So, this is what I have to say.' He clapped his hands together to get their full attention.

'We're all aware that change is part of the natural order of things. Nature's first delight is in changing things.' He smiled and nodded. 'I know what you're thinking – I've been here for over 30 years. There's been little change there!'

They didn't respond, though George could hear their boots shifting and scraping on the floor.

'In times of trouble,' he continued, 'nature brings us nothing we cannot bear. Remember, we do not have to bear up against the future or the past – only against the present.' He glanced at the Jordans, then at the Smiths. He extended his arms and looked towards the rear of the church.

'If we work together, we can thrive and be happy. If we work hard and live in the present, then we will harvest the present. Having said this, I must admit that life is not easy. It's not something we can dance our way through. I reckon life is more like wrestling than dancing – and that's just as well, having seen you lads dance!'

William's brothers grinned and nudged each other.

'As when we wrestle, we must be ready to keep our feet against all odds, no matter what happens to trip us. We must seek neither pity nor applause. And we must not be roused to anger.' He dropped his voice. 'As you know, I myself have been guilty of this at times – and I regret it.' He cleared his throat before resuming his thread.

'Remember, the mark of a true man is in gentleness and courtesy, not in fits of passion. So, don't listen to slander or gossip, and be constant and even in your friendships. I know it's difficult, but bear criticism with a cheerful, open heart. And don't live your lives as if you had a thousand years before you but perform each task as if it were your last. Work with the weather, not against it. I know Ben will agree with me there.' He looked again to the back of the church and waved. 'Thank you, Ben – I'll miss hearing your words of wisdom. I was remembering one of your sayings just this mornin. Ice i' November to bear a duck, rest o' winter is slush an' muck.'

The congregation smiled and turned to peer at Ben. He shuffled on his bench, so pleased to be singled out.

'So, work hard each day. It's all we have. Yesterday has gone. Tomorrow is unknown. Let us pray that we may do nothing but what the Lord approves, that we may accept whatever He assigns us. We put our trust in the Lord. Amen.'

George stood in the porch to shake hands and say a final farewell. Then there was nothing for it but to look forward to a new life in Rudston. As he sat down to enjoy his last Sunday dinner in the vicarage, he knew he'd miss having his daughters and wife with him, even if it was only for a few months. He also knew, of all his daughters, he'd miss Milcah the most. She was more sensitive and considerate than the others, kind to a fault. She'd make someone an excellent wife and would be a lovely mother. Perhaps she'd find a suitable husband in Rudston.

He left Reighton very early the next day so as not to meet anyone on the way. He'd had quite enough of farewells.

On January 18th, George Gurwood was instructed to return to Reighton. Doctor Richard Osbaldeston, vicar of Hunmanby, needed him to sign one final entry in the parish register. George waited patiently in the church with clenched teeth and watched while the long and official declaration was written. It was then read out to him, word for word, in a cultured, monotonous voice.

'Mr George Gurwood, late curate of the chapel of Reighton, one of the chapels of ease of the church of Hunmanby, paid me the present vicar of Hunmanby the sum of 2s 2d for 26 burials, which is called skin pennies, for 26 burials which is the sum of 1d each corpse which is paid to the incumbent of the mother church for having the liberty of being buried in that churchyard.'

Richard Osbaldeston signed it and stepped aside for George to add his signature.

'No, I'm not happy,' George confessed. 'I don't want any misunderstandings over payments and, since I won't be here again and there's a new vicar, I don't want any future wrangling over these skin pennies. I want you to write that this penny has been paid for each corpse while I've been curate here.'

The vicar of Hunmanby shrugged. Nevertheless, he obliged, and added an extra two lines.

George read it but did not add his usual signature. He would only make his mark. His humiliation was not over. He was then told to ride with Richard Osbaldeston to Hunmanby and sign an identical declaration there, one already prepared in that parish register. When he arrived, he found the words had been written in a space on a random page. This time he signed it properly, though it was far from his usual fluent hand. He knew it meant the end of his association with Reighton.

Chapter 48

1720

Throughout January and February, people were unsettled. The departure of the Gurwood family was imminent and no one could get used to the new vicar. John Sumpton arrived for the appointed services and left straight afterwards. Small, portly and red-faced, he irritated his congregation by staring at a point above their heads and speaking through his nose. No one referred to him by name; he was always 'the new vicar'. Even Robert Storey was regretting the change; the vicar showed no interest in the glebe land and avoided questions about both the land and the Bible. The services were a great disappointment, conducted as if the vicar wished he were elsewhere. Old Ben summed up the general opinion.

'New vicar 'as a funny way o' talkin'. 'E's not from round 'ere. An' I bet 'e's never set foot in a field.'

February, always a difficult month to endure at the best of times, was made worse by the previous poor harvest. There was a serious food shortage, and if it were not for the smuggling, many would have starved. The illegal landing of goods continued, and many turned their hand to fetching and hiding brandy, tobacco or French lace – anything they could sell for money to buy food. William grew accustomed to the sight of women at the markets pretending to be with child, the large bulge a perfect disguise for hidden goods.

Sarah Ezard took advantage of the smuggling. She mixed sloe leaves with the tea leaves and sold the mixture on as genuine tea. As for Ben, he became involved because of Princess Patience, the mule he'd trained years ago. The Hunmanby men were using her to carry goods from the beach, and he fretted that she was overloaded and abused.

One morning, Ben found the mule in a terrible state at Uphall. She was safely back in the stable but was sweating and trembling with fatigue. Clouds of steam rose from her back in the frosty air and her head hung low over the cold earthen floor, bare of any straw. It made Ben weep. If Tom had still been working there, this would never have happened. He took off his neckerchief and began to rub her down, talking to her softly as if to a lover.

'It's not right thoo bein' left like this. If I 'ad my way, thoo'd 'ave a better life. Thoo deserves more. Thoo's a princess to me.' As she shivered beneath his hands, he was so sorry that the mule was not his. He couldn't prevent her being worked; neither could he tolerate such misuse. There was only one thing to do – go with her at night, wherever that might be. At least that way he could ensure she was loaded up properly and treated well.

In the middle of February, a Dutch lugger hovered in Filey Bay. It waited a while and then gave a signal to the watcher on the cliffs. Then it sailed further out to sea to wait until dark. Ben did not see the boat, but he noticed that the sails on the Reighton windmill were altered at noon; a landing would be attempted that night. Folk at Hunmanby would get the message and everyone would be prepared when evening came.

Late in the afternoon, William was in the yard at Uphall when he saw Ben leading the mule from the stable.

'Now then, Ben, what are *you* up to?' he shouted, rather puzzled.

'Same as thoo I reckon.' He winked and tapped his nose.

'Don't tell me you're going out tonight and mixing with that rough lot on the beach?'

Ben nodded and led the mule past William. As he was about to leave the yard, he turned. 'Thoo can explain to 'em. Let 'em know *I'll* be lookin' after mule from now on. Per'aps thoo'll be there tonight?'

William didn't answer the question. 'Be careful,' he advised. 'They're not all as friendly as me.'

Ben chose to ignore the warning and carried on walking across the yard. It didn't make any difference once he'd made up his mind.

As William watched the pair go down the street, he was concerned on a few counts. Ben might not be fit for the task, and any slowness could prove costly to the whole enterprise. Also, the Hunmanby lot would not welcome his interference. At the same time, William could understand the attachment to the mule. Ben had slept with her and trained her up, had been able to get that mule to do anything. Perhaps Ben was doing the right thing and might even be useful. Perhaps the evening would pass off with no untoward incidents.

When Ben reached his cottage, he took the mule inside like an honoured guest. He warmed a pan of water for her to drink and found a few oats to feed her. While the mule rested, Ben got himself ready.

First, he undid his shirt and rubbed goose fat onto his chest to keep out the cold. Then he dropped his breeches and massaged more fat onto his thighs. After he'd pulled his breeches up again, he rammed down a few handfuls of loose fleece. He checked that he had the four moles' feet in his pockets for rheumatism and then put on his thick jacket. As he was prone to earache in windy weather, he stuffed lambs' wool round his ears before adding his tarred hat. All he need do now was rub in some of Sarah Ezard's lip ointment. The mixture of mutton fat and candle wax was perfect to protect his cracked lips. For good measure, he smeared the grease over his hands too. He stank a bit, but the mule didn't seem to mind, accustomed to Ben's many odours.

When Ben and Princess Patience left the cottage, the half moon was still high in the south. They set off, heading northwards on the Filey road, aiming towards the stars of the Plough. At times, the wind cleared the clouds from the moon just enough to see the way. They hadn't gone far when a cold breeze blew in from the sea and brought rain and sleet. Soon, they were soaked. Ben wished now that he'd put a tarred cover on the mule, but it was too late to turn back.

They left the road near Hunmanby Moor and turned down a track that led to Flat Cliff Gill. Then they followed the side of the stream, the mule treading more cautiously as the track steepened. From time to time, they stopped and waited for the moon to reappear from the clouds. Once they could see where to put their feet, they edged their way again down the ravine to Butcher Haven.

Ben appreciated why the place was chosen to land goods; it was remote and out of sight between the high cliffs. He waited quietly in the dark of the ravine, believing he was the first to arrive. He was wrong.

Hidden in the dark on the other side of the ravine were over 20 men with donkeys. And they'd seen the mule. The Hunmanby men stayed hidden amid the gorse and brambles. Silent and alert, they looked for signs of activity at sea. The stench of warm goose fat drifted across on the wind. Whispers went round that it must be old Ben with the mule. They were surprised but reckoned he could handle the beast better than most. They waved him over to join them.

As Ben crossed the ravine, he had a good view of the sea. Although sheltered in Filey Bay, the northerly wind caused huge rolling waves to pound up the beach. He peered out to sea, where a tiny light on the Dutch ship reared and plunged. Three Filey cobles were lying off, ready for the transfer of goods, but it would not be easy to beach and unload in such a swell. He hoped there were no honest revenue men nearby to see what went on.

William sat on his horse on the cliff top to the south. He held the reins in one hand while stroking the horse's flank with the other. His dark coat and breeches blended with the night sky. He was as invisible as the Dutch lugger out there somewhere with its tar-blackened sides. A freezing wind ruffled the horse's mane. William pressed his hat down further and pulled his neckerchief up over his mouth. He strained his eyes. There was no sign of a revenue ship, but there'd been so many successful runs that winter that complacency had set in. The Hunmanby landers used to disguise themselves – not anymore. Although William knew each one, he didn't want to meet them face to face.

In the ravine below, Ben stood with the others, the cold stream trickling over his boots as they waited for a signal. He guessed the landers were farm labourers who'd earn far more on such nights than any daytime work. All at once, there was movement, and he saw a lantern swung briefly on the beach. Even that act of signalling to a boat was a punishable offence, yet he reasoned the men around him were well-armed; they had long staves and one had a pistol.

Scanning the beach, William played a waiting game. If he approached the men and they felt threatened in any way, there would be violence. Despite his usual silence and connivance, they could unseat him and do him harm. He shifted uneasily in his saddle. It had never been worth his while to seize goods as he was paid to do – a third went to the King, a third to the informer and only one fifth to the seizing officer. The rest went to cover the court costs. It was much better to know where the stuff would be stored before it was moved on; that was where he got his share, and he trusted that everyone involved understood his role.

He kept his distance on the cliff, waited and watched while the sleet collected and froze on his collar. His nose and cheeks grew numb with cold, yet he remained motionless as a rock at the cliff edge, a solitary black shape against the dark sky. He guessed Ben was down there somewhere. He hoped he was safe.

The men stayed hidden until the last moment. The cobles came in one at a time, waiting for the largest waves to hurl them far up the beach. Then the landers rushed out to unload; it was achieved without speaking, everyone knowing his job. The strong and fit young men carried the tubs of spirit while others loaded the donkeys.

Ben made sure the mule's panniers were balanced and then he joined the queue about to start the long pull to the top of the ravine. He soon regretted his rash decision to help. It was tough going uphill, and the track, if it could be called such, was narrow, wet and slippery. Parts of it were even in the stream itself to avoid overhanging gorse. In the dark, thorns scratched his face, and at times he found himself in a tunnel of briars.

Due to his ability with the mule, Ben was placed almost at the front of the line of donkeys. This meant he had to keep up the pace. Though the mule was sure-footed, Ben slipped and struggled in the mud. The more he tried to keep up, the more his legs shook and the more he stumbled. His ears pounded and he felt dizzy and sick as he fought for breath. Trembling from the exertion, he leant his cheek against the mule's wet shoulder. While he prayed for strength, he couldn't see how he'd ever make it to the top, let alone get to Hunmanby and then back to Reighton. It was stupid to think he was up to it. Though it was freezing cold, sweat dripped from his face. Suddenly, his chest tightened, and his heart was gripped in a vice. He wrenched at his coat buttons as dots of light flashed before him. In a panic, he lunged at the mule for support. He crashed against her and then fell headlong into the stream.

The mule stopped. The donkeys in front carried on up the ravine while the men behind bumped into each other and cursed at the delay. When the mule still refused to move forward, the man next in line went to see what was wrong. He fell over Ben's lifeless body lying in the stream.

Chapter 49

The men took turns to carry Ben's body over their shoulders. They left him at the top of the ravine and a lad was sent to look for William Jordan. The customs officer was bound to be somewhere nearby on the cliff top.

On hearing footsteps approaching, William grew alarmed and wished he still had his pistol. From the gloom came the familiar low whistle of the landers and a lantern appeared. He relaxed as a young voice hailed him.

'What's the problem?' William asked.

The lad waited to catch his breath. 'It's Ben. 'E's collapsed – stone-dead.' William was too stunned to reply. 'So, will tha take 'im back to Reighton?'

'Yes, of course,' William heard himself say.

As he followed the lantern back along the cliff, William thought what a fool he'd been to let Ben take the mule. And what would he say to Sarah Ezard? Or Mary?

When they reached the top of the ravine, the last of the donkeys had finished their climb and were heading towards Hunmanby. Only the mule remained, standing by the side of Ben's body. She kept lowering her head to nudge him.

The lad put down the lantern and scratched his head. 'Damn mule won't leave 'im. They've 'ad to transfer 'er load.'

William knelt down to check if Ben might yet be alive. It was obvious that he wasn't; his eyes were wide open, his face cold as ice. William closed Ben's eyes and then turned to the youth.

'Before you go, help me lift him over my horse.'

'Well, that's a daft idea. Thoo's got a mule 'ere – put Ben across mule. That's what mules are for.'

'No.' William found trouble speaking. 'It's too far back to Reighton. Ben wouldn't want the mule to suffer.'

The lad shrugged. 'It's still daft,' he muttered as they lifted the body and draped it across William's horse.

'You go on home now,' said William. 'I'll take the mule with me.'

It was a long walk back with plenty of time for reflection. Ben had been around for the whole of William's life, like another father. And he'd been as a grandfather to young Mary, had understood her and valued her in a way most others didn't. There'd never be another like him. His throat tightened and his eyes filled with tears at the thought of telling Mary and the boys. But first he must tell Sarah Ezard. God knows how she'd feel, and she'd be the one to wash and lay out the body.

On reaching the village, he went straight to Ben's cottage. He managed to half drag, half carry the body inside and rest it on the table. After rummaging around in the dark, he found a lantern. He blew on the embers of the fire, lit a spill and set the lighted lantern on the table. Then he stood back to get a proper view. He shook his head and smiled. Ben still had his hat on. When he leant over to remove it, he realised why it had stayed on even though Ben's head had been upside down. The hat fitted exactly, moulded to each contour of his skull. William remembered the day Ben made it years ago and the fuss caused. William had been told to wind a strip of cloth round Ben's head. Then Ben had dipped the 'helmet' in tar to make it waterproof.

As William prised off the legendary hat, fluffy bits of wool tumbled out from round the ears. No, William thought again, there'd never be another quite like Ben.

After pulling off Ben's wet jacket and boots, he also removed his shirt. The body was already beginning to stiffen, so he pulled down the breeches as well. The moles' feet fell unnoticed to the floor. William got a sheet to cover the body and placed a pillow under the grizzled head. He stood awhile by the side of the lined face and stroked smooth Ben's few remaining strands of hair. He'd never seen him asleep, had never known him anything but animated whether teasing or grumbling or cursing. Now that he was still and peaceful, it was a different Ben entirely. Before he left, he rested his hand on Ben's shoulder.

'Farewell, my friend.'

He took his time returning the horse and mule to the Uphall stable, putting off what he had to do next. Then, although it was the middle of the night, he knocked on Sarah Ezard's door and let himself in.

'Sarah!' he hissed. 'Are you awake? It's William.'

'Oh my God! Is it one o' thy lads?'

'No. No one's ill – don't worry.' He waited until he heard her getting out of bed. 'I'm afraid I have bad news.'

She waddled over to the fire and poked it to give some light. 'Thoo'd better tell me then an' get it over with.' She sat down on the settle, wondering who might have died.

William stepped forward and sat beside her. He sighed. How he hated to do this.

'I'm sorry,' he whispered, as he held her hand, 'it's Ben. I'm so sorry.' He swallowed and took a deep breath. 'He died tonight – helping that bloody mule, the stupid clod.' He began to cry and, as she held him, he sobbed into her shoulder, the pain and grief of the last few years bursting out.

She remained dry-eyed, staring into the ashy remains of the fire. Already, she was planning the last acts of kindness she would do for Ben in the morning.

When William got home, he undressed and eased himself into bed, trying not to disturb Mary.

She was a light sleeper. 'All went to plan?' she mumbled, hardly listening for a reply. When he didn't answer, she guessed something was wrong and turned over to face him. 'What is it?'

He sighed and then blurted it out. 'Ben's dead.' He felt her body tense. 'It was the walk up the ravine – it was too much for him.'

She raised herself up on one elbow and demanded, 'But why on earth was *he* there?'

'That bloody mule, that's why! That damn mule has been the death of him. He fretted about it being mistreated – and now it's alive, and he isn't.'

Mary leant her head against his shoulder, trying to take it in. She had dealings with Ben nearly every day.

Just knowing he was in the village made everything seem right. Like William, her tears came at the thought of telling others, of breaking it to the boys.

Next morning, Mary braced herself. She waited until the boys had finished their porridge and then reported simply that Ben had died in his sleep during the night. While Francis took it well, John began to cry, partly because he saw his parents so upset.

'We can see him again?' he asked.

'Not really,' answered Mary, 'not like before. We'll always love him though. Think of him happy now he's in heaven.'

Young William sprang up to leave the table so suddenly that the bench rocked. He scowled at everyone, leant forward and grabbed hold of the dog. 'I'm going out,' he snarled.

Mary didn't stop him. 'Don't be long then. It might snow,' she had to shout as he left the room, 'and I'll need you to look after Richard later. There are things I need to do at Ben's.'

Young William returned within the hour. Mary thought him unusually subdued and tired. No doubt he'd been racing on the beach with the dog. She couldn't help him with his feelings about Ben and death; she had enough of her own to deal with. She left him with instructions and went to Ben's cottage.

Sarah Ezard was there and had washed the body already. 'I loved 'im, daft ol' devil that 'e was.' She smiled at Mary. 'It's taken me ages gettin' off ev'ry bit o' goose fat!'

Together, they wrapped Ben in a woollen winding-sheet and knotted it round his feet and above his head.

They left his face visible. Sarah fitted an onion into his mouth and placed a candle in his hands across his breast. Mary put three handfuls of salt in a wooden bowl and set it on his chest above the candle.

'We're about done,' said Sarah. 'I'll just open window an' then folk can come in an' see 'im. An' then I'll whisper to 'is bees, tell 'em their master is gone.'

Mary wondered who would take care of the beehives. They wouldn't be wanted at Uphall; Francis Jordan preferred the kind you could stack together. She changed the subject.

'William will bring the coffin. He's gone to the church to fetch it.'

They stood in silence for a moment and then Sarah gave a huge sigh. 'I wish George Gurwood were still 'ere. It's not right 'avin' another vicar to lay Ben to rest.'

'I don't suppose the new vicar'll be overpleased to ride out mid-week. Perhaps John Gurwood will go and tell him, or William can go.'

'Aye, someone'll 'ave to go.' Sarah wiped her eyes. 'It's bad when we 'ave strangers to bury us.'

When Mary returned home, the smells of Ben's cottage lingered in her hair and clothes; a mixture of tar, tobacco and wood-smoke followed her whenever she moved. At times, she could almost sense the warmth of his arm on hers, like when she helped him up from his chair. Tears welled up again at the thought of not saying goodbye, of not telling him how much she loved to have him around, helping her with the boys, befriending William. She'd never thanked him enough. It was too late now. And he wouldn't see her new baby, due in the summer.

Later that day, as the pale sun dipped behind the hill, Mary took her boys to see Ben. It was their first sight of a dead body. Curious, but also wary of anything to do with death, they crept into the cottage, hiding behind their mother. They stood around the coffin, not daring to peep in.

Young William was the first to speak. 'What has four stiff standers, four dilly danders, two lookers, two crookers and a wig wag?'

'It's a cow!' John shouted with a great smile on his face. Of all Ben's riddles, that was his favourite.

Mary put a hand on his head and ruffled his hair. 'Do you remember what Ben used to say about your head lice when he saw you scratching in bed?'

The two boys grinned and replied in unison. 'Turn over, let young'uns 'ave a feed.' It was good to talk like Ben.

John was getting excited. 'I'll snickersneeze thoo!' he yelled, jumping up and down.

'Shush!' Francis warned. He frowned at them. 'This is a house of mourning now. Talk quietly. Don't go shouting.'

Mary put a hand up. 'He's alright, Francis. Ben wouldn't mind one bit.'

'Ben's dead,' said John matter-of-factly.

'Yes. Ben's dead,' she repeated. She wasn't sure if he fully understood. 'He won't be coming back. Remember what Ben would say – we didn't all come into this world together, an' we can't all leave it together. It was very wise. We will see him again though – in heaven.'

Francis and William were tall enough to peep into the coffin. It didn't look much like Ben, not the Ben they knew.

'Come on, John,' said Mary, 'I'll lift you up so you can say goodbye.'

As soon as John saw the face poking out from the shroud, he announced, 'Mother – I think he's sleeping.'

'No, that's what people are like when they're dead,' she explained. 'He looks very peaceful though, doesn't he?' John nodded and seemed satisfied. 'We can leave him now. Your father's going to stay with him tonight and keep him company.'

On the eve of the funeral, William ate a hasty supper and left at dusk to attend Ben's wake. Mary made him take a couple of stools; Ben's one-roomed cottage was devoid of chairs. He was the first to arrive so relit the candles around the coffin and then prepared a fire. It was as cold inside the cottage as out. He found a bundle of gorse faggots in a corner that made him smile. Ben always kept up a good supply and there'd be enough to last the whole evening. He doubted the fire would ever warm the room enough to affect the body and if the men felt cold, they could keep on their coats.

Once the fire was well alight, he took out his box of tobacco, lit up a pipe and waited for the others. It was silent in the cottage except for the crackle of the burning gorse. He looked around. Apart from the two stools he'd brought, there was only one other stool to sit on. Late arrivals would have to sit on Ben's clothes chest or the meal bin, or else sit on the bed.

His pipe smoke had already filled the room when his father walked in with Dickon. They carried a small cask of ale, donated by Martha Wrench, and they'd remembered to bring tankards. Since the coffin was on the table, they set everything on the earthen floor.

'Grave's been dug,' announced his father. 'A tough job they 'ad – top inches o' soil was frozen.'

Dickon filled their tankards and then peered into the coffin. His lips moved in silent prayer. When he'd finished, he asked what it was tucked under the side of the body.

'Summat's there, William. I can't see what.'

'I don't know.' William put his head in to look. He moved the sheet a little and then grinned. 'You'll never guess – Sarah Ezard's left his moles' feet with him.'

His father laughed. ''E won't be needin' 'em where 'e's goin'. There's no rheumatism in 'eaven. No more stiff knees for 'im.' He raised his tankard. ''Ere's to Ben. 'Is worries an' pains is over.'

At that point, Matthew Smith walked in with a bottle of brandy, also bringing the cold night air into the room. William noticed a light dusting of snow on his hat and coat.

'Is it starting to snow?'

'No, it won't amount to much. As Ben might say, it's too cold for snow.' He stood in front of the fire to warm his hands and then realised there was nowhere for him to sit.

William waved towards the chest by the wall. For once, he had the upper hand. 'You can sit there. It's either that or the bed.'

Matthew, as expected, chose the chest. He settled down with a tankard of ale as John Gurwood entered carrying his fiddle. Soon, others arrived – so many that they did have to sit on the bed or the floor.

William sat by the fire and enjoyed his smoke, glad that it was a wake for the men only. As the tankards of ale were topped up with brandy, the room became no place for women. At first, John played the melancholy tunes of ballads, but as the drink took effect, he played lively jigs and then bawdy songs. The awkwardness and rivalry between William and Matthew dissipated the more they drank. By midnight, the two were singing and swaying together arm in arm. They were satisfied it was the kind of wake Ben would have appreciated.

'Aye,' announced Dickon as they left the cottage, 'we've done 'im proud. An' let's remember what 'e used to say – more rain, more rest, fine weather's not allus best.'

While the men had been singing rowdy choruses, Sarah Ezard had been alone by her kitchen fire drinking toasts to Ben with a bottle of his own mead. She savoured each mouthful, the mature blend of apple and honey produced from his garden by his hand. While she dreaded sitting alone tomorrow at the back of the church, she was grateful for the life they'd shared. One important thing she must see to, for his sake, was to make sure someone cared for the bees.

Next morning, the new vicar arrived from Filey in plenty of time. He had never known Ben and, the weather being so cold and blustery, he aimed to keep the service brief. John Gurwood asked if he could read a passage from the Bible, one that Ben would have liked. He also invited the vicar to food and drink at the vicarage later.

'Fine,' agreed John Sumpton, 'you can read a passage if it's short, but I won't come to the feast afterwards, thank you. I want to be back in Filey before it snows.'

When it was time for the service, the vicar entered the pulpit. Being of small stature, he stood on a block of wood to give him height and then fixed his gaze on the far wall beyond everyone's heads.

Folk thought it was a miserable service, lacking in warmth until John Gurwood went to the front to give his reading. Like the rest of the congregation, he'd known Ben his whole life and knew the kind of wisdom Ben preferred. The passage from Ecclesiastes was perfect and had been his own grandmother's favourite.

'To everything there is a season,' he enunciated slowly, 'and a time to every purpose under the heaven: A time to be born, and a time to die; a time to plant, and a time to pluck up that which is planted.'

William's boys knew Ben as old and grey, weatherbeaten, with a bristly face and rheumy eyes. They knew how he'd sat too close to the fire and rubbed his knees, how his pipe slotted between the gap in his teeth.

The older generation remembered him in his prime, full of vigour, always the first to dance and to help either man or beast. Even when old and with failing health, he'd tried to help the mule.

William and Mary stood in the graveyard afterwards and looked towards Filey, to the bleak, misty landscape devoid of any redeeming features. They were both aware that Ben had been an anchor in their lives, steadying them when they were going adrift; George Gurwood had been another. Now both were gone.

Chapter 50

Ben's cottage belonged to the manor, and it was soon emptied. Though there was no will, there was hardly anything to give away. William took the tools and wood to Uphall, and Sarah Ezard was told she could have anything else. After taking the bottles of mead, she wandered miserably into the garden to find the beehives untouched. Remembering her promise, she loaded them onto Ben's sledge to take home. She also took a couple of buckets, the one stool and the cauldron. Ben's pallet bed, his table and workbench were used for fence repairs. As for the chest of clothes – no one wanted them. When Sarah sifted through them with Mary, they found nothing but things that had belonged to Ben's father. Mary took the blue hat for John to dress up in and cut up the rest of the clothes for patches and rags. The cottage, always sparse, was now completely bare.

The women dropped the latch on the door for the last time and walked away lost in thought. As they stopped to say goodbye at the bottom of St Helen's Lane, Sarah grabbed Mary's arm. There was a wildness in her eyes despite the tears.

'Thoo knows, Mary, I'm oldest i' village now. There's no one left that knew me when I were a lass. Me an' Ben, we 'ad some fun then.'

Mary gave her a hug. 'We all need you. We always will.'

'Oh, aye, I get a bit o' respect an' folk are kind enough.' She brushed a tear from her cheek. 'But there's no one like Ben. I could argue with 'im an' we'd end up laughin'.'

Already Sarah felt like a different person, a stranger to herself. She'd begun to feel so tired. For the first time in her old age, it dawned on her that she was ready to leave this world.

Mary could not get used to life without Ben. Every day she expected to see him saunter up the lane or hear him knocking and opening the door. She began to take John and Richard for long walks. At times she thought she saw Ben in the distance and hurried her steps. She walked halfway to Filey with the ridiculous hope of catching a glimpse of him or at least feeling his presence. If he was in heaven, surely there'd be a sign. As the breeze rustled the dry reeds or a robin sang high in a tree, she wondered if it was because of Ben or that he was there somehow. Not convinced, she'd carry on walking, searching with tears in her eyes and finding no relief. If she was honest, she was beginning to doubt a life after death. She shuddered at her lack of faith. George Gurwood could have helped, but he was in Rudston. The new vicar didn't look the sort to give up his time easily, and anyway, he wasn't here – he was in Filey. There was no consolation.

Less than a week after the funeral, the new vicar came to baptise John Gurwood's son. He stood in the porch afterwards to let everyone file past and shake hands. William and his family were the last to leave. The vicar noticed the strange lopsided gait of young William.

'Cannot anything be done about that?' he asked.

Folk nearby heard and turned their heads, puzzled. What on earth was the vicar talking about? They were surprised to see him pointing at young William's foot. They'd grown so accustomed to the boy's walk that no one paid any heed.

'Can't your lad have a bigger sole put on his boot?'

William and Mary were equally dumbfounded by the intrusion.

Mary then confided in a low voice, 'It's his spine.' She was ashamed to speak about her son's affliction. 'I think it happened when he was just starting to walk.' She muttered something else about the lack of food at the time.

The vicar was about to repeat his idea that a better boot would help when he saw the expression on the boy's face. He realised suddenly that the boy didn't know he had a problem. There was such a cheeky and determined scowl on his face. Perhaps he could look after himself and was at no disadvantage. After all, no one else took any notice of the limp.

'Never mind then,' he concluded and waved them goodbye. Once alone, he smiled to himself. Every village had its oddity. As he watched the family heading to the gate, he noticed the way they treated another of their sons, the one they called John. Fancy, he thought, that family has two oddities.

Though he'd been invited to have dinner at the vicarage, he rode straight back to Filey. Susanna

Gurwood and her daughters were not surprised when the vicar did not arrive. John Sumpton never accepted their invitations. He was a great disappointment, giving the minimum of church services and sacraments.

'Perhaps it's as well we're leaving,' Cecilia decided.

In March, the Gurwood women busied themselves in preparing to quit the vicarage. Milcah took part without any of the relish shown by her sisters. Like Mary, she was seen wandering about the hills and moorland. She stood gazing into streams and often strolled along the cliffs to stare at the horizon. One afternoon, she saw Mary walking ahead and so quickened her step to join her. Both found comfort in the companionship. For a while they walked and chatted about the spring sowing, the new piglets at Uphall and the best places to gather violets. Then Mary stood still and faced Milcah.

'You *really* don't want to leave Reighton, do you?' she asked.

'No, is it that obvious? Mother knows how I feel. She did say there might be a way for me to stay. Nothing else has been said though, and we have to be gone before Easter, before the Good Friday tithes. I don't have many days left.'

That evening at supper, Francis heard his mother speak about Milcah's reluctance to go. He listened with great interest and hoped it was because of him. Perhaps Milcah sensed there was more than friendship between them.

'If she doesn't want to go,' he interrupted, 'then maybe she could stay. I'm sure she could find some employment – and a new home.'

Mary blinked, surprised at his suggestion. 'She can't live with us if that's what you're thinking. She's used to better living that we can give.'

Francis blushed. 'I didn't mean that.' Confused, he got up and poked the fire. As the flames rose, he had an idea. Walking back to the table, he found it difficult to hide his excitement and speak without a grin breaking out.

He put on an innocent air. 'You know her brother's wife has just had another baby? Well, I think they could do with an extra pair of hands. Their other son – he still needs looking after. You know, don't you, Mother, how hard it is to feed a baby and see to the house? And there's the gardening, and you have to make butter and cheese with children under your feet. I can see how hard that is – no end to the work.'

His parents couldn't help but smile; the boy was rambling.

William held up his hand. 'Whoa, Francis, you've said quite enough.' Then, to put his son out of his misery, he added, 'I'll mention it to her mother tomorrow. I won't mention *you* mind, just the idea.'

Francis sat back down at the table, his heart thumping and his hands shaking. He couldn't wait to find out if Milcah would stay.

True to his word, William went to the Gurwoods' next day. He explained the plan, and by evening it was all arranged. Milcah was amazed she hadn't thought of it herself. When the Gurwoods left for Rudston, Milcah would move in and live with her brother as a very welcome houseguest and helper.

At the end of March, Susanna Gurwood and six of her daughters climbed into a wagon with their possessions.

It was a glorious spring morning, not a cloud in the sky. Everyone lined the street to wave them off and folk passed them small gifts. Sarah Ezard had packed a box with jars and bottles containing herbal cures for every possible ailment. She kissed each girl in turn and wished them well.

'Mind them Rudston lads,' she warned with a wink. 'Don't be over fond with 'em. Give 'em an inch an' all that.'

Milcah began to cry. She reached up to clasp each of her sisters' hands in turn. Now that the final day had come, she knew how much she'd miss their company and the many things they did together.

Francis stood close by, dying to hold her hand and comfort her. Perhaps he'd been too selfish wanting her to stay behind, yet his happiness outweighed the guilt. He fidgeted, moving his weight from one foot to the other while the last farewells were made. When the wagon moved off at last, he followed with Milcah as far as the road to Argam. There they stopped and waved one last time before they turned and walked slowly back to Reighton.

Francis held back his joy. What he wanted to do was leap and shout. The sky was so blue, and the fields had never looked so fresh. The hawthorn was greening, its new buds about to open, and birds flitted and sang from every bank. He could have been Adam in the Garden of Eden with Eve at his side. It wasn't true what his mother said – that the vicar leaving and the death of old Ben had ripped the heart out of the village. No, his heart was with Milcah; it was spring and the whole of life was celebrating. Reighton was beautiful and the future was bright. While he felt like singing, he was aware that

Milcah was subdued. She walked with her head down, absorbed in thought. He contained his wild excitement. Whatever happened in the future, Milcah would be there. He forced himself to amble quietly at her side though the glory of spring and young love was in every step. When he waved her goodbye, he bounded home like a young deer.

Book Four

The younger generation is growing up fast. Francis Jordan, only 13, is in love, but the object of his dreams is courted by Uncle Thomas. Without the influence of their previous vicar and his daughters, the men and boys of Reighton follow their desires; it is the weak, the women and the animals that are most vulnerable.

Mary Jordan, in an all-male household, struggles to control her sons' behaviour as well as deal with her husband's reactions on approaching middle age. She finds comfort in John, the simple son who is happy to stay close to home and share her menial tasks. As the smuggling reaches a crisis and troubles escalate, she will need all the help she can get.

About the Author

Joy Stonehouse's father came from Filey. He moved to Hornsea before the war and married Gladys Jordan, a descendant of the Jordans of Reighton. Joy writes under her maiden name; she is known locally as Mrs Gelsthorpe.

Lightning Source UK Ltd.
Milton Keynes UK
UKHW010813261121
394640UK00003B/390